BETTY NEELS

THE ULTIMATE COLLECTION

Betty Neels's novels are loved
by millions of readers around the world,
and this very special *12-volume collection*
offers a unique chance to recapture the pleasure
of some of her most popular stories.

Each month we're bringing you a new volume
containing two timeless classics—irresistible love
stories that belong together, whether they share the
same colourful setting, romantic theme, or follow the
same characters in their continuing lives...

As a special treat, each volume also includes an
introductory letter by a different author. Some of the
most popular names in romance fiction are delighted
to pay tribute to Betty Neels; we hope you enjoy
reading their personal thoughts and memories.

We're proud and privileged to bring you
this very special collection, and hope you enjoy
reading—and keeping—these twelve wonderful
volumes over the coming months!

Volume Eleven

*—with an introduction from a star
of the Medical Romance™ series, author*

Caroline Anderson

**A delightful duet—
two linked stories by Betty Neels:**

*THE PROMISE OF HAPPINESS
CAROLINE'S WATERLOO*

We'd like to take this opportunity to pay tribute to **Betty Neels**, *who sadly passed away last year. Betty was one of our best-loved authors. As well as being a wonderfully warm and thoroughly charming individual, Betty led a fascinating life even before becoming a writer, and her publishing record was impressive.*

Betty spent her childhood and youth in Devonshire before training as a nurse and midwife. She was an army nursing sister during the war, married a Dutchman and subsequently lived in Holland for fourteen years. On retirement from nursing Betty started to write, inspired by a lady in a library bemoaning the lack of romantic novels.

Over her thirty-year writing career Betty wrote more than 134 novels and was published in more than one hundred international markets. She continued to write into her ninetieth year, remaining as passionate about her characters and stories then as she was with her very first book.

Betty will be greatly missed, both by her friends at Harlequin Mills & Boon® *and by her legions of loyal readers around the world. Betty was a prolific writer and has left a lasting legacy through her heartwarming novels. She will always be remembered as a truly delightful person who brought great happiness to many.*

THE ULTIMATE COLLECTION

Volume Eleven

THE PROMISE OF HAPPINESS

&

CAROLINE'S WATERLOO

Two full-length novels

Harlequin Mills & Boon Limited,
Eton House, 18-24 Paradise Road, Richmond, Surrey TW9 1SR

This compilation: THE ULTIMATE COLLECTION
© Harlequin Enterprises II B.V., 2003

First published in Great Britain as:

THE PROMISE OF HAPPINESS © Betty Neels 1979

CAROLINE'S WATERLOO © Betty Neels 1980

ISBN 0 263 83653 3

Set in Times Roman 11½ on 12¾ pt.
141-0503-101168

Printed and bound in Spain
by Litografia Rosés, S.A., Barcelona

Dear Reader

My editor asked me to write a short letter about Betty Neels. 'Good grief,' I said, 'what can I possibly say that hasn't been better said by other people over and over again?' I heard her shrug over the phone. 'How were you introduced to her writing?' she asked, and I laughed. Introduced? No, I was never introduced to Betty's writing. It was always there. It would have been like being introduced to my mother—quite unnecessary.

Not many of us come to be a legend in our own lifetimes, but Betty was, and deservedly. I was privileged to be introduced to her in person once, and she was exactly how I expected—sweet and charming, with an amazing energy. The world of romance is diminished by her passing, but her writing and her memory will live on.

Caroline Anderson

THE PROMISE OF HAPPINESS

by

Betty Neels

CHAPTER ONE

THE ROAD over the moors was lonely, its surface glistening from the drizzle which had been falling since first light. It was still very early; barely six o'clock, but already full daylight by reason of the time of year—the end of June, but as yet there was no sign of the clouds breaking, so that the magnificence of the scenery was a little marred by their uniform greyness.

There were no houses in sight and no cars, only a solitary figure marching briskly on the crown of the road, the thin figure of a girl, wrapped in a shabby old-fashioned raincoat, her hair tied in a sopping scarf. Marching beside her was a black retriever, no longer young, attached to a stout string, and tucked under the other arm was a plastic bag from the top of which protruded a cat's head. It was an ugly beast, made more so by its wetness and a battle-scarred ear, but it was quiet enough, taking no notice of the road but fixing its eyes on the girl's face.

'We're free, my dears,' she told them in a rather breathy voice, because she was walking so quickly. 'At least, if we can get to Newcastle we are. The main road's only another mile; there may be a bus,' she added, more to reassure herself than the animals. 'Anyway, they won't find we're gone for another two hours.'

The dog whimpered gently and she slowed her steps, and said: 'Sorry, Bertie.' Without the animals she could have got away much faster, but the thought hadn't even entered her head. They had been her solace for two years or more and she wasn't going to abandon them. She began to whistle; they were together and hopeful of the future; she had a pitifully small sum in her purse, the clothes she stood up in, by now very wet, and a comb in her pocket—there had been no time

for more; but she was free, and so were Bertie and Pooch.
She whistled a little louder.

She intended to join the A696 north of Newcastle with the
prospect of at least another six miles to go before she reached
the city. She had been walking through moorland, magnificent
country forming a small corner of the National Park, but very
shortly it would be the main road and Newcastle at the end
of it.

The main road, when she joined it presently, was surprisingly free from traffic and she supposed it was too early for
a bus. She began to wonder what she would do when she got
there and her courage faltered a little at the prospect of finding
somewhere to spend the night, and most important, a job. And
that shouldn't be too difficult, she told herself bracingly; she
was a trained nurse, surely there was a hospital who would
employ her and let her live in—which left Bertie and Pooch...
And they would want references... She was so deep in thought
that she didn't hear the big car slowing behind her and then
stopping a few paces ahead. It was a large car, a silver-grey
Rolls-Royce Corniche, and the man who got out of the driving
seat was large too and very tall, with pepper and salt hair and
very blue eyes in a handsome face. He waited until the trio
had drawn abreast of him before he spoke. He said 'good
morning' with casual politeness and looked amused. 'Perhaps
I can give you a lift?' he offered, still casual, and waited
quietly for his answer.

'Well, thank you—but Bertie and Pooch are wet, they'd
spoil your lovely car.' She looked it over before her eyes went
back to his face.

For answer he opened the back door. 'There's a rug—your
dog can sit on it.' He studied Pooch's damp fur. 'Perhaps the
cat beside him, or would you rather have him on your knee?'

'Oh, with me, if you don't mind, it's all a bit strange for
him.'

He opened the door for her and when they were all settled
she said contritely: 'We're all so wet—I'm sorry.'

'It's of no importance. Where can I set you down?' He smiled fleetingly. 'My name's Raukema van den Eck—Tiele Raukema van den Eck.'

'Rebecca Saunders.' She offered a wet hand and he shook it, still with an air of amusement. She really was a nondescript little thing, no make-up and far too thin—her pansy brown eyes looked huge and there were hollows in her cheeks, and her hair was so wet he could hardly tell its colour.

'Where would you like to go?' he asked again, and this time there was faint impatience in his voice.

'Well, anywhere in Newcastle, thank you,' she made haste to assure him. 'I must look for a job.'

'A little early in the day for that, surely?' he queried idly. 'You must have left home early—you live close by?'

'I left home just before four o'clock. It's six miles away, down a side road.'

Her companion shot her a quick glance. He said on a laugh: 'You sound as though you're running away from a wicked stepmother!'

'Well, I am,' said Rebecca matter-of-factly. 'At least, she's not exactly wicked, but I had to run away; Basil was going to drown Pooch and shoot Bertie, you see.'

'I am a very discreet man,' offered Mr Raukema van den Eck, 'if you would care to tell me about it...?'

Her hands tightened on Pooch's fur so that he muttered at her. 'I can't bother you with something that's—that's...'

'None of my business? I have always found that talking to a stranger is so much easier—you see, they are not involved.'

'Well, it would be nice to talk about it...'

'Then talk, Miss...no, Rebecca.'

'People call me Becky, only my stepmother and Basil call me Rebecca.'

He had slowed the car as the country round them was slowly swallowed by the outskirts of the city, and his 'Well?' was encouraging if a little impatient.

'I'm twenty-three,' began Becky, 'my mother died when I

was eighteen and I looked after Father at first and when I
went to Leeds to train we got a housekeeper. Everything was
lovely…' she swallowed a grief which had never quite faded.
'My father married again. He died two years ago and my
stepmother forced me to go home because she said she was
ill and needed me…'

'People don't force anyone in these days,' remarked her
companion.

'Oh, yes, they do.' She wanted to argue with him about
that, but there wasn't much more time. 'She wrote to the Prin-
cipal Nursing Officer and her doctor wrote too. She sent
Basil—he's my stepbrother, to fetch me. She wasn't really
ill—jaundice, but not severe, but somehow I couldn't get
away. I tried once or twice, but each time she told me what
she would do to Pooch and Bertie if I went, and I had no
money.' She added vehemently: 'I don't suppose you know
what it's like not to have any money? It took me almost two
years to save up enough money to get away.'

'How much did you save?' he asked idly.

'Thirty pounds and sixty pence.'

'That won't go far.' His voice was gentle.

'Well, I thought for a start it would pay our bus fares and
breakfast before we look for a job.'

'Will your stepmother not look for you?'

'Probably, but they don't get up until eight o'clock. I call
them every morning—they'd wonder where I'd got to. But by
the time they've asked the housekeeper and looked for me
that will be at least another hour.'

'And what kind of job do you hope to get?'

'Well, nursing, of course, though I suppose I could be a
housekeeper…'

'References?' he probed.

'Oh—if I gave them the hospital at Leeds my stepmother
might enquire there and find out—there isn't anyone else, only
my father's elder brother, and he lives in Cornwall, and I don't

expect he even remembers me.' She turned to look at him. 'I suppose you couldn't…?'

'No, I couldn't.' His tone was very decisive.

She watched the almost empty street and didn't look at him. 'No, of course not—I'm sorry. And thank you for giving us a lift. If you'd stop anywhere here, we'll get out.'

He pulled into the kerb. 'I am a little pressed for time and I am tired, but I have no intention of leaving you here at this hour of the morning. I intend to have breakfast and I shall be delighted if you will join me.'

He didn't sound in the least delighted, but Becky was hungry. She asked hesitantly: 'What about Pooch and Bertie?'

'I feel sure we shall be able to find someone who will feed them.'

'I'm very obliged to you,' said Becky, any qualms melting before the prospects of a good meal.

He drove on again without speaking, threading his way into and across the central motorway, to take the road to Tynemouth and stop outside the Imperial Hotel.

'Not here?' asked Becky anxiously.

'Yes, here.' He got out and opened her door and then invited Bertie to get out too, handing her the string wordlessly before entering the hotel. He was looking impatient again and as she hastened to keep close, reflecting that the hotel looked rather splendid and that probably the porter would take one look at her and refuse to allow her in—especially with the animals.

She need not have worried. Her wet raincoat was taken from her and leaving Pooch and Bertie with Mr Raukema van den Eck she retired to the powder room with her comb to do the best she could with her appearance. And not very successfully, judging by her host's expression when she joined him.

They were shown into the coffee room where a table had been got ready for them and what was more, two plates of food set on the floor beside it. Becky took her seat wonder-ingly. 'I say,' she wanted to know, 'do all hotels do this? I didn't know—breakfast at seven o'clock in the morning and no one minding about the animals.'

Her companion looked up from his menu. 'I don't think I should try it on your own,' he suggested dryly. 'They happen to be expecting me here.' He added: 'What would you like to eat?'

Becky hesitated. True, he drove a Rolls-Royce and this was a very super hotel, but the car could go with the job and he might have intended to treat himself to a good meal. She frowned; it seemed a funny time of day to be going anywhere...

'I'm very hungry,' said Mr Raukema van den Eck. 'I shall have—let me see—grapefruit, eggs and bacon and sausages, toast and marmalade. And tea—I prefer tea to coffee.'

'I'd like the same,' said Becky, and when it came, ate the lot. The good food brought a little colour into her pale thin face and her companion, glancing at her, looked again. A plain girl, but not quite as plain as he had at first supposed. When they had finished she made haste to thank him and assure him that she would be on her way. 'We're very grateful,' she told him, and Bertie and Pooch, sitting quietly at her feet, stared up in speechless agreement. 'It's made a wonderful start to the day. I'll get my coat...would you mind waiting with them while I go? I'll be very quick...you're in a hurry, aren't you?'

'Not at the moment. Take all the time you need.' He had taken a notebook from a pocket and was leafing through it.

Becky inspected her person in the privacy of the powder room and sighed. Her hair had dried more or less; it hung straight and fine down her back, a hideous mouse in her own opinion. She looked better now she had had a meal, but she had no make-up and her hands were rough and red and the nails worn down with housework. She didn't see the beauty of her eyes or the creaminess of her skin or the silky brows. She turned away after a minute or two and with her raincoat

over her arm went back to the coffee room. She was crossing
the foyer when the door opened and three people came in; a
large, florid woman in a too tight suit who looked furious,
and a small, elderly lady, exquisitely dressed, looking even
more furious, and seated in a wheelchair pushed by a ha-
rassed-looking man.

'I am in great pain,' declared the little lady, 'and you, who
call yourself a nurse, do nothing about it! I am in your
clutches for the next few weeks and I do not like it; I wish
you to go.'

The large woman put down the wraps she was carrying.
'Foreigners,' she observed nastily. 'They're all alike. I'm going!'

She took herself off under Becky's astonished stare followed by a gleeful chuckle from the little lady, who said
something to the man behind the chair so that he went out of
the door too. It was then that her eye lighted upon Becky.
'Come here, young woman,' she ordered imperiously. 'I am
in great pain and that silly woman who calls herself a nurse
took no notice. You have a sensible face; lift me up and look
beneath my leg, if you please.'

Becky was an obliging girl; she twitched back the rug covering the lady's knees in preparation for lifting her and saw
why she was in a chair in the first place. One leg was in
plaster, the other one had a crêpe bandage round the knee.
'Which leg?' asked Becky.

'The bandaged one.'

It was a pin which shouldn't have been there in the first
place, its point imbedded behind the lady's knee. Becky made
soothing noises, whisked it out, pocketed it and tucked the
bandage end in neatly. 'That must have hurt,' she said sym-
pathetically. 'Can I help with anything else?'

The little lady smiled. 'No, my dear, thank you. You've
been kind.' The man had come back with a small case under
his arm. 'I'll go straight to my room and they can send up
breakfast.' She waved goodbye and Becky heard her telling

the porter to let her know...she didn't hear any more as the lift doors shut.

She went back to the coffee room and was a little surprised to find that her host seemed in no hurry at all. All the same, she bade him goodbye and marched resolutely to the door. It was still raining outside and she had no idea where to go, but she refused his rather perfunctory invitation to stay where she was for an hour or so; he must be longing to be rid of them by now. She went off down the street, walking as though she knew just where she was going, although she hadn't a clue.

Mr Raukema van den Eck stood where he was, watching her small upright person out of sight. If he hadn't had an appointment he might have gone after her...it was like putting a stray kitten back on the street after letting it sit by the fire and eat its fill... He frowned with annoyance because he was becoming sentimental and he didn't hold with that, and the waiter who had just come on duty hesitated before sidling up to him.

'The Baroness is here, Baron,' he murmured deferentially.

'Just arrived?' He glanced at the man. 'She's in her room? I'll come up at once.'

He ignored the lift, taking the stairs two at a time, to tap on the door which had been indicated to him. It was a large, comfortably furnished room and his mother was sitting, still in her wheelchair, by the window.

'Mama, how delightfully punctual, and was it very inconvenient for you?'

She lifted her face for his kiss and smiled at him. 'No, my dear—Lucy was charming about it when I explained and William took the greatest care of me, and after all we didn't have to leave until six o'clock.'

Her son looked round the room. 'And the nurse?'

His mother's very blue eyes flashed. 'I have given her the sack. A horrible woman; I knew I should not like her when she arrived last night, the thought of spending three weeks in her company made me feel ill, and only a short while ago, as we arrived, I begged her to help me because of the pain and she would not. So I sent her away.'

Her son blinked rapidly, his mind running ahead. Here was a situation to be dealt with and he was due to leave in less than an hour. 'Where was the pain?' he asked gently.

'It was a pin, in the bandage round my knee—at the back where I could not get at it. There was a girl in the foyer—a skinny little creature with enormous eyes; she knew what to do at once when I asked for help. Now why cannot I have someone like her instead of that wretched woman they sent from the agency?'

The faint but well-concealed impatience on the Baron's features was replaced by a look of pleased conjecture. 'And why not?' he wanted to know. 'Mama, will you wait for a few minutes while I see if I can find her? There is no time to explain at the moment—I'll do that later. Shall I ring for a maid before I go?'

It was still raining as he got into the car and slid into the early morning traffic, thickening every minute, but he didn't drive fast. Becky and her companions should be easy enough to see, even in a busy city, but there was always the likelihood that she had gone down some side street. But she hadn't; she had stopped to ask the way to somewhere or other, that was apparent, for the matronly-looking woman she was talking to was pointing down the street. The Baron slid to a halt beside them, wound down his window and said quietly: 'Becky...'

She turned round at once and when she saw who it was her face broke into a smile. 'Oh, it's you,' she observed. 'Are you on your way again?'

He was disinclined for conversation. 'I have a job for you; you'll have to come back to the hotel, I'll tell you about it there.'

He waited while she thanked the woman and then got out into the rain to usher Bertie in and settle her and Pooch beside him.

And he turned the car, he said severely: 'You are far too

trusting, Becky—to accept my word without one single question. I might have been intent on abducting you.'

She gave him a puzzled look. 'But why shouldn't I trust you?' she wanted to know. 'And who in his right mind would want to abduct me?'

'You have a point there.' He threw her a sidelong glance. She looked bedraggled and tired; perhaps his idea hadn't been such a good one after all. On the other hand, some dry clothes and a few good meals might make all the difference. 'That lady you helped in the hotel—she needs a nurse for a few weeks. She liked you, so I said I'd fetch you back so that she could talk to you…'

'References,' said Becky sadly. 'I haven't any, you know—and I can't prove I'm a nurse.'

He had drawn up before the hotel once more, now he turned to her. 'What would you do if you were given the care of someone with ulcerative protocolitis?'

'Oh, that's usually treated medically, isn't it—they only operate when the disease is severe. I've only seen it done once…' She launched into a succinct account of what could be done. 'Is that what I'm to nurse?' she asked.

'No. What do you know about serum viral hepatitis?'

She wrinkled her brow. 'I don't know much about that, only that it's transmitted in three ways…' She mentioned them briefly and he asked quietly:

'The sources?'

She told him those too.

'And what preventative measures can be taken?'

She had to think hard about those, and when she had remembered all six of them she asked: 'Are you examining me?'

'No— You said that you had no references…'

Becky said suddenly: 'Gosh, how silly I am! You must be a doctor.'

'Indeed I am, and due to leave here within the hour, so if we might go inside…?'

For all the world as though she had been wasting his time in light conversation, thought Becky. The whole thing must be a dreadful bore for him. With a face like his and a Rolls to boot, he hardly needed to waste time on someone as uninteresting as herself. But she got out obediently, gathered the animals to her, and went back into the hotel.

The little lady she had helped in the foyer turned to stare at her as she entered the room and then took her quite by surprise by exclaiming: 'Yes, that's the one. How very clever of you to find her, Tiele—we'll engage her at once.' Her eyes fell on Bertie and Pooch. 'And these animals…?'

'I have been thinking about them, Mama, but first let me introduce you. This is Miss Rebecca Saunders, a registered nurse, who has run away from her home with her two—er—companions. Becky, this is my mother, the Baroness Raukema van den Eck.' So that made him a Baron!

Becky had her mouth open to begin on a spate of questions, but he stopped her with an urgent hand. 'No, there is little time for questions, if you don't mind, I will explain briefly. Pray sit down.'

He was obviously used to having his own way; she sat, with Pooch peering out from under her arm and Bertie on her feet.

'My mother, as you can see for yourself, is for the time being unable to walk. She has a compound fracture of tib and fib which unfortunately has taken some time to knit, and a badly torn semilunar cartilage of the other knee. She has had quadriceps exercises for three weeks with some good results, and we hope she may commence active movement very shortly. When she does so, she will need a nurse to assist her until she is quite accustomed to walking on her plaster, and we are satisfied that the other knee will give no further trouble. As you are aware, she had engaged a nurse to go with her, but this arrangement has fallen through and it is imperative that she has someone now—she will be sailing on a cruise ship from this port late this afternoon. Unfortunately, I have to be back in Holland by tomorrow morning at the latest, which means that I must leave very shortly.' He added, as though it were a foregone conclusion: 'The post should suit you very well.'

Becky sat up straight. 'I should like to ask some questions,' and at his impatient frown: 'I'll be quick. Where are we going?'

He looked surprised. 'I didn't mention it? Trondheim, in Norway. I have an aunt living there whom my mother wishes to visit.'

'I have no clothes…'

'Easily remedied. A couple of hours' shopping.'

'What happens when I leave?' She suddenly caught Pooch close so that he let out a raucous protest. 'And what about Pooch and Bertie?' she frowned. 'How can I possibly…'

'You will return to Holland with my mother where it should be easy enough for you to get a job in one of the hospitals. I shall, of course, give you any help you may need. As to the animals, may I suggest that I take them with me to Holland where they will be well cared for at my home until you return there; after that it should be a simple matter to get a small flat for yourself where they can live.'

'Quarantine?'

'There is none—only injections, which I will undertake to see about.'

It all sounded so easy; she perceived that if you were important and rich enough, most things were easy. All the same she hesitated. 'I'm not sure if they'll like it…'

He smiled quite kindly then. 'I promise you that they will have the best of treatment and be cared for.'

'Yes, I know, but supposing…'

'What is the alternative, Becky?' He wasn't smiling now and he sounded impatient again.

The alternative didn't bear thinking about. She couldn't be sure of getting a job, in the first place, and just supposing she should meet Basil or her stepmother before she had found somewhere to live. He was watching her narrowly. 'Not very attractive, is it?' he asked, 'and you have only enough money for a meal—thirty pounds and—er—sixty pence wouldn't buy you a bed for more than three nights, you know.'

His mother looked at Becky. 'My dear child, is that all the money you have? And why is that? And why did you leave your home?'

'With your permission, Mama; you will have time enough to discuss the whole situation. If Becky could decide—now— there are several matters which I must attend to...'

She was annoying him now, she could see that, but what seemed so simple from his point of view was an entirely different matter for her. But she would have to agree; the idea of parting with her pets was unpleasant enough, but at least they would be safe and cared for and after a week or so she would be able to collect them and start a new life for herself. To clinch the matter she suddenly remembered the quarantine laws; she would never have enough money to pay the fees— besides, there was no one and nothing to keep her in England. 'Thank you, I'll take the job,' she said in a resolute voice.

'Good, then let us waste no more time. My mother will explain the details later. What fee were you to pay the nurse you dismissed, Mama?'

Son and parent exchanged a speaking glance. 'Sixty pounds a week with—how do you say?—board and lodging.'

'But that's too much!' protested Becky.

'You will forgive me if I remind you that you have been living in, how shall we say? retirement for the past two years. That is the normal pay for a trained nurse working privately. Over and above that you will receive travelling expenses, and a uniform allowance.' He took some notes from a pocket and peeled off several. 'Perhaps you will go now and buy what you think necessary. Your uniform allowance is here, and an advance on your week's pay.'

Becky took the money, longing to count it, but that might

look greedy. 'I haven't any clothes,' she pointed out, 'so I'd better buy uniform dresses, hadn't I?'

'Yes, do that, my dear,' interpolated the Baroness. 'You can go shopping in Trondheim and buy the clothes you need.'

Becky found herself in a taxi, the Baron's cool apologies in her ear. He intended leaving at any moment; she was to take a taxi back to the hotel when she had done her shopping. 'And don't be too long about it,' he begged her forthrightly, 'although you don't look to me to be the kind of girl who fusses over her clothes.' A remark which she had to allow was completely justified but hardly flattering. She had bidden Bertie and Pooch goodbye and hated doing it, but they had looked content enough, sitting quietly by the Baroness. At the last moment she poked her head out of the taxi window.

'You will look after them, won't you? They'll be so lonely…'

'I give you my word, Becky, and remember that in a few weeks' time you will be able to make a home for them.'

She nodded, quite unable to speak for the lump in her throat.

She felt better presently. The Baron didn't like her particularly, she was sure, and yet she felt that she could trust him and upon reflection, she had saved him a lot of time and bother finding another nurse for his mother. She counted the money he had given her and felt quite faint at the amount and then being a practical girl, made a mental list of the things she would need.

It took her just two hours in which to do her shopping; some neat dark blue uniform dresses, because she could wear those each and every day, a blue cardigan and a navy blue raincoat, shoes and stockings and an unassuming handbag and then the more interesting part; undies and a thin dressing gown she could pack easily, and things for her face and her hair. All the same, there was quite a lot of money over. She found a suitcase to house her modest purchases and, obedient to the Baron's wish, took a taxi back to the hotel.

She found her patient lying on a chaise-longue drawn up to the window, a tray of coffee on the table at her elbow. 'I hope I haven't been too long,' began Becky, trying not to look at the corner where Bertie and Pooch had been sitting.

'No, my dear. Tiele went about an hour ago, and your animals went quite happily with him. I must tell you that he has a great liking for animals and they like him.' Her eyes fell upon the case Becky was carrying. 'You bought all that you require?' She nodded to herself without waiting for Becky to reply. 'Then come and have coffee with me and we will get to know each other. Tiele has arranged for us to be taken to the ship in good time; we will have lunch presently—here, I think, as I do dislike being pushed around in that chair—then we shall have time for a rest before we go. I'm sure you must be wondering just where we are going and why,' she added. 'Give me another cup of coffee, child, and I will tell you. I have been staying with an old friend at Blanchland, but unfortunately within two days of arriving I fell down some steps and injured my legs. Tiele came over at once, of course, and saw to everything, and I remained at my friend's house until I was fit to travel again. I could have remained there, but I have a sister living in Trondheim and as I had arranged to visit her before their summer is over, I prevailed upon Tiele to arrange things so that I might go. I get tired in a car and I suffer badly from air-sickness, so he decided that the best plan was for me to go by ship and since there is time enough, to go in comfort and leisure. We shall be sailing to Tilbury first and then to Hamburg and from there to Trondheim, where I intend to stay for three weeks. By then, with your help and that of the local doctor, I should be able to hobble and be out of this wheelchair. I have no idea how we shall return to Holland—Tiele will decide that when the time comes.'

Becky said: 'Yes, of course,' in a rather faint voice. After two years or more of isolation and hard work, events were crowding in on her so that she felt quite bewildered. 'Where do you live in Holland?' she asked.

'Our home is in Friesland, north of Leeuwarden. I don't live with Tiele, of course, now that I am alone I have moved to a house in Leeuwarden only a few miles from Huis Raukema. I have a daughter, Tialda, who is married and lives in Haarlem. Leeuwarden is a pleasant city, not too large, but you should find work there easily enough—besides, Tiele can help you there.'

'He has a practice in Leeuwarden?'

'Yes, although he doesn't live there.' She put down her cup and saucer. 'I have talked a great deal, but it is pleasant to chat with someone as restful as you are, Becky. I think we shall get on very well together. Tiele says that we must arrange our days in a businesslike fashion, so will you tell me what you think is best?' She opened her bag. 'I almost forgot, he left this for you—instructions, I believe.'

Very precise ones, written in a frightful scrawl, telling her just what he wanted done for his mother, reminding her that she was to take the usual off duty, that she might possibly have to get up at night if the Baroness wasn't sleeping, that she was to report to the ship's doctor immediately she went on board that afternoon and that she was to persevere with active movements however much his mother objected to them. At Trondheim there would be a doctor, already in possession of all the details of his mother's injuries, and he would call very shortly after they arrived there.

He hadn't forgotten anything; organising, she considered, must be his strong point.

'That's all very clear,' she told her patient. 'Shall we go over it together and get some sort of a routine thought out?'

It took them until a waiter came with the lunch menu. The Baroness had made one or two suggestions which Becky secretly decided were really commands and to which she acceded readily enough, since none of them were important, but she thought that they were going to get on very well. The Baroness was accustomed to having her own way but she was nice about it. To Becky, who had lived without affection save for her animal friends, her patient seemed kindness itself. They decided on their lunch and she got her settled nicely in a chair with a small table conveniently placed between them and then went away to change her clothes.

She felt a different girl after she had bathed and done her hair up into a neat bun and donned the uniform dress. She had bought some caps too, and she put one on now and went to join the Baroness, who studied her carefully, remarking: 'You're far too thin, Becky, but I like you in uniform. Have you bought clothes as well?'

'Well, no. You see, I should need such a lot....'

Her companion nodded. 'Yes, of course, but there are some nice shops in Trondheim, you can enjoy yourself buying all you want there. There's sherry on the table, child, pour us each a glass and we will wish ourselves luck.'

Becky hadn't had sherry in ages. It went straight to her head and made her feel as though life was fun after all and in a sincere effort not to be thin any longer, she ate her lunch with a splendid appetite. It was later, over coffee, that her patient said: 'We have a couple of hours still. Supposing you tell me about yourself, Becky?'

CHAPTER TWO

AFTERWARDS, thinking about it, Becky came to the conclusion that she had had far too much to say about herself, but somehow the Baroness had seemed so sympathetic—not that she had said very much, but Becky, who hadn't had anyone to talk to like that for a long time, sensed that the interest was real, as real as the sympathy. She hadn't meant to say much; only that she had trained at Hull because she had always wanted to be a nurse, and besides, her father was a country GP, and that her mother had died five years earlier and her father three years after her. But when she had paused there her companion had urged: 'But my dear, your stepmother—I wish to hear about her and this so unpleasant son of hers with the funny name...'

'Basil,' said Becky, and shivered a little. 'He's very good-looking and he smiles a lot and he never quite looks at you. He's cruel; he'll beat a dog and smile while he's doing it. He held my finger in a gas flame once because I'd forgotten to iron a shirt he wanted, and he smiled all the time.'

'The brute! But why were they so unkind to you? How did they treat your father?'

'Oh, they were very nice to him, and of course while he was alive I was at the hospital so I only went home for holidays, and then they persuaded my father to alter his will; my stepmother said that there was no need to leave me anything because she would take care of me and share whatever he left with me. That was a lie, of course. I knew it would be, but I couldn't do much about it, could I?' She sighed. 'And I had already decided that I would get a job abroad. But then Father died and my stepmother told me that I had nothing and that she wasn't going to give me anything and that I wasn't welcome at home any more, but I went all the same because

Bertie and Pooch had belonged to my father and I wanted to make sure that they were looked after. We still had the housekeeper Father had before he married again and she took care of them as best she could. And then my stepmother had jaundice. She didn't really need a nurse, but she wrote to the hospital and made it look as though it was vital that I should go home—and then Basil came and told me that they had sacked the housekeeper and that if I didn't go home they'd let Bertie and Pooch starve. So I went home. The house was on the edge of the village and Stoney Chase is a bit isolated anyway. They made it quite clear that I was to take the housekeeper's place, only they didn't pay me any wages to speak of and I couldn't go anywhere, you see, because I had no money after a little while—once I'd used up what I had on things like soap and tights from the village shop...'

'You told no one?'

'No. You see, Basil said that if I did he'd kill Pooch and Bertie, so then I knew I'd have to get away somehow, so each week I kept a bit from the shopping—I had aimed at fifty pounds, but then yesterday Basil and my stepmother were talking and I was in the garden and heard them. He said he was going to drown them both while I was in the village shopping the next day, so then I knew I'd have to leave sooner. We left about three o'clock this morning...' She had smiled then. 'The doctor stopped and gave us a lift, it was kind of him, especially as he was in such a hurry and we were all so wet and he didn't even know if I was making up the whole thing.' She had added uncomfortably: 'I must have bored you; I hate people who are sorry for themselves.'

'I should hardly say that you were sorry for yourself. A most unpleasant experience, my dear, and one which we must try and erase from your mind. I see no reason why you shouldn't make a pleasant future for yourself when we get to Holland. Nurses are always needed, and with Tiele's help you should be able to find something to suit you and somewhere to live.'

Becky had felt happy for the first time in a long while.

Their removal to the ship took place with an effortless ease which Becky attributed to the doctor's forethought. People materialised to take the luggage, push the wheelchair and get them into a taxi, and at the docks a businesslike man in a bowler hat saw them through Customs and into the hands of a steward on board. Becky, who had visualised a good deal of delay and bother on account of her having no passport, even though the Baroness had assured her that her son had arranged that too, was quite taken aback when the man in the bowler hat handed her a visitor's passport which he assured her would see her safely on her way. She remembered that the doctor had asked her some swift questions about her age and where she was born, but she hadn't taken, much notice at the time. It was evident that he was a man who got things done.

The Baroness had a suite on the promenade deck, a large stateroom, a sitting room with a dear little balcony leading from it, overlooking the deck below a splendidly appointed bathroom and a second stateroom which was to be Becky's. It was only a little smaller than her patient's and she circled round it, her eyes round with excitement, taking in the fluffy white towels in the bathroom, the telephone, the radio, the basket of fruit on the table. None of it seemed quite real, and she said so to the Baroness while she made her comfortable and started the unpacking; there was a formidable amount of it; the Baroness liked clothes, she told Becky blandly, and she had a great many. Becky, lovingly folding silk undies which must have cost a fortune and hanging dresses with couture labels, hadn't enjoyed herself so much for years. Perhaps in other circumstances she might have felt envy, but she had a wardrobe of her own to gloat over; Marks & Spencer's undies in place of pure silk, but they were pretty and new. Even her uniform dresses gave her pleasure, and if Bertie and Pooch had been with her she would have been quite happy. She finished the unpacking and went, at her patient's request, to find the purser's office, the shop, the doctor's surgery and the restaurant. 'For you may need to visit all of them at some time or other,' remarked the Baroness, 'and it's so much easier if you know your way around.'

It was a beautiful ship and not overcrowded. Becky, while she was at it, explored all its decks, peeped into the vast ballroom and the various bars and lounges, walked briskly round the promenade deck, skipped to the lowest deck of all to discover the swimming pool and hurried back to her patient, her too thin face glowing with excitement. 'It's super!' she told her. 'You know, I'm sure I could manage the wheelchair if you want to go on deck—I'm very strong.'

The Baroness gave her a faintly smiling look. 'Yes, Becky, I'm sure you are—but what about your sea legs?'

Becky hadn't given that a thought. The sea was calm at the moment, but of course they weren't really at sea yet; they had been passing Tynemouth when she had been on deck, but in another half hour or so they would be really on their way.

'Now let us have some room service,' observed the Baroness. 'Becky, telephone for the stewardess, will you?'

The dark-haired, brown-eyed young creature who presented herself a few minutes later was Norwegian, ready to be helpful and friendly. 'I shall have my breakfast here,' decreed the Baroness, 'and you, Becky, will go to the restaurant for yours.' She made her arrangements smoothly but with great politeness and then asked for the hotel manager, disregarding the stewardess's statement that he wouldn't be available at that time. Becky picked up the telephone once again and passed on the Baroness's request, and was surprised when he actually presented himself within a few minutes.

'A table for my nurse, if you please,' explained the Baroness, and broke off to ask Becky if she wanted to share with other people or sit by herself.

'Oh, alone, please,' declared Becky, and listened while that was arranged to her patient's satisfaction. 'We'll lunch here,' went on Baroness Raukema van den Eck, 'and dine here too.'

And when the manager had gone, 'You must have some time to yourself each day—I like a little rest after lunch, so if you settle me down I shall be quite all right until four o'clock or so. I'm sure there'll be plenty for you to do, and I expect you'll make friends.'

Becky doubted that; she had got out of the habit of meeting people and she didn't think anyone would bother much with a rather uninteresting nurse. But she agreed placidly and assured her companion that that would be very nice. 'I've found a library, too,' she said. 'Would you like a book?'

'A good idea—I should. Go and find something for me, my dear, and then we'll have a glass of sherry before dinner. Don't hurry,' she added kindly, 'have a walk on deck as you go.'

It didn't seem like a job, thought Becky, nipping happily from one deck to the other, and it was delightful to be able to talk to someone again. She wondered briefly what the Baron was doing at that moment, then turned her attention to the bookcases.

They dined in the greatest possible comfort with a steward to serve them, and Becky, reading the menu with something like ecstasy, could hardly stop her mouth watering. Her stepmother kept to a strict slimming diet and Basil had liked nothing much but steaks and chops and huge shoulders of lamb; too expensive for more than one, her stepmother had decreed, so that Becky, willy-nilly, had lived on a slimming diet as well, with little chance of adding to her meagre meals because she had to account for the contents of the larder and fridge each morning. Now she ate her way through mushrooms in sauce rémoulade, iced celery soup, cold chicken with tangerines and apple salad, and topped these with peach royale before pouring coffee for them both. She said like a happy little girl: 'That was the best meal I've ever had. I used to think about food a lot, you know, when you're always a bit hungry, you do, but I never imagined anything as delicious as this.' She added awkwardly: 'I don't think you should pay me as

much as you said you would, Baroness, because I'm not earn-
ing it and I'm getting all this as well...it doesn't seem quite
honest...'

'You will be worth every penny to me, Becky,' her patient
assured her, 'and how you managed to bear with that dreadful
life you were forced to lead is more than I can understand.
Besides, I am a demanding and spoilt woman, you won't get
a great deal of time to yourself.'

Which was true enough. Becky found her day well filled.
True, she breakfasted alone in the restaurant, but only after
she had spent half an hour with the Baroness preparing that
lady for her own breakfast in bed. And then there was the
business of helping her patient to dress, getting her into her
wheelchair and taking her to whichever part of the ship she
preferred. Here they stayed for an hour or so, taking their
coffee, chatting a little and enjoying the sun. Becky read aloud
too, because the Baroness said it tried her eyes to read for
herself, until half an hour or so before lunch when Becky was
sent off to walk round the decks or potter round the shop and
buy postcards at the purser's office for the Baroness. They
were to dock at Tilbury in the morning and as the ship
wouldn't sail for Hamburg until the late afternoon the Baroness had suggested that Becky could go up to London and
do some shopping and rejoin the ship after lunch. But this
Becky declined to do; so far, she considered, she hadn't
earned half her salary. She had been hired to look after her
patient and that she intended to do. Instead, the two of them
spent a peaceful day in the Baroness's stateroom playing be-
zique, and taking a slow wander round the deck on the quiet
ship. But by tea time the passengers were coming aboard and
the pair of them retired once more to the little balcony leading
from the suite, from where they watched the bustle and to-
ing and fro-ing going on below them.

They sailed soon afterwards and Becky, leaving her patient
with a considerable pile of mail to read, went on deck to watch
the ship leave. She hung over the rails, determined not to miss

a thing, and it was half an hour before she tore herself away from watching the busy river scene and returned to the stateroom. The Baroness was telephoning, but she broke off what she was saying to tell Becky: 'It is Tiele—making sure that we are quite all right.' And at Becky's look of surprise: 'He's back in Friesland, and I'm to tell you that Pooch and Bertie have settled down very well.' She nodded dismissal and Becky slipped away to her own cabin.

She had collected all the literature about the voyage that she could lay hands on, and now she sat down and studied it; Hamburg next and then Trondheim. There was a whole day at sea first, though, and more than a day between Hamburg and Trondheim. She began to read the leaflet she had been given and only put it down when her patient called to her through the slightly open door.

At Hamburg the Baroness declared her intention of going ashore. The purser, summoned to the cabin, assured her that a taxi should be arranged without difficulty, that help would be at hand to wheel the chair down the gangway and that the Baroness need have no worry herself further. To Becky, accustomed to doing everything for herself, it seemed the height of comfort. And indeed, when the ship docked there was nothing for her to do beyond readying her patient for the outing and then walking beside the chair while a steward wheeled it carefully on to the quay. There were several busloads of passengers going on shore excursions and they had been advised by the purser to get back before these returned or the new passengers began to embark. 'Plenty of time,' said the Baroness easily. 'We will drive round the city, take a look at the Binnenalster and the Aussenalster and the driver can take us to a confectioner's so that you can buy me some of the chocolates Tiele always brings me when he comes here.'

She was arranged comfortably in the taxi, accorded a courteous farewell by the officer on duty whom she warned not to allow the ship to leave until her return, and was driven away, with Becky sitting beside her.

It was all very exciting; first the journey through the dock area, which the Baroness didn't bother to look at, but which Becky found absorbing, and then presently the shopping streets and a brief glimpse of the inner lake. 'It is much prettier once we have crossed the Kennedybrucke,' said the Baroness. She said something to the driver in German and he slowed down to take the pleasant road running alongside the lake, its calm water gleaming in the sunshine, the well kept villas in their splendid grounds facing it. Becky's face lighted up and a little colour came into it. 'Oh, this is super!' she declared. 'I had no idea…'

Her companion cast her a glance full of sympathy, but all she said was: 'I think you will like Trondheim better, although it is a great deal smaller, of course.'

They circled the lake slowly before going back to the shopping centre where the driver parked outside a confectioner's whose windows displayed extravagantly boxed sweets of every sort, and Becky, obedient to her patient's request, went rather hesitantly inside. There were no difficulties, however. She was perfectly understood, her purchases were made and paid for and with several prettily wrapped boxes she got back into the taxi. It surprised her very much when the taxi stopped once more and the driver got out, went into a café and emerged presently with a waiter carrying a tray with coffee and cream cakes. The tray was set carefully upon Becky's knees and they were left to take their elevenses in peace. 'I like my little comforts,' explained the Baroness placidly. And get them too, thought Becky admiringly.

Their return to the ship was as smooth as their departure had been. A steward was by the taxi door almost before it had stopped and the Baroness was bestowed carefully into her wheelchair once more. Only when she was quite comfortable did she open her handbag and pay the driver—generously too, if the smile on his face was anything to go by. Becky, trotting along beside the chair, wondered what it must be like to be rich enough to command all the attention and comfort one required without apparent effort. Probably one got used to it and took it as a matter of course; thinking about it, she remembered that the Baron hadn't seemed surprised when she had accepted the job he had offered her out of the blue. She was deeply grateful to him, of course, but at the same time she couldn't help wondering what he would have done if she had refused.

The Baroness was tired after their outing, so she elected to take a light lunch in her stateroom and then rest, sending Becky down to the restaurant for her own lunch while she ate hers. Becky found the place quite full, for a good many more passengers had boarded the ship that morning. She sat at her table, set discreetly in a corner, and ate a rather hurried meal, in case the Baroness should want her the minute she had finished her own lunch, and then slipped away, smiling rather shyly at the waiter as she did so. She hadn't quite got used to being waited on.

The Baroness was drinking her coffee but professed herself quite ready to rest. Becky made her comfortable on the sofa along one wall, covered her with a rug and sat down nearby because her patient had asked her not to go away for a little while. 'I'm expecting a call from Tiele,' explained the Baroness, 'and if you would stay until it comes through...' She closed her eyes and dozed while Becky sat, still as a mouse, listening to the exciting noises going on all around them—people talking, music coming from somewhere, but faintly, the winch loading the luggage, an occasional voice raised in command or order. It was all very exciting; she contemplated her new shoes and thought about the Baron, his mother, the journey they were about to make, Norway, about which she knew almost nothing, and then the Baron again. It was a pity he didn't like her, but very understandable, and it made his kindness in taking care of Bertie and Pooch all the greater; it couldn't be much fun doing kindnesses to someone you didn't care a row of pins for. Her thoughts were interrupted by the faint tinkle of the telephone, and she picked it up quickly with a glance at the still sleeping Baroness. Her hullo was quiet and the Baron said at once: 'Becky? My mother's asleep?'

'Yes, but I think she would like me to wake her, if you would wait a moment.'

He didn't answer her but asked: 'You're settling down, I hope? No snags? You won't give way to seasickness or anything of that sort, I hope?' She heard him sigh. 'You didn't look very strong.'

Becky's voice stayed quiet but held indignation. 'I'm very strong,' she told him quite sharply, 'and as the sea is as calm as a millpond, I'm not likely to be seasick.'

'You seem to have a temper too,' remarked the Baron. 'As long as you don't vent it on my mother…'

'Well,' breathed Becky, her chest swelling with rage under the neat dress, 'I never did! As though I would! And I haven't got a temper…'

'I'm glad to hear it. Bertie and Pooch are quite nicely settled.'

'I'm so glad—I've been worrying about them just a little; you're sure…?'

'Quite. Now if you would wake up my mother, Nurse?'

She was to be nurse, was she? And what was she to call him? Baron or doctor or sir? She crossed the room and roused the Baroness with a gentle touch on her shoulder and that lady opened her eyes at once with a look of such innocence that Becky didn't even begin to suspect that her patient had been listening to every word she had uttered.

She went to her cabin while mother and son carried on a quite lengthy conversation and spent ten minutes or so doing things to her face. She had bought make-up, the brand she had always used when she had money of her own to spend, and now she was enjoying the luxury of using it. She applied powder to her small nose, lipstick to her too large mouth, and tidied her hair under her cap and then studied her face. Nothing remarkable; no wonder her employer had dismissed her with the kind of casual kindness he would afford a stray cat.

She sighed and then adjusted her expression to a cheerful calm at the sound of her patient's voice calling her.

The rest of the day passed pleasantly enough with the Baroness remarkably amenable when called upon to do her exercises. The moment they got on shore at Trondheim, Becky had been told to instruct her in the use of crutches, something she wasn't looking forward to over-much. The Baroness could be a trifle pettish if called upon to do something she didn't fancy doing, and yet Becky already liked her; she had probably spent a spoilt life with a doting husband and now a doting son, having everything she wanted within reason, but she could be kind too and thoughtful of others, and, Becky reminded herself, she had a wonderful job; well paid, by no means exhausting and offering her the chance of seeing something of the world.

There were almost two days before they would arrive at Trondheim, and Becky found that they went too quickly. A good deal of time was spent on deck, the Baroness in her wheelchair, Becky sitting beside her while they carried on a gentle flow of small talk. There was plenty to talk about; the distant coastline of Sweden and then Norway, their fellow passengers, the day's events on board; there was so much to do and even though neither of them took part in any of them, it was fun to discuss them. The Captain was giving a cocktail party that evening, but the Baroness had declared that nothing would persuade her to go to it in a wheelchair; they would dine quietly in her stateroom as usual, and Becky didn't mind; she had nothing to wear and the idea of appearing at such a glittering gathering in a nurse's uniform didn't appeal to her in the least. All the same, it would have been fun to have seen some of the dresses...

The Baroness liked to dress for the evening. Becky, helping her into a black chiffon gown and laying a lacy shawl over her knees, wished just for a moment that they had been going to the party, it seemed such a waste...

It wasn't a waste. Instead of the sherry which the steward

brought to the stateroom, he carried a bottle of champagne in an ice bucket, and following hard on his heels was the Captain himself, accompanied by several of his officers, and they were followed by more stewards bearing trays of delicious bits and pieces, presumably to help the champagne down. Becky, with a young officer on either side of her, intent on keeping her glass filled and carrying on the kind of conversation she had almost forgotten existed, found life, for the first time in two years, was fun.

When the gentlemen had gone the Baroness sat back in her chair and eyed Becky. 'You must buy yourself some pretty clothes,' she observed. 'You won't always be on duty, you know—I know there was no time in Newcastle to do more than get the few essentials, but once we are in Trondheim you shall go shopping. Tiele gave you enough money, I hope?'

Becky thought with still amazed astonishment of the notes in her purse. 'More than enough,' she explained. 'A week's salary in advance and money to buy my uniforms and—and things.'

'A week's salary? What is that? Let me see, sixty pounds, did we not say? What is sixty pounds?' It was lucky that she didn't expect an answer, for Becky was quite prepared to tell her that for her, at least, it was a small fortune. 'When we get to Trondheim you will have your second week's wages—not very much, but I daresay you will be able to find something to wear.'

Becky thought privately that she would have no difficulty at all, although she had no intention of spending all that money. It was of course tempting to do so, but she had the future to think of; she supposed her present job would last a month or a little longer and even though she managed to get another job at once, there would be rent to pay if she were lucky enough to find somewhere to live, and food for herself and the animals until she drew her pay. All the same she allowed herself the luxury of planning a modest outfit or two. They would arrive at Trondheim the next day and a little thrill of excitement ran through her, just for the moment she forgot the future and the unpleasant past; Norway, as yet invisible over the horizon, was before her and after that Holland. Perhaps later she would be homesick for England, but now she felt secure and content, with almost the width of the North Sea between her and her stepmother and Basil.

She fell to planning the little home she would make for herself and Bertie and Pooch and was only disturbed in this pleasant occupation by the Baroness, who had been reading and now put down her book and suggested a game of dominoes before the leisurely process of getting ready for bed.

The next day was fine and warm, the sea was calm and very blue and the shores of Norway, towering on either side of the Trondheimsfjord, looked magnificent. Becky, released from the patient's company for an hour, hung over the rail, not missing a thing; the tiny villages in the narrow valleys, the farms perched impossibly on narrow ledges half way up the mountains with apparently no way of reaching them, the camping sites on the edge of the water and the cosy wooden houses. It was only when Trondheim came into sight, still some way off on a bend of the fjord, that she went reluctantly back to the Baroness. She had packed earlier, there was little left to do other than eat their lunch and collect the last few odds and ends, but there would be ample time for that; the Baroness had elected to wait until the passengers who were going on the shore excursions had left the ship; they would have to go ashore by tender, and Becky knew enough of her patient by now to guess that that lady avoided curious glances as much as possible.

The passengers were taken ashore with despatch and wouldn't return until five o'clock. Becky, sent on deck to take a breath of air while her patient enjoyed a last-minute chat with the ship's doctor, the purser and the first officer, watched the last tender returning from the shore. Trondheim looked well worth a visit and she longed to get a closer look. It was nice to think that she would have two or three weeks in which to explore it thoroughly. There was a lot to see; the cathedral, the old warehouses, the royal palace, the Folk Museum...she pitied the passengers who had just gone ashore and who would have to view all these delights in the space of a few hours. One of the young officers who had come to the Baroness's cabin joined her at the rail. 'You get off here, don't you?' he asked in a friendly voice. He glanced at her trim uniform. 'Will you get time to look around Trondheim?—it's a lovely old place.'

'Oh, I'm sure I shall—I don't have to work hard, you know. The Baroness is kindness itself and I get free time each day just like anyone else.' She smiled at him. 'I loved being on board this ship.'

He smiled back at her; he was a nice young man with a pretty girl at home waiting to marry him and he felt vague pity for this small plain creature, who didn't look plain at all when she smiled. He said now: 'Well, I hope you enjoy your stay in Norway. Do you go back to Holland with the Baroness?'

'Yes, just for a little while, then I'll get a job there.'

He looked at her curiously. 'Don't you want to go back to England?'

She was saved from answering him by the stewardess coming in search of her to tell her that the Baroness was ready to go ashore now. Getting that lady into the tender was a delicate operation involving careful lifting while Becky hovered over the plastered leg, in a panic that the tender would give a lurch and it would receive a thump which would undo all the good it had been doing. But nothing happened, the Baroness was seated at last, the leg carefully propped up before her and Becky beside her, their luggage was stowed on board, and they made the short trip to the shore. Here the same procedure had to be carried out, although it wasn't quite as bad because there were no stairs to negotiate. Becky nipped on to the wooden pier and had the wheelchair ready by the time the

Baroness was borne ashore. Escorted by a petty officer, they made their way off the pier to the land proper.

There were a lot of people about and a couple of officials who made short work of examining their papers before waving them on to where a Saab Turbo was waiting. The lady sitting in the car got out when she saw them coming, not waiting for her companion, and ran to meet them. She was a small woman, a little older than the Baroness and very like her in looks. The two ladies embraced, both talking at once, and only broke off when the elderly gentleman who had been in the car reached them. The Baroness embraced him too and embarked on another conversation to stop in the middle of a sentence and say in English: 'I am so excited, you must forgive me, I had forgotten my dear Becky. She has looked after me so very well and she is going to stay with me until I return home.' She turned to Becky standing quietly a few paces away. 'Becky, come and meet my sister and brother-in-law. Mijnheer and Mevrouw van Denne—he is Consul here and will know exactly the right places for you to see while you are here. And now if I could be put in the car...?'

An oldish man joined them and was introduced as Jaap the chauffeur, between them Becky and he lifted the Baroness into the back seat where she was joined by the Consul and his wife while Becky, having seen the chair and the luggage safely stowed in the boot, got in beside Jaap.

She tried to see everything as they went through the city, of course, but she would have needed eyes all round her head. But she glimpsed two department stores and a street of pleasant shops with other streets leading from it and she had the palace pointed out to her, an imposing building built entirely of wood, then they were in a wide street with the cathedral at its far end. But they didn't get as far as that; half way down Jaap turned into a tree-lined avenue with large houses, before one of which he slowed to turn again into a short drive and stop before its solid front door. They had arrived. Becky drew a deep breath to calm herself. It would never do to get too excited; she was a nurse and must preserve a calm front, but her eyes shone with delight and her pale face held a nice colour for once. The Baroness, watching her with some amusement, decided that she wasn't only a nice girl, she was—just now and again—quite a pretty one, too.

CHAPTER THREE

THE HOUSE WAS surprisingly light inside and furnished with large, comfortable furniture. The whole party crossed the hall and went into a lofty sitting room with a splendid view of the cathedral in the distance, and the Baroness, still talking, was transferred from her wheelchair to a high-backed winged chair while coffee and little cakes were served by a cheerful young woman whom the Baroness's sister introduced as Luce. She added, smiling at Becky, 'And you do not mind if we call you Becky?' Her English was as good as her sister's.

'Please do,' said Becky, and was interrupted by her patient with: 'And tomorrow morning, my dear, you shall go to the shops as soon as you have helped me, and buy yourself some pretty clothes. It is a good idea to wear uniform, I know, but now you will get some free time each day and then you will want to go out and enjoy yourself.'

Her three companions turned to look at her kindly, but she could also see doubt in their elderly faces. If she had been pretty, she thought wryly, she would probably have a simply super time, as it was she would have to content herself with a round of museums and places of interest. She gave herself a mental shake, appalled at her self-pity; good fortune was smiling on her at last, and she had no need to be sorry for herself. She agreed with enthusiasm tempered with a reminder that exercises for the day hadn't yet been done and since the family doctor was going to call that evening, it might be as well if they were done and over before he arrived—a remark which was the signal to convey the Baroness to her room on the ground floor. It was a charming apartment and extremely comfortable with a bathroom leading from it and on the other side of that, a smaller but just as comfortable room for Becky. The exercises over, she settled her patient back into a chair by the window and prepared to unpack, a task which was frequently interrupted by her companion who was watching the traffic in the distance and declared that she could see the coachloads of passengers off the ship on their way to the cathedral. 'You must go there,' she declared. 'It is quite beautiful—I should like to see it again myself.'

'Then we'll go together,' said Becky instantly. 'It's no distance. I'll push the chair—the exercise will do me good.'

The Baroness was doubtful. 'Tiele said that you weren't to do too much heavy lifting—he seems to think you're not very strong.'

Becky gave a snort. 'Then he's mistaken—I'm as strong as a horse! When I was at home I used to do almost all the housework; it was quite a big house, too, with miles of flagstoned floors and stairs to polish and heavy furniture to shift about.'

'Disgraceful!' the Baroness sounded indignant. Your stepmother should be brought to justice for treating you in such a way.' She considered a moment. 'Of course, the maids at home have a good deal of housework to do, but they are well paid and none of them is overworked.' She turned away from the window and watched Becky hanging a black velvet dress in the wardrobe. 'What clothes will you buy?'

'Well, I thought a couple of cotton dresses because it's warm, isn't it? I thought it would be much cooler...'

'It can be cool, but a cotton dress or two could be useful—get a jacket or something to wear with them—what else?'

'Slacks? Some thin tops, perhaps a sweater, some light shoes or sandals...'

'A pretty dress for the evening, of course. Two.'

Becky, who hadn't had a new dress for so long, heaved a sigh of great content.

The Baroness was unusually docile the following morning; she allowed Becky to assist her to dress, did her exercises with exemplary perfection, the while discussing Doctor Iversen's visit. He had come just before dinner on the previous evening and he knew so much about the Baroness's injuries that Becky felt sure that the Baron had taken care to give him every last detail. He applauded her progress, agreed that the exercises should be stepped up and went away again, promising to call in two days' time bringing with him some gutter crutches so that the Baroness might start to walk again. 'The quicker you are on your feet the better,' he had pointed out. 'You are here for two—three weeks? Then by the time you leave us, Baroness, I believe you will be able to manage very well.' He had given Becky one or two instructions in his excellent English, and smiled at her very kindly.

Becky walked to the shops. The city was spread widely and easy to find one's way about. There were two department stores, Mevrouw van Denne had told her—Sundt & Co in Kongens Gate and Steen & Strom, Olav Tryggvasonsgate, fairly close to each other. She prowled happily round them in turn and finally returned to the Consul's house, laden with parcels, all of which she had to undo and display their contents to the Baroness, who had been stationed strategically in the hall, waiting for her. Two cotton dresses and a cardigan to go with them, blue slacks and a couple of cotton tops, sensible flat sandals and a pair of pretty slippers, a flowered cotton skirt and a lace-trimmed blouse to go with it, and a pale green jersey dress, very simple but, as the Baroness remarked approvingly: 'In excellent taste.' She added: 'Is that all, Becky?'

Becky had spent just about all the money she had, but she didn't say so. When she had her next pay she would buy another dress perhaps, but from now on she was determined to save as much as she could. Her job here in Norway was more like a holiday; once she got to Holland and got work in a hospital there she would need all the money she could spare—there would be food for herself and the animals, lodgings and light and heating and all the other mundane things which cost money; besides, the clothes she had bought had been rather expensive. 'I'll look around,' she told the Baroness placidly, 'and when I see something nice I'll buy it,' a statement with which the Baroness was in complete agreement since that was something she had always been able to do herself.

The Baron telephoned again that evening and this time Becky was called to speak to him. She faithfully relayed Doctor Iversen's remarks, assured him that his mother was doing very nicely and was surprised, when she had finished, to be asked if she was enjoying herself and having enough time in which to see the city for herself.

She told him she had plenty of free time and enquired about Bertie and Pooch. 'They're in excellent condition and perfectly happy. Have you had a free day yet, Becky?'

'Me? No—what would I do with it?' she asked him in a matter-of-fact voice. 'I'm very happy, and the Baroness is a perfect patient.'

Which wasn't quite true; her patient liked her own way and was used to getting it and she could be imperious at times, but Becky liked her. The work wasn't arduous; she considered that she was overpaid and the question of a day off hadn't entered her mind.

'You will probably meet someone of your own age,' persisted the Baron, 'and wish to spend a day with them—there are some interesting trips you can make...'

'I don't think I'll meet anyone—in any case,' she reminded him severely, 'I'm not on holiday, you know.'

But during the next week or so it seemed as though she was. True, the Baroness took up the major portion of her day; the crutches had to be mastered and since her patient had taken exception to them on the grounds that they were clumsy and ugly, it took a good deal of coaxing to get her to use them. But after the first few days she began to make progress, although her confidence was so small that she refused to go anywhere, even across the room, without Becky beside her, but as there was a constant stream of visitors to the house, Becky was able to get an hour here and an hour there. She met people too. The Consul lived fairly quietly, but there was a good deal of coming and going between the Consulates, small dinner parties, coffee in the morning, people dropping in for tea in the afternoons, and since the Baroness couldn't go out to any great extent, the visits were more frequent. The Baroness was meticulous in introducing Becky to anyone and everyone who called, and despite her protests, she attended all the dinner parties and was treated more like a daughter of the house than a nurse. And she was liked by everyone too, although she didn't realise that herself. As the Baroness said to her sister: 'Becky may be a plain girl, but she has charm and a restful manner and the sweetest smile. She is also a splendid nurse. I must tell Tiele to see that she gets a really good job when we get back. The child deserves it after these last few wretched years.'

The two ladies, quite carried away, discussed the matter at some length.

Becky, true to her promise, took the Baroness to the cathedral. It was a bright sunny day and not too warm and the journey there wasn't too arduous. The Nidras Cathedral loomed before them, its dark granite exterior almost forbidding. It was dark inside, too, but its beautiful windows softened the darkness to a dim peace which Becky found soothing as well as awe-inspiring. And once inside they joined one of the groups of visitors being led round by students, picturesque in their long red gowns, addressing their audiences with apparently no difficulty at all in whatever language was needed. Becky, on the fringe of their group because of the awkwardness of the wheelchair, missed a good deal of what was said and made up her mind to go again, on her own, and this she was able to do the very next day when several ladies came for coffee and she was dismissed kindly by the Baroness and told to go and enjoy herself until lunch time. And this time she kept well to the fore in the group following the guide so that she missed nothing at all, inspecting the Gothic interior to her heart's content, treading the dark passages behind the altar to see the spring in the walls and then going all round the outside to admire the great building. It gave her a taste for sightseeing and after that she visited the wooden houses along the waterfront and the *veits*, the narrow medieval lanes between the main streets, as well as paying a visit to Stiftsgaarden, the large wooden palace in the middle of the city. There was only one place she hadn't managed to visit; the Folk Museum on the outskirts of Trondheim. It was too far to walk in the brief periods of freedom she had and even if she treated herself to a taxi she would be worrying all the time that she would be late back; the Baroness was a dear, but she liked everyone to be punctual, although it wasn't one of her own virtues.

The Baron telephoned regularly, sometimes asking to speak to her, but more often or not sending some casual message about Bertie and Pooch. In another week they would be going to Holland and she could hardly wait to see her old friends again, although she felt regret that she had seen so little of Norway. She had loved every minute of it and she had been luckier than she had deserved. The thought of a new job and freedom went to her head like strong drink, so that she bought a knitted top and skirt in a pleasing shade of old rose, just because she found it pretty. She tried it on again that evening when she was getting ready for bed and pranced around her room, her mousey hair done in an elaborate whirl and her best shoes on her feet. Life was fun, she told herself.

It was still fun in the morning; it was glorious weather and she put on her uniform dress and cap with something like regret; a cotton dress would have been so much more suitable, but the Baroness had old-fashioned ideas about nurses; she liked Becky in uniform unless she was free. She perched her cap tidily, made sure that her face was nicely made up and went along the hall as was her custom to get the post for the Baroness and fetch the coffee tray which would be in readiness on the sitting room table. It was still early, barely eight o'clock, and the house was quiet. She whistled softly as she went and, still whistling, opened the sitting-room door.

The last person she had expected to see was standing in the big bay window, hands in the pockets of his beautifully cut trousers, looking out into the street. He turned as she paused in the doorway and gave her a long, considering look. 'Good morning, Becky,' said the Baron.

'Well!' said Becky, and was annoyed to find herself blushing. 'Good morning—I didn't expect to see you...'

'Why should you?' he asked coolly. 'I didn't tell you I was coming.' He smiled across the room, not at her but at someone else. He wasn't alone; there was a tall, graceful girl sitting on the arm of a chair in a corner of the large room. She was wearing slacks and a loosely belted tunic and looked exactly as Becky longed to look and never did. She was pretty too, with strong features and bright blue eyes, and when she turned them on Becky it was very plain to see that she was the Baron's sister. She smiled now in a friendly way while the Baron contented himself with a brief glance before turning his head to look out of the window again.

'You're surprised to see us,' he commented idly. 'Tialda, this is Becky, who is looking after Mama.' He nodded vaguely in his sister's direction. 'Becky, this is my sister Tialda.'

Becky said how do you do and pondered her reason for feeling so relieved when she had realised that it was the Baron's sister and not some girl-friend; she had no reason to feel relief. She frowned a little and the Baron said briskly: 'We have decided to take a short holiday here.'

'Oh? Well, that's nice.' Becky felt the inadequacy of her words and beamed at them warmly to make up for it.

The girl's smile deepened. 'You said she was plain,' she observed to her brother. 'A half starved mouse.'

He gave Becky another look. 'And so she was—it must be the food and the fresh air.' He gave Becky a bland smile. 'You filled out very nicely, Becky.'

He was impossible! Becky hated him, although she didn't

hate him in the same way as she hated Basil. There was a difference, like hating a thunderstorm and something nasty under an upturned stone...

'If you have finished discussing me,' she said haughtily, 'I'll tell the Baroness that you're here.' At the door she paused to say: 'Such manners!'

Tialda crossed the room and tucked an arm under her brother's. 'And that puts you in your place, my boy.' She looked up at him. 'We were abominably rude, you know—I shall apologise; I think she's rather a sweetie.'

He smiled down at her. 'Yes? She would be disappointed if I did. She is grateful—rather touchingly so—because I rescued her, but that doesn't prevent her having a rather poor opinion of me. I fancy that I'm overbearing as well as rude and too much given to getting my own way.'

'What a nice change from girls melting all over you, though you're quite nice really.'

Tialda turned round as the door opened and Becky came in. 'The Baroness would like you to go in immediately,' she announced in a cold little voice. 'It's the door on the right of the stairs. Would you like your coffee with her or later?'

Tialda had crossed the room to stand before her. 'I'm sorry I was rude,' she said gently, 'it was unforgivable of me; you've been so kind to Mama, I hope you'll not mind too much.' She held out an exquisitely manicured hand. 'I should like to be friends.'

Becky took the hand in her own small capable one. She said rather gruffly: 'I don't mind a bit, really I don't, especially as it was true. And it would be nice to be friends.' She looked up and caught the Baron's eye fixed on her and saw the mocking light in it.

He threw up a protesting hand and said silkily: 'Don't look at me like that, Becky—I have no manners, you know.'

But when she saw him next he wasn't silky at all, he was impersonally polite, just like a consultant doing a round of a ward; it was 'If you please, Nurse,' or 'Lift the leg, will you,

Nurse?' or 'Be so good as to hand me that tendon hammer, Nurse.' Just as though he'd never seen her before in his life! And she for her part behaved exactly as she sensed he expected her to, a quiet, well-trained nurse, only speaking when spoken to, anticipating his wants a split second before he voiced them, waiting ready with the crutches so that his mother could demonstrate her progress, re-bandaging the injured knee with neat speediness... Doctor Iversen was there too, and the two men conferred together, occasionally turning to her for information while the Baroness sat on a chair between them, looking impatient. At length she asked with some asperity:

'Well, will you not tell me how I progress? All this solemn talk...is it so necessary? I am a little bored.' She glanced at Becky. 'I expect Becky is too, but of course she has been trained not to show it.'

Her son laughed at her. 'Allow us a little self-importance, Mama,' he begged, 'and yes, we're delighted with your progress. You have done very well indeed, there's no reason why you shouldn't use your leg normally provided you're careful—you'll have to wear a supporting bandage for a little longer, of course, and in a couple of weeks the plaster on the other leg can come off. We'll see to that when we get home.' He looked at Becky. 'I hope you will stay with my mother for a week or so in Holland—just until she can walk with a stick. It will give you time to get another job, too.'

Becky said yes, thank you, relieved that she would have a little time in which to get used to the idea of working in a foreign land and to find herself somewhere to live. She did a few rapid sums in her head and decided that she wouldn't buy anything else but save every penny. Rent in advance, she thought worriedly, and food and probably bus fares...'Becky,' said the Baron softly, and she realised that he had said her name several times. 'I was only saying,' he said patiently, 'that the exercises might be lengthened considerably...'

She was kept busy for the rest of the morning. The Baroness was excited and impatient and wanted to skip her usual routine, which Becky wouldn't allow, but she recovered her good humour presently when everyone gathered for drinks before lunch and over that meal she dominated the table with her amusing conversation, and afterwards she declared that she would have her rest in the drawing room so that she could gossip with Tialda, and Becky could have an hour off and go to Sundt and match up the embroidery silks. 'And don't be long, my dear,' she added. 'You said you would massage my shoulders.'

Becky whisked away, changed into one of the cotton dresses and walked to the shops. She would have liked more time; it was exactly the kind of weather in which to take a long walk—she could have gone down to the harbour and watched the coastline express come in, a daily event of which she never tired; it fired her imagination that the miniature liner went to and fro together with its sister ships every day of the year, whatever the weather, calling at each small village all the way to Kirkenes on the very border of Russia. One day, she promised herself, she would make the journey, but now she did her errand and hurried back, to thread the Baroness's needle because the little lady declared that her eyesight was worsening and then go to her room to fetch a shawl she wanted Tialda to see. It was after their afternoon tea, while Becky was encouraging the Baroness to put her weight on the almost sound leg, that her son joined them, and presently, when the exercises were finished and the Baroness was sitting once more and Becky had gone to find Tialda so that her mother could continue their pleasant chat, he asked: 'Has Becky had any days off, Mama? You have been here two weeks as well as several days on board ship.'

The Baroness looked unhappy. 'Oh, dear—I did tell you that I would see that she had a day, or was it two—each week, but somehow I forgot, and she is such a sweet little thing and such good company...she has had several hours each day, though, most afternoons, you know.'

'And have you had to rouse her at night, my dear?'

'Once or twice—if I have wanted a drink or could not sleep.' She looked a little shamefaced. 'Have I been selfish, Tiele?'

He bent to kiss her cheek. 'No, my dear, but I think we might arrange a few days for her, don't you agree? I was talking to Iversen, he knows of a nurse who will come in each day and look after you while Becky has her little holiday.'

'Of course, dear. But where will she go?'

The Baron got to his feet and strolled to the window. 'Tialda thinks it might be a good idea if we drove over to Molde and took Becky with us. For three—perhaps four days, and when we come back she can get you ready to come back with us. Do you think you could manage the car journey if we spend three nights on the way? We'll make you comfortable in the back of the car and you'll have Becky.'

'I shall enjoy it,' declared his parent. 'Is it very far?'

'Seven hundred miles, perhaps a little more. We'll stop whenever you're tired and we can cross from Kristiansand to Hirtshals and drive down from there.'

'I wonder what Becky will say?' asked his mother.

'I'll let her know this evening,' he said carelessly. 'I thought we might go tomorrow—it's only a hundred and seventy miles or so. We can leave after lunch—I don't suppose she'll need much time to put a few things in a bag.'

The Baroness looked at him thoughtfully. 'No,' she said at length, 'the child has pitifully few things to put into a bag, she has bought almost no clothes since we have been here.'

'Very sensible of her. She's presumably saving for her future comfort.'

'Don't you like her?'

He laughed gently. 'It depends what you mean by that, Mama. I like Becky, she's a good nurse, and she's gone through a nasty patch, but she's hardly a beauty, is she? and her conversation hardly sparkles. Shall we say that she's not quite my type—I'm not attracted to thin mice.'

It was a pity that Becky heard him as she came back into the room. The self-confidence she had so painfully built up since she had been with the Baroness oozed out of her sensible shoes and her face went rigid in an effort to compose it to a suitably unaware expression. She was aware that she was being looked at quite searchingly, but her voice was nicely normal as she informed her patient that Tialda would join them in a few minutes. She didn't look at the Baron at all, but murmured some vague nothing at the Baroness and made for the door. The Baron reached it at the same time, held it open for her and followed her into the hall, shutting the door behind him. 'A few words with you?' he suggested, and Becky, boiling with rage and humiliation behind her quiet face, said 'certainly' in a voice just as quiet. It seemed likely that he was going to give her the sack or at least express displeasure at something or other. After all, she had just heard him...her face didn't alter, but her eyes spoke volumes.

'No, you're not getting the sack,' observed the Baron disconcertingly. 'On the contrary, I am delighted with my mother's progress and the care you have given her—she never ceases to sing your praises. You have had no days off, I believe? I'm sorry about that, my mother forgot about them, but you shall have them at once. Tialda and I are going to drive over to Molde for a few days tomorrow, and we should like you to come with us. We shall leave after lunch.'

Becky stared at his tie, because that was on a level with her eyes. Nothing, she told herself fiercely, would make her do any such thing—the arrogance of the man, throwing her a holiday with the careless concern of one throwing a bone to a hungry dog! She went bright pink and said: 'No, thank you,' in a tight voice.

'Oh—why not?' He spoke easily as though he didn't much mind.

'You wouldn't enjoy my company.'

'Probably not,' he sounded amused, 'but Tialda wants you

to come, you'll be company for each other and leave me in peace.'

Becky eyed him thoughtfully. He might have saved her from Basil and her stepmother, but she couldn't for the life of her think why. She perceived then that she was a convenience to him; his sister had looked considerably younger than he, it was more than likely that he would be glad to share her society with someone else. She couldn't very well refuse— besides, he had been the means of her starting a new life as well as saving Bertie and Pooch from a horrid fate. 'When do you want me to be ready?' she asked.

'Sensible girl! After lunch tomorrow. Don't bother with clothes, something to travel in and a dress for the evening.'

Which was about all she had anyhow.

They left immediately after lunch the following day with brother and sister sitting together and Becky, looking small and a little lost, in the back of the Rolls. She had had a busy morning, explaining just how the Baroness liked things done, to the Norwegian nurse who was to take her place while she was away—a very pretty girl with excellent English and dark curly hair. The Baron had talked to her for quite a time and as they drove away from the house he remarked: 'Margarethe seems a charming girl, Mama will enjoy her company. Come to that, I'd quite enjoy her company myself.'

Tialda laughed and Becky, who had had a glass of claret with her lunch as well as sherry before it and was feeling quite reckless in consequence, observed tartly: 'Quite your type in fact, Baron Raukema.'

His eye caught and held hers in the mirror above his seat. 'I wondered if you overheard me yesterday. It seems that you did.' She stared at him like a mesmerised rabbit and only a sudden spate of traffic saved her, as he had to keep his eyes on the road.

But that was all he said about it. Presently, free of Trond-heim and on the road south, he began to tell her about the country they were passing through and with Tialda joining in, the conversation seemed nothing but a rather lighthearted resumé of their holiday, to which Becky added only a guarded remark from time to time. But presently she began to relax. Tialda was full of fun, telling her of their previous holidays in Molde: 'Winter sports, you know, Becky—we have been several times; last year we came with my husband, Pieter.' She sighed loudly. 'He is away in America for a few weeks and I miss him.' The sigh turned to a laugh. 'I have to put up with Tiele instead and he is only a brother, you understand.'

They were driving quite fast now through magnificent country, the Rolls making light of the steep road and the hairpin bends. 'Where shall we stop for tea?' asked the Baron. 'I told the hotel we'd get there some time before dinner; we've time enough, although the road climbs a bit presently.'

Becky, looking a little nervously out of the window, considered that the road was doing that already. She didn't fancy heights, but there was so much to see and with Tialda keeping up a continuous chatter, she had no time to worry about that. The Baron's blue eyes encountered hers once more in the mirror. 'Enjoying it?' he wanted to know.

'Oh, yes, it's—it's—I've never seen anything like it.' The words were commonplace enough, but her eyes shone with excitement and there was a faint colour in her cheeks. She had washed her hair the night before and now, tied back neatly, it hung in a pale brown cloud round her shoulders, making her eyes look darker than they really were and although her cotton dress was ordinary enough, it was a pretty green check which showed up her creamy skin. She looked a very different girl from the waif he had encountered and befriended, thought Tiele; he must remember to see that she got a good job when they got back...

Becky stared out at the towering mountains. She was getting used to the scenery now and she had no reason to feel nervous. The Baron was a superb driver, taking no risks but keeping up a good speed with nonchalant calm while Tialda kept up a ceaseless stream of chatter; what they would do, where they would go, what they would buy. 'You've no idea how glad I am to have you here, Becky,' she remarked happily. 'You see, I've just started a baby and Tiele wouldn't have any idea what to do if anything were to go wrong...'

'But the—the Baron is a doctor,' exclaimed Becky.

'Not that kind of a doctor. He's a physician—hearts and lungs and things.'

'Oh, I see,' said Becky politely. She saw very well. She was still the nurse in the Baron's employ—he might call it days off, but she had merely switched from one patient to the other. She glanced at the broad back in front of her and frowned at it. He was a domineering man who was manipulating her to suit himself under the guise of the generous offer of a holiday. She should have felt very angry, but all she felt was very sad.

They stopped for tea at an hotel built on a terrifying curve half way up a mountain, and Becky was surprised at its luxurious appearance. It wasn't all that large, but it was built in a chalet style and there was a lake behind it in whose steel blue waters the mountains were reflected. She paused at the door to take in the view while Tialda hurried inside, intent on tea, and the Baron, who had been with her, turned back and came to stand beside Becky. 'It's not like that at all,' he explained in a gentle voice which took her by surprise. 'I haven't brought you along for convenience, and strange though it may seem, I am quite capable of dealing with any emergency which Tialda might spring on me. You're here for a short holiday, Becky—I want you to enjoy it.'

'You don't like thin mice,' Becky reminded him coldly.

His eyes twinkled and his smile very nearly made her change her mind about him. 'I'm not sure about that any more.' He eyed her without haste. 'And you aren't so thin, you know.'

He took her arm and turned her round and walked her into

the hotel where they found Tialda happily deciding which of the splendid array of cakes offered her she should choose.

'You'll get fat,' observed her brother.

'I have to keep my strength up. Becky, sit here by me—isn't it lucky that we don't have to diet or anything dreary like that? I shall eat two cream cakes.'

Becky ate two as well while the Baron sat back drinking his tea and making do with a small slice of plain cake, entertaining them with light conversation the while.

They reached Molde in the early evening and the Baron slowed to idle through the little town so that Becky had time to look around her. And there was plenty to see. Molde lay on the north bank of a fjord with mountains towering behind it and the fjord before it, its calm water besprinkled with a great many islands and beyond them in the distance, the Molde Panorama—eighty-seven mountains, snow-capped, providing a magnificent backdrop to the charming little place. Becky, almost twisting her neck off in order to see everything, allowed her gaze to drop finally on to the street they were driving through; the main street, lined with shops and filled with people on holiday and ending presently at the quay side, where it changed abruptly into a pleasant road lined with villas. They didn't go as far as this, though. The Baron drew up opposite the quay, said 'Here we are,' and got out.

The hotel was modern and large, overlooking the fjord, and after the bright sunshine outside the foyer looked cool and welcoming. And the Baron was known there; they were taken at once to their rooms overlooking the loch, each with a balcony. Becky, after a quick look round the comfortable apartment, went straight outside. There was a ferry coming in and a good deal of bustle on the quay only a few hundred yards away, and coming up the fjord from the open sea was a liner, its paintwork gleaming in the evening sun. She rested her elbows on the balcony rail and watched its speedy approach until the Baron's voice, very close, interrupted her.

He was on the balcony next to hers, doing just as she was

doing. 'Nice, isn't it?' he asked mildly. 'I've been here several times and I never tire of it. What shall we do first? Drinks and dinner and then a stroll? We can explore the town to-morrow.'

'But you must know it very well already?' said Becky practically.

'Oh, I do—but there's always a certain smug satisfaction in showing people around when you know it all and they don't.'

She laughed then and he said: 'You should laugh more often, Becky—there's no reason why you shouldn't now, you know.' He smiled at her and nodded. 'I'm going to have a shower and change. About half an hour suit you? Tialda takes ages...'

He went into his room and Becky stood where she was and didn't say a word. She should laugh more often, should she? Was he implying that she was dull and incapable of enjoying herself? What was it he had said? No beauty and no sparkle. She went inside herself. What did he suppose she had to laugh about, in heaven's name?

CHAPTER FOUR

THEY DINED AT a table in the window and as the restaurant overlooked the quay, they had a splendid view of the liner berthing for the night and its passengers streaming ashore. The little town was lighted now, although the mountains beyond the fjord still had their snow-capped summits gilded with the very last of the sun. It was a little paradise, thought Becky, sipping her sherry and staring out at it all. She turned when the Baron spoke; he was sitting opposite her, his elbows resting on the table, his hands clasped before him. He had nice hands, large and well-shaped and with well-kept nails; they looked, she decided, very dependable.

'Daydreaming?' he asked idly, and she went a little pink because she must have seemed rude, ignoring her companions.

'No, just a bit overcome with the scenery.'

He nodded. 'We'll go across to Hjertoya beach tomorrow—it's on that island straight ahead. You swim?'

She nodded. 'But I haven't got a swimsuit.'

'And I want a bathing cap,' declared Tialda. 'We'll go out early, Becky, and get them.' She picked up the menu. 'What shall we eat?'

The food was mouthwatering; Becky settled for crabmeat cocktail, chilled strawberry soup, Virginia ham with rum and raisin sauce with a salad on the side because the Baron assured her that that was essential to her good health, and by way of afters blueberry pie with whipped cream. She and Tialda drank a delicious white wine, but the Baron took red wine with his tenderloin steak and brandy with his coffee. They went for a stroll afterwards; just along the main street, past the modern town hall and the whitewashed church above it.

'We'll go in there tomorrow,' promised the Baron. 'It was

rebuilt after the Germans destroyed it during the war—it's beautiful.'

Becky wandered along in a pleasant dream. It was cool and she hadn't got a jacket with her because she hadn't got one; and who would dream of wearing a navy blue cardigan with the flowered shirt and the lacy blouse? And when the Baron wanted to know if she were warm enough she was quite emphatic about saying that she was, and if his mouth twitched a little at seeing her little shivers, she didn't see it.

They took a water taxi across the fjord to the bathing beach the next morning, and Becky had never been so happy. She was a good swimmer and the water was surprisingly warm. She forgot that her swimsuit was a cheap one-piece, its complete lack of glamour highlighted by Tialda's expensive beach outfit, she forgot that her future was precarious to say the least, she even forgot the amused glance the Baron had flung at her as she had waded into the water and struck out into the calm blue waters of the fjord; just for the present, life was everything she could wish for. She tired presently and turned on to her back to rest, and found the Baron idling alongside her. 'Who taught you to swim?' he wanted to know.

'My father.' She remembered the look of amusement and turned over and began to swim back to the beach. 'I'll go and keep Tialda company,' she called as she passed him. But she couldn't escape him; he kept beside her without difficulty, so that they arrived at the beach together to find Tialda half asleep in the sun. 'Oh, good,' she greeted them, 'you're back—I'm dying for something long and cool to drink. Tiele, be a darling and find something,' and when he had gone: 'There's a café half way up the beach. Becky, what a wonderful swimmer you are.' She chuckled. 'You've surprised Tiele—I expect he thought you could only paddle like me.' She rolled over and smiled at Becky who had dropped on to the sand beside her. 'Gosh, I'm hungry! I hope Tiele buys something to eat as well.'

He had; they drank lemonade and munched delicious outsize buns, thick with currants and then had one more swim before taking the taxi back again for lunch. And in the afternoon they strolled through the town to the church, where Becky wandered off by herself to enjoy its whitewashed walls and small vivid stained glass windows and the big colourful cross behind the simple altar—quite different from the cathedral at Trondheim but in its way just as magnificent. She found the others outside presently, sitting on the wall of the terrace overlooking the town and the fjord with the mountains beyond. There were roses everywhere and their scent filled the still warm air, and Becky, sniffing appreciatively, said: 'Oh, I'd like to come back here—I always imagined Norway to be cold and grey, and it's not at all...'

'It is in the winter, although this is one of the warmer spots, that's why the roses are so abundant—Molde is called the Town of the Roses, did you know that? Becky, do you want to do any shopping? Tialda wants some hand-painted woodwork, supposing we go and look for it now?'

And so the day passed pleasantly enough, and the day after it, and Becky made the most of every minute of them. Right at the back of her mind was the unhappy thought that the Baron was a little bored by it all; he was charming and thoughtful and patient, but every now and then she caught that faint look of amusement on his face when he looked at her. She was annoyed by it but sad too; she could just imagine what he thought of her: a dowdy girl who wore cheap clothes and didn't know how to make the best of herself—and she wasn't really like that, but after two years of no money, no make-up and nothing new to wear it was difficult to splash out, for always at the back of her mind was the fear that it wouldn't last; that she would find herself with no job and no money again, and he was so secure himself that he would never have known the insecurity that not having money brought with it.

They went back on the fourth day after a last lunch overlooking the quay and the lovely fjord, the boot filled with painted wooden knick-knacks which Tialda had taken a fancy to, and a great armful of roses which the Baron had bought just to prove, he pointed out, that they had been to Molde. And Becky had bought something too; a delicate glass vase to hold one rose; it had been expensive but she hadn't been able to find anything else, and besides, the Baroness seemed to have everything she could possibly want.

She found herself in the front seat beside the Baron when they left, to be entertained by him with a gently amusing conversation for the entire journey, and when, at the end of it, she tried to thank him for her holiday he just as gently ignored her, so that after one or two attempts she gave up, sensing his faint impatience with her.

'I'm glad you enjoyed it,' he observed carelessly. 'And now you face the herculean task of getting my mother organised to leave the day after tomorrow.'

Which somehow reduced her to the status of a wage-earner in his household. Which, after all, she was.

Indeed, she was kept so busy upon her return that she hardly saw him or Tialda during the next day. The Baron had friends to visit in Trondheim and took Tialda with him, and as he was out for dinner on the following day and was so late for lunch that she had it alone, by reason of Doctor Iversen's visit, she saw him only briefly. But they met unexpectedly only a few hours before they were to leave; the Baroness had told Becky to have an hour or two off while she enjoyed a last gossip with her sister, and Becky had seized the opportunity to go to the cathedral just once more. And there, standing quietly in a corner admiring its sombre magnificence, she had been joined by the Baron. He said nothing at all, only nodded, faintly smiling, and after an awkward moment or two she had given an abrupt nod in answer and walked away. But he had been at the door when she reached it and together they crossed the flagstones and went through the gate which led to the front of the cathedral.

'I hardly expected to find you here,' remarked the Baron.

It seemed that he intended to walk back with her. 'Why not?'

'I should have imagined that a last round of the shops would have been more to your liking.'

'Why?'

He stopped to look at her in surprise. 'Well, girls like shopping, don't they? Don't you?'

'I love it,' declared Becky promptly, 'but I can see shops in any town, but I can't see Trondheim Cathedral anywhere but here.' She walked on briskly, annoyed with herself because she had sounded like a prig and annoyed with her companion for not saying another word until they reached the house, when all he said was: 'We leave directly after lunch, so will you do the last-minute chores now? Someone will be up for the luggage in about ten minutes.'

She had whisked upstairs and in the teeth of the Baroness's complaints that she hadn't finished with her jewel case, beauty box, a selection of hats—one of which she still had to decide upon—and several pairs of shoes, she did as her employer had asked and then changed into uniform, rammed her hair under her cap in a very severe fashion, and trod downstairs to search for the handbag the Baroness had left somewhere but couldn't remember where, and when she met the Baron in the hall she gave him such a stern look that he opened his eyes very wide indeed. Tialda had seen the look as she came out of the sitting room and when Becky had gone back upstairs she slipped a hand into her brother's arm, grinning up at him.

'What does it feel like?' she wanted to know. 'You're—how old? thirty-eight—and ever since I can remember girls have fallen over themselves to get you interested. You've never bothered with any of them—well, not many, anyway, and here's Becky...'

'I'm not interested in Becky either, Tialda.' The Baron's voice was soft and very gentle and his sister said hastily:

'I didn't say you were, so don't come the big brother over

me.' She giggled: 'All the same, she'll make some man a very good wife one day; he'll have to put his slippers on in the house and exercise the dog and bring her tea in bed—oh, and of course she'll have children, very well behaved ones.'

The Baron frowned faintly, but his voice was light. 'Which is more than we can expect from your brats; you were a most unpleasant little girl.'

She beamed up at him. 'Wasn't I? But I'm nice now.' She reached up and gave him a sisterly peck on the cheek. 'There are an awful lot of nice girls around,' she wheedled. 'Surely there's one you fancy?'

'I fancy any number,' he told her blandly, 'but not to marry. Besides, I've no time for a wife—there is so much work...'

'Pooh! You find time to take Nina van Doorn out—she only has to pout at you and roll those eyes. It would save a lot of time and trouble if you married her...'

'Would you like that, Tialda?'

'No—I can't stand the girl, but that's natural, she outshines the lot of us with all that gorgeous hair, we none of us stand a chance. I wonder how Becky will feel when she sees her...'

'Why Becky?'

'I don't suppose you've looked at her long enough to see that she's plain—nice eyes, but her face is too thin and pale, and she drags all that hair back... Oh, well, I must go and throw the last few things in, I suppose.'

Tialda wandered off, leaving her brother staring at nothing and frowning again.

It said much for the Baron's powers of persuasion that the party left exactly at the time he had suggested. His mother, never very punctual and used to having her own way, had thought of a dozen things which had to be done at the last minute; friends she wanted to say goodbye to once more, even a letter to write, to all of which her son had a suitable answer, so that the Rolls, with Becky and her patient in the back, the luggage safely stowed and he driving with Tialda beside him, took the road south in the early afternoon sunshine.

Because of the Baroness's leg, still in plaster, and her dislike of long car journeys, they travelled only as far as Otta, about a hundred and fifty miles away, and here they put up for the night. The Baroness was inclined to be demanding in a charming way and already declaring that she ached all over, was giddy from looking at so many mountains and convinced that she would be unable to go on the next morning. Becky soothed her in a motherly fashion, put her to bed and saw to it that she had her dinner brought to her there, and then, because she was still a little querulous, suggested a game of cribbage. They were deeply immersed in this when the Baron and Tialda came to enquire why Becky hadn't gone down to dinner and it seemed sensible to relinquish her chair to the Baron and go with Tialda, who declared that she was quite able to eat her dinner for a second time if Becky wanted company.

And all the Baroness's discomforts had disappeared by morning. The Baron waited patiently while Becky helped her patient to ready herself for the day, stowed her into the car carefully, and set off once more. They had the whole day before them, which was a good thing since they had a great distance to go; Kristiansand was some three hundred and eighty miles distant and the roads, although good, were in many parts mountainous, but as the Baron pointed out, he had done the trip several times, he knew the road and provided they stopped frequently for his mother's benefit, he saw nothing out of the way in attempting such a long trip in country where half that distance was considered a fair day's driving. And he was right; there was little traffic as it was early for the tourists and the Baroness, kept amused by Becky, felt no discomfort. They stopped in Drammen for lunch and Brunkeberg for tea, and arrived at Kristiansand in good time to rest before a late dinner. And the following morning there was no hurry; they were to go on the midday ferry to Hirtshals, drive the hundred and fifty odd miles to Vejle and go on again in the morning.

Another three hundred and fifty miles; Becky doing sums on the back of an envelope was staggered at the amount of ground they were covering. Normally, she supposed that they would have all been bone-weary by now, but they stopped frequently and had nothing to do each evening but have their dinner and go to bed, although it wasn't quite as easy for her as all that, because her patient needed a good deal of attention at the end of the day and exercises had to be done, however unwilling the Baroness was to do them. But the Baron showed no signs of tiredness. He drove superbly and nothing appeared to disturb his calm. The journey had been well organised before they set out and he knew exactly when and where to stop, and although he took it for granted that Becky would have her hands full he was careful of her comfort. She wouldn't have missed their journey for all the tea in China. She was sorry that it was almost over and her job with it, as the Baroness was making steady progress; within a week of their return she would have the plaster off and exchange her crutches for a stick and then, Becky supposed, she wouldn't be needed any more.

That the Baron would find her a job she never doubted, but working in hospital might not be as pleasant as living in the lap of luxury with the Baroness. She consoled herself with the thought that she would have Bertie and Pooch again and it would be fun making a home for the three of them. She had no reason to complain, she told herself firmly, and concentrated upon seeing as much of Denmark as possible as they drove down from the ferry. It was entirely different from Norway and as on parts of the road at least there was no speed limit, she managed to get only brief glimpses of the country, but in the towns and villages where the Baron had to slow down, she had ample chance to look around her. Everything was very neat and clean and she admired the rolling farmland with beech woods and pine plantations dotted here and there, and she was charmed with Vejle although she saw very little of it. The Baroness was tired and cross and it took Becky a long time and a good deal of her patience to settle the little lady for the night. But she was her charming self in the morning, eager to start, for as she pointed out to Becky: 'We shall be home this evening, my dear. I know it's quite a journey, but Tiele has promised that I shall eat dinner under his roof tonight.'

'Isn't it your roof too?' asked Becky.

'No—I lived there while my husband was alive, but now I live in our town house in Leeuwarden—quite close, you know. But Tiele wishes me to spend the night at Huis Raukema.'

So they set off once more on the last lap of the journey; another three hundred and sixty miles, six hours' travelling, the Baron assured them, and frequent stops. 'For we have all day to kill,' he pointed out. 'It's not yet eleven o'clock and I told Willem to expect us in time for dinner.' He looked at Becky. 'Someone should have warned you that I enjoy driving. On my own I should have travelled much faster...'

'I am enjoying the journey very much,' Becky told him sedately.

It was exciting to cross into Germany and then later, into Holland at last. The country looked rather like Denmark although the farms were larger with enormous barns at their backs and great herds of cows grazing in the flat water meadows. They bypassed Groningen and once clear of the city took a country road running north, side by side with a wide canal, but after a while the Baron turned off to the west, cutting across the flat countryside until they reached another canal bordered by trees. It was a peaceful landscape with small villages, each with its church dominating it and dykes encircling the low-lying land. Leeuwarden lay somewhere ahead, Becky supposed, but there was no sign of it at present. Perhaps this was a short cut...

The Baron, who had been travelling fast along a familiar road, slowed the car presently and Becky, watching the canal slip past them, exclaimed with delight when she saw the narrow arm of water leading from it. It was lined with trees too and as well as that there were cottages along the water's edge, half hidden from the road and in the distance a church. 'Oh, that's really very pretty,' declared Becky to no one in particular.

'You like it? That's where we're going,' said the Baron. He kept on driving though and it was a minute or two before he turned into a narrow lane which led off the road towards the canal and the village on the other side of the water. They had to cross a bridge to reach it, a quaint affair which opened for boats and barges to pass; Becky was still looking back at it as they reached the first few cottages.

The village was small, peaceful and pretty, its church large enough to accommodate ten times the number of its inhabitants. The road wound past it and into a small wood fenced in, and after a minute or two the Baron turned the car for the last time into a sanded drive between thick shrubs and trees. 'Home,' said the Baroness softly.

Home, decided Becky, peering in front of her, was a place of splendour, standing proudly at the end of the drive; a large square house backed by a semi-circle of trees—one of every species, she thought flippantly, gazing at their variety and lowering her gaze to take in the velvet lawns and the flower beds blazing with colour. The drive ended in a sweep and the Baron brought the Rolls to a gentle stop before the shallow steps leading to a massive porch and double doors, already opening. Becky got out, bent on making herself useful, and while Tialda ran excitedly up the steps she gathered the Baroness's bits and pieces and followed the Baron at a more sober pace. There was an elderly man at the door, but beyond a brief reply to his greeting, the Baron with his mother in his arms didn't pause on his way. He crossed the lofty wide hall, with Willem ahead of him to open one of the many doors leading from it, and strode through it with Becky on his heels, very wishful to stop and look around her but not daring to. Just inside the door he paused for a second, which did give her a chance to

see that the room was large, beautifully furnished and despite
that contrived to look cosy, but when she heard him speak
she brought her gaze back to the broad shoulders in front of
her.

'Nina!' said the Baron in a voice she hadn't heard before.
'I didn't expect you to be here.'

Becky heard a trill of laughter and skipped a couple of steps
to one side so that she could see round the massive back
before her. In the centre of the room stood a girl—a beautiful
creature with golden hair brushed into the fashionable untidy
mop, and exquisite features. She was wearing a dress of some
soft material in palest blue with a full skirt and a tiny bodice
which showed off her slenderness to perfection and she was
smiling confidently across the room at the Baron.

'Is it a lovely surprise?' she wanted to know, quite sure
that it was, and waited while he made his mother comfortable
in one of the straight-backed armchairs by the open french
window before crossing the room and lifting her face to his.
Becky looked away as he bent his head to kiss her and wished
that she wasn't there. This couldn't be his wife; he had never
mentioned one—his fiancée, then...

'Nina,' said the Baron formally, 'this is Miss Rebecca
Saunders who is looking after Mama. Becky, Juffrouw Nina
van Doorn.'

The girl murmured something in her own language and
Becky's face went wooden because she guessed it was some-
thing about her, but then Juffrouw van Doorn smiled and said
How do you do so pleasantly that she decided that she had
been mistaken, but she had no opportunity to think about this
as the Baron went on smoothly: 'Becky, will you go upstairs
and make sure that my mother's room is quite ready for her?
You'll find someone in the hall to take you up—I'll bring the
Baroness up in ten minutes. She should have supper in bed,
I think.'

Becky was only too glad to escape. Somehow it wasn't
quite what she had expected, but of course after the carefree

weeks with the Baroness, she had rather forgotten her position in the household. And she had wanted to go at once to see Bertie and Pooch. She swallowed disappointment and went out of the room to where a nice-faced middle-aged woman was waiting.

'Sutske,' she said, and smiled, and Becky put out a hand.

'I'm the nurse,' she said, hopeful that she would be understood.

'Zuster Saunders,' nodded the housekeeper cheerfully, and beckoned her to follow.

The staircase was at the back of the hall, its graceful wings branching left and right to the gallery above. Sutske didn't hurry and Becky had time to look about her as they went, her head over one shoulder as they climbed. The hall was square, its crimson wall hangings divided by white-painted wall pillars picked out with gold, a circular window in the roof high above her head lighted it and the polished wood floor was spread with thin silk rugs. It looked very grand, and the gallery when they reached it was just as grand; the walls were all white here and in place of rugs there was a thick crimson carpet. Becky paused a second to look down into the hall before following the housekeeper to one end of the gallery where that lady opened a door and ushered her inside. This was to be the Baroness's room, then, a vast apartment with windows on two walls, a canopied bed, a number of very comfortable chairs, a marquetry tallboy and a graceful sofa table under one of the windows with a triple mirror upon it.

Left alone, Becky, in a panic that the Baroness would arrive before she was ready for her, turned back the bed, plumped up the pillows and went to see what was behind the three doors in the room. A bathroom, splendidly appointed in the same soft pinks and blues as the curtains and coverlet, an enormous clothes closet, in which she saw that the Baroness's things for the night were already disposed, and the last door, leading into a small lobby with another open door at its end. Another bedroom which would be hers, she surmised, much smaller but every bit as charming. She didn't waste time exploring further, but went to put out soap and sponge, her patient's night things, and lay her brushes and combs on the dressing table. And just in time, for the door was thrust open and the Baron walked in, carrying his mother.

He didn't speak to Becky, only nodded vaguely before he went again, and his mother said dryly: 'Now he can go back to Nina...' She stopped and went on in quite a different voice: 'Dear Becky, you have everything ready—I'm a little tired. Tiele says something on a tray—he told Sutske to send it up in about an hour.'

Perhaps Becky was more tired than she knew, but the hour seemed very long, and indeed by the time the Baroness was sitting up in bed with a dainty supper on the bed table before her, she was as worn out as her patient and a good deal more hungry, and over and above that was the urge to go in search of Bertie and Pooch. No one had mentioned them yet, and with the beautiful Nina downstairs it was hardly likely that the Baron would remember them. After what seemed an age the Baroness was settled for the night and Becky, leaving one small lamp alight, went softly from the room with the tray.

It was very late, possibly everyone had gone to bed and although Tialda had been in to say goodnight some time ago, declaring that she was going to bed too and reminding Becky that there would be some supper for her downstairs, Becky had not the least idea where to go for it. If she found the kitchen there might be coffee, though, and at the same time she would have a quick look for Bertie and Pooch...perhaps it wasn't quite the thing to prowl around the house in that fashion, but she felt that she had excuse enough; besides, she wasn't likely to meet anyone.

She met the Baron; he was coming in through the front door as she gained the last stair and since she could hear the whine of a receding car, she concluded that his visitor had just left. He frowned when he saw her and said: 'Good lord, are you still up?'

It would hardly be her ghost and she was tempted to say so. 'Yes,' she told him briefly, and made for the back of the hall where she had noticed a baize door.

'You don't have to carry trays in this house.' The Baron's voice had an edge to it.

'There's no one about,' she pointed out matter-of-factly.

'Then I'll ring for someone...'

Becky quite forgot who he was. 'Indeed you won't,' she told him roundly. 'Getting people out of their beds at this hour—do you know how late it is?'

He didn't need to answer, for the great Friesian wall clock creaked into life and chimed midnight in a mellow old voice. 'You've had supper?' he asked carelessly as he turned away.

'No.'

He was beside her then, taking the tray from her. 'My dear girl, what a thoughtless man I am!'

'No, not really—Tialda came and told me that there would be supper downstairs for me; your mother was very tired— too tired to settle easily. She's asleep now.'

He stood looking down at her, the tray balanced on one hand. 'I'm afraid I have neglected you all. We will go to the kitchens now and see what we can find.'

Becky was suddenly cross as well as tired, nothing had been quite what she expected; the grandeur of the house and she had thought that at least someone would have mentioned Bertie and Pooch. 'Thank you,' she said snappily, 'I shall do very well—I'm not in the least hungry,' which was a lie, 'but I should like to know if Bertie and Pooch are all right, Baron.'

'Oh, God—that too! Forgive me, Becky. Of course they're all right—I'll take you to them now.'

He put a hand on her back and swept her along and through the baize door, down some steps and into a large kitchen, equipped to the last skewer and still somehow looking delightfully old-fashioned. There was an Aga stove along one wall and on the rug before it were Bertie, Pooch and a Great Dane. All three animals turned round, half asleep, and then bounded to their feet and rushed across the kitchen, the Great Dane to hurl herself at the Baron, Bertie and Pooch to cover Becky with joyful licks, pushing and shoving her in their efforts to greet her properly after such a long time. She sank on to the floor and let them have their way while the tears ran down her cheeks. They hadn't forgotten her, and very soon they could set up house somewhere and she wouldn't have to leave them again. She forgot her companion completely, but presently he bent down, plucked her to her feet, ignoring the tears and remarked cheerfully: 'There's coffee—it's always on the stove in case I have to go out at night—and I've found some rolls and butter and cheese and there's a salad in the fridge.'

He sat her down at the scrubbed wooden table in the middle of the kitchen and poured coffee for them both while the Great Dane trod quietly at his heels.

Becky drank some of the coffee, wiped her eyes and found her voice. 'Thank you very much, Baron, for taking such good care of them.' And at his non-committal grunt: 'What do you call your dog?'

'Lola.'

'Why do you call her that?'

'What Lola wants, Lola gets,' quoted the Baron. 'She rules this place with a rod of iron, although she's as gentle as a lamb. Your two get on very well with her.' He buttered a roll and put some salad on a plate. 'And now eat your supper—such as it is.'

Becky ate, with Pooch on her lap and Bertie sitting as close to her as he could get, the Baron plying her with food and coffee while he carried on a conversation which really needed no reply from her, which gave her time to resume her usual composed manner. But presently she had had enough and began to pile the supper things tidily.

'Oh, leave that,' he spoke impatiently, 'someone will see to it in the morning.'

Becky went on collecting plates and cups and saucers. 'My

stepmother and Basil did that—left things for the morning. You have no idea how beastly it is to come downstairs and find a lot of dirty crockery to wash up.'

'No, I haven't, and I can assure you that there are sufficient staff in my household to find the task bearable—and may I remind you, Becky, that this is my house and I do exactly what I wish in it, and I expect its other occupants to do as I ask.'

His self-assurance was a little daunting. She said uncertainly: 'Oh, you do?' and beyond gently laying the china in her hands on the tray, she stopped what she was doing. There was no point in annoying him; she seemed to do that easily enough anyway. She got up, wished Bertie and Pooch goodnight and directed them back to their rug, and went to the door where she turned to say: 'Goodnight, Baron.'

'Why do you persist in calling me Baron?' he asked testily.

'Well, you are,' she said reasonably. 'Thank you for my supper and for taking such good care of Bertie and Pooch.'

He had been sitting at the table but he reached the door at the same time as she did. 'Tiele, perhaps?' he asked persuasively.

'Certainly not—you're my employer, and it wouldn't be right.'

He shrugged his shoulders. 'Please yourself.'

He bent his head suddenly and kissed her as she passed him.

CHAPTER FIVE

THE BARONESS WAS tired the next morning. Becky, leaving her propped up against the pillows, having her breakfast, went to find the Baron and tell him so. She had seen him earlier from the window, astride a great horse, returning from an early morning ride—he looked rather splendid on horseback, she conceded, wondering at the same time whether he worked the normal long hours of a doctor or held a part time post at some hospital. In any case, since he was a doctor, he could decide if his mother was fit to get up. Personally, Becky considered that the little lady had exhausted herself on their long journey and needed at least a day in bed, if not two. She found him in the small breakfast room, a small, panelled apartment at the side of the house, having been shown there by Willem, and as she went in, just for a moment she felt shy, remembering the previous evening, but only for a moment. His kiss hadn't meant a thing and it certainly couldn't have been because she had looked attractive, more the sort of comforting kiss one would give an old lady who had lost her purse... She gave him a polite good morning and asked him, still very politely, if he could spare the time to see his mother. 'Before you go to work,' she explained, just to make it quite clear.

'Ah—bent on getting my nose to the grindstone again, are you? Well, I have two more days of my holiday, and when my mother is staying with me,' he added blandly, 'I visit her every morning after breakfast.'

Becky took no notice of the way he was looking down his high-bridged nose at her—very intimidating, but she wasn't going to be intimidated.

'I supposed that you would be going to work, Baron.'

'Then I suggest that you give up supposing and wait until you are told.'

She gritted her little white teeth and without answering him, walked out of the room. Two could be rude!

The Baroness wouldn't have finished her breakfast yet. Becky hadn't had hers either and she had no idea where to go for it—the kitchen, perhaps. There would be some sort of servants' hall, she supposed, and Tialda on the previous evening had told her that her supper was downstairs—besides, it was a splendid chance to see Bertie and Pooch.

Sutske was there with two young women and they all looked up and smiled as Becky went in. She smiled back and stood still while Bertie and Pooch made much of her, and since no one had said anything about breakfast she went through the open door at the back of the kitchen, into the yard at the back of the house. It was almost encircled with outbuildings, its cobbled surface uneven and worn by countless footsteps. Becky walked briskly to where an open archway led to the grounds beyond and was on the point of continuing down the back drive when the Baron popped up beside her, apparently coming from one of the great barnlike buildings on either side of her.

'You walked away,' he remarked mildly. 'I was on the point of asking if you would care to breakfast with me.'

She stood to answer him, Pooch under one arm, Bertie pressed to her side.

'Thank you, no. If you would tell me where I'm to have my meals…?'

He lifted his eyebrows. 'My dear girl, with us, of course—where else?'

She eyed him stonily. 'I was waiting to be told,' she said sweetly.

He laughed then and caught her by the arm and turned her round to walk her back into the house. He called something to Sutske as they went through the kitchen and when they reached the breakfast room Willem was laying a place for her. Bertie and Pooch had come too and at the door Becky paused. 'Do you mind the animals?' she asked diffidently.

'Not in the least. Lola is under the table if you care to look.'

He drew out a chair for her and sat down himself. 'You're worried about my mother?'

'Not worried exactly; she's tired—it was a long journey and although she loved every minute of it, I think it exhausted her.'

'We'll keep her in bed for today, then, and tomorrow as well. If she's quite rested then, you can go back with her on the day after that.'

Becky buttered a roll and laid a wafer of cheese on it, wondering if she could ask about Bertie and Pooch, but before she could frame a suitable request, the Baron spoke. 'You'll take the animals with you, of course. Lola will miss them—so shall I and the rest of us here. Will they be all right in a strange house until you leave my mother?'

'Oh, yes. They'll go wherever I do.' She hesitated. 'How do I get another job? The Baroness isn't going to need me for much longer, is she? Would you mind if I started looking for something before I leave?'

'You will remain with my mother for at least another week, perhaps longer, and I will see to it that you have somewhere to go, and work in one of the hospitals, either in Leeuwarden or Groningen.'

She blinked. He seemed very sure about it, but it was a relief to know that she wouldn't have to worry about that herself. She still had to make herself familiar with Holland and its ways, let alone the language, which sounded impossible at the moment. She thanked him and asked if Tialda was all right. 'She looked tired last night; if she wants to spend a day in bed I don't mind looking after her,' she offered.

'I looked in on her on my way down this morning; she's fine—plans to go shopping, I believe. She's going to stay here for a while. Pieter—her husband—will be back in another two weeks.' He was interrupted by the telephone and he got up to answer it and Becky got up too. As she did so she heard him say: 'Nina...' and although she couldn't have understood a

word if she had remained, she swept Pooch up in her arms
and with Bertie at her heels, left the room.

She didn't see him for the rest of that day. He had visited
his mother, but she had left them together and when she returned he had merely left a message that his suggestions made
at the breakfast table were to stand.

She didn't see him on the following day either; as she
dressed that morning she had seen him ride away with Lola
beside him and when he had gone up to visit the Baroness,
Becky herself was eating a solitary breakfast with Willem to
look after her and the animals for company. And since the
family doctor came to see the Baroness just before lunch and
stayed for a long time, there was no question of either Becky
or her patient going to that meal. Doctor van Diessen was
elderly, with a weatherbeaten face and twinkling blue eyes.
He had known the family for so long that he was more of a
friend than a doctor to them. He finished his examination of
the Baroness although, as he observed, the legs were nothing
to do with him—specialists would see to those very shortly.
But he pronounced her very fit and agreed that there was no
reason why she shouldn't return to her own home the next
day if she wished. 'You have this excellent young lady to
look after you, and Tiele to watch over you both.' He beamed
at them both and went away to find Tiele, refusing an invitation to stay for lunch because he had more patients to see.

But the Baron didn't lunch alone. Becky, looking idly out
of the Baroness's window, saw a Mercedes sweep up the drive
and stop by the front door. Nina van Doorn got out, wearing
slacks and a silk shirt which made Becky green with envy
and before she had closed the car door the Baron was beside
her. Becky turned away. They were well suited, the pair of
them, she told herself. The Baron might be kind and when he
remembered, thoughtful of others, but he was too self-assured,
naturally so, for he had far too much of the world's goods;
and Nina seemed to have been cast in the same mould. And

why are you worrying? Becky asked herself crossly. In another couple of weeks you'll never set eyes on them again.

The Baroness lunched in bed and Becky, summoned by the ever-attentive Willem, went downstairs presently and ate another solitary meal before settling her patient for a nap and going off duty for an hour or two. She changed into one of the cotton dresses she had bought in Trondheim and went to fetch Bertie and Pooch, and because she seemed to want to come too, Lola. The grounds round the house were parklike, and she left the formal gardens and wandered in the landscaped fields surrounding them, Pooch on his lead and the two dogs running free. They made for a little copse which bordered the boundary along one side and Becky, delighted to be free for a little while, didn't hurry. The sun was warm on her, her surroundings were idyllic and she had time to think.

But not for long. She had reached the copse and was wandering along one of its paths among the trees when she rounded a curve and saw the Baron and Nina van Doorn, deep in conversation, just ahead of her, Lola saw them too and launched herself at her master in a few great leaps, putting her paws on his shoulders to gaze into his face, and close behind her, not to be outdone, came Bertie, a good deal slower and much less agile and content to rub himself round the Baron's elegantly trousered legs. He didn't appear to mind in the least, although he told both beasts firmly to get down, but Nina minded very much. She had backed away, crying out something in a quite different voice from her usual cool tones, and when she saw Becky she began on her, remembering in her sudden rage to speak English.

'You!' she cried. 'You, with these animals—take them away at once, how dare you bring them here!' She rounded on the Baron. 'You know how I cannot bear them, they spoil my clothes.' Her voice soared. 'And don't dare laugh! Tell that girl to take them away—the servants should know better...'

The Baron's voice was soothing but amused. 'Don't be silly, Nina, they'll not harm you, and I think you have not recognised my mother's nurse. She is hardly to be blamed, she had no idea that you had such a dislike of dogs and cats.'

Becky had Bertie beside her again and Pooch tucked firmly under one arm. She said quietly: 'If Lola will come with me, I'll take her back with me. I'm sorry we disturbed you, Juffrouw van Doorn.'

Nina turned her back without answering and the Baron spoke quietly to Lola, who gave him a reproachful look, went to join Bertie and then followed Becky obediently back the way they had come.

It was a rather subdued little party that went back to the house. Becky had been shocked by the other girl's ill-temper and rudeness and the animals, sensing her feelings, had lost their enjoyment of a scamper. But it was much too soon to return to the house. Becky prowled round the gardens, seeking a quiet spot, and found one eventually; a rough patch at the bottom of the walled kitchen garden, nicely hidden by a row of raspberry canes and shaded by a mulberry tree. She settled on the grass, wound Pooch's lead round her wrist, warned the dogs to behave themselves and shut her eyes. Half an hour later, while she was still in that strange world between sleeping and waking, the dogs' sudden barking brought her upright. The Baron was standing just inside the raspberry canes, looking down at her.

She stared back at him, her brown velvet eyes still drowsy with sleep. 'Oh, lord,' she exclaimed crossly, 'can't we come here either?' She rubbed her eyes like a sleepy child. 'How did you know we were here?' She started to struggle to her feet, but the Baron put out a large restraining hand and sat down beside her.

'It happens to be my hiding place. When I was a small boy and had done something wrong—and that was very often—I used to come here; for some reason no one ever thought of looking behind the raspberries. I come here even now with Lola.'

He stretched out his great length on the grass and Lola lay down beside him. 'I'm sorry that Juffrouw van Doorn was so upset. She had no intention of being rude—she simply didn't recognise you. She hates most small animals…'

Becky didn't speak. She was thinking that even if she had been one of the servants she would have resented Nina's tone of voice.

'She is a very beautiful girl,' went on the Baron, choosing his words. 'I suppose that is why she cannot bear to have a golden hair out of place or the tiniest crease in her clothes.' His eyes fell to Becky's dress, rumpled and creased where the dogs had lolled on her. 'When a girl is as beautiful as Nina, she would not wish to spoil it in any way.'

Becky, for want of anything better to say, agreed politely, stroking Pooch's rather tatty fur as he lay curled in her lap.

'You're not envious of her?' enquired her companion softly.

'Me?' Becky thought about it. 'No, I don't think so. Of course it must be wonderful to know you're so lovely that everyone turns around to look at you and to know that all men are ready to eat out of your hand, but I wouldn't like it if I didn't like Pooch and Bertie and had to fuss about my clothes…'

'Juffrouw van Doorn hardly fusses,' remarked the Baron coldly, and Becky said hastily:

'Oh, I wasn't being personal. She's quite the most beautiful creature I've ever seen. You must think you're the luckiest man alive.'

'Oh? Why?' His silky voice should have warned her.

'Well, you're going to marry her…' She looked up and caught his icy stare. 'Well, it's none of my business,' she mumbled, going red.

'No, it isn't.' He had sat up, leaning his back against the tree, his casual friendliness all gone. 'This seems a good opportunity to discuss my mother and your future. She will return to her own home tomorrow and you with her, of course. I have arranged for her to be seen two days later; the plaster will be removed and if everything is satisfactory, she should be able to manage very well with a stick. I should be obliged if you will stay with her for a further week, during which time I will see about a job for you and find you somewhere to live. Have you any preference—surgical or medical?'

The red in Becky's cheeks had faded and she looked quite pale again despite her days in the sun. It was like accepting charity and it stuck in her throat; he was carrying out his promise because he had said that he would help her and he wouldn't go back on his word. Charity could be very cold.

She said at once, her pleasant voice without expression, 'I like medical work, thank you, but I'll take whatever there is going.'

He nodded and got to his feet. 'No, don't get up—bring Lola in when you come, will you? I'll see what there is and my secretary will let you know.'

Becky watched him go unhurriedly towards his house. It was a pity, she reflected, that he was so taken with Nina. She wouldn't be any good for him; they both liked their own way far too well—though perhaps if he loved her very much, he would let her do exactly as she wanted. Becky scowled at the thought—no dogs, no cats, certainly no horses or donkeys, probably no children; sticky fingers would anger Nina just as much as muddy paws. Becky swept her still too thin arms round the necks of her astonished companions and gave them a throttling hug. Poor Lola, poor kitchen cats; she hoped the Baron would find a kind home for them.

She saw very little of him for the rest of that day and on the following afternoon, after a hectic morning persuading the Baroness to pack the few things she had needed while she was staying with her son, collecting Bertie and Pooch, putting her own small possessions in her case, they drove away in an elderly Cadillac, driven by an equally elderly chauffeur; both

of them candidates for a museum, thought Becky, skipping
into the front seat while Bertie, on his best behaviour, sat on
the floor at the Baroness's feet. The Baron saw them off, Lola
beside him, and his mother, reclining rather awkwardly in the
back of the car, remarked comfortably: 'Of course, it's ridiculous to say goodbye. We live so close to each other and in
any case he comes to see me frequently on his way to and
from the hospital.'

Becky plucked up the courage to ask exactly what the
Baron did.

'My dear child, has no one told you? Chests and hearts, my
dear, just as his father before him. He has beds in Leeuwarden
and Groningen and he goes frequently to London and Edin-
burgh and Birmingham—for consultations, you know. He
works too hard, and it seems a pity that he should waste so
much of his free time with someone as unsuitable as Nina van
Doorn.'

To which bit of outspokenness Becky replied with a murmur. It was nice to think that someone else shared her views,
though.

The Baroness lived in the centre of Leeuwarden in a beautiful old house in a quiet street lined with equally beautiful
houses. Its door was opened by a slightly younger Willem,
who Becky quickly learned was indeed that old man's brother,
and he passed them carefully on to a severe and very tall
woman rejoicing in the name of Jikke, who instantly took
charge of the Baroness while at the same time welcoming
Becky with an unexpectedly sweet smile and a complete lack
of surprise at the sight of Bertie and Pooch. Becky beamed
back at her, happily unaware that the Baron had made sure
that his mother's household would accept the two animals in
an amiable manner.

The party entered the house through an imposing lobby
which in turn led to a narrow hall, stretching endlessly back
to a gracefully curved staircase at its end, and lined on both
sides with doors. With Jikke leading the way, Pooch under

one arm and the Baroness on the other, Becky slowly walked half its length before the housekeeper opened a pair of doors and ushered them into a small panelled room, very cool and dim by reason of it having only one small leaded window. Its floor was of polished wood with a handsome rug before an old-fashioned and elaborate stove, and several high-backed armchairs arranged casually, interspersed by small tables holding charming lamps. There were bookshelves too and high on a shelf above the panelling, rows of Delft plates and dishes. It looked as though no one had touched it since it was first furnished, centuries ago, thought Becky, bidding Bertie sit while she set Pooch carefully beside him.

The Baroness smiled at her. 'We'll have tea before we do another thing,' she declared, for all the world as though she would be doing the unpacking and putting away of her many possessions, 'and then I shall have my exercises before dinner. I've not asked anyone for this evening—indeed, I shall not do so until this wretched plaster is taken off. I daresay we can amuse ourselves for two days, Becky.' She allowed Becky to make her more comfortable in her chair and arrange the offending limb just so before saying: 'Ring the bell, will you? Ulco speaks English and he will tell you where your pets may sleep. You had better go with him when he comes.'

Which Becky did, through the hall again and a narrow wooden door, thick enough to withstand a siege, down a pair of steps and into a semi-basement kitchen, a nice old-fashioned place, fitted out cunningly with every modern device. It had a number of doors leading from it, and one of them revealed a roomy cupboard with a dog basket, comfortably blanketed.

'We thought that this is good, Zuster—if your dog and cat will sleep here—with an open door and you to lay them down before bed. We will not disturb them in the morning, but you will take them into the garden at the back?'

'Oh, splendid,' agreed Becky. 'I'll be down early, if no one minds?'

Ulco smiled at her. 'No one will mind, Zuster, and we take good care of them.'

She was really a lucky girl, mused Becky, as she sped back to the Baroness. Wherever would she have found someone who didn't object to animals, let alone went out of their way to accommodate them?

They had their tea, she and her patient, and then Becky left her patient to be taken upstairs where a cheerful young girl was already unpacking the Baroness's luggage in a vast room with an elaborate plastered ceiling and William and Mary walnut furniture. The curtains were a dusky pink and matched the bedspread and the white carpet was soft underfoot. Becky gave a willing hand in the disposing of her patient's wardrobe, smoothing silk and lace with a careful hand, loving the feel of it, and presently when they were finished the girl beckoned her to follow her through a door leading from the room which led directly into another bedroom. It was large too, simply furnished with white-painted bed, dressing table and tall chest, but it too had a thick carpet and easy chairs and enchanting little bedside lamps. The curtains were the same pink as in the Baroness's room and the bedspread was quilted rose-patterned chintz. There were books on the table by the bed too; Becky heaved a sigh of pure happiness and set about unpacking her own few garments.

It seemed very quiet after the Baron's great house and Becky found herself listening for his firm footstep around the place and his voice, never loud but clear and decisive. She was surprised at her pleasure when he arrived the following evening, walking in on the pair of them, the Baroness sitting in her lovely drawing room, stitching at her petit-point while Becky patiently unravelled silks for her.

'How very domestic,' was his comment as he joined them, and when Becky got up to leave them together: 'No, stay for a while, please—this concerns you, Becky.' He eased himself into a great armchair and stretched out his legs before him. 'Mama, I have arranged for you to be seen tomorrow afternoon at two o'clock. At the hospital—it will be easier there, as they will need the plaster shears to take that off your leg. You'll be seen in the orthopaedic consulting room and de Vries will make quite sure that everything is exactly as it should be. You will have to be X-rayed, of course, but there will be no waiting around. I shall be there for part of the time, but I have to be in Groningen in the morning, so don't expect me too early, will you.' He turned to look at Becky. 'You heard all that, Becky, is there anything else you want to know?'

'No, thank you, Baron.'

'I shall be obliged if you refrain from calling me Baron at the hospital—I prefer to be called Doctor.'

'Just as you wish, Doctor.' She sounded very meek.

'I sometimes suspect that you are laughing at me,' he observed blandly. And when she didn't answer: 'I should like to talk to my mother alone, if you wouldn't mind...'

Becky skipped off to the kitchen where Pooch and Bertie had taken up residence as though they had lived there all their lives, and carried them off for a run in the narrow garden. It was a pleasant place, shaded by trees and bright with flowers and with a swing, long since forgotten, in one corner behind a hornbeam hedge. Becky sat herself on it with Pooch held firmly on her lap and idled to and fro in the sun. The swing squeaked each time she sent it back and forth; a pleasant sound, mingling with the birds around her and the chiming clocks in the city. She closed her eyes and allowed her thoughts to wander. She had some money saved now; once she had somewhere to live and a job she would buy some clothes. She began to reckon how long it would take her to save enough to buy a real silk shirt just like the one Nina van Doorn had been wearing...

'Good lord,' said the Baron behind her, 'that swing hasn't been used since Tialda was a little girl and screamed her head off if I wouldn't push her. Do you want to be pushed?'

'No, thank you—Pooch is on my lap, I don't think he

would like it.' She got out of the swing. 'I'll go back to the Baroness.'

'Do you get your free time, Becky?'

'Oh, rather,' she lied briskly without looking at him. 'Leeuwarden is just the kind of place I would choose to live in…'

'That is fortunate,' his voice was bland, 'since it is to be your home. Jikke has a sister living on the other side of the city; she has an old house, converted into flats—I'm told that the top one is empty and she would be prepared to let you have it. She has no objections to animals provided they behave themselves. I will take you to see it tomorrow evening. This evening is impossible, I'm afraid, as I have an engagement.'

Nina, said Becky soundlessly to herself, and aloud: 'That's very kind of you, Doctor, but if you give me the address I'm sure I can find it on my own.'

'I have no doubt of that, but Mevrouw Botte speaks no English and you, I imagine, speak very little Dutch.'

'I have a dictionary,' said Becky with dignity, 'and I'm learning as fast as I can.'

'Yes, well—I doubt if you can learn sufficient to bargain with Mevrouw Botte by tomorrow evening. I'll call for you at half past six—I have already spoken to my mother.'

There was precious little time to think about it. By tea time the next day Becky was tired and irritable, although she hid that successfully from the Baroness. That little lady had been at her most trying; because she had been unable to decide what she should wear, they had very nearly been late for the appointment at the hospital and there had been a further delay when they reached it because she recalled suddenly that Willem's sister was in one of the wards, and she desired to see that lady first. It took tact and patience on Becky's part to explain to her that time to a consultant was precious, especially when he had made a special journey to see her—not to mention the houseman in attendance and a nurse or two.

In the end the plaster had been successfully removed,

Becky had escorted her patient to X-Ray and then delivered her into the hands of Professor de Vries again. The examination had taken a long time, for he and the Baroness were very old friends and spent a good deal of time reminiscing about their youth. It wasn't until the Baron joined them that they got down to business, and Becky, asked to relieve the hospital nurse while she went to her tea and quite worn out with holding up X-rays, taking scribbled notes from the professor to various people whose whereabouts she had the greatest difficulty in finding in the vast and splendid new building, and supporting her patient when she was required to take a few steps, as well as fetching glasses of water, a fan because it was too hot, retrieving a mislaid handbag and encouraging her patient each time she declared that she was tired to death and couldn't they continue on the following day, could have fallen on his neck with relief. Not that she would have dared do any such thing. Somehow on his home ground, as it were, he looked unapproachable; older and remote, very much the consultant. He didn't notice her anyway; she doubted if he knew that she was there; she did as she was told and when they had finally finished, put the Baroness to rights once more, got her stick and waited patiently to see what would happen next.

The Baron had escorted them out to the car, a firm arm under his mother's, with Becky trotting behind, making sure that the Baroness used her stick and didn't just wave it about as she was prone to do. They had a small posse of people hovering behind them; Out-Patients Sister, the Orthopaedic Registrar and houseman, a couple of nurses and a porter in case he was needed. The Baroness thanked them all graciously, was settled in her car by the Baron and with a thankful Becky beside her, had been borne home once more.

And now Becky was free to get ready for her evening. The Baroness had a friend to see her and was quite content to let her go directly after they had had tea. Becky went up to her room after she had taken Bertie and Pooch for a quick walk,

and surveyed her scant wardrobe. It would have to be the
green jersey. It had been a warm day, but the evening was
overcast and cooler. She got ready slowly and then had to
hurry over her face and hair because it was almost half past
six and she fancied that the Baron didn't like being kept waiting. Probably he waited hours for Nina, she thought as she
sped downstairs and into the hall.

He came out of the drawing room as she reached it, wished
her good evening and with a sidelong glance at the green
dress, suggested that they should waste no time, but he
stopped as they reached the door where Ulco was hovering.
'I feel that Bertie and Pooch should be with us. Wait here.'

He was back very quickly, with Pooch's battered head
sticking out from under an arm, and Bertie walking sedately
beside him. 'Lola's already in the car,' he told her.

Mevrouw Botte's house was ten minutes' drive away, in
the centre of a narrow street of similar houses, all of them
facing a canal with a line of trees and a wall beyond. It was
quiet and had the advantage of being within fifteen minutes'
walk from the hospital, and as Becky got out of the car she
knew at once that she could be happy living in it. It remained
to see if she felt the same way about Mevrouw Botte.

She did. That lady was at the door waiting for them, a
small, bustling woman dressed in sober black, her hair
strained back into a tidy knob from a round face whose most
striking feature was a pair of boot-button eyes.

The Baron ushered his party into the narrow hall, introduced everyone, exchanged a few remarks with Mevrouw
Botte and then stood aside to allow Becky to follow her up
the steep narrow staircase.

There was a small landing on the first floor, with two doors,
and on the second floor the landing was still smaller, so that
the two doors were very close together, but the third landing
was so minute it afforded nothing more than a foothold in
front of its one door which Mevrouw now opened with a
flourish.

The room within was surprisingly large, for it ran from the back to the front of the house, with a window at one end, and a door at the other. It was simply furnished with a disguised bed along one wall, a small round table with two chairs, a rather shabby easy chair, a little desk and a mirror over it. There were two doors side by side along the inner wall. One opened on to a cupboard of a kitchen, very neat and spotlessly clean, the other revealed a minute shower room. Becky beamed round her with delight; here was home at last.

'How much?' she asked breathlessly. 'Shall I be able to afford it?'

'Er—I'll ask Mevrouw Botte.' He said something to her which caused her black eyes to snap with amusement as she answered him, and then turned to Becky. The sum he mentioned seemed a great deal to her, but he added: 'You will earn three times as much as that each week. Would you be able to manage, do you think?'

'Oh, yes, I know I can. Does she really not mind Bertie and Pooch?'

The Baron smiled. 'Not in the least—you will see that there is a very small balcony outside the door and she will provide a large box in which they can sleep.' He glanced around him. 'It will be rather warm here, I fancy, and in the winter you will have to have some kind of heating. You wish to take it?'

'Yes, please. Would she like a week's rent in advance?'

'I imagine so—I believe that is the usual custom. You will be coming—let me see—a week today. Do you want her to do anything for you? Milk isn't delivered and nor is bread, but there are one or two shops close by.'

'Washing,' said Becky suddenly, and went to look at the balcony; very small with a high wall and a clothes line already stretched across it. There was room for the animals to sit there too—she would be able to go to work and leave the door open. The wall was too high for them to climb over; besides, they were both too elderly to entertain any such idea.

She went back to where the Baron and Mevrouw Botte

were talking quietly together and got out her purse. 'And she will call each week for the rent,' explained the Baron. 'You feel you can cope with the language?'

Becky nodded. 'Oh, yes. I'll learn—I have to, you see.'

They bade Mervouw Botte goodbye and trailed down the stairs again and out to the car. On the way back the Baron told her that he had made an appointment to see the Directrice of the hospital on the following afternoon. 'A medical ward,' he explained. 'Women's, day duty, although you will have to do your share of night duty later on. You will be given Dutch lessons, although you will find that most of the staff speak English more or less.' He told her her salary too; it sounded a lot of guldens; probably she would be able to save quite a lot and buy some clothes. She became lost in a daydream for which she was roused by the Baron's impatient voice begging her to pay attention. 'For I am a busy man,' he reminded her, 'with no time to tell you everything twice.'

Becky said she was sorry in a meek voice and concentrated on all the do's and don'ts he was detailing for her benefit, and when they drew up before the Baroness's house once more she started to thank him. But she was barely halfway through her little speech when he cut her short quite curtly.

'My dear girl, don't make such a thing about it.' He glanced at his watch. 'I'm already late for an appointment...'

Becky had whipped out of the car, opened the door for Bertie and with Pooch over her arm poked her head back through the window.

'With Juffrouw van Doorn? If I'd known, Baron—Doctor—and what does it matter anyway?—I wouldn't have wasted your time. Still, I daresay you'll enjoy the rest of the evening all the more,' she added obscurely.

Her eyes were huge in her small face and dark with sudden temper. She withdrew her head before he could say anything and crossed the pavement and rang the door bell, wishing very much to have a good cry although she wasn't exactly sure why. Ulco's solemn kindly presence prevented her, though.

CHAPTER SIX

THE WEEK flew by. The Baroness, while delighted that Becky had a job and somewhere to live, was a little peevish at the idea of her leaving. True, she had an abundant staff only too happy to fulfil her every whim, as Becky pointed out to her, but that proved to be no argument with her patient. 'I liked you the moment I set eyes on you, my dear,' declared the Baroness, 'and I am going to miss you. You will, of course, visit me whenever possible.'

And Becky, used by now to the little lady's imperious ways, said that yes, of course she would. 'I'm only a short walk away,' she pointed out, 'and I shall get off duty like everyone else.'

She had gone for an interview at the hospital, feeling scared, not because she wasn't sure if she could manage the job—she was sure of that, but worried that her tiny smattering of Dutch might decide the authorities against her. It was a tremendous relief to find that everyone, from the Directrice to the Home Warden who showed her over the Nurses' Home and where she could change each day, spoke English. She would have lessons in Dutch starting on the very first day and she would be expected to work hard at them and speak Dutch whenever possible. To start with, the Directrice explained, she would do routine work on the ward with another nurse until she felt that she was able to deal with patients on her own. 'And that shouldn't be long,' declared the Directrice cheerfully. 'It is amazing how quickly one learns if one applies one's mind to it.'

Becky had gone back to the Baroness's house with a dictionary and a book of Dutch medical terms, which she was delighted to find weren't so very different from the English ones—indeed, several of them were English. She had seen the

Baron on the way, driving along the narrow street in his beautiful car. If he had seen her he gave no sign and she really hadn't expected her to; she had been rude and he must think her wretchedly ungrateful. Although she had tried to thank him...

She had met the beautiful Nina too. She had gone into the city to do a small errand for the Baroness and coming out of the shop she had come face to face with Nina. She had smiled and said Hullo and been cut dead for her pains. But Nina had recognised her; her blue eyes had slid from Becky's tidy, mousey hair, down her cheap cotton dress, and come to rest on the sandals she had bought at Bata's.

And when, on her last day as the Baroness's nurse, she was about to leave for her new home, Nina and the Baron arrived together as she was waiting in the hall for the taxi, she remembered that look and her small determined chin went up. Nina nodded casually as she passed her, but the Baron stopped.

'Ah, yes, of course you start your new job tomorrow,' he remarked. 'Is everything OK?'

'Yes, thank you.' Becky gave him the briefest of glances and bent to adjust Bertie's collar.

'You're waiting for the car?'

Ulco answered for her, speaking in Dutch, and the Baron's reply sounded vexed. 'There is no need for you to have a taxi. I'll drive you over to Mevrouw Botte's house now.' He frowned down at Becky. 'There has been some misunderstanding.'

'No, there hasn't,' Becky told him, aware that Nina had paused on her way to the drawing room and was listening. She came back to them now and put a lovely useless hand on the Baron's arm. 'Tiele, don't hinder Nurse—you heard her say that she was waiting for a taxi. Your mother is expecting us...'

The Baron's mouth could look exactly like a steel trap. He said quietly: 'Will you tell Mother, Nina? I shan't be more than ten minutes or so.' And then to Becky: 'I must apologise, Becky, it was not intended that you should leave like this.' He picked up her bag and nodded to Ulco, an interested spectator, to carry her case outside, and when she would have protested, took her arm, pausing only long enough at the door for Ulco to wish her goodbye.

'My mother has said goodbye to you?' he wanted to know as he opened the car door and ushered Bertie in.

'Yes, thank you.' Becky remembered that lady's tearful farewell and smiled faintly. The Baroness had been in no state to order the car or ask Becky how she was going to get to her new home; she had pressed a small flat parcel into Becky's hands and kissed her and then burst into tears. If it hadn't been for the faithful Jikke, Becky wouldn't have got away.

The short journey was accomplished in silence, with Becky sitting very upright with Pooch tucked firmly under her arm. At Mevrouw Botte's front door the Baron got out, fished out Bertie and went to hammer on the knocker before he went to help Becky, hampered by a rather restless Pooch, out. 'Upstairs with you,' he commanded, 'leave your bags, I'll bring them up.'

So Becky, with Bertie trailing behind her and Pooch craning his neck to see his new surroundings, went up the stairs behind Mevrouw Botte and on the top landing, received her key and was ushered into her very own flat.

It was, if anything, cleaner and neater than on her previous visit and on the table was a vase of summer flowers with a card tied to it. It read simply: 'Welcome to your home, Becky,' and she was bending to admire the bouquet when the Baron walked in with her things.

'Aren't they lovely?' She turned an excited face to him, quite forgetting that they had had little to say to each other. 'Whoever could have put them there? Would it be Mevrouw Botte?' She frowned. 'But she doesn't know that my name's Becky, and I'm sure it's not the Baroness...'

'Why are you sure?'

She went pink. 'Well—she has no reason to do so.' She went on, making it brief: 'Thank you for bringing me, although it was quite unnecessary.'

He smiled faintly. 'Have you enough money, Becky? My mother remembered to pay you before you left?'

The pink deepened. 'I've quite enough money, thank you.'

'But you haven't been paid.' He smiled again. 'My mother never remembers anything.' He took a note case from his pocket and counted out notes and laid them on the table. 'If ever you need help or money, I hope you will ask me, Becky.'

It was the last thing she would ever do! If she hadn't needed the money she would have given it back to him with the greatest of pleasure; it only served to highlight the gulf between them. She gave a little gasp when he said softly: 'I get paid too, Becky—you don't have to look like that.'

He went to the door. 'I shall see you from time to time at the hospital, I daresay. I hope that you will enjoy your work and be happy here.'

She said thank you in a quiet little voice; he might dislike her and find her a nuisance, but he was the last link between her and the sheltered life she had been leading for the past month. She had a ridiculous urge to ask him to stay—just for a little while—while she got used to the idea of being on her own, but she had hindered him long enough; he would want to dash back to his Nina. He waited by the door for a moment as though he expected her to say more than that, and when she didn't speak he went away.

But there was too much to do for her to be lonely for long. Mevrouw Botte had stocked her cupboard with milk and enough food to feed them that evening and the following morning; she looked it over with satisfaction before unpacking her case, arranging the animals' box to their satisfaction and then, because it was still a warm light evening, introducing them to the balcony. It was quite late by the time they had had their suppers and tidied up, and she had turned the bed into a bed again and gone as silently as possible down the stairs with them both to take a walk in the nearby small park.

It was a far cry from the luxurious bedroom she had been sleeping in, but it was an even further cry from her unhappy life in her stepmother's house. Becky curled up in her narrow bed and slept, though not before stifling a pang of regret for the pleasant life she had been leading. 'At least I know now how the other half lives,' she told herself, and Bertie and Pooch, disturbed by her voice, muttered back at her.

She was on duty at half past seven in the morning, which meant getting up at six o'clock, taking Bertie and Pooch for their walk, having a quick breakfast and walking to the hospital, but she would be home before four o'clock, with the whole evening to call her own. She skipped along the narrow pavement in the fresh bright morning, eager to start but a little nervous too.

But she need not have been; she had barely had time to change into her white uniform dress and tuck her hair under the plain white cap before a big girl with very fair hair and blue eyes shot into the cloakroom where the living out nurses changed and begged her, in English, to go with her. The hospital was light and airy and modern. Becky, who had trained in a hospital which was a veritable nest of small passages and endless staircases, found herself whisked into a life and borne upwards to a wide corridor lined with closed doors. 'Administration,' breathed her guide, and added in a friendly voice: 'My name is Riet—Riet van Blom.' She paused to hold out a hand which Becky shook.

'I'm Rebecca Saunders—Becky everyone calls me.'

They smiled at each other as Riet stopped before a door and knocked on it. Before she sped away she said hurriedly: 'I see you at coffee. I work also on the medical wards.'

Becky turned the handle and walked in. The Directrice sitting behind the desk in the severely furnished office was elderly, small and very round, with a severe hairstyle which made no attempt to keep up with fashion and very bright blue eyes. She wished Becky good morning and bade her sit before refreshing her memory from the papers before her.

'Doctor Raukema gives you a good reference,' she observed, 'and it is upon this I offer you the post of diploma'd nurse on the medical wards. You already know your salary; I told you during your first interview, and your working hours will be told to you by the Hoofd Zuster of your ward. Your Dutch lessons will commence immediately—they will be given during your duty hours, but you will be expected to study during your free time as well. If at the end of a month you are unable to reach the not very high standard we have set, then I am afraid we shall no longer be able to employ you.' She smiled suddenly. 'But I think there is little likelihood of that.' She rang a little bell and a door opened to reveal an elderly woman in a dark blue uniform. 'Juffrouw Markela will take you to your ward. I hope that you will be very happy with us.'

Becky murmured suitably and followed Juffrouw Markela from the office, glad that one hurdle had been crossed. It proved to be the first of many that morning, though; the wards looked the same; small six-bedded rooms leading off from a central area where the nurses' station stood, but there were any number of them and it was difficult at first to distinguish one from the other. All the doors looked alike, and so did the patients lying in their beds. Becky, flying rapidly behind Riet, discovered after the first panic that it was rather like the hospital had been at Leeds. The six ladies in the first ward she went into were all suffering from chest infections and it really didn't matter what it might be called in Dutch, the condition was exactly the same as she had nursed countless times in England, so that it didn't matter so very much that she could understand only one word in twenty or so; the routine was the same.

It was the same in all the wards and after a little while she began to gain some confidence, especially as some of the patients could speak a little English. And during the coffee break, she went downstairs with the cheerful Riet and met several more nurses, all of whom seemed prepared to accept her as one of themselves. She went back, much heartened by their friendliness, to plunge into the round of treatments, the giving of medicines and the making of beds.

She was going down to her dinner with two other nurses when she saw the Baron coming up the stairs they were going down. He was accompanied by his registrar, several house-men, a clerk bearing an armful of notes and a fierce-looking lady whom Becky took to be the social worker. She stood a little on one side to allow the party to pass her on the stairs and the Baron glanced at her briefly, accorded her the slightest of smiles as he drew level and continued on his way. Becky stared after him; she hadn't really expected him to stop, but she had hoped that he might.

She was tired when she reached her little flat that afternoon, but she forgot that in the delight of seeing Bertie and Pooch, sitting contentedly on the balcony, obviously nicely settled in. They all had tea and then she changed into a cotton dress and took them both for a walk in the park. It was cooler now and everyone was hurrying home from work. Becky climbed the stairs once more and once in her flat found herself wishing that she had a radio to break the quiet. But she didn't need one, she reminded herself. She had her Dutch lessons to study; she had had her first lesson that afternoon and it was all-important that she should learn that language as quickly as possible. She took a chair on to the balcony and with the animals sprawled at her feet, spent the next hour or so with her head in her books.

The next day was easier. She was on duty at ten o'clock until six in the evening, which meant that she could take Bertie and Pooch for their airing before going to the local shops for her food. It was a long time to leave her pets alone, al-though they had often had to spend whole days hidden away when Basil was in one of his tempers and Becky hadn't thought it safe for them to be at large, at his mercy. She fed them, tidied her little home and walked to work. And when she got off duty that evening she was too tired to do more than the usual walk in the park, make herself tea and toast, and go to bed early.

And the next day she was tired too, for she had late duty; from one o'clock until eight in the evening, but she was getting into the swing of the work now and it was easier, and Sister Tutor had been pleased with her progress with her Dutch lessons. She went to bed well content and lay for a little while going over her day.

She had seen the Baron again, for old Mevrouw Fiske, a heart patient, had had a mild coronary during the afternoon and the houseman, hastily summoned with the panic team, had been preceded by Doctor Raukema. It was Becky who had seen the old lady's sudden collapse, pressed the panic bell, flung the pillows to the ground, and with the patient flat on the bed, begun cardiac massage. By rights the patient should have been laid on the floor, but that was beyond her strength, and someone else should have been administering oxygen. Becky, working away at manual compression, sixty times a minute, had no time to worry about anything else. The panic bell should bring help within seconds, and it did—the panic team, running from their various duties, the houseman on duty, who had just left the floor and had further than anyone else to run, and the Baron, who happened to be passing the ward when Becky pressed the bell. Well ahead of everyone else, he had the patient on the floor and had taken over from Becky with a brief order for her to start mouth-to-mouth resuscitation before the team and its trolley arrived. The anaesthetist took over from Becky then and at a kindly nod of dismissal from Hoofd Zuster Witma, she slipped away, back to the six-bedded ward on the other side of the corridor where she had been going in the first place. It had been sheer luck that she had happened to peer into Mevrouw Fiske's room as she went past...

She was arranging Juffrouw Drummel in her chair, preparatory to making that lady's bed before the three o'clock cup of tea came round for the patients, when the half-open door was thrust open and the Baron walked in. He wished the six inmates a pleasant good day and then crossed the ward to where Becky was making the bed.

'Mevrouw Fiske has recovered,' he told her, watching her mitre a corner very neatly.

Becky straightened up. 'I'm very glad, sir—thank you for coming to tell me.' She was still holding the blanket, ready to turn it down neatly.

He frowned at her. 'Naturally I would tell you; your prompt action undoubtedly saved her life.' He turned on his heel, wished the patients goodbye with great courtesy and went away. 'For all the world as though I were to blame for the whole thing!' muttered Becky darkly, giving the pillows a tremendous pummelling.

Before she slept she cried a little, although she had no idea why.

She was on duty at ten o'clock the next morning. She was beginning to get into the routine now and it was astonishing how many words she had picked up, mispronounced for the most part and heavily frowned upon by Sister Tutor if she uttered them during her lesson period, but she no longer felt so foreign, and the nurses were friendly too and the registrar had stopped and asked her how she was getting on. With Bertie and Pooch nicely settled for the day, she sped to work.

She hurried home just as quickly that evening. It had seemed a long day and a hot one, but now the evening was a little cooler; she would take her pets for their usual walk in the park and have scrambled eggs for her supper... She climbed the stairs slowly. Her day had been heavy, the wards were full and because she had to be doubly sure of everything, nursing, as it were, in another language, as well as saying everything twice so that even her monosyllabic remarks could be understood, her work was that much harder. All the same she was happy; her steps quickened as she reached the third landing and got out her key. She could hear Bertie breathing deeply under the door and Pooch uttering the raucous miaouw which was his welcome to her. She opened the door to meet their delighted onslaught.

She fed them first and then, with the promise of a walk, went to take a shower and change into a dress. She was getting a little tired of her scanty wardrobe now; she would buy herself something new in another week, once she had had her first pay packet, in the meantime the blue cotton would have to do. She brushed her hair and left it loose and dug bare feet into sandals. She hadn't bothered overmuch with make-up, it was too warm, but she applied lipstick hurriedly and went in search of Bertie's lead. She was on her knees with her head under the divan when someone knocked on the door and she called '*Kom binnen.*' It would be Mevrouw Botte who had promised her some eggs from her daughter's farm.

It wasn't Mevrouw Botte. The Baron strolled in, eyed Becky's lower half sticking out from under the divan and remarked severely: 'You should never tell anyone to come in unless you know who it is, Becky.'

She came out backwards, the lead in her hand, and got to her feet, quite unembarrassed because somehow she never was with him. 'Well, I thought it was Mevrouw Botte with the eggs,' she explained. 'Who else would come here?'

'I would perhaps,' suggested her visitor blandly, and she said quickly:

'Oh, lord—have I done something wrong on the ward? I do try to be careful, but it's such a frightful language, isn't it?'

He agreed gravely and assured her that there was nothing amiss. 'Indeed, everyone is very pleased with your progress.' He looked around him. 'You're comfortable here?'

'Yes, thank you.' Becky looked at him, wondering why he had come.

'Good. I thought that we might go out this evening so that I can catch up on your—er—career.'

She was so surprised that she couldn't think of anything to say. Why should he bother to climb all those stairs just to ask her that when he could have done it much more easily at the hospital?

'Well, that's very kind of you, but I'm not...I haven't anything to wear.'

The Baron's face remained bland, showing no sign of the rapid changes he was making in his plans for the evening.

'You look just right to me for a picnic.'

Becky's face cleared. 'Oh, a picnic!' She added soberly: 'But I can't, thank you all the same—Bertie and Pooch, you know, they've been shut up all day and I've promised them a walk in the park.'

'Lola's in the car, they can come too.' He opened the door. 'I've a message from Sutske for Mevrouw Botte—I'll wait for you downstairs.' He paused. 'I quite forgot, Tialda sends her love. If you're free tomorrow she wants to take you out to lunch. Can you manage that?' He smiled faintly at her happy nod. 'And my mother—she sends her love also—she wishes you to have tea with her. Tialda will arrange that, I expect.'

He shut the door quietly behind him and Becky listened to his feet on the stairs. She still couldn't imagine why he had called to see her unless it was a sense of duty, which it most likely was. She put Pooch's harness on and fastened the lead on Bertie's elderly neck, then went out of her little flat, locking the door carefully and with a sense of pride at being able to do so.

The Baron had possessed himself of Mevrouw Botte's telephone and when Willem answered he had given instant and crisp directions: Willem was to cancel the table the Baron had booked for that evening at the exclusive hotel Borg de Breedenburg and ask Sutske to come to the telephone at once. 'I want a picnic basket for two,' he told his housekeeper, 'cold supper and coffee, and tell Willem to put in a bottle of that Moselle—the sweet one.' He had listened patiently to Sutske's scolding voice and when she had finished: 'Dear kind Sutske, you know you don't mean a word of it.'

There was a snort at the other end. 'And you know you never drink that sweet Moselle...'

'Just for this once I'm going to, Sutske, do your best—you can have fifteen minutes.'

Sutske snorted again. 'You're no better than when you were a little boy,' she observed sternly and added: 'Willem will be waiting with it, Baron.'

He was in the hall, looking as though he had been waiting for quite some time by the time Becky got there.

It was only a little more than twenty miles to the Baron's house and the road was a good one; the animals shared the back seat and Becky, sitting in front, made polite conversation. It was difficult to think of something to talk about; she didn't think that her companion would be interested in her day-to-day activities, for they hadn't amounted to much so far. She worried away at the weather like a dog with a bone and felt relief when he turned in at the gates and stopped outside the house. 'To collect the picnic,' he told her blandly, and got out to speak to the waiting Willem.

The picnic basket was stowed away in the boot, Willem accorded her a nice smile and retreated to the steps as the Baron started the Rolls. When it was quite out of sight he made his slow way back to the kitchen to remark to Sutske: 'I have never known the master so kindly disposed towards a young lady so lacking in looks and chic, not that she isn't a very nice young lady indeed.' He added deliberately: 'Depend upon it, he is sorry for her.' He heaved a sigh. 'When I think of all the beautiful young ladies he has been interested in...'

'It isn't always looks,' observed Sutske darkly, 'though the child could do with more flesh on her bones. I've put in plenty of good food. I wonder where they're going?'

Becky was wondering too. The Baron, carrying on an easy conversation, had taken a side road leading to the coast to the north of his home, presently he turned again on to a narrow dyke road winding between the fields, which led to wooded country a mile or so ahead of them.

'This is pretty,' observed Becky. 'I like trees,' and then, as he turned into an open gateway and on to a sandy lane: 'Oh—isn't this private?'

The Baron's voice was casual. 'Yes, but I know the owner—he has no objection to my coming here.'

A favourite picnicking place for the Baron and Nina, perhaps? Becky stifled a sigh and looked around her. The lane had opened out to a broader road running between meadows, and nicely sheltered by a variety of trees a house stood a little to one side. It was a farmhouse, spick and span with new paint and shining windows and geraniums encircling it like a glowing necklace. As they passed it Becky craned her neck to see it.

'Is it really a farm? It looks so—so well cared for.'

'It is, and it's a farm—pedigree cattle and horses.'

'Your friend's lucky. How lovely to live here—animals and trees—lovely for children.'

'He's not married.'

'He doesn't live here all alone, surely?' She added: 'What a waste!'

'Well, no—he comes here at weekends and during holidays.'

'Oh, poor man—does he work very hard and live away from here, then?'

'He works hard, yes—but he has another house. Probably when he marries he will come out here more often.'

He volunteered no more information but followed the lane away from the meadows back into the trees and surprisingly, on to the dunes with the flat calm sea beyond.

'Oh, it's heaven,' declared Becky. 'Is this where we're going to picnic?'

'I thought it might do. Take Pooch for his walk while I unload the food—the dogs can amuse themselves.'

She wandered off with Pooch ambling along beside her.

The air was warm still and smelled of the sea and the trees around her. The sky was a pale, pearly blue and the only sounds were the birds and the happy barking of the dogs. It was perfect, thought Becky, and wondered why she felt vaguely sad. She had no chance to pursue this further though, because the Baron's voice bade her come and eat her supper. She went at once. He had been kind, wasting his evening on her, but she knew better than to keep him waiting.

Sutske had performed miracles in the time the Baron had allowed her; chicken legs wrapped in foil, tiny pork pies, minute sausages, crisp rolls filled with ham and dishes of salad and icecream in a container. There was coffee too in a thermos jug and the Moselle, packed in its own cooler. Becky sipped it with pleasure and pronounced it delicious, and her companion, swallowing his with no pleasure at all, blandly agreed with her.

Becky sat on the sand, the dogs lolling against her, Pooch on her lap. The sea air had brought colour into her face and the breeze had whipped her hair around her shoulders. The Baron, watching her, was of the opinion that although she hadn't a great deal to be happy about, she was probably the happiest person he had come across for a long time. She looked up and smiled at him. 'All this lovely food,' she said happily, 'although they feed us awfully well at the hospital.'

He filled her plate and passed it to her. 'Ah, yes—tell me about it,' he begged. There was quite a lot to tell, after all, and they had eaten almost everything by the time she had finished answering his questions and, a little hazy with the wine, she leaned back against Bertie's stout body and sighed with content. 'This is the nicest picnic I've ever had,' she told him.

'You make a habit of them?' enquired her companion lazily.

'When I was a little girl, yes—my mother and father and I. Not—not since then.' She kept her voice bright so that he didn't have to feel sorry for her. 'But we picnicked at Molde, didn't we? And that was lovely—I never imagined I'd see Norway; it's funny how life changes suddenly and everything's different...' She glanced up and saw that he was frowning. She was boring him, rambling on about nothing—she had neither good looks nor conversation. She sat up and began to collect the remains of their meal with him watching her in silence until she had everything neatly packed away, and when she gave him an enquiring look he got to his feet, ushered the dogs back into the car and held the door open for her and Pooch. He hardly spoke as he drove back, but at her door he got out too, opened her door and caught Bertie by his collar. Becky paused on the step, feeling shy and awkward because she didn't know why he had become so silent and withdrawn. All the same she thanked him for her evening, to have her thanks cut short by his brief: 'I'm coming up.'

The little place was too warm when they reached it and smaller than ever with the Baron taking up so much room. Becky switched on the little reading lamp and said rather defiantly: 'It's rather warm, but it'll be cosy in the winter. Would you like a cup of coffee?'

He was leaning against the door, staring at her. 'Thank you, no. You've filled out very nicely, Becky.'

She was so surprised at this that she stared at him, her mouth open, and then: 'You don't mean that I'm getting fat?'

The horror in her voice made him laugh. 'No—only that you're no longer a thin mouse.'

She had nothing to say to that. After a moment she said: 'It was a lovely evening, thank you very much. Bertie and Pooch liked it too.'

'And I, Becky? Do you think that I liked it?'

His voice was too silky for her liking but she answered him seriously: 'Yes, you did, to begin with, and then I began to bore you, didn't I? The wine, you know—I'm not used to it and it made me chatty. I'm sorry it was a wasted evening for you.'

'You're wrong.' His voice was so mild that it didn't sound

like his at all. 'I enjoyed every single moment of it, Becky.' He took a step forward and swept her to him with one great arm, kissed her hard and went away, leaving her standing there staring at the closed door. She could hear him running down the stairs, his footsteps getting fainter and fainter. They had died away into silence before she spoke. 'I'm a fool!' she cried, and turned to face Bertie and Pooch, watching her from their box. 'Oh, my dears, do you know what's happened? I'm in love with him—with Tiele—Baron Raukema van den Eck—and I might just as well have fallen in love with the moon!' And she burst into tears.

CHAPTER SEVEN

SHE CRIED FOR quite a time, with the animals crowding up close to her, uneasy at the way she was carrying on, but presently she sniffed, blew her red nose and mopped her face. 'You see,' she explained, 'we can't go back to England; I haven't enough money to put you in quarantine and I'd have to get a job, and supposing I met Stepmother or Basil?' She shivered at the thought. 'Besides, I'm happy here, and so are you. I'll just have to keep out of his way, won't I?'

The very idea sent the tears flowing again, so that Pooch, who had wormed his way on to her knees, had to shake his tatty old head free of them.

But presently Becky pulled herself together; crying never did any good. She washed her puffy face and tidied her hair, made a pot of tea and went to bed. And her companions, aware of her misery, broke her strict rule about not getting on to the bed, and crowded on to it with her, making her hotter than ever but offering a silent sympathy which sent her to sleep.

She need not have worried about keeping out of the Baron's way. She didn't see him at all for several days and when she did—on his ward rounds—his austere 'Good morning, Zuster Saunders' would have choked off even the most thick-skinned. She saw him one evening too, driving through the city with Nina beside him, looking utterly beautiful, so that any small silly hopes she had been cherishing died a quick death. She had hurried home, with Bertie plodding along beside her, and spent the evening working away at her Dutch lessons.

She had formed some sort of a plan by now; she would give herself six months in which to learn enough Dutch to make her quite confident of getting another job and move to some other part of Holland. As far away from the Baron as possible, and he need never know where she had gone—probably he wouldn't realise that she had, anyway. In the meantime she made the best of her days. She enjoyed her work now, she had quickly discovered that it was very much the same as it had been in England. Certainly the patients weren't any different even though they spoke a different language. She had made friends too among the nurses and some of the housemen stopped to pass the time of day with her. And the Hoofd Zuster, apparently carved from the same block of granite as the elderly martinet Becky had worked under at Leeds, actually had a heart of gold despite the fact that her tongue was as sharp as a razor and she had the eye of a hawk; she was kind and patient with Becky, never even smiled at her strange mangling of the Dutch language, and after the first week or so, paid her the compliment of speaking to her in Dutch. Not that Becky always understood her; instructions often had to be repeated in English, but at least she was learning, and learning fast.

She had been to tea with the Baroness too, fearful of meeting the Baron there, but he had been at the hospital and despite her hostess's entreaties to stay after tea and meet him, Becky had invented an invitation to the cinema that evening, and left in good time. The Baroness had been kind, and interested in her progress, although a good deal of the visit had been taken up with her own detailed account of her convalescence. She was walking well with a stick now and enlarged at some length on the shopping expeditions she had been able to make. 'Such a pity that Tialda has gone back to den Haag,' she told Becky. 'Pieter came back earlier than she had expected, so of course she went at once.' She sighed. 'So nice to see the child happily married. If only Tiele would marry too—though not,' she added strongly, 'Nina van Doorn.'

'She's a very lovely girl,' offered Becky, putting her paper-thin cup and saucer down because her hand was shaking at the mere thought.

'I know that,' declared the Baroness impatiently. 'It is most unfortunate that she knows it too—her good looks are more important to her than anything or anyone else. Do you know, my dear, that she takes two hours or more to dress? And her clothes—she has far too many.'

That from the Baroness, who had several vast wardrobes full herself, struck Becky as amusing, although she took care not to smile. After all, the little lady sitting opposite her might be spoilt and wilful, but she was kindness itself. Becky said placatingly: 'Well, I don't suppose that your son will mind—he'll be so proud of her.' And then because she couldn't bear to go on talking about him any more, she made her excuses, hurrying through the streets, anxious not to meet the Baron.

But she had to meet him sooner or later. Only a few days later she was on duty when he came into the ward, and because the other nurses were at their coffee, Becky was told to join the procession behind him to fulfil the humble duty of pulling curtains round the patient to be examined, support her while the examination took place, and arrange the bedclothes just so afterwards. It was unfortunate that the patients to be seen that day were, for the most part, well built ladies who needed heaving up against their pillows and sustained there while the Baron went carefully over their chests. It was difficult to keep out of his way while he was doing so and even harder to keep her head from bumping his and quite impossible upon occasion to prevent their hands touching. Becky's small nose twitched at the expensive cologne the Baron favoured and did her best to ignore him, something he had no difficulty in doing. She might not have been there; even when he looked at her, his blue eyes went right through her to some distant point of concentration while he probed and poked gently. And indeed, she had proof of this later that day, when she met him on the stairs. He had stopped to bid her a courteous good day and added: 'How are you getting on, Becky? I haven't seen you lately.'

She had steadied her breath and replied that she was getting on very well, thank you, before ducking her head awkwardly at him and galloping past him to lose herself in the blessed hordes of people milling round in Outpatients where she had been sent to help out for the afternoon.

The fine weather broke a few days later, the blue sky shut out by great storm clouds hovering menacingly, occasionally drenching everyone beneath them with warm rain. Becky, plodding home wet and tired, decided that she would rather suffer the heat of her little flat than be cool and have no view from its windows but wet roofs. It was only a little past six o'clock, but it was ominously dark and still. There would be a storm soon, she decided, and hurried even faster. She was standing in the doorway shaking herself like a wet dog, when the basement door opened and Mevrouw Botte joined her. Becky smiled and greeted her and wondered why she looked so very agitated; she was casting about for the right words to ask when her landlady spoke. 'Bertie—' she began, and went on slowly so that Becky would understand. 'He has gone, one hour, two hours ago. It is my fault, Miss Saunders, I went to your flat to close the door because of the rain, you understand, and he ran from the room and before I could get downstairs he had disappeared.' She added: 'The cat is safe.'

Becky stood saying nothing, thinking of all the awful things which could have happened to old Bertie, wandering about in a strange town and not even understanding if someone spoke to him. She had taken off her raincoat to shake it, but now she put it back on again. She said in her slow awkward Dutch: 'I'll go and look for him, he can't be very far away—perhaps he's in the park.'

She went back up the street, looking down the narrow *steegs* leading from it as she went and crossing to the canal side to peer down its banks. And in the park, she combed every bush and corner, whistling all the time and listening for Bertie's gruff old voice. But there was no sign of him and she forced herself to stand a minute and consider where he might be. Run over, lying in some gutter; wounded and unable to move, taken by someone and sold to a laboratory...her mind boggled at horrors and returned to normal good sense again. He was a sensible dog, even though old, so possibly he was sheltering from the rain and if she didn't find him soon she would go to the police station. She went back to the house to find Mevrouw Botte hovering unhappily on her doorstep and shaking her head mournfully, and stopping only to ask her to keep an eye open for him, Becky hurried off again. Bertie liked water, he had once or twice ventured down the canal's banks to gaze at its murky waters at close quarters. She walked the length of the street, whistling and calling and searching every inch of the canal before running down a side street leading to a much wider thoroughfare bisected by a much wider canal, frequently crossed by bridges. She was running over the first of these when she ran full tilt into the Baron.

'What the devil are you doing?' he demanded, 'tearing along like a street urchin!'

Becky hardly stopped. 'Bertie's lost.' She got another yard or two before he took her by the arm and swung her round.

'No, don't pull away like that—when did he go?'

'About two hours ago—Mevrouw Botte isn't sure. He ran through the door when she went to close the windows.' She gulped. 'I've searched the park and the street.' She tugged at her arm. 'Let me go, do!' She ended on a small shriek because the storm broke then with a vivid flash of lightning and a great rumble of thunder which drowned every other sound.

The Baron turned up the collar of his Burberry. 'You go down that side, I'll search this—we'll find him, Becky. You're not afraid of the storm?'

She was terrified, but her terror was quite wiped out by anxiety for Bertie. She shook her head and started off down the deserted street, peering through the pelting rain, searching the canal as well as every doorway and alley. She could see the Baron on the other side, doing exactly the same thing, and it made her feel a little better. He had disappeared down a *steeg* when she reached the next bridge, larger than the rest, its supports crowded with a mass of broken wood, old boxes and tangles of wire, caught up in a hopeless mess until someone should come and clear them away. It was so gloomy now that she couldn't see very clearly right under the bridge, but her heart gave a leap when she heard a faint whine. She clambered down to the canal's edge and saw Bertie, wedged in with all the rubbish. She whistled encouragingly and called him, but he only whined again, and another flash of lightning which made her cringe with fright showed her that he was unable to get free.

The water looked filthy; she peeled off her soaking raincoat and slid off the bank and began to swim towards the bridge. She was almost there when she remembered that it would have been a good idea to have warned the Baron; he would come out of his *steeg* and see that she wasn't on the opposite bank. She could shout, of course, but the chance of getting a mouthful of the vile water she was swimming through was too great. She reached the first of the old spars which comprised the perimeter of the flotsam upon which Bertie was trapped, and trod water.

He was delighted to see her although he didn't bark. From what she could see of him, he was soaking wet and tired out. She took a deep breath and shouted: 'I'm here!' and nearly let go of her spar when the Baron said quietly from behind her, 'A good thing I saw you sliding into the water. I take it Bertie's trapped in some way.'

They worked their way closer to Bertie, who showed his teeth for a moment and then kept still while the Baron gently prised him loose from the wire, the wood and a couple of nasty rusty nails embedded in his hind leg.

'Right,' he said at length, 'it's impossible to see if he's injured in any other way. I'll swim him back—you go and get your raincoat and come over the bridge.'

Becky hadn't spoken; she had been so happy to have found Bertie again that she hadn't really noticed the slimy water or the storm raging around her. But now the thought of going even those few yards and then chancing more lightning and thunder appalled her. Her teeth chattered with her fright and the Baron said briskly: 'Go on, you'll catch your death of cold if you don't look sharp.'

So she swam back and crawled up the bank and put on her raincoat which seemed a bit silly since she was wet to the bone, and then ran back over the bridge, gasping and wincing at the storm and almost knocked over by the rain.

The Baron was waiting for her with Bertie over one shoulder. At Becky's scared look he said hearteningly: 'He's not too bad, but he's limping and it will be quicker to carry him. Thank God it isn't far.'

He tucked his free hand under her arm and started off, not speaking at all excepting when they got to Mevrouw Botte's door when he let her go to push her gently inside before him. 'Lord, how we smell!' he exclaimed, and Becky was surprised to see that he was laughing. She burst out laughing too and Mevrouw Botte, waiting for them anxiously in the open doorway, looked at them both with astonishment. She would have asked a lot of questions, but the Baron cut her short with a smile and began mounting the stairs, Becky in front and Bertie, moaning gently, still draped on his shoulders. On the tiny landing he took the key from her hand and opened the door, pushed her before him and then laid the dog carefully on the hearthrug.

'Warm water and soap,' he demanded unhurriedly, 'and I'll wash some of this stuff off me before I begin on Bertie. While I'm seeing to him supposing you have a shower and get into something dry?'

He took off his jacket and went to the sink and Becky exclaimed: 'Your raincoat...'

'I'll telephone Willem presently; he can fetch it.' He grinned suddenly. 'You look simply frightful, my dear, but you're a very brave girl.'

It wasn't the kind of compliment a girl would appreciate,

but it was better than nothing, she supposed. 'Now get those wet things off,' he ordered.

'Yes—but Bertie…?'

'He'll do, I fancy. I'm going to clean him up and then send for the vet.'

She took slacks and a sweater from the cupboard and presently, her hair still damp round her shoulders, joined him on the floor by Bertie.

The Baron had done a good job on the old dog. He was clean and almost dry and his wounded leg was lying on what Becky recognised as one of Mevrouw Botte's pillowcases. She asked urgently: 'Shall I telephone now? And what about you?'

His mouth twitched faintly. 'No. I'll telephone—the vet and Willem, he can bring me some clothes. I'll ask Mevrouw Botte if I can use her shower. I'll be back before the vet goes.'

Left alone Becky hugged Bertie gently, fed an impatient Pooch and tidied up the mess the Baron had made. She had only just finished this when the vet arrived—a cheerful young man who introduced himself as de Viske and began work on Bertie without more ado. 'Tiele around?' he wanted to know.

'He's downstairs, changing his clothes—he came into the canal too, you see.'

Mijnheer de Viske didn't see at all; it wasn't like Tiele to go grovelling around in canals, but he supposed there had been some good reason for it. He asked: 'Did the dog fall in the water?'

'Well, we don't know—he was lost and then we found him caught up in a lot of flotsam under a bridge.'

He would get the story out of Tiele later. In the meantime he examined Bertie, cleaned his injured leg, put a couple of stitches in and gave him an antibiotic. 'He'll do,' he pronounced finally. 'Keep him quiet for a day or two. I'll come round and take another look in a day or two—Tiele's got my telephone number if you should want me before then.'

Becky thanked him, wondering if she should tell him that

she wasn't on those sort of terms with the Baron; she was wondering, too, how best to say so when that gentleman, in slacks and a sweater, came in, to engage Mijnheer de Viske in a brief conversation before he left. Becky, who had expected the Baron to go at the same time, was nonplussed when he sat himself down in a shabby, comfortable easy chair by the empty stove, lifted Pooch on to his knee and asked in the mildest of voices if there was any coffee.

And when she said yes, she would make it straight away: 'And I hope you can make it in the Dutch way—it's mostly undrinkable in England.'

She hurried to assure him that Mevrouw Botte had taught her exactly how to make it and went into her little kitchen, to pop out a minute later to answer the knock on the door. It was Willem bearing a tray loaded with bottle and glasses. He wished her good evening in a benign voice, expressed the hope that she was none the worse for her adventure and still speaking English informed his master that he was about to return to Huize Raukema; that he had found the raincoat, fetched the Rolls from the hospital where it had been parked, and added in an expressionless voice: 'And Juffrouw van Doorn, Baron, is there any message for her?'

The Baron gazed at his elderly friend and servant, looking remarkably put out. He said something which sounded like the worst kind of swear words in a forceful voice, and Becky was sorry that she couldn't understand them. It was obvious that Willem did, though, from the shocked look on his face. But the Baron recovered quickly. He said blandly: 'Ah, yes— I had forgotten, think up something for me, will you, Willem? If you could tell her that I have been unavoidably detained— and she had better go without me, and make my excuses.'

'Very good, mijnheer.' Willem's face was as bland as his master's as he poured the brandy, asked if there was anything else he could do and bade them both good evening.

'He's very nice,' pronounced Becky. 'Have you had him a very long time?'

The Baron handed her a glass. 'Legend has it that I sat on his knee as a baby.'

Becky tried to imagine her companion as a baby and failed completely. 'I'm sorry your evening has been spoilt; I hope Juffrouw van Doorn won't be too upset.'

'She will be livid,' he observed with calm. 'Drink your brandy, it will prevent you catching cold.' He leant over Bertie for a moment and listened to the dog's snores. 'He'll be all right now.'

Becky sipped her brandy, wrinkling her nose. 'This tastes very peculiar.'

Not a muscle of the Baron's face moved. He would hardly have described his best Napoleon brandy as peculiar. He said merely: 'I think that it is a taste that one acquires.' He got up from his chair, putting Pooch gently on the floor, and went to stand by the door. 'You are still happy at the hospital? It has seemed to me that the work may be too heavy for you...'

She felt herself grow pale; she hadn't been satisfactory after all, and she had been trying so hard. 'No, I don't mean that you aren't able to do the work—you seem to be getting on very nicely, I merely meant that the patients you heave up and down their beds seem to be at least three times your size. I thought that old Mevrouw Kats would have had you on the floor...'

Becky went red where she had been white before. She hadn't thought he had seen her and he had. 'I'm very strong.' She took another sip of the brandy, and then another. She didn't like the taste, but it was deliciously warming. A pleasant cosy haze slowly enveloped her; she had tried very hard during the last few days to forget the Baron, but it had been of no use, of course, and the effort had given her a perpetual headache and kept her awake at night, but now she suddenly felt quite cheerful.

'I haven't thanked you yet,' she said chattily. 'I—we're awfully grateful—it would have been quite a job prising Bertie loose on my own.' She took another sip. 'I didn't know you walked...I mean, you always seem to be going or coming in your car.' She added, to make it quite clear: 'Sometimes I see you going back from the hospital, you often have Juffrouw van Doorn with you.'

He stared at her, his eyes very blue. 'Yes?'

The brandy had gone to Becky's head. 'You really shouldn't marry her, you know—she's not the wife for you.'

The Baron shifted his position slightly and took a drink. 'Should I not?' he queried softly. 'Pray give me your advice, my dear girl.'

His voice should have warned her, but she was now in a state of euphoria beyond heeding that. Her eyes had grown very dark and round and she spoke with careful deliberation. 'Someone kind and loving who would take no notice of your bad temper; who'd look after you and make sure that you had enough sleep, and...'

'My God!' exploded the Baron. 'And this paragon? Will she be as beautiful as she is good? Clever and amusing and exciting too, I suppose.' He paused and went on bitingly, his eyes like blue ice: 'Or should she be a skinny creature with no conversation—such as yourself, Rebecca?'

It seemed as though all the blood in her body was rushing to her face. She felt her cheeks burn, but worse than that was the humiliation. Her ever-returning hopes that he might like her were buried under it. He didn't like her, but did he have to be so cruel, even though she had been a fool to talk to him like that? It was entirely her own fault, she shouldn't have drunk that brandy. She made herself meet his eyes without flinching.

'Of course she would be beautiful and amusing because you—you never look at anyone less than that, do you? But she could be kind too.' She drew a breath and put the empty glass down carefully on the crochet mat Mevrouw Botte considered correct to display on the table. She said miserably, wishing she could still her unruly tongue: 'I'm sorry I said that, it was only because I like you so much that I did it. I'd like you to be happy...' Her voice trailed away under his mocking look.

'You're drunk, my dear. A glass of brandy and probably no supper. Go to bed and sleep it off. I should keep to tea, if I were you.' He put his glass down beside hers, wished her goodnight and ran down the stairs, in such a hurry he didn't shut the door behind him. Becky shut it slowly and then went and sat by the dozing Bertie. Presently Pooch came to sit with her and she stayed there a long while, so unhappy that she was quite beyond tears.

She made tea later, saw to Bertie's and Pooch's needs and got ready for bed. She was on the point of putting out the light when Mevrouw Botte knocked on the door and when Becky opened it, handed her a note.

'Willem,' she said, and pointed downstairs. It was a brief missive, telling her, in the Baron's careless unintelligible scrawl, that he had arranged with the hospital that she should take her days off on the next two days so that Bertie might have the necessary attention. It had no beginning and no end, just his initials.

She told herself that she must be grateful for his thoughtfulness and went to bed, where she spent an almost sleepless night wondering how she would feel when she saw him again. Absolutely ghastly, she supposed.

The two days went slowly. She tended Bertie, who was making a remarkable recovery, easing him up and down the stairs twice a day with Pooch under her arm, doing a little household shopping and trying out her Dutch, and working at her lessons. The weather had cleared after the storm, but it was cooler now, so that the little room under the roof was quite bearable, besides, she could take a chair on to the balcony when she felt inclined. But it was dull too and she couldn't be bothered to cook, so that on the third day, when she went back to work, she had got thinner and there were dark shadows under her eyes because she hadn't been sleeping. She tried not to think about meeting the Baron; she would

have to sooner or later, she knew that, but it would be easier
if it were during a ward round when he had no need to address
her. Perhaps Fate would be kind, she thought hopefully, as
she darted down the corridor on her way to the changing
room.

Fate was nothing of the sort. Coming towards her was the
Baron. And why here? she thought wildly; it doesn't lead
anywhere but the cloakrooms and Nurses' Home. She took a
few deep breaths so that by the time he had reached her she
was able to say good morning in a quiet voice. She had had
every intention of not stopping, indeed, she had passed him
when he caught her by the shoulder and brought her to a halt.

'How is Bertie?' he wanted to know.

'Very much better, thank you. Mr de Viske is coming this
afternoon to see him.' She wriggled a little under his hand.
'I'm on duty...'

'Not so fast. My mother has Tialda staying with her, and
they would like you to go to tea. Tomorrow?'

'I'm sorry, it's my two to eight.'

'In that case, make it lunch. Ulco shall fetch you at half
past eleven—my mother will be lunching at noon. You will
be taken back in good time so that you can look in on Bertie
before you go on duty.'

'I don't think...' began Becky weakly.

'She will be delighted to see you again,' said the Baron
smoothly, 'and Tialda is only here until tomorrow evening.'
He nodded briefly and was gone before she could say another
word.

She saw him later on the round, of course; he included her
in his general good morning to the small group of people
waiting to accompany him. It was a pity that several of the
patients were even heavier than Mevrouw Kats and one of
them stone deaf into the bargain. Becky was forced to raise
her voice so that she might give instructions to the old dear,
tying her tongue in knots over the grammar while the Baron

stood at the foot of the bed, looking impassive and, she had
no doubt, laughing his head off.

She was ready in good time the next morning, although she
wasn't absolutely sure that the Baron had meant a word of
his invitation. But Ulco arrived exactly at half past eleven,
expressed his pleasure at seeing her again and ushered her
into the Cadillac, as though she were royalty. Indeed, on the
short journey to the Baroness's house, he told her that she
had been very much missed and that everyone would be glad
to see her again.

And the Baroness's greeting bore this out. She declared that
she didn't see nearly enough of Becky and that something
must be done about it, and when Tialda joined them presently
she hugged Becky with real pleasure, declaring that she would
have to pay her a visit in den Haag before the summer was
out. So it was a cheerful little party which sat down to a
delicious lunch presently, and Becky, after her uninspired diet
of fruit and bread and cheese and too many cups of tea, ate
with appetite. Just at first she had been on tenterhooks, afraid
that the Baron would join them, and it was a relief when
Tialda mentioned that she had met Nina in town and been told
that Tiele was taking her to lunch. 'At least,' went on Tialda,
'she invited herself—she told me so. I wish Tiele would exert
himself…she practically lives with him, and only because he's
too lazy to do anything about it. He won't marry her, of
course—he's not quite such a fool, but I just wish he'd fall
in love with someone else.' She smiled at Becky. 'Have you
made any friends yet, Becky?'

'Well, I'm getting to know some of the nurses—it'll be
better when I can speak Dutch properly.'

'Oh, good—I must come and see your flat one day, but
now Pieter's back I don't have much time.'

Becky said she didn't suppose that she had and asked the
Baroness how she was getting on—an endless topic which
lasted until it was time for her to leave. 'If you don't mind?'

she asked her hostess. 'You see, I must just pop in and make sure Bertie is all right.'

The Baroness kissed her. 'And next time you must come for the day and bring Bertie and Pooch. Tialda, you must try and come too.'

Ulco was waiting in the hall. So was the Baron, and when she stopped short: 'Well, don't look so surprised, Becky—I happened to be passing and it seemed good sense to pick you up.' He ushered her through the door Ulco had opened for them and opened the door of the Rolls. Nina was in the front seat. She turned her head and nodded without speaking as Becky got in and when Tiele was beside her again, spoke to him in Dutch, making Becky well aware that she was being given a lift and nothing more. Although the Baron didn't seem to consider that to be the case, because he asked her how she thought his mother was getting on, wanted to know if Bertie had quite recovered and even made one or two observations about the hospital, so that Nina had no chance to join in the conversation. At Mevrouw Botte's door he stopped, remarking: 'I'll wait for you, Becky—is ten minutes enough?'

She was already out of the car as he came round to her door. 'Thank you, but I'll walk.' She was breathing rather fast and her colour was high; Nina hadn't even bothered to turn her head when she had wished her goodbye.

'Why?' He smiled faintly. 'You'll be late on duty.'

'I prefer to be that than—than...I suppose you think it's funny to watch her snubbing me—I expect you think I deserve it, too. Probably I do. Thank you for the lift.'

She couldn't walk away because he had taken her by the arm. Now he turned and said something to Nina which made that young lady sizzle with temper. 'I've told Nina that she can wait if she likes to. Let's go up.'

But before he did he took the ignition key out of the car and put it into a pocket, blandly ignoring both girls' astonished faces.

Inside the flat he sat down, watching Becky putting food

out and opening the door on to the balcony. 'And let me
assure you, Becky, that I don't find Nina's behaviour towards
you in the least funny. I'm not sure what I find it.' He bent
to lift an impatient Pooch on to his knee. 'That's not quite
true, but there is no time to discuss it now. Are you ready?'

Nina had gone by the time they reached the car. 'Get in
front,' begged the Baron. 'We can talk shop until we get to
the hospital.'

Which they did in a comfortable casual fashion, brought to
an end when they were crossing the vast entrance hall together.

'I should prefer it if you were to call me Tiele,' said the
Baron à propos nothing.

Becky would have stopped if he had given her the chance,
but as he didn't she contented herself with a long look at him.
'Quite impossible—you're a Baron and a doctor, and I worked
for you...'

'I wish you wouldn't keep throwing Baron at me in that
inflexible fashion; I was Tiele first, you know. Besides, you
told me that you liked me...'

She marched on, not looking at him, her cheeks glowing.
'I like you, too, Becky.' His voice was beguiling.

She said stonily: 'Yes, I know. I heard you telling your
mother that in Trondheim—you liked me, but I wasn't your
cup of tea.'

'And I was quite right—but I do believe that you're my
glass of champagne, Becky.'

They had come to a halt now, for she had to turn down a
corridor leading to the back of the hospital and he was going,
presumably, to the consultants' room. In any case, a houseman
was hovering, only kept at bay by the Baron's dismissing
wave of the hand.

'I don't understand you at all,' declared Becky severely.

'I'm not sure that I understand myself.' He added sharply:
'You've got thin again, are you eating enough?'

'Yes, thank you. I-I expect it's the warm weather.'

He nodded, thinking about something else. Then: 'You have enough money?'

Becky was vexed to feel her cheeks grow hot again. 'Yes, thank you.'

'And yet you seem to have very few clothes. I thought girls spent a lot of money on clothes.'

Her eye caught the clock; she had about three minutes in which to change and present herself on the ward. 'Oh, we do, but I-I'm saving up for something.' She gave a funny indecisive little nod, said goodbye and flew along the corridor. If he had asked what she was saving up for she would have had to tell a fib—she was normally an honest girl, but to look him in the eye and tell him that she was saving every cent so that she could get away from him just wasn't on.

CHAPTER EIGHT

BECKY SAW a good deal of the Baron during the next week; they seemed to be forever meeting on stairs and along corridors and he came to the ward frequently, often on his own, and twice he left when she did, offering her a lift home which she accepted, because although her head reminded her of her resolve not to see him unless she was forced to, her heart urged her to turn a deaf ear to such advice. And on the second occasion he had suggested, vaguely, she had to admit, that he would take her to dine at a famous castle hotel—Borg de Breedenburg, which was at Warffum, a village about fifteen miles north of Groningen. On the strength of his suggestion she had gone out the very next day and bought a dress, a pretty flowered cotton voile which cost a good deal more than she could afford, telling herself that she was a fool to have taken him seriously.

An assumption which proved to be only too true. She didn't see him at all for two days and on the third day, although he did a ward round, he didn't appear to see her. She had hardly expected him to stop and speak to her on the ward, but he could surely have managed a smile. She went down to her dinner in a temper, made worse by her unhappiness. He had forgotten, or worse, merely made a casual remark which hadn't meant a thing. She pranced down the staircase, frowning fiercely, and walked right into Wim Tolde, one of the junior housemen who had from time to time spoken to her. He stopped now and caught her by the arm.

'Hey, what is wrong with you, Zuster Becky? So cross, and such a frown.' He smiled at her kindly. 'You are having a bad day?' And when she nodded: 'Then something must be done—I have tickets for the concert in the Town Hall this evening, my girl-friend cannot come and I would be glad if you will accompany me instead; I do not like to be alone.'

Becky hesitated; she accepted the fact that he was asking her because he wanted someone to go with, not because it was her as a person, but he was a nice boy, still scared stiff because he had only just qualified, and it would be an excuse to wear the new dress, too. She said that yes, she would like to go very much, thank you.

Wim seemed pleased. 'I must go now.' He turned on his heel and called over his shoulder: 'I will be at the front entrance at seven o'clock. Do not be late—I don't want to miss a single moment...'

Becky wondered why he suddenly looked so uncomfortable, staring over her shoulder and then hurrying away and she turned round to see. The Baron was quite close, a few yards from her; he must have heard every word. He said quietly: 'You are going out this evening?'

Becky nodded. 'Yes. To a concert.' And then because he looked so bad-tempered about it, added defiantly: 'I like going out, too.'

'Meaning?'

'Just exactly that, sir.'

He frowned down at her. 'You go out often? I somehow imagined...' He looked quite fierce. 'I hope you choose your friends carefully, Becky.'

She said steadily: 'You have been very kind to me, I can't forget that, but you don't have to feel responsible for me any more, you know—I'm making my own life now.'

She couldn't tell from his face what he was thinking; it was impassive as it so often was. He said merely: 'Of course, Becky,' and went past her, up the stairs.

There was no pleasure in putting on the new dress. She had bought it because she was going out with Tiele, and now she wasn't and there was really no reason to dress up for Wim; he already had a girlfriend and besides, she hadn't the least interest in him. All the same she met him with a cheerful smile exactly on time and walked with him to the Town Hall, listening to his rather pompous remarks about his work. He was going to carve a career for himself, he told her, so that he and his Elsa could get married; he had done well in his exams and very soon his superiors would realise how clever he was—another year on the medical side and then a junior partnership if he could get the money together. 'Of course, Doctor Raukema van den Eck could help me. He has great influence—he knows everybody of importance...' Wim puffed out his chest. 'One day I shall be as important as he is, too, although of course I am not of the *Adel*.'

'Surely that doesn't have anything to do with being a good doctor?'

'No, of course not, but he has much money and is greatly respected.' He added honestly: 'He is also a very good doctor.'

'I had noticed.'

The Gemeente Huis was packed. It wasn't until they were seated in the middle of the seats on the ground floor that Becky saw that there was a gallery encircling them above; presumably the élite were to sit there, as there were flowers arranged along the balcony's edge and the seats looked more comfortable than the hard wooden one she was seated on. She accepted the programme Wim handed to her and read it slowly, realising with horror that it was chamber music, something she had never enjoyed, moreover the works of Bach, Handel and somebody called Antonio de Cabezon, of whom she had never even heard, predominated throughout the lengthy programme. She was a little cheered to see that there was a list of vocalists at the end. A little singing would help the evening along and at least she could study the lady singers' dresses.

Sitting silently beside Wim, who was taking no notice of her at all, she listened to an unaccompanied work by Bach for violin and cello and presently cautiously looked around her. Everyone there was gazing raptly at the group of players on the platform—that was, everyone but the Baron. She saw him at once, sitting behind a bank of nicely arranged carnations, next to a stout lady who had her eyes shut. He was staring down at her and even in the semi-dark he looked badtempered. Becky returned her gaze to the players, composing her unremarkable features into what she hoped was a look of intense interest, and kept it like that until the music ended, when she clapped just as heartily as those around her, though for a different reason.

'A splendid rendering,' pronounced Wim. 'Bach expressed his deeper thoughts in such works, do you not think so?'

Becky looked wise and said, oh, yes, of course and kept her interested gaze on him while he went over the performance, note by note. When the lights were lowered and the musicians were well and truly into the next item she turned her head very slowly and peered upwards. The Baron was staring down at her again and she allowed her eyes to turn casually from one side to the other as though she hadn't seen him, before riveting them on the platform once again. It was a long composition and except for a nervous cough from time to time, she could have heard a pin drop. The audience was attentive, nobody around her moved a muscle. Presently she looked down on to her lap and allowed her thoughts to wander. Now if it had been Sibelius or Shostakovich or Brahms she would have loved every moment of it. She sighed soundlessly; she had no culture; she knew very little about anything and in a country where everyone seemed to speak English as easily as their own tongue, she was the complete ignoramus. The lights went up and she concentrated on trying to understand what Wim was saying about the origin of chamber music: 'And it is singing next,' he told her. 'You will enjoy that.'

The soloists filed on to the platform, a stout man in white tie and tails and two ladies in flowered tents. Becky had no doubt at all that they had excellent voices, but as they sang in German and it was a madrigal, she found her interest wandering. She turned a little in her chair so that she could peep upwards without it noticing. The Baron was sitting back with his eyes closed and now she saw Nina, until that moment hidden behind a massive arrangement of summer flowers next to him. She was looking bored and for once Becky felt strongly sympathetic towards her, although the feeling didn't last long. Even at that distance she looked shatteringly lovely.

The singing ended, giving way to an interval during which almost everyone went into the foyer where there was a bar, but Wim stayed where he was, pointing out that there was such a crowd that their chance of getting anything to drink was small; they might just as well sit quietly where they were and discuss the performance. As far as Becky could see, everyone in the gallery had disappeared. Perhaps they were privileged and had a bar of their own… She lent an attentive ear to Wim's knowledgeable remarks and wondered if he would take her to supper afterwards—or at least a cup of coffee; she had had only a snatched tea and she was famished.

She managed not to look up once during the second half of the concert and even when the lights went on at its end she kept her eyes fixed on the people around her. Wim looked at his watch. 'It's after ten o'clock,' he told her. 'We'd better get a tram; I'm on early duty in the morning.'

Becky agreed, outwardly cheerful while her insides rumbled, and followed him through the press of people to the street outside. When a hand fell on her shoulder she jumped, trod on someone's foot, apologised and turned round.

'A delightful concert, was it not?' queried the Baron courteously. 'Such splendid voices, and I particularly enjoyed the oboe.' Wim had stopped, looking awkward, and the Baron went on smoothly: 'Ah, young Tolde, is it not? You are together? I'll give you a lift back.'

He bore them inexorably forward, to be joined by Nina who had been talking to a group of people on the pavement. She looked annoyed when she saw them and still more annoyed when the Baron said briskly: 'Nina, I'm going to drop these two off.' They had reached the Rolls and he was opening

doors and stuffing them inside so that no one had a chance to
say much. 'I'll go to your place first. I'm afraid we'll have to
call off supper, Nina, something's come up and I must get
back to the hospital.' He turned round and addressed Wim.
'You first, Tolde. We can go past the hospital on the way.'
He seemed to have forgotten Becky.

Nina had a good deal to say, but Becky's Dutch wasn't up
to understanding it, but she was annoyed, that was certain.
She sat rigid presently while the Baron drove through Leeuwarden, deposited Wim at the hospital gates and then drove
on again to a quiet street where he pulled up before a block
of modern flats and got out with Nina. He wasn't gone long,
and when he got back he drove off again without speaking to
Becky, still sitting in the back. She wondered if she should
give a polite cough or say something light like: 'I'm still here,'
or 'I can walk home from here,' when he asked: 'Are you
hungry, Becky?'

She said yes before she could stop herself and he said:
'Good, so am I—let's eat.'

'But you've got to go to the hospital—you said something
had come up...'

'So it has, but not at the hospital. It's too late to go to
Waffum—we'll go to 't Pannekoekhuysje and eat pancakes.'

Which they did—enormous ones, a foot across, liberally
sprinkled with crisp fat bacon, and lavishly damped down
with black treacle. Becky, who hadn't believed the Baron
when he had described what he had ordered for them both,
took a first mouthful in some doubt and then quickly decided
that she had never tasted anything so suitable for an empty
stomach. They washed it down with lager because, as it was
explained to her, that was the correct drink to have with a
spek Pannekoek. They didn't bother to talk much to begin
with. Only when they were half way through did Becky put
down her knife and fork and observe: 'This is absolutely delicious!'

'Ah, but you should eat it on a raw winter's day when the

frost's thick on the ground and your feet are frozen—there's nothing like it then.'

Becky tried to imagine Nina sitting in her place, making inroads into the wholesome fattening food on her plate, and found it impossible. The Baron's voice interrupted her thoughts. 'You enjoyed the concert this evening?'

She cast around for an answer that wasn't exactly a fib. 'Well—I don't know much about Bach or—or madrigals...'

'And yet you appeared to be deeply absorbed—perhaps it was the flowered tents which interested you so much.'

Her eyes widened with laughter. 'Oh, that's what I called them too—they were, weren't they?'

'Why did you go?' The Baron lifted a finger and ordered coffee.

'Well, I thought it would be nice to go out.' She sounded wistful without knowing it. 'I didn't know what kind of concert it was, though. If it had been Brahms or Sibelius I'd have loved it.'

'Ah—a romantic. I must say I prefer them myself—the madrigal has never been my favourite form of music.'

'Then why did you go?'

When he answered 'Because you did,' she goggled at him in amazement.

'But Nina was there, I saw her...'

'The poor girl! She had been expecting to visit one of her dear friend's birthday party.'

Becky giggled despite herself. 'Do you mean to say you took her to the concert without her knowing she was going?'

'Something like that.' He smiled at her and her heart melted against her ribs. 'Why?' she asked in a whisper.

He stared at her across the table, his eyes very blue and bright. 'You know, Becky, I do believe that we are at last establishing a good relationship—isn't that the modern jargon? Do you realise that we have been sitting here for upwards of an hour without a cross word to show for it? I must be a reformed character.' He didn't give her a chance to answer him but went on smoothly:

'Has de Viske been to see Bertie?'

It seemed best to ignore the first part of his remark. 'Yes—he's pleased with him, he told me that Bertie was a fine healthy dog for his age—he gave me some pills for him. He looked at Pooch too, he said he might as well while he was there.' She frowned faintly, thinking of the bill which hadn't come yet; she shouldn't have bought the new dress—a thought instantly cancelled out by the Baron's quiet:

'I like that thing you're wearing—you should wear pretty things more often, Becky.'

She finished her coffee and didn't say anything. Probably he had no idea what it cost to live, especially when you had two animals and were trying to save. 'If you don't mind, I think I ought to go home. I'm on at ten o'clock and I must take Bertie for his walk first and I've the shopping to do. Thank you for my supper.'

In the car he asked her: 'Do you like young Tolde?'

'Like him? He's all right, and he was kind when I first started work—stopped to talk to me and showed me where the dining room was when I got lost. His girl-friend couldn't come this evening and he just wanted company.'

The Baron said: 'Ah, just so.' He sounded so satisfied that she glanced at his profile in surprise, but it gave nothing away.

When they reached Mevrouw Botte's house he got out too. 'I'll take Bertie to stretch his legs while you make the coffee,' he told her, and followed her up the stairs.

Becky had had no intention of asking him in for coffee, but she found herself getting the pot from the kitchen shelf and going through the careful ritual. It was ready when he got back with Bertie, who sat down at once and looked starved until she offered a biscuit, which meant that Pooch had to have something too. The Baron poured milk into a saucer and then accepted his coffee. 'A very pleasant evening,' he pronounced, 'and full of surprises.'

'Surprises? I don't think I was surprised.'

'They were all surprises for me,' he told her, which explained nothing, and put his coffee cup down. 'You're growing into quite a pretty girl, Becky.'

She shook her head sadly. 'No, I'm not, thank you all the
same.' She added quite fiercely: 'I wish I were beautiful, so
that everyone stared at me...'

She looked away, ashamed of her outburst so that she didn't
see his smile.

'There are so many kinds of beauty—have you ever looked
in a small hidden pool in a wood, Becky? It's full of beauty,
but it's not in the least spectacular, only restful and quiet and
never-endingly fascinating.' He got up and wandered to the
door. 'Someone said—and I've forgotten who-''Beauty is
nothing other than the promise of happiness.'' That's very
true, you know.'

He put out an arm and pulled her close and kissed her
gently. 'Good night, my pretty little mouse.'

A remark which gave Becky a sleepless night.

It was silly to get up ten minutes earlier so that she could
take pains with her face and hair, especially as the Baron
wasn't to be seen all day—nor the day after, for that matter.
On the third day, while she was having coffee with some of
her new friends, she ventured to ask casually if Doctor Raukema van den Eck had beds in other hospitals.

'But of course,' she was told. 'He has beds in Groningen,
and he goes often to Utrecht and Leiden, for he lectures also.
And as well as that he goes often to England; he is a busy
man. He is in England now, I think.'

'And does the so lovely Nina van Doorn go with him?'
asked a voice, and Becky let out a relieved breath which she
hadn't known she had been holding when someone else said:
'No, because I saw her yesterday with a man—he was old, at
least fifty, and fat. They were being driven in a Mercedes
limousine.'

The speaker turned to Becky. 'You have met this Nina?

She is very beautiful, is she not? She is also greedy for money, therefore she is always to be seen with Doctor Raukema, who has a great deal of it. But perhaps this fat man has more. I hope so.' There was general laughter in which Becky joined, praying quietly that the fat man would be a multi-millionaire. The Baron might be rich, but surely not as rich as all that.

He was back the next morning, coming on to the ward with his usual followers. Becky had seen him through the linen room door while she sorted sheets for the beds which had to be made up for the new admissions, so she stayed where she was until she judged that he would be well started—she could sneak up and along the other side and into the side ward.

Which she did, and since he had his back to her, she felt safe in assuming that he hadn't seen her. She wasn't quite sure why she didn't want to meet him, for she loved him so much that she felt that she could never see enough of him, anyway. Possibly because the last time they had met he had called her a pretty little mouse. She turned her thoughts resolutely away from him and began a conversation with the student nurse who was helping her, a rather tiresome type who took pleasure in pointing out Becky's many faults on every occasion. She was being called to task quite severely because she had got her tenses mixed as usual, when Zuster Trippe stopped rather suddenly, letting the blanket fall. Becky swept her side tidily up the bed, mitred the corner neatly and said, her Dutch all wrong as usual: 'Why do you stop? You can't have finished grumbling at my mistakes...'

She was aware that the other girl was put out about something, indeed she had never seen her look so uncomfortable. The Directrice, thought Becky, who had a wholesome regard for that lady, and turned round smartly.

The Baron was in the doorway, watching silently, his registrar and houseman and the Hoofd Zuster peering round him, as though she and Zuster Trippe were putting on an exhibition of bedmaking for their benefit.

The Baron inclined his head politely. 'Zuster Saunders, I

wish to speak to you.' He advanced into the ward. 'And I must compliment you on the improvement in your Dutch,' he gave Zuster Trippe a cold look as he spoke. 'I trust that you get all the help and encouragement you need.' He spoke softly to the Hoofd Zuster, who said something in her turn to everyone there, and Becky watched them all go away. She went a little pale; she had done something awful, although she couldn't think what—or perhaps Bertie was ill, or Pooch... She raised troubled eyes to his face and said quickly: 'Oh, what have I done? Or is it the animals...?'

The Baron seated himself on the side of a newly made-up bed. 'Why must you always imagine that I am the bearer of bad news?' he wanted to know with some asperity. 'That nurse was rather on the snappy side, wasn't she? What had you been doing?'

'Getting my grammar wrong—she fancies herself as a teacher, I think.'

'Your grammar is admittedly a little peculiar, but your accent is good,' and when she said eagerly: 'Oh, is it really? I am glad...' he asked: 'Why are you so anxious to speak our language, Becky?'

She could hardly tell him that it was because she wanted to understand every word he uttered and even be able to answer him so that he would be able to understand her. 'Oh, I don't know,' she mumbled.

He hitched up his elegant trousers and stared at a shoe. 'My mother is to go to London in three days' time—I want her to see Mr Lennox...' Becky knew of him; a famous orthopaedic surgeon whose opinion was sought all over the world. 'We're old friends,' went on the Baron. 'I want to make sure that everything is as good as it ever will be before she plunges back into her busy little life. She gardens, you know, not just a weed or two and picking flowers; she's quite capable of taking the spade from the gardener and using it, and she has this thing about digging the potato crop too. My father was able to manage her in the nicest possible way, I'm not as successful—she has done what she wants all her life, bless her, and it would be cruel and impossible to stop her. All the same, I'd like her looked at before she surprises us with some new idea. Last year it was country dancing...'

Becky smiled. 'It's nice to find someone who doesn't moan about getting elderly. I don't think I've ever met anyone who enjoyed life as she does.'

'You like her, Becky?'

'Yes, immensely.' She added silently: 'And I like you too, Tiele, as well as loving you.'

'That's good. She has agreed to go to London, but only if you will go with her. Tialda offered, but Pieter isn't keen on her travelling around too much, and in any case, my mother had already decided that she wanted you to go.'

Becky folded a pillow case neatly. 'That's very nice of her and I'd have loved to have gone, but I'm here, aren't I?'

'Don't worry about that—I've already spoken to the Directrice, she has no objection—it will only be for three days.'

'Oh, but I can't leave Bertie and Pooch...'

He said patiently: 'Of course not. They can spend the time at my home with Lola. Willem will look after them—they know their way about there.'

'How do we go?'

'I shall drive, of course.' He sounded surprised at her question. 'We can take the night ferry from the Hoek.' He got up from the bed. 'Today's Friday; Willem will collect you at eleven o'clock on Monday and bring you all out to Huize Raukema, we'll leave after lunch.' He sauntered to the door.

'Will I be staying at the hospital?' asked Becky.

'No. My mother will be examined on Tuesday afternoon, probably X-rayed then and possibly have a final check-up on the Wednesday. We shall return on the Thursday. You will of course accompany her to the hospital.'

He had gone before she could say anything else. He had said that she wouldn't be staying at the hospital; she supposed it would be an hotel, in which case would her wardrobe stand up to it? The vexed question kept her mind occupied while she finished off the beds, but after that she was too busy to think about it.

At lunch, as she was sitting with the other nurses of the ward, someone asked her what Doctor Raukema had wanted. 'He never talks to any of the nurses, though I suppose as you nursed his mother you know each other well.' There was faint envy in the voice.

'Well, no, not really,' said Becky, painstakingly truthful. 'His mother has to go to London to be examined and she wants me to go with her.'

There was a murmur of interest. 'And you go, naturally, Becky?'

'Doctor Raukema asked me if I would; it's only for a few days.'

'You are a lucky girl—will you have much free time?'

Becky remembered the Baroness's habit of forgetting things like off duty and whether she had had her lunch, and all the errands she wanted done. She smiled because despite that she was fond of the little lady. 'No, I don't expect I shall,' she admitted.

She decided against buying another dress; her slowly growing hoard of guldens was too precious and she doubted very much if she would wear it. She packed the green jersey dress, the flowered cotton skirt and the blouse that went with it and then recklessly went to C & A and bought a second one in very pale green with a ruffled collar and long sleeves ending in matching ruffles.

She was ready and waiting for Willem when he arrived. Mevrouw Botte, quite excited about the whole thing, toiled up the stairs to tell Becky he was there and then insisted on carrying her case down for her while Willem, who had come along at a more leisurely pace, took Bertie's lead, which left Becky, clutching Pooch, to go downstairs quite uncluttered. It gave her a lovely feeling, just as though she were beautiful and important, and somehow Willem contrived to go on making her feel like that in the car. He was driving a Porsche which he explained was used by the Baron occasionally, although he preferred the Rolls. 'And that's a very good car, Miss Saunders,' said Willem surprisingly, 'but for myself, I like something sporty.'

Becky digested this in silence; Willem hardly looked like a demon driver. Presently she asked: 'Doesn't the Baron like driving a fast car?'

They were already clear of Leeuwarden, racing along the road. 'Him drive fast? Why, I taught him to drive, Miss Saunders, when he was a lad. He's a great one for speed—you should just see him in that Rolls of his when he's on his own.'

'You've known him a long time, haven't you, Willem?' She hoped they would go on talking about the Baron for a long time; it was lovely to find out about him, and Willem, she was delighted to discover, was nothing loath. The journey passed pleasantly for both of them. It was only a pity that they reached the gates of Huize Raukema before Willem had finished telling her about the Baron's more youthful days.

The master of the house wasn't home; Becky gathered from Sutske that he was seeing a patient, and the Baroness was expected shortly. With Bertie and Pooch ambling ahead of her, very much at home, she was led to the sitting room, its doors open to the garden beyond, and given coffee and a selection of the day's newspapers. She was painstakingly translating the small ads when the Baron arrived. The house was too large and solidly built for her to hear more than a murmur of voices, but she was quite sure who it was, for Bertie and Pooch were already hurrying to the door.

The Baron stopped to pull Bertie's ears, sweep Pooch up into an arm and warn Lola not to get excited and then came across the room to her with a brisk 'Good morning, Becky, everything is all right, I hope?' He sat down opposite her. 'I'm sorry I wasn't home when you arrived—a last-minute urgent case. Ah, here's Willem with more coffee. Be mother, will you, Becky?'

She poured the coffee from a tall silver pot into delicate white and lilac cups—early Delft and so old she was terrified of breaking something. She concentrated hard on what she was doing because she felt shy of him. Now if she had been beautiful and sure of herself like Nina van Doorn...

'What are you thinking about, Becky?' asked her companion. 'You look sad and excited all rolled into one. Is it a secret?'

She drew a breath. 'Yes.' And then, because she had to talk about something else and anyway she had been worrying away at something which had puzzled her for days: 'When we had that picnic—in the grounds of that dear little country house—whose was it?' And when he didn't answer at once: 'Was it yours, too?'

He passed his cup for more coffee and settled himself more comfortably. 'Yes, Becky, it is my house. And since you're so curious about it—I didn't want to tell you then—I had a feeling it might spoil the evening, you see. I...'

He didn't finish because the door was flung open and Nina came in. She looked lovelier than ever because she was in a towering rage. Beyond a furious look at Becky she didn't bother with her, but almost ran across the room to the Baron, who had got to his feet unhurriedly and was showing, Becky was relieved to see, no signs of alarm, nor was his calm shattered under the torrent of words Nina was pouring out. It was a pity that she spoke in Dutch, for Becky longed to know what she was so angry about. When she finally drew breath the Baron spoke—unhurriedly and as far as Becky could judge, good-humouredly, but Nina didn't like whatever he said. She raised her voice to an ugly shout and addressed Becky, who was none the wiser, added a rider to the Baron and rushed out of the room.

'Well,' said Becky in an interested voice, 'what was all that about?'

'You,' said the Baron, and before she could get her mouth

open to ask more, the door opened again and his mother came in.

In the bustle of getting the Baroness comfortably settled in a chair, pouring more coffee, retrieving the shawls, scarves and handbag which she had cast down on her way from the door to the sitting room, Becky had little time to ponder the Baron's reply. And when she did, sitting in the Rolls beside him while he drove them all down to the Hoek, she came to the conclusion that Nina had been upset because she wasn't a member of the party. It was a pity that no one had mentioned her. Lunch had been a pleasant meal with the Baroness bearing the lion's share of the conversation, and afterwards Becky had gone to the kitchen to bid Bertie and Pooch goodbye, and when she rejoined mother and son in the drawing room, the Baroness was talking about the weather. The Baron, for some reason, was looking amused.

They travelled in great comfort, but then Becky couldn't imagine the Baron doing anything else, and certainly not his mother, but it was pleasant, when they stopped briefly for tea, to have instant attention and smiling service. They stopped for dinner too, at Saur's in den Haag, and Becky thanked heaven silently that she was wearing the green jersey; it was hardly *haute couture* but it passed muster in a crowd, and the crowd was fashionable. Presumably the Baron had booked a table, for there was no delay for them, they had their drinks and were served at once; iced soup followed by lobster and a salad because the Baron had recommended them and washed down by a dry white wine. And Becky was persuaded to sample a waffle smothered in whipped cream for dessert and topped with strawberries before their coffee. She would have liked to have spent more time in den Haag, one day, she promised herself. She would go there on a day off and have a good look round.

They reached the Hoek shortly after, and here again there was no waiting about. The car was driven aboard, the Baroness made comfortable in her stateroom, the steward warned as to what time they were to be wakened in the morning and by that time the ferry was already at sea. Becky, rather disappointed at the total absence of the Baron, went to the cabin next to the Baroness's and got ready for the night. The Baroness was already asleep when she crept in to see if she wanted anything; Becky left a dim light on, opened the door between them, and went to bed herself.

They breakfasted in their cabins and it was only as the ferry was docking that the Baron appeared, to wish them both good morning and swept them down into the car. True, he enquired as to whether they had had a good night, but he was so deep in thought that Becky kept a still tongue in her head and even suggested, once they were clear of Customs, that she should travel in the back with the Baroness—a suggestion nipped in the bud with a: 'What for?' from the Baron, uttered in a tone of voice which really didn't need an answer.

They were in London by mid-morning, and Becky, who wasn't familiar with the city, watched idly from the window as they threaded their way through the traffic, but she couldn't help but see that they were passing through the most elegant streets and squares. When the Baron finally stopped in Carlos Place and she got out of the car, aided quite unnecessarily by a porter, she saw that they were outside the Connaught Hotel. She might not know her London well, but she had heard about some of its famous hotels. She thought with vexation of her inadequate wardrobe as she took the Baroness's arm and went into the splendid foyer. But only for a moment or so. After all, her clothes didn't really matter; she had come as companion to the Baroness and it wasn't likely that she would spend much time in its restaurant or public rooms. She watched the Baron getting things arranged without fuss and was wafted with her companion to the third floor, where a suite of rooms had been booked for them—a sitting room, an enormous bedroom for the Baroness with a smaller one for herself, bathrooms, and a room for the Baron. She still wasn't very happy about her clothes, but she unpacked for the Baroness and herself, assisted that lady to tidy herself and sat her down in the sitting room until the Baron should join them.

CHAPTER NINE

THEY HAD LUNCH in the hotel's restaurant and although Becky had suggested diffidently that mother and son might like to lunch alone while she had something in their sitting room, she had been met with such a blazing look from the Baron that she had stopped in mid-sentence. 'Do you not wish for our company?' he had asked her coldly, and when she had tried to explain, getting her lack of the right clothes hopelessly mixed up with the fact that she was only there as a companion anyway, and hadn't expected...she had been cut short with such arrogance that she had remarked severely:

'Well, you have no need to be so nasty about it. I was trying to make it easier for you and the Baroness—after all I'm only...'

'If you say that just once more,' said the Baron explosively, 'I shall do you an injury! Just because your stepmother and stepbrother treated you like a maid-of-all-work it doesn't mean to say that I, or my mother, intend to do the same. You will take your meals with us, Becky.'

She had been so taken aback by his arrogance that she had agreed meekly.

The arrogance had disappeared by the time they were shown to their table; the Baron was all smooth charm, putting her at ease with a skill only seconded by his parent. Becky found herself enjoying every moment—the excellent food, the rich surroundings, the waiter's attention. She began to sparkle just a little and when they had finished went off with the Baroness to assist that lady to make herself comfortable for an afternoon's rest. That done, she wandered into the sitting room and went to look out of the windows. London—the best part of London, flowed smoothly past her downbent gaze; she was so absorbed that she didn't hear the Baron come in until he joined her. She jumped nervously, intent as always on keeping a cool front towards him.

'Oh, I expect you want to sit here—I've heaps of things I can do in my room, I'll...'

His hand came out and fastened gently on her arm. 'Becky, why do you always behave as though I'm an ogre?' He sighed. 'I've said some horrible things to you, haven't I? And now I discover that I didn't mean one of them.'

He smiled down at her and her heart rocked. She said stupidly: 'Oh, it doesn't matter,' and was inordinately vexed when he replied blandly: 'I know it doesn't.'

His hand tightened on her arm. 'Come and sit down while I tell you what has been arranged.' And when she was seated beside him: 'Mother will be seen by Mr Lennox tomorrow morning at ten o'clock. It will be your job to see that she is ready to leave here by half past nine, stay with her at all times while she is there and bring her back here. It is possible that he may wish to see her briefly in the afternoon; we shan't be leaving until the following evening, in any case. At half past three this afternoon I shall drive you both to the hospital where she will have her X-rays done. I'm afraid you will have to come back by taxi because I have an appointment at four-thirty and may not be ready in time to fetch you. I've already arranged for it to be waiting for you; the hall porter will see to that. I thought it might be pleasant to go to a theatre this evening—I've got tickets. We'll dine early—seven o'clock should be time enough.'

'Oh, but...' began Becky, and then, completely reckless: 'That would be very nice, but have I time to go and buy a dress? I mean, I didn't expect to go out.'

He glanced at his watch. 'You have one hour exactly, take a taxi there and back.' He added reflectively: 'I was beginning to wonder just what you were saving your money for, Becky.'

She felt her cheeks redden. She could hardly say: 'To get away from you, my darling Tiele,' but instead she murmured something about having had no time and got to her feet. 'I promise I'll be back,' she told him breathlessly. 'Is it—will it be black tie, do you think?'

His mouth twitched just a little. 'Oh, yes—we're celebrating my mother's return to good health, are we not?'

From a visit years ago, Becky remembered that Fenwick's was in Bond Street, and that wasn't too far away. 'I'll go now,' she decided, and made for the door. The Baron had no difficulty in keeping up with her; he ushered her into the lift, escorted her to the pavement, told the doorman to get a taxi and handed her in. 'Where do you go?' he asked her.

'Well, Fenwick's, it's at the other end of Bond Street.'

He spoke to the driver, gave him some money, and put his head through the window. 'Buy something pretty,' he advised her, 'and I've settled with the man.'

Fenwick's didn't seem to have changed very much. Becky made her way to the gown department and set about the serious business of buying something pretty. It would have to be practical too, since it was an extravagance she didn't mean to repeat for a long time. She found what she wanted before long; a wide skirt in palest grey patterned with delicate pink roses and a pale pink crépe blouse to wear with it. It cost more than she had bargained for, and she still had sandals to buy. Luckily there was quite a bit of the hour left; she hurried into Oxford Street and found exactly what she wanted—pale grey sandals with high heels. They were on the bargain rack outside the shop and although they looked like leather, they were plastic and very flimsy, but they would do. She almost ran into the street to find a taxi, terrified of being late.

At the hotel the doorman helped her out, assured her that he would pay the driver and called a boy to carry her parcels up to her room, where, with five minutes to spare, she had a quick look at the dress and hung it up before presenting herself in the sitting room.

'Ten minutes,' said the Baron. 'If you will start on my mother now.' He had been sitting by the window with his

eyes shut, but now he got to his feet and wanted to know if
she had had a successful time at the shops.

'Oh, yes, thank you,' said Becky happily, and went away
to get the Baroness on to her feet.

At the hospital the Baron handed them over to a young
man in a white coat who was introduced as Jimmy Mathers,
before he excused himself and went back to the car, leaving
Becky and the Baroness to be escorted to the X-ray department. The Baroness was inclined to be peevish and it took all
Becky's tact to get her to do as she was asked. It was tedious,
complained the little lady, having to come to the hospital—
surely it could have been done at the hotel, and just when she
wanted her tea...

Becky promised tea, explained with patience why it was
really better to attend the hospital and pointed out that the taxi
was waiting for them the moment they were ready.

'Oh, well,' sighed the Baroness, 'let us get it over and done
with, then.' She handed Becky her handbag and stick. 'You
will come with me tomorrow, won't you, my dear?'

'Of course, Baroness. Now if you will just lie down here—
I'll help you...'

They were back at the hotel, half way through tea, when
the Baron joined them. He refused tea, saying that he had
already had it, and he stayed only a few minutes, explaining
that he had to go out again. 'But don't forget that we are
dining at seven o'clock,' he warned, as he went.

Becky dressed with care but no waste of time; the Baroness
had taken longer than usual, complaining that her legs ached,
so that Becky had spent quite a while massaging them before
helping her patient to dress. Now, wriggling into her outfit,
she thanked heaven that her hair-style was a simple one and
her make-up just as simple. The dress looked nice. She twirled
to and fro before the wall mirror, looking closely at the sandals; at a distance and unless they were inspected very closely,
they didn't look cheap at all. With a final pat to her already

smooth hair, she went along to the sitting room. The Baroness would be waiting...

She wasn't, but the Baron was, standing with his back to the room, looking out of one of the windows. Her heart danced at the sight of his broad shoulders, elegant in his black jacket, and it danced even harder when he turned round.

'I always thought you were nice to look at,' he told her softly. 'You look very pretty, Becky—indeed, I might say beautiful.'

She paused in the doorway feeling shy and happy and sad all rolled into one.

'Thank you, but it's not true, you know. I mean, when you think of Juffrouw van Doorn...'

'But I'm not thinking of her.'

Her eyes were very dark. 'Yes—well, I think you should be. I mean...'

'Just what do you mean, Becky?'

She was pleating a fold of her skirt in nervous fingers, wishing she had never started this conversation. 'She's so beautiful,' she managed at last.

'Do you know what I told her that day she came—you remember? just before we left home?' He strolled across the room to stand before her, staring down into her upturned face.

She thought how very blue his eyes were. 'No.'

'I told her that I was going to marry you.' He stooped and kissed her. 'No, don't say a word; you're going to tell me that you don't believe it, and I'm not surprised, I didn't believe it myself at first. Just get used to the idea, Becky.'

She had no words and no breath, and perhaps it was just as well that the Baroness came into the room at that moment, demanding with charming persistence that someone should give her a drink. Becky was given a glass too and drank its contents, not having the least notion what it was. She had no idea what she ate at dinner either; she sat in a dreamlike state answering when she was spoken to, avoiding Tiele's eye, prudently refusing more than one glass of the champagne he had ordered; she was muddled enough as it was.

She became even more muddled as the evening wore on. Nothing in the Baron's manner bore out his astonishing remarks to her before dinner; he treated her with a placid friendliness which made her wonder if she had dreamed the whole thing—only, she told herself, no one could dream up a kiss like the one he had given her. She sat between mother and son, her eyes on the stage, seeing nothing of the play, and feeling so peculiar that she began to wonder if it was the champagne. But it wasn't the champagne, she knew that when Tiele possessed himself of her hand, holding it gently in a cool, firm grip.

But he said nothing. They went back to the hotel when the play was over and had a light supper in the restaurant and presently the Baroness said that she really would have to go to bed and Becky, terrified of being left alone with Tiele although it was the one thing she most wanted to happen, accompanied her to her room and helped her to her bed. Tiele had bidden them both goodnight, and if Becky had hoped secretly that he would suggest that she should join him again, she took care not to admit it, even to herself.

He had gone out when she went along to the sitting room in the morning. She made a quick breakfast and then spent the next hour making sure that the Baroness would be ready to leave at half past nine—something which was achieved, but only just. The Baron returned punctually, wished them a cheerful good morning and without waste of time drove them to the hospital. Becky, studying him covertly, could see no signs of a man in love, especially with herself. He handed them over to the care of the Orthopaedic Ward Sister, observed that he would see them later, and went away.

Mr Lennox was a thorough man. The Baroness, examined exhaustively, was allowed to leave about noon with the request that she should return that afternoon. 'A final test or two,' said Mr Lennox soothingly. 'Let your nurse bring you back at three o'clock. There will be no need for her to wait, I shall have the pleasure of driving you back to your hotel myself.'

There was no sign of the Baron when they got back to the hotel. They lunched in the sitting room, discussing the morning's activities, and after the Baroness had rested Becky called a taxi and took her back to the hospital, prudently leaving a note for the Baron.

It was well after three o'clock by the time Becky had satisfied herself that the Baroness was in good hands and that Mr Lennox really did intend to take her back later. 'Go and enjoy yourself, my dear,' begged the Baroness. 'They tell me that I shan't be leaving here for an hour—why not do some shopping? If I'm not back by five o'clock, you can telephone...'

Becky bade her a cheerful goodbye. She wasn't going to do any shopping; she was going to get on a bus and go to the nearest park and walk, perhaps that would clear her head. She went briskly through the entrance, across the forecourt and on to the crowded pavement—right into the arms of Basil.

The shock sent the colour from her cheeks and rendered her dumb. She could only stand and stare at him, grinning down at her with a look of vindictive triumph. It was only when he put a hand on her arm that she tried to wrench it away and couldn't.

'Not so fast, Rebecca.' Basil's voice was as smooth and nasty as it had always been. 'What a gift from heaven, my dear, dear Rebecca! Mother isn't really up to running the house, you know, and somehow the housekeepers we engage don't stay more than a week or two. She'll be delighted to see you again—you shall come back with me...'

'I won't!' said Becky fiercely. 'And you can't make me. I've a good job and I'd rather die than go back.'

'At the hospital, are you? Well, it shouldn't be too hard to cook up some reason why you should come home, but it would be far better for you, little stepsister, if you came quietly with me now.'

She gave another tug and his grip tightened. She didn't like the idea of making a scene, it would mean the police, probably, and that would involve the Baroness and Tiele. At the thought of him she said desperately: 'Oh, Tiele!'

The Baron, standing on the other side of the street watching, frowned. He had been on the point of going into the hospital, waiting for the traffic to allow him to cross. Now he didn't wait, but dodged between buses and taxis and cars and gained the pavement in time to hear Basil say: 'Don't be a fool, Rebecca! You can't make a scene here—come along...'

The Baron's voice, very soft, sent Becky's heart soaring. 'Not so fast, my friend. Rebecca stays where she is.' He added in a voice which sent shivers down her back: 'You are the unspeakable Basil, I take it?'

Basil went a rich plum colour. 'And who are you?' he blustered. 'What right have you to interfere?'

'All the right in the world, my good fellow; Rebecca is going to be my wife.' His hand closed like a vice on Basil's arm and plucked it away from Becky. 'You mentioned making a scene—I have no inhibitions about doing so; if you are not out of my sight in ten seconds, I'll make a scene you will never forget.'

It was amazing how very quickly Basil melted into the unnoticing passers-by. Becky, very pale still, stood shivering, and Tiele slid a vast arm round her shoulders.

'A nice cup of tea,' he observed placidly, 'is just what we need.' But when Becky looked at his face, his eyes weren't placid at all, they were dark blue with rage.

She said apologetically: 'I'm sorry—he took me by surprise, and I was frightened. I'm all right now...'

'Are you indeed? The colour of watered milk and shaking like a fairy in a snowstorm.'

'You're angry.'

His smile warmed her. 'Yes, but that cup of tea will soothe me back to my usual arrogant, ill-mannered self.'

She closed her eyes for a moment. 'Don't say that—it's not true.' She opened them to tell him: 'I called you and you came.'

'Let us say rather that kindly providence arranged for me to be on my way to meet you at the hospital—I was on the other side of the street.' He took his arm from her shoulders and put a hand under her arm. 'There's an Olde-Worlde Tea Shoppe in the next street—it's rather out of its environment and it's run by a dragon with a light hand at pastry.'

Becky, who had been wanting to cry, giggled instead. 'I don't suppose you know the first thing about pastry.'

He walked her down a narrow turning, round a corner and into a quiet little cul-de-sac, unexpected and almost rural in the centre of the city. The tea room was at its end, sandwiched between a narrow house with window boxes and a tiny dress shop called 'Angel's Boutique'. There weren't many people sitting at the small round tables, and the Baron chose one at a window, so that he could sit on the window seat. 'For I doubt if these chairs are up to my weight,' he explained, and then turned to smile with tremendous charm at the light-handed dragon, already hovering.

'Tea, if you please,' he begged her in a voice as charming as his smile, 'and some of your little cakes—and perhaps a plate of thinly cut bread and butter.'

'Tea is not tea without bread and butter,' observed the dragon severely. 'I am glad that there are some people who know what is right and proper.' She sent a chilling glance at the two girls sitting close by, with a dish of eclairs between them and no bread and butter in sight. When she had gone Tiele remarked: 'I'll wager my table silver that she's been someone's nanny.'

Becky was feeling better. 'The bread and butter bit? Yes, I think you're right. Tiele, do you think he'll come back for me?—Basil?'

He stretched a hand across the table and took hers in its secure grasp. 'No, my darling, he won't come back again, and I shall be there if he does.'

'Oh, why do you...' She broke off as the dragon arrived with a tray and arranged everything just so before leaving them again.

Just as though she had finished the sentence he answered her: 'You are my darling. Becky, it took me a little while to discover it—and to admit it—but now I find that I cannot live without you, nor do I wish to.'

He poured the tea for them both and passed her a cup. 'Drink that, my dearest heart—you've had a bad fright.' He hadn't let go of her hand and she took no notice of the tea, only sat there staring at him.

'Nina?' she spoke under her breath.

'She loved my money, Becky darling, not me.'

Becky heaved a deep sigh. 'I love you,' she said simply. 'But didn't you l-love her at all?'

He shook his head. 'No. I took her out a good deal; she amused me... But I don't want to be amused in that way, darling— Oh, I shall laugh at you a dozen times a day, but we shall share our laughter.'

He was interrupted by the dragon who swept up to the table, wanting to know if the bread and butter wasn't to their liking. 'Because you've eaten none of it,' she pointed out severely.

Tiele charmed her with another smile. 'It is quite perfect,' he told her. 'We are about to eat every morsel.'

She smiled then, looking at them in turn. 'Well, you don't have to hurry,' she said as she went away.

Becky was made to eat her tea then and when she tried to get her hand back Tiele engulfed it even more tightly. 'No, you'll have to manage with the other one,' he told her. 'I've been wanting to hold your hand for a long time, and now that I have it, I don't intend to let it go.'

Becky obediently ate her bread and butter. Half way through the second slice she said: 'It doesn't seem true...I can't believe… Tiele, I'm plain and I haven't any pretty clothes and I'm not witty—and your big house terrifies me even though I love it.'

He lifted her hand and kissed it gently. 'You're the most beautiful girl in the world and I'm going to give you all the pretty clothes you could possibly want. I don't like witty girls with shrill voices—you have a lovely voice, my darling.' He grinned at her. 'And when the house has some children in it, it won't seem so large.'

He poured more tea and Becky, suddenly on top of her world, took one of the cakes he was offering her. She said a little shyly: 'People in love aren't supposed to eat…'

'Then we will be the exception to the rule, my love.'

Presently they bade the dragon goodbye and wandered out into the street. There was no one about, only the dragon watching them through a window.

'We must go back,' said Becky. 'Your mother will wonder what has happened.'

'No, she won't—she knows that I'm going to marry you.'

'Are you?' asked Becky demurely. 'I haven't been asked yet.'

The words were no sooner out of her mouth before she was in his arms.

'Dare to say no,' said the Baron, and gave her no chance to say anything at all. Being kissed like that, thought Becky hazily, took all one's breath; to try to speak would be a waste of time. She kissed him back instead, and the dragon, looking fiercer than ever, wiped away a sentimental tear and nodded her head with satisfaction.

CAROLINE'S
WATERLOO

by

Betty Neels

'Beauty is nothing other
than the promise of happiness.'

Stendhal

CHAPTER ONE

THE NARROW brick road wound itself along narrow canals, through wide stretches of water meadows and small clumps of trees and, here and there, a larger copse. Standing well away from the road there were big farmhouses, each backed by a great barn, their mellow red brick glistening in the last rays of the October sun. Save for the cows, already in their winter coats, and one or two great horses, there was little to be seen and the only other movement was made by the four girls cycling briskly along the road. They had come quite a distance that day and now they were flagging a little; the camping equipment each carried made it heavy going, and besides, they had lost their way.

It had been easy enough leaving Alkmaar that morning, going over the Afsluitdijk and into Friesland, pedalling cheerfully towards the camping ground they had decided upon, but now, with no village in sight and the dusk beginning to creep over the wide Friesian sky, they were getting uneasy.

Presently they came to a halt, to look at the map and wonder where they had gone wrong. 'This doesn't go anywhere,' grumbled the obvious leader, a tall, very pretty girl. 'What shall we do? Go back—and that's miles—or press on?'

They all peered at the map again, one fair head, two dark ones and an unspectacular mouse-brown. The owner of the mouse-brown hair spoke:

'Well, the road must go somewhere, they wouldn't have built it just for fun, and we've been on it now for quite a while—I daresay we're nearer the end than the beginning.' She had a pretty voice, soft and slightly hesitant, perhaps as compensation for her very ordinary face.

Her three companions peered at the map again. 'You're right, Caro—let's go on before it's quite dark.' The speaker, one of the dark-haired girls, glanced around her at the empty landscape. 'It's lonely, isn't it? I mean, after all the towns and villages we've been through just lately.'

'Friesland and Groningen are sparsely populated,' said Caro, 'they're mostly agricultural.'

The three of them gave her a tolerant look. Caro was small and quiet and unassuming, but she was a fount of information about a great many things, because she read a lot, they imagined with a trace of pity; unlike the other nurses at Oliver's, she was seldom invited to go out by any of the young doctors and she lived alone in a small bedsitter in a horrid shabby little street convenient to the hospital. She had any number of friends, because she could be relied upon to change off-duty at a moment's notice, lend anything needed without fuss, and fill in last-minute gaps. As she was doing now; the nurse who should have been in her place had developed an appendix and because four was a much better number with which to go camping and biking, she had been roped in at the last minute. She hadn't particularly wanted to go; she had planned to spend her two weeks' holiday redecorating her room and visiting art galleries. She knew almost nothing about art, but she had discovered long ago that art galleries were restful and pleasant and there were always other people strolling around for company, even though no one ever spoke to her. Not that she minded being alone; she had grown up in a lonely way. An orphan from childhood, the aunt she had lived with had married while Caro was still at school and her new uncle had never taken to her; indeed, over the years, he had let it be known that she must find a home for herself; her aunt's was too small to house all three of them. If she had been pretty he might have thought differently, and if she had tried to conciliate him he might have had second thoughts. As it was, Caroline hadn't seen her aunt for two years or more.

'Well, let's get on,' suggested Stacey. She tossed her blonde hair back over her shoulders and got on to her bike once more, followed by Clare and Miriam with Caro bringing up the rear.

The sun seemed to set very rapidly and once it had disappeared behind them, the sky darkened even more rapidly. But the road appeared to run ahead of them, clearly to be seen until it disappeared into a large clump of trees on the horizon. There were distant lights from the farmhouse now, a long way off, but they dispelled the loneliness so that they all became cheerful again, calling to and fro to each other, discussing what they would eat for their supper and whose turn it was to cook. They reached the trees a few minutes later, and Stacey, still in front, called out excitedly: 'I say, look there, on the left—those lights—there must be a house!' She braked to take a better look and Clare and Miriam, who hadn't braked fast enough, went into her, joined seconds later by Caro, quite unable to stop herself in time. She ploughed into the struggling heap in front of her, felt a sharp pain in her leg and then nothing more, because she had hit her head on an old-fashioned milestone beside the cycle path.

She came to with a simply shocking headache, a strange feeling that she was in a nightmare, and the pain in her leg rather worse. What was more, she was being carried, very awkwardly too, with someone supporting her legs and her head cradled against what felt like an alpaca jacket—but men didn't wear alpaca jackets any more. She tried to say so, but the words didn't come out right and she was further mystified by a man's cockney voice close to her ear, warning someone to go easy. She wanted to say, 'My leg hurts,' but talking had become difficult and when she made her eyes open, she could see nothing much; a small strip of sky between tall trees and somewhere ahead lights shining. She gave up and passed out again, unaware that the awkward little party had reached the house, that Stacey, obedient to the cockney voice, had opened the door and held it wide while the others carried her inside. She was unaware too of the size and magnificence of the hall or of its many doors, one of which was flung open with some

force by a large man with a sheaf of papers in his hand and
a scowl on his handsome features. But she was brought back
to consciousness by his commanding voice, demanding
harshly why he was forced to suffer such a commotion in his
own house.

It seemed to Caro that someone should speak up and explain, but her head was still in a muddle although she knew
what she wanted to say; it was just a question of getting the
words out. She embarked on an explanation, only to be
abruptly halted by the harsh voice, very close to her now.
'This girl's concussed and that leg needs attention. Noakes,
carry her into the surgery.' She heard his sigh. 'I suppose I
must attend to it.'

Just for a moment her addled brain cleared. She said quite
clearly: 'You have no need to be quite so unfeeling. Give me
a needle and thread and I'll do it myself.'

She heard his crack of laughter before she went back into
limbo again.

She drifted in and out of sleep several times during the
night and each time she opened her eyes it was to see, rather
hazily, someone sitting by her bed. He took no notice of her
at all, but wrote and read and wrote again, and something
about his austere look convinced her that it was the owner of
the voice who had declared that she was concussed.

'I'm not concussed,' she said aloud, and was surprised that
her voice sounded so wobbly.

He had got to his feet without answering her, given her a
drink and said in a voice which wasn't going to take no for
an answer: 'Go to sleep.'

It seemed a good idea; she closed her eyes.

The next time she woke, although the room was dim she
knew that it was day, for the reading lamp by the chair was
out. The man had gone and Stacey sat there, reading a book.

'Hullo,' said Caro in a much stronger voice; her head still
ached and so did her leg, but she had stopped feeling dreamlike.

Stacey got up and came over to the bed. 'Caro, do you feel better? You gave us all a fright, I can tell you!'

Caro looked carefully round the room, trying not to move her head because of the pain. It was a splendid apartment, its walls hung with pale silk, its rosewood furniture shining with age and polishing. The bed she was in had a draped canopy and a silken bedspread, its beauty rather marred by the cradle beneath it, guarding her injured leg.

'What happened' she asked. 'There was a very cross man, wasn't there?'

Stacey giggled. 'Oh, ducky, you should have heard yourself! It's an enormous house and he's so good-looking you blink...'

Caroline closed her eyes. 'What happened?'

'We all fell over, and you cut your leg open on Clare's pedal—it whizzed round and gashed it badly, and you fell on to one of those milestones and knocked yourself out.'

'Are you all right? You and Clare and Miriam?'

'Absolutely, hardly a scratch between us—only you, Caro—we're ever so sorry.' She patted Caro's arm. 'I've got to tell Professor Thoe van Erckelens you're awake.'

Caro still had her eyes shut. 'What an extraordinary name...'

Her hand was picked up and her pulse taken and she opened her eyes. Stacey had gone, the man—presumably the Professor—was there, towering over her.

He grunted to himself and then asked: 'What is your name, young lady?'

'Caroline Tripp.' She watched his stern mouth twitch at the corners; possibly her name sounded as strange to him as his did to her. 'I feel better, thank you.' She added, 'It was kind of you to sit with me last night.'

He had produced an ophthalmoscope from somewhere and was fitting it together. 'I am a doctor, Miss Tripp—a doctor's duty is to his patient.'

Unanswerable, especially with her head in such a muddled

state. He examined her eyes with care and silently and then spoke to someone she couldn't see. 'I should like to examine the leg, please.'

It was Stacey who turned back the coverlet and removed the cradle before unwinding the bandage which covered Caro's leg from knee to ankle.

'Did you stitch it?' asked Caro, craning her neck to see.

A firm hand restrained her. 'You would be foolish to move your head too much,' she was told. 'Yes, I have cleaned and stitched the wound in your leg. It is a deep, jagged cut and you will have to rest it for some days.'

'Oh, I can't do that,' said Caro, still not quite in control of her woolly wits, 'I'm on duty in four days' time.'

'An impossibility—you will remain here until I consider you fit to return.'

'There must be a hospital...' Her head was beginning to throb.

'As a nurse you should be aware of the importance of resting both your brain and your leg. Kindly don't argue.'

She was feeling very peculiar again, rather as though she were lying in a mist, listening to people's voices but quite unable to focus them with her tired eyes. 'You can't possibly be married,' she mumbled, 'and you sound as though you hate me—you must be a mi—mi...'

'Misogynist.'

She had her eyes shut again so that she wouldn't cry. He was being very gentle, but her leg hurt dreadfully; she was going to tell him so, but she dropped off again.

Next time she woke up it was Clare by the bed and she grinned weakly and said: 'I feel better.'

'Good. Would you like a cup of tea?—it's real strong tea, like we make at Oliver's.'

It tasted lovely; drinking it, Caroline began to feel that everything was normal again. 'There's some very thin bread and butter,' suggested Clare. Caro devoured that too; she had barely swallowed the last morsel before she was asleep again.

It was late afternoon when she woke again. The lamp was already lighted and the Professor was sitting beside it, writing. 'Don't you have any patients?' asked Caroline.

He glanced up from his writing. 'Yes. Would you like a drink?'

She had seen the tray with a glass and jug on it, on the table by her bed. 'Yes, please—I can help myself; I'm feeling fine.'

He took no notice at all but got up, put an arm behind her shoulders, lifted her very gently and held the glass for her. When she had finished he laid her down again and said: 'You may have your friends in for ten minutes,' and stalked quietly out of the room.

They crept in very silently and stood in a row at the foot of the bed, looking at her. 'You're better,' said Miriam, 'the Professor says so.' And then: We're going back tomorrow morning.'

Caro tried to sit up and was instantly thrust gently back on to her pillow. 'You can't—you can't leave me here! He doesn't like me—why can't I go to hospital if I've got to stay? How are you going?'

'Noakes—that's the sort of butler who was at the gate when we fell over—he's to drive us to the Hoek. The bikes are to be sent back later.'

'He's quite nice,' said Clare, 'the Professor, I mean—he's a bit terse but he's been a perfect host. I don't think he likes us much but then of course, he's quite old, quite forty, I should think; he's always reading or writing and he's away a lot—Noakes says he's a very important man in his profession.' She giggled, 'You can hardly hear that he's Dutch, his English is so good, and isn't it funny that Noakes comes from Paddington? but he's been here for years and years—he's married to the cook. There's a housekeeper too, very tall and looks severe but she's not.'

'And three maids besides a gardener,' chimed in Miriam. 'He must be awfully rich.'

'You'll be OK,' Stacey assured her, 'you'll be back in no time. Do you want us to do anything for you?'

Caro's head was aching again. 'Would you ask Mrs Hodge to go on feeding Waterloo until I get back? There's some money in my purse—will you take some so that she can get his food?'

'OK—we'll go round to your place and make sure he's all right. Do you have to pay Mrs Hodge any rent?'

'No, I pay in advance each month. Is there enough money for me to get back by boat?'

Stacey counted. 'Yes—it's only a single fare and I expect Noakes will take you to the boat.' She came a bit nearer. 'Well, 'bye for now, Caro. We hate leaving you, but there's nothing we can do about it.'

Caro managed a smile. 'I'll be fine—I'll let you know when I'm coming.'

They all shook hands with her rather solemnly. 'We're going quite early and the Professor said we weren't to disturb you in the morning.'

Caroline lay quietly after they had gone, too tired to feel much. Indeed, when the Professor came in later and gave her a sedative she made no demur but drank it down meekly and closed her eyes at once. It must have been quite strong because she was asleep at once, although he stayed for some time, sitting in his chair watching her, for once neither reading nor writing.

She didn't wake until quite late in the morning, to find Noakes' wife—Marta—standing by the bed with a small tray. There was tea again and paper-thin bread and butter and scrambled egg which she fed Caro with just as though she were a baby. She spoke a little English too, and Caro made out that her friends had gone.

When Marta had gone away, she lay and thought about it; she felt much more clear-headed now, almost herself, but not quite, otherwise she would never have conceived the idea of getting up, getting dressed, and leaving the house. She couldn't stay where she wasn't welcome—it was like her uncle all over again. Perhaps, she thought miserably, there was something about her that made her unacceptable as a guest. She was on the plain side, that she already knew, and perhaps because of that she was self-effacing and inclined to be shy. She had quickly learned not to draw attention to herself, but on the other hand she had plenty of spirit and a natural friendliness which had made her a great number of friends. But the Professor, she felt, was not one of their number.

The more she thought of her scheme, the more she liked it; the fact that she had a considerable fever made it seem both feasible and sensible, although it was neither. She began, very cautiously, to sit up. Her head ached worse than ever, but she ignored that and concentrated on moving her injured leg. It hurt a good deal more than she had expected, but she persevered until she was sitting untidily on the edge of the bed, her sound foot on the ground, its stricken fellow on its edge. It had hurt before; now, when she started to dangle it over the side of the bed, the pain brought great waves of nausea sweeping over her.

'Oh, God!' said Caro despairingly, and meant it.

'Perhaps I will do?' The Professor had come softly into the room, taking great strides to reach her.

'I'm going to be sick,' moaned Caro, and was, making a mess of his beautifully polished shoes. If she hadn't felt so ill she would have died of shame, as it was she burst into tears, sobbing and sniffing and gulping.

The Professor said nothing at all but picked her up and laid her back in bed again, pulling the covers over her and arranging the cradle just so over her injured leg before getting a sponge and towel from the adjoining bathroom and wiping her face for her. She looked at him round the sponge and mumbled: 'Your shoes—your lovely shoes, I'm so s-sorry.' She gave a great gulp. 'I should have gone with the others.'

'Why were you getting out of bed?' He didn't sound angry, only interested.

'Well, I thought I could manage to dress and I've enough money, I think—I was going back to England.'

He went to the fireplace opposite the bed and pressed the brass wall bell beside it. When Noakes answered it he requested a clean pair of shoes and a tray of tea for two and waited patiently until these had been brought and Noakes, accompanied by a maid, had swiftly cleared up the mess. Only then did he say: 'And now suppose we have a little talk over our tea?'

He pulled a chair nearer the bed, handed her a cup of tea and poured one for himself. 'Let us understand each other, young lady.'

Caroline studied him over the rim of her cup. He talked like a professor, but he didn't look like one; he was enormous and she had always thought of professors as small bent gentlemen with bald heads and untidy moustaches, but Professor Thoe van Erckelens had plenty of hair, light brown, going grey, and cut short, and he had no need to hide his good looks behind a moustache. Caro thought wistfully that he was exactly the kind of man every girl hoped to meet one day and marry; which was a pity, because he obviously wasn't the marrying kind...

'If I might have your full attention?' enquired the Professor. 'You are sufficiently recovered to listen to me?'

Her head and her leg ached, but they were bearable. She nodded.

'If you could reconcile yourself to remaining here for another ten days, perhaps a fortnight, Miss Tripp? I can assure you that you are in no fit condition to do much at the moment. I shall remove the stitches from your leg in another four days and you may then walk a little with a stick, as from tomorrow, and provided your headache is lessening, you may sit up for a period of time. Feel free to ask for anything you want, my home is at your disposal. There is a library from which Noakes will fetch a selection of books, although I advise you not to read for a few days yet, and there is no reason why you should not sit in the garden, well wrapped up. You will drink no alcohol, nor will you smoke, and kindly refrain from watching television for a further day or so; it will merely aggravate your headache. I must ask you to excuse me from keeping you company at any time—I am a busy man and I have my work and my own interests. I shall of course treat you as I would any other patient of mine and when I consider you fit to travel, I will see that you get back safely to your home.'

Caro had listened to this precise speech with astonishment; she hadn't met anyone who talked like that before—it was like reading the instructions on the front of a medicine bottle. She loved the bit about no drinking or smoking; she did neither, but she wondered if she looked the kind of girl who did. But one thing was very clear. The Professor was offering her hospitality but she was to keep out of his way; he didn't want his ordered life disrupted—which was amusing really; now if it had been Clare or Stacey or Miriam, all pretty girls who had never lacked for men friends, that would have been a different matter, but Caroline's own appearance was hardly likely to cause even the smallest ripple on the calm surface of his life.

'I'll do exactly as you say,' she told him, 'and I'll keep out of your way—you won't know I'm here. And thank you for being so kind.' She added: 'I'm truly sorry about me being sick and your shoes...'

He stood up. 'Sickness is to be expected in cases of concussion,' he told her. 'I am surprised that you, a nurse, should not have thought of that. We must make allowances for your cerebral condition.'

She looked at him helplessly. Underneath all that pedantic talk there was a quite ordinary man; for some reason, the professor was concealing him. After he had gone she lay back on her pillows, suddenly sleepy, but before she closed her eyes she decided that she would discover what had happened to make him like that. She must make friends with Noakes...

She made splendid progress. The Professor dressed her leg the next morning and when Marta had draped her in a dressing gown several sizes too large for her, he returned to lift her into a chair by the open window, for the weather was glorious and the view from it delightful. The gardens and the house were large and full of autumn colours, and just to lie back with Marta tucking a rug over her and settling her elevenses beside her was bliss. She had been careful to say very little to the Professor while he attended to her leg; he had made one or two routine remarks about the weather and how she felt and she had answered him with polite brevity, but now he had gone and despite his silence, she felt lonely. She sipped the warm milk Marta had left for her and looked at the view. The road was just visible beyond the grounds and part of the drive which led to it from the house; presently she heard a car leaving the house and caught a glimpse of it as it flashed down the drive: an Aston Martin—a Lagonda. The Professor must have a friend who liked fast driving. Caro thought that it might be rather fun to know someone who drove an Aston Martin, and even more fun to actually ride in one.

She was to achieve both of these ambitions. The Professor came as usual the following morning after breakfast to dress her leg, but instead of going away immediately as he usually did he spoke to Juffrouw Kropp who had accompanied him and then addressed himself to Caro.

'I am taking you to the hospital in Leeuwarden this morning. You are to have your head X-rayed. I am certain that no harm has come from your concussion, but I wish my opinion to be confirmed.'

Caro eyed him from the vast folds of her dressing gown. 'Like this?' she asked.

He raised thick arched brows. 'Why not? Juffrouw Kropp will assist you.' He had gone before she could answer him.

Juffrouw Kropp's severe face broke into a smile as the door closed. She fetched brush and comb and make-up and produced a length of ribbon from a pocket. She brushed Caro's hair despite her protests, plaited it carefully and fastened it with the ribbon, fetched a hand mirror and held it while Caro did things to her face, then fastened the dressing gown and tied it securely round Caro's small waist. Like a well-schooled actor, the Professor knocked on the door, just as though he had been given his cue, plucked Caro from the bed and carried her downstairs where Noakes stood, holding the front door wide. The Professor marched through with a muttered word and Noakes slid round him to open the door of the Aston Martin, and with no discomfort at all Caro found herself reclining on the back seat with Noakes covering her with a light rug and the Professor, to her astonishment, getting behind the wheel.

'This is never your car?' she asked, too surprised to be polite.

He turned his head and gave her an unfriendly look. 'Is there any reason why it shouldn't be?' he wanted to know, coldly.

She said kindly: 'You don't need to get annoyed. It's only that you don't look the kind of man to drive a fast car.' She added vaguely: 'A professor...'

'And no longer young,' he snapped. 'I have no interest in your opinions, Miss Tripp. May I suggest that you close your eyes and compose yourself—the journey will take fifteen minutes.'

Caroline did as she was bid, reflecting that until that very moment she hadn't realised what compelling eyes he had; slate blue and very bright. When she judged it safe, she opened her eyes again; she wasn't going to miss a second of the ride; it would be something to tell her friends when she got back. She couldn't see much of the road because the Professor took up so much of the front seat, but the telegraph poles were going past at a terrific rate; he drove fast all right and very well, and he didn't slow at all until she saw buildings on either side of them and presently he was turning off the road and stopping smoothly.

He got out without speaking and a moment later the door was opened and she was lifted out and set in a wheelchair while the Professor spoke to a youngish man in a white coat. He turned on his heel without even glancing at her and walked away, into the hospital, leaving her with the man in the white coat and a porter.

How rude he is, thought Caro, and then: poor man, he must be very unhappy.

She was wheeled briskly down a number of corridors to the X-ray department. It was a modern hospital and she admired it as they went, and after a minute or so, when the white-coated man spoke rather diffidently to her in English, showered him with a host of questions. He hadn't answered half of them by the time they reached their destination and she interrupted him to ask: 'Who are you?'

He apologised. 'I'm sorry, I have not introduced myself. Jan van Spaark—I am attached to Professor Thoe van Erckelens' team. I am to look after you while you are here.'

'A doctor?'

He nodded. 'Yes, I think you would call me a medical registrar in your country.'

The X-ray only took a short while, and in no time at all she was being wheeled back to the entrance hall, but here, to her surprise, her new friend wished her goodbye and handed her over to a nurse, who offered a hand, saying: 'Mies Hoeversma—that is my name.'

Caro shook it. 'Caroline Tripp. What happens next?'

'You are to have coffee because Professor Thoe van Erckelens is not quite ready to leave.'

She was wheeled to a small room, rather gloomy and austerely furnished used, Mies told her, as a meeting place for visiting doctors, but the coffee was hot and delicious and Mies, although her English was sketchy, was a nice girl. Caro, who had been lonely even though she hadn't admitted it to herself, enjoyed herself. She could have spent the morning there, listening to Mies describing life in a Dutch hospital and giving her a lighthearted account of her own life in London, but the door opened, just as they had gone off into whoops of mirth over something or other, and the porter reappeared, spoke to Mies and wheeled Caro rapidly away, giving her barely a moment in which to say goodbye.

'Why the hurry?' asked Caro, hurriedly shaking hands again.

'The Professor—he must not be kept waiting.' Mies was quite serious; evidently he had the same effect on the hospital staff as he had on his staff at home. Instant, quiet obedience—and yet they liked him...

Caroline puzzled over that as she was whisked carefully to the car, to be lifted in by the Professor before he got behind the wheel and drove away. Jan van Spaark had been there, with two other younger men and a Sister, the Professor had lifted his hand in grave salute as he drove away.

He seemed intent on getting home as quickly as possible, driving very fast again, and it was a few minutes before Caroline ventured in a small polite voice: 'Was it all right—my head?'

'There is no injury to the skull,' she was assured with detached politeness. 'Tomorrow I shall remove the stitches from your leg and you may walk for brief periods—with a stick, of course. You will rest each afternoon and read for no more than an hour each day.'

'Very well, Professor, I'll do as you say.' She sounded so meek that he glanced at her through his driving mirror. When she smiled at him he looked away at once.

He carried her back to her room when they reached the house and set her down in the chair made ready for her by the window. 'After lunch I will carry you downstairs to one of the sitting rooms. Are you lonely?'

His question took her by surprise. She had her mouth open to say yes and remembered just in time that he wanted none of her company.

'Not in the least, thank you,' she told him. 'I live alone in London, you know—I have a flat, close to Oliver's.'

He nodded, wished her goodbye and went away—she heard the car roar away minutes later. Not a very successful morning, she considered, although he had wanted to know if she were lonely. And she had told a fib—not only was she lonely, but the flat she had mentioned so casually was in reality a bedsitter, a poky first floor room in a dingy street... She was reminded forcibly of it now and of dear old Waterloo, stoically waiting for her to come back. She longed for the sight of his round whiskered face and the comfort of his plump furry body curled on her knee. 'I'm a real old maid,' she said out loud, and then called, 'Come in,' in a bright, cheerful voice because there was someone at the door.

It was Noakes with more coffee. 'And the Professor says if yer've got an 'eadache, miss, yer ter take one of them pills in the red box.'

'I haven't got a headache, thank you, Noakes, not so's you'd notice. Has the Professor gone again?'

'Yes, miss—Groningen this time. In great demand, 'e is.'

'Yes. It's quiet here, isn't it? Doesn't he ever have guests or family?' Noakes hesitated and she said at once: 'I'm sorry, I had no right to ask you questions about the Professor. I wasn't being nosey, though.'

'I know that, miss, and I ain't one ter gossip, specially about the Professor—'e's a good man, make no mistake, but 'e ain't a 'appy one, neither.' Caro poured a cup of coffee and waited. 'It used ter be an 'ouse full when I first come 'ere. Eighteen years ago, it were—come over on 'oliday, I did, and took a fancy ter living 'ere after I met Marta. She was already working 'ere, kitchenmaid then, that was when the Professor's ma and pa were alive. Died in a car accident, they did, and he ups and marries a couple of years after that. Gay times they were, when the young Baroness was 'ere...'

'Baroness?'

Noakes scratched his head. 'Well, miss, the Professor's a baron as well as a professor, if yer take my meaning.'

'How long ago did he marry, Noakes?' Caroline was so afraid that he would stop telling her the rest, and she did want to know.

'It was in 1966, miss, two years after his folk died. Pretty lady she was, too, very gay, 'ated 'im being a doctor, always working, she used ter say, and when 'e was 'ome, looking after the estate. She liked a gay life, I can tell you! She left 'im, miss, two years after they were married—ran away with some man or other and they both got killed in a plane crash a few months later.'

Caro had let her coffee get cold. So that was why the Professor shunned her company—he must have loved his wife very dearly. She said quietly: 'Thank you for telling me, Noakes. I'm glad he's got you and Mrs Noakes and Juffrouw Kropp to look after him.'

'That we do, miss. Shall I warm up that coffee? It must be cold.'

'It's lovely, thank you. I think I'll have a nap before lunch.'

But she didn't go to sleep, she didn't even doze. She sat thinking of the Professor; he had asked her if she were lonely, but it was he who was the truly lonely one.

CHAPTER TWO

THE PROFESSOR TOOK the stitches out of Caro's leg the next morning and his manner towards her was such as to discourage her from showing any of the sympathy she felt for him. He had wished her a chilly good morning, assured her that she would feel no pain, and proceeded about his business without more ado. Then he had stood back and surveyed the limb, pronounced it healing nicely, applied a pad and bandage and suggested that she might like to go downstairs.

'Well, yes, I should, very much,' said Caro, and smiled at him, to receive an icy stare in return which sent the colour to her cheeks. But she wasn't easily put off. 'May I wear my clothes?' she asked him. 'This dressing gown's borrowed from someone and I expect they'd like it back. Besides, I'm sick of it.'

His eyebrows rose. 'It was lent in kindness,' he pointed out.

She stammered a little. 'I didn't mean that—you must think I'm ungrateful, but I'm not—what I meant was it's a bit big for me and I'd like...'

He had turned away. 'You have no need to explain yourself, Miss Tripp. I advise you not to do too much today. The wound on your leg was deep and is not yet soundly healed.' He had left her, feeling that she had made a mess of things again. And she had no sympathy for him at all, she assured herself; let him moulder into middle age with his books and his papers and his lectures!

With Marta's help she dressed in a sweater and pleated skirt and was just wondering if she was to walk downstairs on her own when Noakes arrived. He held a stout stick in one hand and offered her his arm.

'The Professor says you're to go very slowly and lean on

me,' he advised her, 'and take the stairs one at a time.' He smiled at her. 'Like an old lady,' he added.

It took quite a time, but she didn't mind because it gave her time to look around her as they passed from one stair to the next. The hall was even bigger than she had remembered and the room into which she was led quite took her breath away. It was lofty and square and furnished with large comfortable chairs and sofas, its walls lined with cabinets displaying silver and china and in between these, portraits in heavy frames. There was a fire in the enormous hearth and a chair drawn up to it with a small table beside it upon which was a pile of magazines and newspapers.

'The Professor told me ter get something for yer to read, miss,' said Noakes, 'and I done me best. After lunch, if yer feels like it, I'll show yer the library.'

'Oh, Noakes, you're all so kind, and I've given you all such a lot of extra work.'

He looked astonished. 'Lor luv yer, miss—we enjoy 'aving yer—it's quiet, like yer said.'

'Yes. Noakes, I've heard a dog barking...'

'That'll be Rex, miss. 'E's a quiet beast mostly, but 'e barks when the Professor comes in. Marta's got a little cat too.'

'Oh, has she? So have I—his name's Waterloo, and my landlady's looking after him while I'm away. It'll be nice to see him again.'

'Yes, miss. Juffrouw Kropp'll bring coffee for you.'

It was indeed quiet, sitting there by herself. Caroline leafed through the newspapers and tried to get interested in the news and then turned to the magazines. It was almost lunchtime when she heard the Professor's voice in the hall and she sat up, put a hand to her hair and then put on a cheerful face, just as though she were having the time of her life. But he didn't come into the room. She heard his voice receding and a door shutting and presently Juffrouw Kropp brought in her lunch tray, set it on the table beside her and smilingly went away again. Caro had almost finished the delicious little meal when she heard the Professor's voice again, speaking to Noakes as he crossed the hall and left the house.

She was taken to the library by a careful Noakes after lunch and settled into a chair by one of the circular tables in that vast apartment, but no sooner had he gone than she picked up her stick, eased herself out of her chair and began a tour of the bookshelves which lined the entire room. The books were in several languages and most of them learned ones, but there were a number of novels in English and a great many medical books in that language. But she rejected them all for a Dutch- English dictionary; it had occurred to her that since she was to spend several more days as the Professor's guest, she might employ her time in learning a word or two of his language. She was deep in this task, muttering away to herself when Noakes brought a tea tray, arranged it by her, and asked her if she was quite comfortable.

'Yes, Noakes, thank you—I'm teaching myself some Dutch words. But I don't think I'm pronouncing them properly.'

'I daresay not, miss. Tell yer what, when Juffrouw Kropp comes later, get 'er ter 'elp yer. She's a dab hand at it. Nasty awkward language it is—took me years ter learn.'

'But you always speak English with the Professor?'

'That's right, miss—comes as easy to 'im as his own language!'

Caroline ate her tea, feeling much happier now that she had something to do, and when Juffrouw Kropp came to light the lamps presently, she asked that lady to sit down for a minute and help her.

Caro had made a list of words, and now she tried them out on the housekeeper, mispronouncing them dreadfully, and then, because she was really interested, correcting them under her companion's guidance. It whiled away the early evening until the housekeeper had to go, leaving her with the assurance that Noakes would be along presently to help her back to her room.

But it wasn't Noakes who came in, it was the Professor,

walking so quietly that she didn't look up from her work, only said: 'Noakes, Juffrouw Kropp has been such a help, only there's a word here and I can't remember...'

She looked round and stopped, because the Professor was standing quite close by, looking at her. She answered his quiet good evening cheerfully and added: 'So sorry, I expected Noakes, he's coming to help me up to my room. I'd have gone sooner if I'd known you were home.'

She fished the stick up from the floor beside her and stood up, gathering the dictionary and her pen and paper into an awkward bundle under one arm, only to have them removed immediately by the Professor.

He said stiffly: 'Will you dine with me this evening? Since you are already downstairs...'

Caroline was so surprised that she didn't answer at once, and when she did her soft voice was so hesitant that it sounded like a stammer.

'Thank you for asking me, but I won't, thank you.' She put out a hand for the dictionary and he transferred it to the other hand, out of her reach.

'Why not?' He looked annoyed and his voice was cold.

'You don't really want me,' she said frankly. 'You said that I wasn't to—to interfere with your life in any way and I said I wouldn't.' She added kindly: 'I'm very happy, thank you, I've never been so spoiled in all my life.' She held out her hand; this time he gave her the dictionary.

'Just as you wish,' he said with a politeness she found more daunting than coldness. He took the stick from her, then took her arm and helped her out of the room and across the hall. At the bottom of the staircase he picked her up and carried her to the wide gallery above and across it to her room. At the door, he set her down and opened it for her. His 'Goodnight, Miss Tripp' was quite without expression. Caroline had no way of knowing if he was relieved that she had refused his invitation or if he was angry about it. She gave him a quiet goodnight and went through the door, to undress slowly and get ready for bed; she would have a bath and have her supper in her dressing gown by the fire.

Marta came presently to help her into the bath, turn down the bed and fuss nicely round the room, and after her came one of the maids with her supper; soup and a cheese souffl with a salad on the side and a Bavarian creme to follow. Caroline didn't think the Professor would be eating that, nor would he be drinking the home-made lemonade she was offered.

The house was very quiet when she woke the next morning and when Marta brought her her breakfast tray, she told her that Noakes had gone with the Professor to the airfield just south of the city and would bring the car back later.

'Has the Professor gone away?' asked Caroline, feeling unaccountably upset.

'To England and then to Paris—he has, how do you say? the lecture.'

'How long for?' asked Caro.

Marta shrugged her shoulders. 'I do not know—five, six days, perhaps longer.'

Which meant that when he came home again she would go almost at once—perhaps he wanted that. She ate her breakfast listlessly and then got herself up and dressed. Her leg was better, it hardly ached at all and neither did her head. She trundled downstairs slowly and went into the library again where she spent a busy morning conning more Dutch words. There didn't seem much point in it, but it was something to do.

After lunch she went into the garden. It was a chilly day with the first bite of autumn in the air and Juffrouw Kropp had fastened her into a thick woollen cape which dropped around her ankles and felt rather heavy. But she was glad of it presently when she had walked a little way through the formal gardens at the side of the house and found a seat under an arch of beech. It afforded a good view of her surroundings and she looked slowly around her. The gardens stretched away on either side of her and she supposed the meadows beyond belonged to the house too, for there was a high hedge beyond them. The house stood, of red brick, mellowed with age, its many windows gleaming in the thin sunshine; it was large with an important entrance at the top of a double flight of steps, but it was very pleasant too. She could imagine it echoing to the shouts of small children and in the winter evenings its windows would glow with light and guests would stream in to spend the evening…not, of course, in reality, she thought sadly; the Professor had turned himself into a kind of hermit, excluding everyone and everything from his life except work and books. 'I must try and make him smile,' she said out loud, and fell to wondering how she might do that.

It was the following morning, while she was talking to Noakes as he arranged the coffee tray beside her in the library, that they fell to discussing Christmas.

'Doesn't the Professor have family or friends to stay?' asked Caro.

'No, miss. Leastways, 'e 'olds an evening party—very grand affair it is too—but 'e ain't got no family, not in this country. Very quiet time it is.'

'No carols?'

Noakes shook his head. 'More's the pity—I like a nice carol, meself.'

Caro poured out her coffee. 'Noakes, why shouldn't you have them this year? There are—how many? six of you altogether, aren't there? Couldn't you teach everyone the words? I mean, they don't have to know what they mean—aren't there any Dutch carols?'

'Plenty, miss, only it ain't easy with no one ter play the piano. We'd sound a bit silly like.'

'I can play. Noakes, would it be a nice idea to learn one or two carols and sing them for the Professor at Christmas—I mean, take him by surprise?'

Noakes looked dubious. Caroline put her cup down. 'Look, Noakes, everyone loves Christmas—if you could just take him by surprise, it might make it seem more fun. Then perhaps he'd have friends to stay—or something.'

It suddenly seemed very important to her that the Professor should enjoy his Christmas, and Noakes, looking at her earnest face, found himself agreeing. 'We could 'ave a bash, miss. There's a piano in the drawing room and there's one in the servants' sitting room.'

'Would you mind if I played it? I wouldn't want to intrude...'

'Lor' luv yer, miss, we'd be honoured.'

She went with him later that day, through the baize door at the back of the hall, down a flagstoned passage and through another door into a vast kitchen, lined with old-fashioned dressers and deep cupboards. Marta was at the kitchen table and Juffrouw Kropp was sitting in a chair by the Aga, and they looked up and smiled as she went in. Noakes guided her to a door at the end and opened it on to a very comfortably furnished room with a large table at one end, easy chairs, a TV in a corner and a piano against one wall. There was a stove half way along the further wall and warm curtains at the windows. The Professor certainly saw to it that those who worked for him were comfortable. Caroline went over to the piano and opened it, sat down and began to play. She was by no means an accomplished pianist, but she played with feeling and real pleasure. She forgot Noakes for the moment, tinkling her way through a medley of Schubert, Mozart and Brahms until she was startled to hear him clapping and turned to see them all standing by the door watching her.

'Cor, yer play a treat, miss,' said Noakes. 'I suppose yer don't 'appen to know *Annie Get Yer Gun*?'

She knew some of it; before she had got to the end they were clapping their hands in time to the music and Noakes was singing. When she came to a stop finally, he said: 'Never mind the carols, miss, if yer'd just play now and then—something we could all sing?'

He sounded wistful, and looking round at their faces she

saw how eager they were to go on with the impromptu sing-
song. 'Of course I'll play,' she said at once. 'You can tell me
what you want and I'll do my best.' She smiled round at them
all; Noakes and Marta and Juffrouw Kropp, the three young
maids and someone she hadn't seen before, a quite old man—
the gardener, she supposed. 'Shall I play something else?' she
asked.

She sat there for an hour and when she went she had promised that she would go back the following evening. And on
the way upstairs she asked Noakes if she might look at the
piano in the drawing-room.

She stood in the doorway, staring around her. The piano
occupied a low platform built under the window at one end,
it was a grand and she longed to play upon it; she longed to
explore the room too, its panelled walls hung with portraits,
its windows draped with heavy brocade curtains. The hearth
had a vast hood above it with what she supposed was a coat
of arms carved upon it. All very grand, but it would be like
trespassing to go into the room without the Professor inviting
her to do so, and she didn't think he would be likely to do
that. She thanked a rather mystified Noakes and went on up
to her room.

Lying in bed later, she thought how nice it would be to
explore the house. She had had glimpses of it, but there were
any number of closed doors she could never hope to have
opened for her. Still, she reminded herself bracingly, she was
being given the opportunity of staying in a lovely old house
and being waited on hand and foot. Much later she heard
Noakes locking up and Rex barking. She hadn't met him yet;
Noakes had told her that he was to be kept out of her way
until she was quite secure on her feet. 'Mild as milk,' he had
said, 'but a bit on the big side.' Caroline had forgotten to ask
what kind of dog he was. Tomorrow she would contrive to
meet him; her leg was rapidly improving, indeed it hardly hurt
at all, only when she was tired.

Her thoughts wandered on the verge of sleep. Would the

Professor expect to be reimbursed for his trouble and his professional services, she wondered, and if so how would one set about it? Perhaps the hospital would settle with him if and when he sent a bill. He wouldn't be bothered to do that himself, she decided hazily; she had seen a serious middle-aged woman only that morning as she crossed the hall on her way to the library and Noakes had told her that it was the secretary, Mevrouw Slikker, who came daily to attend to the Professor's correspondence. Undoubtedly she would be businesslike about it. Caro nodded her sleepy head at this satisfactory solution and went to sleep.

She walked a little further the next day, following the paths around the gardens and sitting down now and again to admire her surroundings. She wondered if the Professor ever had the time to admire his own grounds and thought probably not, he was certainly never long enough in his own house to enjoy its comforts and magnificence. She wandered round to the back of the house and found a pleasing group of old buildings grouped round a courtyard, barns and stables and a garage and a shed which smelled deliciously of apples and corn. It was coming out of this interesting place that she came face to face with an Old English sheepdog. He stood almost to her waist and peered at her with a heavily eyebrowed whiskered face. 'Rex!' she cried. 'Oh, aren't you a darling!' She extended a closed fist and he sniffed at it and then put an enormous paw on each of her shoulders and reared up to peer down at her. He must have liked what he saw, for he licked her face gently, got down on to his four feet again and offered a head for scratching. They finished their walk together and wandered in through a little side door to find Noakes looking anxious.

'There you are, miss—I 'opes yer 'aven't been too far.' His elderly eyes fell upon Rex. ''E didn't frighten yer? 'E's always in the kitchen with Marta in the mornings. I'll take 'im back...'

'Oh, Noakes, please could he stay with me? He's company and ever so gentle. Is he allowed in the house?'

'Lor' yes, miss. Follows the Professor round like a shadow, 'e does. Well, I don't see no 'arm.' He beamed at her. 'There's a nice lunch for yer in the library and Juffrouw Kropp says if yer wants 'er this afternoon she's at yer disposal.'

So the day passed pleasantly enough, and the following two days were just as pleasant. Caro did a little more each day now; the Professor would be back in two days' time, Noakes had told her, and she had to be ready to leave then. She had no intention of trespassing on his kindness for an hour longer than she needed to. Of course she would have to get tickets for the journey home, but that shouldn't take long, and Noakes would help her and perhaps the Professor would allow him to drive her to the station in Leeuwarden; she had already discovered that the train went all the way to the Hoek—all she would need to do was to get from it to the boat. She had mentioned it carefully to Noakes when he had been clearing away her supper dishes, but he had shaken his head and said dubiously that it would be better to consult the Professor. ''E may not want yer to go straight away, miss,' he suggested.

'Well, I should think he would,' she told him matter-of-factly, 'for I'm quite well now and after all, he didn't invite me as a guest. He's been more than kind to let me get well here and I mustn't stay longer than absolutely necessary.'

Noakes had shaken his head and muttered to himself and then begged her to go down to the sitting-room and play for them all again—something she had done with great pleasure, for it passed the evenings very nicely. When she was on her own she found that she had an increasing tendency to think about the Professor—a pointless pastime, she told herself, and went on doing it nonetheless.

It rained the next day, so that she spent a great deal of it in the library, with Rex beside her, poring over her dictionary. She was making progress, or so she thought, with an ever lengthening list of words which she tried out on members of the staff. All rather a waste of time, she knew that, but it passed the days and in some obscure way made the Professor a little less of a stranger. She went earlier than usual to play the piano that day, perhaps because the afternoon was unnaturally dark and perhaps because she was lonely despite Rex's company. And Noakes and his staff seemed pleased to see her, requesting this, that and the other tune, beating time and tra-la-ing away to each other. Presently, with everyone satisfied, Caroline began to play to please herself; half forgotten melodies she had enjoyed before her aunt had married again and then on to Sibelius and Grieg, not noticing how quiet everyone had become; she was half way through a wistful little French tune when she stopped and turned round. 'Sorry, I got carried away,' she began, and saw the Professor standing in the doorway, his hands in his pockets, leaning against the door frame.

He didn't smile, indeed, he was looking coldly furious, although his icily polite: 'Pray don't stop on my account, Miss Tripp,' was uttered in a quiet voice.

Caroline stood up rather too hard on the bad leg so that she winced. 'You're angry,' she said quickly, 'and I'm sorry—I have no right to be here, but you're not to blame Noakes or anyone else—I invited myself.'

She wanted to say a great deal more, but the look of annoyance on his face stopped her. She wished everyone goodnight in her newly acquired Dutch and went past him through the door and along the passage. He caught up with her quite easily before she could reach the staircase, and she sighed soundlessly. He was going to lecture her and she might as well have it now as later; perhaps she might even get him to see that no harm had been done, indeed he might even be glad that his staff had enjoyed a pleasant hour.

She turned to face him. 'It's a pity you frown so,' she said kindly.

He looked down his splendid nose at her. 'I have very good

reason to frown, Miss Tripp, and well you know it. I return home unexpectedly and what do I find? My butler, my housekeeper, my cook, the maidservants and the gardener being entertained by you in the servants' sitting-room. Probably if I had come home even earlier I should have found you all playing gin rummy in the cellars.'

She made haste to reassure him. 'Not gin rummy—it was Canasta, and we played round the kitchen table—just for half an hour,' she added helpfully. 'You see, I'm learning Dutch.'

His fine mouth curved into a sneer. 'Indeed? I cannot think why.'

Caroline said in her quiet hesitant voice: 'Well, it's something to do, you know. I'm quite well, you see.'

His voice was silky and his voice cold. 'Miss Tripp, you have disrupted my household—when one considers that I have done my best to help you and I find your behaviour intolerable.'

She stared back at him, her lip caught between her teeth, because it was beginning to tremble. After a long moment she said: 'I'm sorry, Professor.'

He turned on his heel. 'I'm glad to hear it—I hope you will mend your ways.'

He went into his study without another word and she went to her room, where she sat on her bed to review the situation. The Professor was going out to dinner that evening, she had heard Noakes say so—to one of his grand friends, she supposed, where the girls knew better than to play the piano in the servants' room and said things to make him smile instead of frown. Oh well...she got up and went across to the tallboy where her few possessions were housed and laid them on the bed, fetched her duffle bag from the cupboard and began to pack. She did it neatly and unhurriedly. There was plenty of time; she would eat her supper alone presently, as she always did, and when everyone had gone to the kitchen for their own meal, she would slip away. She would have to leave a letter. She frowned a long while over its composition, but at length it was done, neatly written and sealed into an envelope. She would have to leave it somewhere where Noakes wouldn't find it at once. The Professor's study would be the best place, he always went straight there when he came home, shutting himself away in his own learned lonely world—for he was lonely, Caroline was sure of that.

She finished her packing and went down to her supper which this evening had been set in the dining room, a richly sombre place. She felt quite lost sitting at the great oval table surrounded by all the massive furniture, but she made a good meal, partly to please Noakes and partly because she wasn't sure when she would have the next one. And Noakes was uneasy, although the Professor, he assured her, hadn't been in the least angry—indeed, he had hardly mentioned the matter. Noakes hoped—they all hoped—that tomorrow she would play for them again, but first he would ascertain if the Professor objected to her visiting the servants' sitting-room.

Caroline made some cheerful reply, finished her meal, mentioned that she would go to bed early and went upstairs. When she crept down half an hour later there was no sound. Everyone was in the kitchens by now and she wouldn't be missed, probably not until the morning, or at least until the Professor came home, and that would be late. She had put on her anorak, counted her money carefully and carried her bag downstairs before going to the study and putting the letter on the Professor's desk. She paused in the doorway for a last look; his desk was an orderly clutter of papers and books and his chair was pushed to one side as though he had got up in a hurry. She sighed deeply, closed the door gently, picked up the duffle bag and went to the door. Her leg was aching a little and she had bandaged it firmly because as far as she knew she would have to walk quite a distance before she could get a bus—the nearest village wasn't too far away, she had found that out from Juffrouw Kropp. If there wasn't a bus she would have to thumb a lift.

She put out a reluctant hand and opened the door. It was

heavy, but it swung back on well-oiled hinges, revealing the Professor, key in hand, about to open it from outside. Caro, taken completely by surprise, stood with her mouth open, gaping at him. He, on the other hand, evinced no surprise, nor did he speak, merely took her duffle bag from her, put a large hand on her chest and pushed her very gently back into the house, and then just as gently shut the door behind him. Only then did he ask: 'And where were you going, Caroline?'

'Home—well, the hospital, actually.' He had never called her Caroline before—no one called her that, but it sounded rather nice.

'Why?' He stood blocking her path, the duffle bag on the floor beside him.

It seemed silly to have to explain something to him which he already knew all about. 'I've upset your household: I can quite see that I've been a perfect nuisance to you. I'm very grateful for all you've done for me—and your kindness—but I'm quite able to go back now and... Well, thank you again.'

His harsh laugh made her jump. Quite forgetting to be meek, she said severely: 'And there's no need to laugh when someone thanks you!'

'It strikes me as ironic that you should express gratitude for something you haven't had. I cannot remember being kind to you—I merely did what any other person would have done in similar circumstances, and with the minimum of trouble to myself. If I had been a poor man with a wife and children to care for and had offered you help and shelter at the cost of my and their comfort, that would have been quite a different kettle of fish. As it is, I must confess that I have frequently forgotten that you were in the house.'

Caro didn't speak. A kind of despair had rendered her dumb; her head was full of a mixed bag of thoughts, most of them miserable.

He put out a hand and touched her cheek awkwardly. 'Have you been lonely?'

Living in a bedsitter had taught her not to be lonely. She shook her head, still feeling the touch of his finger.

'And you will be glad to get back—to your flat and your friends. I doubt if you will be allowed to work for a little while.'

She had found her voice at last. It came out in a defiant mutter: 'I shall be awfully glad to get back.'

The gentleness had gone out of his voice; it sounded cold and distant again, just as though he didn't care what she did. 'Yes—I see. But be good enough to wait until the morning. I will arrange a passage for you on the night ferry tomorrow and Noakes shall drive you to the Hoek and see you on board.'

Caroline said stiffly: 'Thank you.'

'You have sufficient money?'

She nodded dumbly.

'Then go to bed.' His eye had caught her bandaged leg. 'Your leg is worse?'

'No. I—I put a crepe bandage on it because I thought I might have to walk for a bit.'

He stared at her without expression, then: 'Come to the study and I will take a look and if necessary rebandage it.'

He prodded and poked with gentle fingers, dressed it lightly and said: 'That should see you safely to Oliver's—get it looked at as soon as you can. It will do better without a dressing.' He held the study door open and offered a hand. 'Goodbye, Caroline.'

His hand was cool and firm and she didn't want to let it go.

'Goodbye, Professor. I shall always be grateful to you—and I'm sorry that I—I disturbed your peace and quiet.'

Just for a moment she thought he was going to say something, but he didn't.

CHAPTER THREE

CARO ARRIVED BACK at Meadow Road during the morning and the moment she opened the door of number twenty-six, Mrs Hodge bounced out of her basement flat, avid for a good gossip.

'Your friends came,' she said without preamble, 'said you had a bad cut leg and concussion; nasty thing concussion; you could 'ave died.' She eyed Caro's leg with relish and then looked disappointed, and Caro said almost apologetically:

'I don't need a bandage any more. Thank you for looking after Waterloo, Mrs Hodge.'

'No trouble.' Mrs Hodge, a woman who throve on other people's troubles, felt her sympathy had been wasted. 'Your rent's due on Monday.'

Caro edged past her with the duffle bag. 'Yes, I know, Mrs Hodge. I'll just see to Waterloo and unpack and then go back to the hospital and see when I'm to go back.'

She went up the stairs and unlocked the door at the back of the landing. Not one of Mrs Hodge's best rooms, but it was quieter because it overlooked back yards and there was a tiny balcony which was nice for Waterloo.

He came to meet her now and she picked him up and laid him on her shoulder while he purred in her ear, delighted to have her back. Caroline sat down on the divan which did duty as a bed at night and looked around her.

The room was small and rather dark and seemed even more so after the Professor's spacious home; she had done the best she could with pretty curtains and cushions and a patchwork cover for the divan, but nothing could quite disguise the cheap furniture or the sink in one corner with the tiny gas cooker beside it. Caro, not given to being sorry for herself, felt a lump in her throat; it was all such a cruel contrast... She missed them all, the Professor, even though he didn't like her, Noakes and Marta, Juffrouw Kropp... She had been utterly spoilt, waited on hand and foot, and she, who had never been spoilt, had loved it. Right up until the moment she had gone on board, too, with Noakes seeing to her bag and getting her magazines to read and having a word with someone or other so that she had a super cabin to herself and a delicious meal before she had gone to bed. She had tried to pay him, but he had said very firmly that the Professor would deal with that later. Caroline had hoped that although he had said goodbye to her, she would have seen the Professor again before she left, but he had left the house after breakfast and wasn't back when she went away, with the entire staff gathered at the door to see her off.

She roused herself, gave Waterloo a saucer of milk and put on the kettle; a cup of tea would cheer her up and when she had drunk it she would unpack, dust and tidy her room and go round to Oliver's, and on the way back she would buy a few flowers to brighten up the place.

In the office at Oliver's, standing in front of Miss Veron's desk, she was astonished to hear from that lady that the Professor had written a letter about her, suggesting in the politest manner possible that she should have a few days' sick leave before she resumed work on the wards.

'A good idea, Staff Nurse,' said Miss Veron kindly. 'I expect you would like to go home or visit friends—suppose you report for duty in five days' time? You'll go back to Women's Surgical, of course. I'm sure Sister will be glad to see you.'

Caro thanked her and walked slowly back through the busy streets to Meadow Road, stopping on the way to do some shopping and indulge in the extravagance of a bunch of flowers. She would have been glad to have gone straight back to work, for she had no family and although she had a number of friends, to invite herself to go and stay with them was something she had never even dreamed of. So she spent the next four days giving her room an extra clean, reading the books she fetched from the library and talking to Waterloo. She hadn't let anyone at the hospital know that she was back; they would have been round like a flash with offers to go to the cinema, invitations to go out to a meal—morning coffee. But most of them had boy-friends or family and she shrank from being pitied; only a few of her closest friends knew that she had no family and that she hated to talk about it. Actually she need not have worried about being pitied, for she turned a bright face to the world; those who didn't know her well considered her a self-sufficient girl bent on a career, and her close friends took care never to mention it.

She went back on duty on the fifth morning, but she didn't see her friends until the coffee break when they all met in the canteen. The precious fifteen minutes was spent in answering questions; Clare, Stacey and Miriam were all there, wanting to know how she had got on, whether her leg was quite better, whether she had enjoyed herself, whether the Professor had entertained her...

'Well, not to say entertain,' observed Caro. 'He was very kind to me and saw to my leg and took me to be X-rayed at the hospital in Leeuwarden. I—I kept out of his way as much as I could—I mean, he is an important man, Noakes says, and had very little leisure.'

'I could go for him,' said Stacey. 'A bit old, perhaps, but very elegant and a man of the world, if you know what I mean, if only he'd come out from his books and lectures. He must have been crossed in love!'

Caro didn't say anything. She wasn't going to tell them about his wife; it was all a long time ago and besides, it had been a confidence on Noakes's part. She shuddered, imagining the Professor's cold rage if he ever discovered that she knew about his past unhappiness, and Miriam, noticing it, asked: 'What's worrying you, Caro? Is the ward busy?'

Caro was glad to change the subject and talked about something which lasted them until it was time to return to their wards.

Women's Surgical was busy all right; what with Sir Eustace Jenkins' round, a twice-weekly event which was stage-managed as carefully as any royal procession; yesterday's operations cases still attached to drips and tubes and underwater pumps and needing constant care and attention, and over and above these, the normal ward routine of dressings and escorting to X-Ray, Physiotherapy and the usual thundering round looking for notes and Path. Lab. forms which somehow always got mislaid on round days. Caro, hovering at Sister's elbow, ready to interpret that lady's raised eyebrow, shake of the head, or lifted finger and smooth her path to the best of her ability, was quite glad when it was dinner time. She left Sister to serve the puddings and went down to the first meal, queuing for her portion of steamed cod, mashed potato, and butter beans, and devouring it with the rest of her friends at speed so that there would be time to go over to the home and make a pot of tea.

She had more tea presently in Sister's office, having been bidden there to be told that Sister would be going on holiday in a week's time and Caro would be taking over the ward. 'Just for two weeks,' Sister Pringle smiled a little. 'Good practice for you, Caro—you're in the running for my job. I'm leaving to get married in a few months' time and they're keen to get someone who's likely to stay for a few years. After all, I've been here for eight years—they wanted me to stay on, but I've had enough of being a career girl. I'll make way for you.'

Caro, not sure if this was a compliment or an admission that she was unlikely to get married, thanked her superior nicely and hoped that she would be adequate while left in charge.

'Well, I can't see why not—Sir Eustace likes you and you have a nice way with the student nurses. There are some heavy cases coming in, though, and it'll be take-in week...'

Caro bowed her head obediently over the notes Sister had before her. She wouldn't mind being busy, if she kept her thoughts occupied sufficiently she didn't have time to think about the Professor—a bad habit she had got into, and one which she must conquer even if only for her own peace of mind.

But she continued to think about him a great deal, picturing him alone in that great house, leading a hermit's life. It was a pity, she told Waterloo that evening as she cooked their supper, that he couldn't find some beautiful girl, exactly suited to him, and fall in love with her and get married. No sooner had she thought that than she left the sausages in the pan to fry themselves to a crisp because following hard on its heels was the second thought—that there was nothing in the world she would like more than to be that girl. Only she wasn't beautiful and she certainly wasn't suited to him; she had annoyed him excessively and he must have been delighted to see the back of her.

She sat down on the divan with Waterloo tucked under one arm. On the other hand, if she were given the chance, she would make him happy because that, she knew all at once, was what she wanted to do more than anything else in the world. She gave a watery chuckle. A more ill-suited pair than herself and the Professor would be hard to find, and why, oh, why had she fallen in love with him? Why couldn't it have been someone she might have stood a faint chance of attracting: someone insignificant and uninteresting and used to living on not much money, just sufficiently ambitious to wish to buy his own semi-detached in a suburb and keep his job, recognising in her a kindred spirit.

Only she wasn't a kindred spirit. She hated her narrow life, she wanted to be free; she wasn't sure what she wanted to do, but certainly it wasn't to be tied to a man who didn't look higher than a safe job.

She went on sitting there, oblivious of the sausages and Waterloo's voice reminding her about his supper, lost in a happy daydream where she was beautiful, well dressed and the apple of the Professor's eye. A changed Professor, of course, enjoying the pleasure of life as well as his work, discussing his day with her, planning it so that he could see as much of her as possible—wanting to be with her every minute of his leisure. She would play to him on that beautiful piano in his grand drawing room, in a pink organza dress, and when he came into his house each evening she would meet him in the hall with their beautiful children around her. It was all absurd and impossible and very real in her mind's eye: if it hadn't been for the smell of burning sausages it might have gone on for hours. As it was, she came back to reality, removed the charred bits from the pan, opened a can of beans, fed Waterloo and made tea before going round to the local library to change her books. She came back with Fodor's Guide to the Netherlands and then spent the evening reading about Friesland, with the Professor's handsome severe features superimposed on every page.

Sister departed a week later, thankfully handing over the ward keys to Caroline with the heartfelt wish that she would be able to manage. 'Not that you're not capable,' said Sister, 'but it's take-in tomorrow.' She added happily: 'We shall be on Majorca—and in swimsuits—can you imagine it? In November, too.'

But there was no time to be envious of Sister Pringle. Take-in weeks were always busy, and this particular one was worse than usual. Several young women were admitted with black eyes, broken noses, cracked bones and severe contusions after taking part in a demonstration march about something or other and falling foul of a rival faction on the way. These had been followed by two victims of a gas explosion in one of the small terraced houses close to the hospital, and no sooner were they settled in their beds than an old lady who had fallen over in the street and cut her head was admitted for observation. Caro found her hands full and they remained like that for most of the week. She sighed with relief when she went off duty on the seventh day. After midnight they would have comparative peace on the ward; she would catch up with the paper work, see to the off- duty and have time to chat to each of the patients as she took round the post—and the nurses should be able to catch up on their off-duty. She rose from her bed at the beginning of the second week of Sister's absence in the pleasant expectation of an uneventful week.

And so it was for the first few hours. The nurses, happy in the knowledge that there would be no urgent call to ready a bed for yet another emergency, began on the morning's routine with a good will and Caro, having fulfilled her ambition to have a nice long chat with each patient in turn, organised the day's tasks, made a sortie to the X-ray department with the firm determination to discover the whereabouts of a number of missing films, and answered the telephone at least a dozen times, before she settled herself in the office to puzzle out the off-duty for the following two weeks. She was half way through this tedious task when there was a knock on the door and before she could say anything, it was opened and Professor Thoe van Erckelens stalked in.

Caroline didn't speak, she was too surprised—and besides, after the first second or two, her heart raced so violently that she had no breath. She just sat where she was and stared at him with huge hazel eyes.

'Ha,' observed the Professor, 'you are surprised to see me.'

He looked ill-tempered, tired too. It was an awful waste of one's life to love a man who didn't care a row of pins for one. She took a steadying breath and said in her quiet voice: 'Yes, Professor, I am. I expect you have a consultation here? Shall I…?'

He came right into the office and shut the door. 'No, I came to see you.'

She opened her eyes and her mouth too. 'Whatever for?' She went on earnestly: 'I can't really spare the time unless you wanted to see a patient—there's Mrs Possett's dressing and two patients to go for X-ray.'

He dismissed Mrs Possett with a wave of his hand. 'What I have to say will take five minutes—less.'

Caroline folded her small, nicely cared for hands in her lap and gave him her full attention. He didn't move from the door. 'Will you marry me, Caroline?'

She stayed very still. After a moment she asked: 'Me? Is this a joke or something, Professor?'

'No, and if you will be good enough to give me your full attention and not interrupt I will explain.'

She glanced around her just to make sure that she wasn't dreaming. The office was much as usual, its desk an orderly muddle of forms and charts and papers, chilly, foggy air coming in through the open window, the radiator as usual gurgling gently into tepid warmth. The only difference was the Professor, taking up most of the available space and apparently suffering from a brain storm. She said in a tranquil voice which quite masked her bewilderment: 'I'm listening,' and made herself look at him. She was rewarded by a forbidding stare.

'I'm forty,' he told her almost angrily. 'I have been married before—thirteen years ago, to be precise. My wife left me for another man within two years of our marriage and she—both of them—were killed in an accident a year later. I have had no wish to marry again.' He shrugged huge shoulders, 'Why should I? I have my work, enough money, a well run home and there are always girls—pretty girls if I should wish for female company.'

He paused to study her and she flinched because no doubt he was comparing her homely face with the young ladies in question. 'However, after you had left my house I missed you—my household miss you. They have worn gloomy faces ever since you left—quite ridiculous, of course—even Rex and the cats…' He paused again, searching her quiet face as though he were trying to discover what there was about her that could disrupt his organised life. Presently he went on. 'You are an extraordinary girl,' he declared irritably, 'you have no looks, no witty conversation, quite deplorable clothes—and yet I find that I am able to talk to you—indeed,

I find myself wishing to discuss the various happenings of my day with you. I am not in love with you and I have no wish to be; I need a calm quiet companion, someone sensible who isn't for ever wanting to be taken out to dinner or the theatre, nor demand to know where I am going each time I leave the house. I need... I need...'

'A sheet anchor,' supplied Caro in a sensible voice. 'No demands, no curiosity, just a—someone to talk to when you feel inclined.'

He looked surprised. 'You understand then; I have no need to explain myself further. And above all, no romantic nonsense!' He gave her a bleak look which wrung her soft heart. 'You will have a pleasant life; the servants are already devoted to you and you will have my friends and sufficient money. And in return I ask for companionship when I need it, someone to sit at my table and play hostess to my guests and run my home as I like it. Well?'

Caro studied his face. He meant every preposterous word of it and he expected her to say yes then and there. I must change him just a little, she thought lovingly, he must be got out of his lonely arrogant world and learn to enjoy himself again—he must have been happy once. Aloud she said in a tranquil voice: 'I must have time to think about it.'

'Time? Why should you need time? You have no family.' He looked deliberately round the little room. 'And nothing but a hard-working future.'

Here was another one who took it for granted that no one wanted to marry her. 'You make it sound like a bribe,' she told him.

His mouth was a straight bad-tempered line. 'Nothing of the sort. I have offered you marriage. I hope that I am not such a hypocrite that I pretend affection for you—liking, yes; you annoy me excessively at times and yet I must admit that I like you. Well?'

She smiled a little. 'I'll tell you tomorrow. I must sleep on it.'

'Oh, very well, if you want it that way. I thought you were a sensible girl.'

'I am, that's why I have to think about it.'

There was a knock on the door and he opened it, glaring at the student nurse standing outside so that she sidled past him uneasily.

'It's all right, Nurse,' said Caro soothingly. 'What's the matter?'

'Mrs Skipton's dressing's down ready for you to see, Staff.'

'I'm coming now,' she smiled reassuringly, and the nurse retreated, casting an interested eye upon the Professor as she went—a remarkably handsome man even though he looked as black as a thundercloud.

He closed the door with a snap behind her and then stood in front of it so that although Caro had got to her feet she was forced to a halt before him. 'I do have to go,' she told him mildly.

He opened the door. 'I'll see you tomorrow, Caroline.'

She walked past him into the ward, looking as serene as she always did while her insides turned somersaults. The nurse who had been to the office rolled her eyes upwards and shrugged her shoulders for the benefit of the junior nurse with her. 'Poor old Staff,' she murmured, 'as prim as a maiden aunt even with that gorgeous man actually talking to her!'

'I'll have the forceps, Nurse,' said Caro briskly. She had seen the look and rightly guessed at the murmur. It would be fun, she mused as she deftly removed the rubber drain from Mrs Skipton's shrinking person, to see the girl's face when she announced her engagement to the Professor.

Because she was going to marry him, she had no doubts about that, and not for any of the reasons he had given her, either. He hadn't even thought of the only reason which mattered—that she loved him.

It was typical of the Professor not to mention when and where he would see her on the following day. Caroline spent the whole of it in a state of pleasurable excitement, one ear cocked for the telephone, and her eyes sliding to the ward door every time it opened. In the end she went off duty after tea, telling herself that he had forgotten all about her, thought better of it, or what seemed more likely, she had dreamed the whole thing. She explained this to Waterloo at some length as she gave him his supper and then went to peer into the cupboard and see what she could cook for her own meal. A tin of soup, she decided, and then a poached egg on toast with a pot of tea. And while she had it she would finish that interesting bit in Fodor's Guide about Friesland having its own national anthem. She knelt to light the gas fire, but before she could strike a match there was a knock on the door. Her heart shot into her mouth, but she ignored it; the Professor had no idea where she lived and she hoped and prayed that he never would. It would be her landlady, she supposed, and went to open the door.

She had supposed wrong. It was the Professor, looming large on the narrow landing. The sheer size of him forced her to retreat a few steps so that he was inside before she could say a word. He stood looking around him unhurriedly and asked: 'This is your flat?'

'Good evening,' said Caro, and didn't answer him.

He turned his eyes on to her then. 'I've annoyed you—probably you didn't wish me to know that you lived in a bedsitter in this truly deplorable neighbourhood.'

'It's convenient for Oliver's.' She added indignantly: 'It's my home.'

His eyes lighted on Waterloo, waiting impatiently for the fire to be lighted. 'Your cat?'

'Yes—Waterloo. I found him there when he was a kitten.'

'He will of course return with us to Huis Thoe.'

She had scrambled to her feet. 'But I haven't said I'd...marry you.'

'Perhaps we might go somewhere and have dinner and discuss it.'

She stared at him, wondering if there was another girl in

the world who had had such a dry-as-dust proposal. Her first
inclination was to refuse, but she was hungry and soup and
an egg weren't exactly gastronomic excitements. 'I'll have to
change,' she said.

'I will wait on the landing.' He opened the door and a
strong aroma of frying onions caused his winged nostrils to
flare. He didn't speak, only gave her an eloquent look as he
closed it quietly.

There wasn't much choice in the rickety wardrobe, but the
few clothes she had were presentable although the Professor
had called them deplorable. How would he know anyway,
leading the life he did? Caroline put on a plain wool dress of
dark green, combed her hair, did things to her face, found her
good wool coat, her best shoes, her only decent handbag, gave
Waterloo a saucer of food and assured him that she wouldn't
be long, and left the room. The Professor was standing quietly,
but giving the impression of an impatient man holding his
impatience in check with a great effort, and she could hardly
blame him; the smell of onions had got considerably worse.

They went down the narrow stairs and out into the street
where he took her by the arm and hurried her on to the opposite pavement. 'The car is at Oliver's,' and at her quick
questioning glance, 'and if you are wondering why I didn't
go and fetch it while you were changing I will admit to a fear
that if I did so you might have changed your mind and disappeared by the time I had got back.'

Caroline paused to stare up at him in the dusk. 'Well, really—is that your opinion of me? I would never dream of...'

'I am aware of that; it was merely a remarkably silly notion
which entered my head.'

He wasn't going to say any more than that. They walked
the short distance in silence and he opened the door of the
Aston Martin for her. Settling himself beside her, he remarked: 'I've booked a table at the Savoy Grill Room.'

'Oh, no!' exclaimed Caro involuntarily. 'I'm not dressed...'

'The Grill Room,' he reminded her, and glanced sideways at her. 'You look all right to me.'

She had the idea that he hadn't the vaguest notion of what she was wearing; probably he never would have, for he never really looked at her for more than a few seconds at a time. If it came to that, very few did.

The Grill Room was full and she felt shy of her surroundings as they went in, but they were shown at once to their table and although she would have preferred one in a quiet corner where she could have been quite unnoticed, nothing could have bettered the attention they received.

She sipped at the sherry she had been given and studied the menu, mouthwateringly lengthy; she settled for salmon mousse, tournedos, saut straw potatoes and braised celery and when it came ate it with appetite, replying politely to her companion's desultory conversation as he demolished a grilled steak. She enjoyed the Beaujolais he offered her too, but prudently refused a second glass, which was just as well, for the sherry trifle was deliciously rich. It was when the waiter had cleared the table and set coffee before them that the Professor abandoned his dinner table conversation and asked abruptly: 'Well, you've slept on it, Caroline, and now I should like your answer. Is it yes or no?'

She handed him his coffee cup without haste. He had asked a plain question, he was going to get a plain answer. 'Yes.'

She watched his face as she spoke and found it rather daunting to see his calm expression quite unchanged. 'Very well, we can now make plans for our marriage. As soon as possible, don't you think?'

'Very well, but I have to give in my resignation at Oliver's, Prof... What am I to call you?'

He smiled a little. 'Radinck. If you have no objection, I can arrange that you leave very shortly. We can be married here by special licence. Do you wish to invite anyone? Family? Friends?'

'I have an aunt—no one else—she's married now and I

don't think she will want to come to the wedding. I expect some of my friends from the hospital would like to come to the church.'

'I'll see about it and let you know. Have you sufficient money to buy yourself some clothes?'

Caroline thought of her little nest-egg, hoarded against a rainy day. 'Yes, thank you.'

He nodded. 'You can of course buy anything you want when we return, but I presume you will want something for the wedding.' His voice held a faint sneer.

'I won't disgrace you,' she told him quietly, and was pleased to see him look a little taken aback. If she hadn't loved him so much she would have been furious.

He begged her pardon stiffly and she said kindly: 'Oh, that's all right—it'll be super to have some decent clothes.' She wrinkled her forehead in thought. 'Something I can travel in and wear afterwards...'

He passed his cup for more coffee. 'Perhaps I should point out to you that you can buy all the clothes you want when you are my wife. I—we shall live comfortably enough.' He sat back in his chair. 'Now as to the actual wedding...'

He had thought of everything; the arrangements for her to leave, the obtaining of the marriage licence, giving up her bedsitter, a basket for Waterloo's comfortable transport to Holland. There would be no honeymoon, he told her, and that didn't surprise her at all, honeymoons were for two people in love, but she was surprised when he said: 'We will go tomorrow and buy the wedding rings and I will give you your engagement ring—I brought it over with me but forgot to bring it with me this evening.'

She didn't know whether to laugh or cry at that.

Radinck took her back to Meadow Road presently, waiting at her front door while she climbed the stairs and unlocked her own door. His goodnight had been casual and, to her ear, faintly impatient. Probably he found her boring company, but in that case why did he want to marry her? Probably he was tired. She got ready for bed, made a pot of tea because she was too excited to sleep and sat in front of the gas fire with Waterloo beside her, politely listening while she recounted the evening's happenings to him.

She was off in the evening again the next day and she supposed Radinck would meet her then; certainly there was no time to go buying wedding rings during the day—but apparently he thought differently.

Caroline had got well into the morning's routine when he came on to the ward with Sir Eustace, and Caro, hastily pulling down her sleeves, went down the ward to meet them, wondering which patient they wanted to see.

They wished her good morning and Sir Eustace said jovially: 'Well, Staff Nurse, I am delighted at the news that you are to marry. I haven't come to do a round, only to beg the pleasure of giving you away.'

Caro pinkened. 'Oh, would you? Would you really? I did wonder... I haven't got any relations...'

'I shall be delighted—Radinck will let me know the day when you've decided it.' He beamed at her. 'And now I must go to theatre—I'm already late.'

She escorted him to the door and went back to the Professor, who hadn't said a word after his good morning and in answer to her look of enquiry he observed: 'It is rather public here, perhaps we might go to the office for a minute.'

She led the way, offered him a seat which he declined and sat down at the desk. 'I will be outside at twelve o'clock,' he told her. 'You will go to your dinner then, I believe? We can go along to Apsleys and get the rings and have a quick lunch somewhere.'

'But I'll be in uniform—there's only an hour, you know—there'll never be time... I don't mind missing lunch.'

'Put a coat over your uniform. I'll see that you get back on duty on time.' He took a small box out of a pocket. 'This was my mother's—she had small hands, like yours, and I hope it will fit.'

He opened the box and took out a great sapphire ring set in a circle of rose diamonds and when she held out her hand, slipped it on to her finger. It fitted exactly. Caro, who was inclined to be superstitious, thought it was a good omen.

She thanked him for it and longed to throw her arms round him and kiss him, but instead she said: 'It's very beautiful: I'll take great care of it.'

He nodded carelessly. 'You will wish to get on with your work—I'll meet you at noon.'

He had gone before she could do more than nod.

It wasn't entirely satisfactory going out in her winter coat which was brown and didn't match her black duty shoes and stockings. She had made her hair tidy and powdered her nose, but rushing down to the front door of the hospital she thought crossly that all the girls she knew would have refused flatly to go out looking so ridiculous; but there again, she reminded herself, Radinck considered she dressed deplorably anyway; he wouldn't notice.

If he did he said nothing, merely stowed her in the car and drove smoothly to Apsleys where they must have expected him, for they were attended to immediately by a quiet-voiced elderly man, who said very little as he displayed rings of every variety before them.

The Professor gave them a cursory glance. 'Choose which you prefer, Caroline,' he suggested. He sounded bored, and just for a moment resentment at his lack of interest at what should be an important event to them both almost choked her, but her common sense came to her rescue; why should he be interested? Buying the ring was to him only a necessary part of getting married. She picked a perfectly plain gold one and the man measured her finger and found her one to fit it before doing the same for the Professor. While he was away wrapping them up, Radinck said quietly: 'You aren't wearing your ring.'

'It's in the box in my pocket. I haven't had a chance—I

mean, I can't wear it on duty and I forgot to wear it now—
I'm not used to it yet.'

'Will you put it on?'

She did so, and when the man came back he saw it and
smiled nicely at her. It made her feel much better and almost
happy.

It hadn't taken much time: there was more than half an
hour before she had to return to the ward, but when the Professor turned the car back in the direction of Oliver's she
supposed that he had decided that there wasn't time for even
a snack lunch and in all fairness she had said that she wouldn't
mind missing her lunch. But in Cheapside he slowed the car,
parked it and walked her into Le Poulbot where it seemed
they were expected.

'I took the liberty of ordering for you since we have only
a short time,' observed Radinck, 'filets de sole Leonora and
a glass of white wine to go with it, and perhaps a sorbet.'

She was surprised at his thoughtfulness and stammered her
thanks. 'But it means you have to rush over lunch too,' she
pointed out.

'I'm not in the habit of sitting over my meals,' he observed.
'When one is by oneself it is a waste of time—one gets into
bad habits...'

Caroline resolved silently to get him out of them even if it
took her a lifetime and took care not to chat while they ate.
Actually she longed to talk; there was so much she wanted to
know, but she would have to wait: when he had made all the
arrangements he would doubtless tell her. She was surprised
when he asked: 'Which day do you wish to choose for the
wedding?'

She said with some asperity: 'Well, how can I choose until
I know when I'm to leave and when you want to go back to
Holland?'

He waved aside the waiter and sat back to watch her eating
her sorbet.

'Ah, yes—I saw your Senior Nursing Officer this morning.

You may leave in five days' time—by then I shall have the licence, would any day after that suit you?'

She felt a surge of excitement at the very idea. 'That's...' she counted on her fingers, 'Sunday. Would Tuesday suit you? That would give me time to pack my things. Will you be here until then?'

He shook his head. 'I'm going back tomorrow—there are several patients I have to see. I'll come back on Sunday and see you then. Would you like to go to an hotel until the Tuesday?'

She was surprised again. 'That's very kind of you, but I'll stay in Meadow Road if you don't mind—Waterloo, you know.'

'Ah, yes, I had forgotten.' He glanced at his watch. 'We had better go.'

His leavetaking was casual. No one looking at the two of them, thought Caro, would have guessed that they were going to be married within a week. She watched him get into his car and drive away, her eyes filled with tears. She knew nothing about him; where he was staying, what he was doing in London, if he had friends...the only thing she was sure of was that she loved him enough to bear with his ways.

FIVE DAYS, Caro discovered, could last for ever, especially when one didn't know what was going to happen at the end of them. The Professor had said he was going to see her on Sunday, but once again he had forgotten to mention time or place. True, she had enjoyed several hours of shopping which had left her very satisfied and reduced her nest-egg to a few paltry pounds, all the same she wished very much that Sunday would come.

And finally come it did and Caro, burdened with a variety of presents from her friends and fellow nurses, left Oliver's early in the afternoon. She had several hours of overtime due to her and Sister Pringle, generous after her holiday, had told her to go early rather than wait until six o'clock. She had been surprised to find her staff nurse engaged and on the point of leaving, but she had been pleased too; Caro got on well with everyone in her quiet way and she would be missed. She would miss her life at Oliver's too, she thought, as she crossed the busy street in front of the forbidding exterior and made her way to Meadow Road, but she wasn't daunted at the idea of living in another country; she would have lived wherever Radinck was and not complained.

She fed Waterloo, made herself a pot of tea and spread her packages on the bed—an early morning tea-set from Stacey, Miriam and Clare, a tea-cosy from the nurses on the ward, a bright pink bath towel from the ward maid and the orderlies and some handkerchiefs from Sister Pringle, and over and above these, a cut glass vase from all her friends. She admired them at length, for with no family of her own, presents had been few and far between. After she had had her tea she went to the wardrobe and looked at the new clothes hanging there. Her wedding outfit, covered in a plastic wrapper, took up most of the room; it was a rather plain fine wool dress in a warm amber colour which, if the weather should prove cold, would go very well under her winter coat. She had bought a small velvet hat to go with it, rather expensive shoes and gloves and a leather handbag. Not even the Professor would be able to find fault with them, she considered. She had bought a suit too, a multi-coloured tweed with a Marks and Spencer sweater to go with it, and more shoes, a sensible pair for walking in, and new undies and slacks. She would have liked some new luggage to pack them in, but her case, although shabby, was quite adequate and she wanted a few pounds in her purse; Radinck had talked about an allowance in a cool voice which had made her determined not to make use of it until she was forced to.

He arrived just as she was making toast for her tea. The afternoon had turned wet and chilly and Caroline had drawn the curtains and got out the Fodor's Guide once more. She was sitting on the wool rug she had made for herself, the bread toasting on a fork, Waterloo sitting beside her, when Radinck thumped on the door. No one else thumped like that. She knew who it was and called to him to come in. She didn't get up but went on with her toast-making, saying merely: 'Hello, Radinck, would you like some tea? I'm just going to make it.'

'Thank you, that would be nice.' He took off his car coat and sat down in the shabby chair beside the fire.

'Have you just arrived?' she asked.

'Yes, they told me at Oliver's that you had left.' His eyes lighted on the presents still laid out on the divan and he looked a question.

'Wedding presents,' said Caro cheerfully, turning her toast. 'I've never had so many things all at once in my life.'

He said, 'Very nice,' and dismissed them. 'You are ready for Tuesday?'

'Yes, I think so.' She buttered the toast and got up to put the kettle on.

Radinck looked tired and even more severe than usual and so aloof that Caroline didn't dare to utter the words of sympathy crowding into her head. Instead she made the tea, poured him a cup and put it, with the toast, on a stool by his chair, and then set about making more toast.

Presently when he had drunk his tea and she had given him a second cup she asked in her soft voice: 'You haven't changed your mind? You really want me to marry you, Radinck? One often gets ideas that don't work out...'

'I still want to marry you, Caroline.' He had relaxed, leaning back eating his toast, stroking Waterloo who had got on to his knee. 'I thought that we might go out for dinner.'

'Thank you, that would be nice.'

'And tomorrow? I have to be at the hospital in the morning, but perhaps we might go out in the afternoon. You have finished your shopping?'

'Yes, thank you—I have only to pack.'

He nodded. 'They are all delighted at Huis Thoe. You realise that we have to return by the night boat on Tuesday?'

'Yes.' She bit into her toast, trying to think of something to add and couldn't. She was astonished when he asked:

'What is the colour of your dress?'

'The one I've bought for the wedding? I suppose you'd call it dark amber.' She took a sip of tea and went on: 'I know you aren't interested in what I wear, it's a very plain dress— quite nice, you know, but no one's likely to take a second look at me, if you see what I mean.'

He raised his thick eyebrows. 'And is that your ambition? I have always understood that women—especially young ones—like to be noticed.'

'Not with a face like mine, they wouldn't,' Caro assured him.

He eyed her gravely. 'Your figure is not displeasing,' he observed, and sounded almost as surprised at his words as she was.

He didn't have to wait on the landing this time. She had

adopted the old-fashioned idea of wearing her best clothes on Sundays even if she wasn't going anywhere; it made the day seem a little different from all the others, so she was ready when Radinck suggested that they should go.

This time he took her to the Connaught Hotel Restaurant and because it was Sunday evening her green wool dress didn't seem too out of place, and she really wouldn't have minded; she had the sapphire on her finger, proclaiming that she had some sort of claim on her companion—although judging by the looks she received from some of the younger women sitting near them, it wasn't at all justified—besides, she was hungry. She did full justice to the cheese soufflé— as light as air, followed by filets de sole princesse and rounded off by millefeuille from the sweet trolley, all nicely helped down by the champagne the Professor had ordered. Caro wasn't very used to champagne; she wasn't sure if she liked it, but with the second glass she assured her companion that it was a drink which grew on one, and although she hadn't intended to make him laugh, he actually did.

She spent the next morning packing her clothes and putting her small treasures and ornaments, carefully wrapped, into a large cardboard box.

She was quite ready when Radinck called for her, dressed in the new suit, her face carefully made up. It was most gratifying when he remarked casually: 'You look nice—is that new?'

She told him yes, reflecting that it had been worth the scandalous price she had paid for it at Jaegers; a lukewarm compliment but still a compliment.

They went to the Connaught again and when she observed how very nice it was, the Professor agreed pleasantly enough. 'I stay here if I'm in England for a few days,' he told her, and she fell to wondering where he went if his stay was protracted. Her thoughts must have been mirrored on her face, for after a pause he said:

'I have a small house in Essex, but it is hardly worth going there unless I'm over for a week or more.'

'What exactly do you do?' she asked carefully. 'That's if you don't mind telling me.'

He didn't answer her at once but remarked testily: 'Why is it that so many remarks you make appear to put me in the wrong, Caroline?' and before she could deny this: 'I am a physician, specialising in heart conditions, and the various diseases consequent to them.'

'But you lecture?'

'Yes.'

'And of course you're a consultant as well. Do you travel a great deal?'

He frowned a little. 'What a great many questions, Caroline!'

She agreed cheerfully. 'But you see, Radinck, if I ask them now, you'll never have to answer them again, will you?'

'That is true. I hope you don't expect to travel with me? I'm used to being alone—I concentrate better.'

She eyed him with pity wringing her heart, but all she said was: 'Of course I don't—I haven't forgotten that I'm to be a sheet-anchor.'

He gave her a hard suspicious look which she met with a clear friendly gaze.

She hadn't asked what they were doing with the rest of the afternoon. She expected to be taken to Meadow Road, but it seemed that Radinck had other plans, for after lunch he left the car at the hotel and hailed a taxi. It cost Caro a great effort not to ask him where they were going, but she guessed that he was waiting for her to do just that. In the taxi he said: 'I have a wedding gift for you, but I wish you to see it first—it may not please you.'

She would have been a moron not to have been pleased, she thought presently, standing in front of the triple mirror in an exclusive furrier's shop. Mink, no less—ranch mink, he had carefully explained, because he thought that a coat made from trapped animals might distress her. It was a perfect fit, and when she remarked upon this he had told her casually that Clare had very kindly supplied her measurements.

She thanked him quietly and sincerely, careful to do it while the sales lady wasn't there. 'I can wear it tomorrow,' she told him. 'I was going to wear my winter coat...'

She understood then that for his wife to return to Huis Thoe in anything less than a mink coat would have upset everyone's idea of the fitness of things. She reflected with some excitement that she would be expected to dress very well, go to the hairdressers too and use the kind of make-up advertised so glossily in *Harpers* and *Vogue*. It struck her then that she was going to be a baroness—ridiculous but true. Just for a moment she quailed at the thought, but then her sensible head told her that it didn't matter what either of them were if they could love each other—and she already did that; it was just a question of getting Radinck to fall in love with her. She wasn't quite sure how she was going to do it, but it would be done.

Leaving the shop Radinck observed: 'I hope you will be pleased. I thought it would be pleasant if we gave a small dinner party for your friends and Sir Eustace and my best man this evening. At the hotel in my rooms there; we shall have to leave directly after we have been married tomorrow, so there is no question of giving a lunch party then.'

'How nice,' said Caro faintly. 'C-can I wear this dress?'

'Certainly not. It will be black ties—your three friends are wearing long dresses. Have you no evening gown?'

She shook her head. 'Well, no—you see I don't go out a great deal.' Not at all, she added silently, but pride stopped her from saying so aloud.

'In that case tell me where you would like to buy a dress and we'll go there now.'

'Oh, I couldn't...'

He said coolly: 'Don't be so old-fashioned, Caroline—it is perfectly permissible for a man to buy his future wife a dress should he wish to do so. We will go to Fortnum and Mason.'

Caro goggled at him. 'But I've never been there in my life—not to buy anything.'

'Then it's time you did.'

He was there and she was getting out of the car before she could think of any argument against this and was led unresisting to the Dress Department where the Professor, looking more severe than ever, was instantly attended to by the head sales lady.

Having made his wishes clear he took himself off to a comfortable chair and left Caro to be led away by the sales lady to go through a selection of dresses which were all so stunning that she had no idea what she wanted.

It was the sales lady who pointed out that green was a good colour for hazel eyes and furthermore she had just the thing to suit, and if that wasn't to madam's taste, there was a charming honey-coloured crêpe or a grey crêpe-de- chine...

Caro, almost delirious with excitement, tried them all on in turn and settled for the green; organza over silk with full sleeves gathered into tight buttoned cuffs and a low ruffled neckline. And when the sales lady suggested that she might like some rather pretty sandals to go with it, she agreed recklessly. She told Radinck about the sandals as they left the shop. 'I had no evening shoes,' she explained gravely, 'so I hope you don't mind. They were rather expensive.'

She hadn't been able to discover the price of the dress; the sales lady had been vague and she had watched Radinck sign a cheque without showing any signs of shock. She hoped that it hadn't been too expensive, but it wasn't until later that evening while she was dressing that she saw its label; a couture garment, and her mind boggled at the cost.

They had tea presently in a tiny shop all gilt and white paint, with the most heavenly cakes Caro had ever eaten, and on the way back she thanked him fervently and then went scarlet when he said coldly: 'You have no need to be quite so fulsome in your thanks. I have hardly lavished a fortune upon you, Caroline.'

She turned her head and looked out of the car window, wanting to burst into tears; the last thing she must ever do before him. She said brightly, proud of her steady voice, 'How dark it grows in the afternoons—but I like winter, don't you?'

She didn't see his quick glance at her averted face. 'You will be able to skate on the canal near Huis Thoe if it freezes enough.' His voice was casual and quite different from the biting tones he had just used. Caroline supposed she would learn in time—not to mind when he snubbed her, not to mind when he was cold and distant; there would surely be times when they could talk together, get to know each other. It would take time, but after all, he had said that he liked her.

He had to go back to the hospital that evening. He left her at Meadow Road, said that he would call for her at half past seven and drove away, leaving her to tell Waterloo all about it, wash her hair, do her face and put on the new dress. She had been ready and waiting half an hour or more before he returned, pleased with her appearance and hoping that he would be pleased too.

His cool 'very nice!' when he arrived was rather less than she had hoped for and his further: 'The dress is pretty,' although truthful, hardly flattered her, but she thanked him politely, tucked Waterloo up in his box and picked up the new fur coat. It was almost frightening how the touch of his cool hands on her shoulders as he held it for her sent her insides seesawing.

The evening was a great success; Clare, Miriam and Stacey had been fetched by the best man whose name Caro, in her excitement, didn't catch, although she remembered afterwards that he had said that he had an English wife who had just had a baby, and Sir Eustace and his wife arrived a few minutes after them. They all looked very elegant, Caro considered, drinking champagne cocktails in the elegant room Radinck had taken her to; her friends did credit to the occasion and sadly seemed on better terms with their host than she did. Just as he did with them. It was strange, she mused a little cloudily because of the champagne, that he should want to marry her when she never amused him, but there again, she couldn't imagine any of them allowing him to lead the quiet, studious life he seemed to enjoy. But her low spirits didn't last for long; the ring was admired, as was the coat, and her friends' pleasure at her change of fortune was genuine enough. And Lady Jenkins, under the impression that it was a love match and knowing that Caro had no parents, became quite motherly.

They dined late and at leisure at the round table set up in the Professor's sitting room at the hotel. Iced melon was followed by lobster Thermidor and rounded off with ices, trifle and charlotte russe. They drank champagne and over coffee the Professor observed that it hardly seemed right to have a wedding cake before the wedding, but he had done his best to substitute that with petits fours, covered in white icing and decorated with silver leaves and flowers.

It was almost midnight when the party broke up and everyone went home, cracking jokes about seeing them at the church in the morning. When they had all gone, Caro put on her coat once more and was driven back to Meadow Road, making polite conversation all the way. She only stopped when Radinck remarked: 'You're very chatty—it must be the champagne.'

He didn't sound annoyed, though, only a little bored, so she said, 'Yes, I expect it is,' and lapsed into silence until they reached the house. He got out first, opened her door and went with her up the stairs, to take the key from her hand and open the door. The contrast after the spacious elegance of the hotel room was cruel, but he didn't say anything, only gave her back her key, cautioned her to be ready when he came for her in the morning and wished her goodnight.

'Goodnight,' said Caro hurriedly, because she hadn't thanked him yet and he seemed in a hurry to be gone. 'It was a delightful dinner party, thank you, Radinck.' And when he muttered something she added: 'I'll be ready when you come.'

She smiled at him and shut the door quite briskly, leaving him on the landing. She loved him so very much, but she mustn't let that weaken her resolve to alter his stern outlook on life. She suspected that he was a man who had always had his own way, even to shutting a door when he wanted to and not a moment before. A small beginning, but she had to start somewhere.

She slept dreamlessly with Waterloo curled up in a tight ball on her feet and was up much earlier than she needed to be, and true to her word, she was dressed and ready when Radinck came for her. Waterloo and her luggage were to be collected after the ceremony. Caroline cast a look round the little room and followed Radinck down the stairs to the car. The drive to the church was a short one and they hardly spoke. At the door she was handed over to Sir Eustace waiting in the porch and given a small bouquet of rich yellow roses which the Professor took from the back of the car. He nodded briefly at her and just for a moment she panicked, staring up at him with eyes full of doubt, and he must have seen that, for he smiled suddenly and she glimpsed the man under the calm mask and all her doubts went. If he could smile like that once, he could do it again, and she would make sure that he did. She took Sir Eustace's arm and walked firmly down the aisle to where Radinck, towering over everything in sight, waited for her.

She had no clear recollection of the ceremony. The best man had given her an encouraging smile as she reached Radinck's side, but the Professor didn't look at her at all. Indeed, he looked rather grim during the short service. Only as he put the ring on her finger he smiled slightly. She wanted to smile too, but she didn't; she would have to remember to remain friendly and undemanding quite without romantic feelings; he didn't hold with romance. That was something else which she had to alter.

There was to be no wedding breakfast. Everyone said good-bye in the church porch and Caro got into the car beside

Radinck, not feeling in the least married and resolved to change his life for him. Indeed when Clare put her head through the window and exclaimed: 'Good lord, you're a baroness now!' she started to deny it and then declared: 'I'd forgotten that— Oh, dear!' She looked so woebegone at the idea that Clare laughed at her.

The Professor didn't intend to waste time; Caro's luggage was put in the boot, Waterloo, in a travelling basket, was arranged on the back seat, and with a hurried word to Mrs Hodge, who looked aggrieved because it hadn't been a proper wedding at all, Caro settled herself tidily beside the Professor. Afterwards, she had no very clear recollection of the journey either. They travelled by Hovercraft from Dover and although they stopped for lunch and again for tea, she had no idea what they had talked about or what she had eaten. The Professor had laid himself out to be pleasant and she had been careful not to chat, answering him when he made some observation but refraining from discussing the morning's ceremony. It was he who asked her if she had been pleased with her wedding, in much the same manner as someone asking if she had enjoyed her lunch, and she told him yes, it had been very nice— a colourless statement, but she could think of nothing better to say. She did enquire the name of the best man and was told he was Tiele Raukema van den Eck, not long married to an English girl. 'You must meet her,' suggested the Professor casually. 'She's rather a nice little thing—they've just had a son.'

It seemed there was no more to be said on the subject. Caro sat quietly as they sped northward and wondered if Noakes and the other servants would be glad to see her. Radinck had said that they had missed her, but going back as the lady of the house was quite a different kettle of fish.

She need not have worried. They were greeted with wide smiles and a great deal of handshaking and when that was done, Noakes led them into the drawing room where, on a small circular table in the centre of the room, was a wedding cake. Caro stopped short and gave a delighted laugh. 'Radinck, how kind of you to think of...'

She looked at him, still laughing, and saw at once that she had been mistaken. He was as surprised as she was—it must have been Noakes.

He was standing in the doorway with Juffrouw Kropp and Marta and the others grouped around him, waiting to be praised like eager children. Caro hoped that they hadn't heard her speak to Radinck; she turned to them now. 'Noakes, all of you—what a wonderful surprise! We're both thrilled; it is the most beautiful cake. Thank you—all of you.' She went on recklessly: 'I'm going to cut it now and we'll all have a piece with some champagne. We were going to have the champagne anyway, weren't we, Radinck?'

She turned a smiling face towards him, her eyes beseeching him to act the part of a happy bridegroom. After all, it was only for once; every other night he could go to his study and spend the evenings with his books.

He met her look with a mocking smile she hoped no one else saw. 'But certainly we will drink champagne,' he agreed. 'Noakes, fetch up half a dozen bottles and get someone to set out the glasses. And thank you all for this magnificent cake.' He repeated it all in Dutch and there was handclapping and smiling and a good deal of bustling to and fro until the champagne had been brought and they went to cut the cake. Caroline, handed the knife by Noakes and alone with the Professor at the table for a moment, said softly; 'I'm afraid it's the custom for us both to hold the knife...'

His hand felt cool and quite impersonal and touched her only briefly. He was disliking the happy little ceremony very much, she knew that; perhaps it reminded him of his first wedding. He'd been in love then...

They ate the cake and drank the champagne and presently Juffrouw Kropp took Caroline upstairs to her room to tidy herself for dinner. It was a different bedroom this time; a vast apartment in the front of the house with an equally vast bed with a brocade coverlet to match the blue curtains and beautiful Hepplewhite furniture. A bathroom led from it and on the other side a dressing room, another bathroom and another bedroom, all leading one to another. Juffrouw Kropp beamed and smiled before she went away, and left alone, Caro explored more thoroughly; it was all very splendid but comfortable too. She tidied herself, did her hair and went downstairs again to join Radinck in the drawing-room, where they made conversation over their drinks before going in to dinner.

Marta had excelled herself with little spinach tarts, roast duckling with black cherries and a bombe surprise. Caro, desperately maintaining a conversation about nothing much, ate some of everything although she had no appetite, because Marta would be upset to see her lovely dishes returned to the kitchen half eaten, and she drank the hock Noakes poured for them, a little too much of it, which was a good thing because it made her feel falsely cheerful.

They had their coffee in the drawing-room and Noakes went away with a benign smile which drew down the corners of the Professor's mouth so that Caro, now valiant with too much drink, said cheerfully: 'You've hated every minute of it, haven't you, Radinck? But I'm going to my room in a few minutes, only before I go I'd like to thank you for giving me such a nice wedding.' She added kindly: 'It's only this one evening, you know, you won't have to do it ever again. You asked me not to disturb your life, and I won't, only they all expected...' She pinkened faintly. 'Well, they expected us to look—like...'

'Exactly, Caroline.' He had got to his feet. 'I'm only sorry that I didn't think of the wedding cake.' He smiled at her: it was a kind, gentle sort of smile and it held a touch of impatience. She said goodnight without fuss and didn't linger. She thought about that smile later, as she got ready for bed. It had been a glimpse of Radinck again, only next time, she promised herself, he would smile without impatience. It might take a long time, but that was something she had.

She woke early while it was still almost dark. She had opened the door to the verandah outside her room before she got into her enormous bed, and Waterloo, after a long sound sleep on her feet after his lengthy journey and hearty supper, was prowling up and down it, talking to her. She got up, put on her new quilted dressing gown and slippers and went to join him.

The sky was getting paler every minute, turning pink along the horizon; it was going to be a lovely November day, bright and frosty. Somewhere Caroline could hear Rex barking and the sound of horses' hooves and then Radinck's whistle to the dog. So that was what he did before breakfast. She vowed then and there to learn to ride.

One of the maids, Ilke, brought her her early morning tea presently, and told her smilingly that breakfast would be at half past eight, or would she rather have it in bed?

Caro elected to go downstairs. She had never had her breakfast in bed, for there had been no one to bring it to her, and the idea didn't appeal to her very much. She bathed and put on her suit and one of the Marks and Spencer sweaters and went down to the hall. It was absurd, but she wasn't sure where she was to breakfast. When she had been staying in the house she had seen only the library, the drawing-room and the dining-room, but there were several more doors and passages leading from the hall and she had no idea where they led. She need not have fussed; Noakes was waiting to conduct her to a small, cosy room leading off the hall, where there was a bright fire burning and a table laid ready for her. Of the Professor there was no sign and she thought it might sound silly if she asked Noakes where he was, so she bade him a smiling good morning, and while she made a good breakfast, listened to his carefully put advice.

'There's Juffrouw Kropp waiting ter show yer the 'ouse, ma'am, and then Marta 'opes yer'll go to the kitchens and take a look at the menu, and anything yer wants ter know yer just ask me. We're all that 'appy that yer're 'ere, ma'am.'

'Noakes, you're very kind to say so, and I'm happy too. When I've found my feet we must have some more singing—I still think we should do something about Christmas, don't you?' She remembered something. 'And, Noakes, I want your help. Is there someone who can teach me to ride? I—I want to surprise the Professor.'

His cheerful face spread into a vast smile. 'Now ain't that just the ticket—the Professor, 'e rides a treat, great big 'orse 'e's got, too, but there's a pony as is 'ardly used. Old Jan'll know—I'll get 'im to come and see yer and I'll come wiv 'im.'

'Thank you, Noakes—it must be a secret, though.' Caroline finished her coffee and got up from the table. 'I'm going to fetch Waterloo and take him round the house with Juffrouw Kropp, then he'll feel at home. Where's Rex?'

'Gone with the Professor. Most days 'e does, ma'am.'

It took all of two hours to go over the house. She hadn't realised quite how big it was, with a great many little passages leading to small rooms, and funny twisted stairs from one floor to the next as well as the massive front staircase. She would have got lost if it hadn't been for Juffrouw Kropp, leading her from one room to the next, waiting patiently while she examined its contents, and then explaining them in basic Dutch so that Caro had at least some idea of them. They were all beautifully furnished and well-kept, but as far as she could make out, never used. A house full of guests, she dreamed to herself, all laughing and talking and dancing in the evening in that lovely drawing-room and riding out in the mornings, with her riding even better than the best there. She sighed and Juffrouw Kropp asked her if she were tired, and when she shook her head in vigorous denial, preceded her downstairs to visit the glories on the ground floor.

The drawing-room she knew, also the library and the morning-room. Now she was conducted round a second sitting-room, furnished with deep armchairs, a work table from the Regency period, several lamp tables and two bow-fronted display cabinets. A lovely room, but not used, she felt sure. Well, she would use it. There was a billiard room too, a garden room and a small room furnished with a desk and chair and several filing cabinets—used by the secretary, Caroline supposed. There was a luxurious cloakroom too and a great many large cupboards as well as several rooms lined with shelves and a pantry or two.

She hoped she would remember where each of them was if ever she needed it, although she couldn't think why she should. The first floor had been easy enough; her own room and the adjoining ones took up half the front corridor and most of one side, and the half a dozen bedrooms and their bathrooms on that floor took up the rest of its space; the smaller rooms and passages she would have to explore later.

She drank her coffee presently, concentrating on what she had seen, reminding herself that it was hers now as well as Radinck's and he would expect her to be responsible for his home. She had no intention of usurping Juffrouw Kropp's position, but it was obvious that even that experienced lady expected her to give orders from time to time.

The kitchens she already knew, but now it was a question of poking her mousy head into all the cupboards and lobbies and dressers while it was explained to her what was in all of them and then, finally, she was given a seat at the kitchen table and offered the day's menu. Noakes translated it for her while Marta waited anxiously to see if she would approve, and when that had been done to everyone's satisfaction, Noakes led her back to the smaller sitting-room, where she had decided to spend her leisure and where after a few minutes Jan was admitted.

Noakes had to act as go-between, of course, but Jan agreed readily enough to teaching her. The pony, he agreed with Noakes, was just right since the Baroness was small and light. Caro, who had forgotten that she was a baroness, felt a little glow of pleasure at his words. They decided that she should begin the very next morning, and well pleased with herself, she got her coat and took herself off for a walk.

She lunched alone, since the Professor didn't come home, and in the afternoon she curled up in the library and had another go at her Dutch. She would have to have lessons, for she was determined to learn to speak it as quickly as possible, but in the meantime she could at least look up as many words as she could. She and Juffrouw Kropp were to go through the linen cupboard on the following morning. She would make her companion say everything in her own language and she would repeat it after her; she would learn a lot that way. And tomorrow she would get Noakes to drive her into Leeuwarden so that she could buy some wool and fill her time with knitting. More flowers about the house too, she decided, and an hour's practice at the piano each day. There was more than enough to keep her busy.

She went upstairs to change after her solitary tea; she put on her wedding dress again and then went to the drawing-room to wait for Radinck, taking a book with her so that it wouldn't look as though she had been there ages, expecting him.

When he did get home, only a short time before dinner, she wished him a cheerful good evening, volunteered no information as to her day, hoped that he had had a good one himself and took up her book again. He had stressed that she wasn't to interfere with his way of living and she would abide by it. She accepted a drink from him and when he excused himself on the plea of work to do before dinner, assured him that she didn't mind in the least.

They met at the dinner table presently and over an unhurried meal talked comfortably enough about this and that, and as they got up to go into the drawing-room for their coffee Caro said diffidently: 'Don't come into the drawing-room unless you want to, Radinck. I'll get Noakes to bring coffee to your study.'

He followed her into the room and closed the door. He said

irritably: 'I'll take my coffee where I wish to, Caroline. I'm sure you mean well, but kindly don't interfere.' He glared down at her. 'I shall be going out very shortly.'

Her voice was quite serene. 'Yes, Radinck. Do you like your coffee black?' She poured it with a steady hand and went to sit down, telling herself she wasn't defeated, only discouraged.

CHAPTER FIVE

THE DAYS PASSED, piling themselves into a week. Caro, awake early as usual by reason of Waterloo's soliloquy as he paced the balcony, sat herself up against her lace-trimmed pillows and began to assess the progress she had made in that time. Nothing startling, she conceded, ticking off her small successes first: her riding lessons had proved well worth the effort. She had got on to Jemmy, the pony, each morning under Jan's eagle eye and done her best while her tutor muttered and tutted at her and occasionally took her to task in a respectful manner, while the faithful Noakes translated every word. And she had learned the geography of the house, having gone over it several times by herself and once or twice with Juffrouw Kropp, learning the names of the various pieces of furniture from that good lady.

She had applied herself to her Dutch too; even though she had little idea how to converse in that language she had worried her way through a host of useful words. Besides all this, she had got Noakes to drive her to Leeuwarden, where she had bought wool and a pattern and started on a sweater for Radinck's Christmas present; probably he would never wear it, but she was getting a lot of pleasure from knitting it, although as the instructions were in Dutch she had had to guess at a good deal of the pattern and enlist Juffrouw Kropp's help over the more difficult bits.

Her eyes fell on Waterloo, who having finished his early morning exercise, was sitting in the doorway washing his elderly face; he at least was happy with the whole house to roam and a safe outdoors with no traffic threatening his safety, and she shared his opinion. The grounds round the house were large and beyond the red brick wall which encompassed them were water meadows and quiet lanes and bridle paths. Caroline had roamed at will during the week, finding her way around, going to the village where she was surprised to be greeted by its inhabitants. She still found it strange to be addressed as Baroness and she had had a struggle to answer civilly in Dutch, but smiling and nodding went a long way towards establishing a sort of rapport.

But with Radinck she had made no progress at all. He was polite, remote and continued to live his own life, just as though she wasn't there. True, once or twice he had discussed some interesting point regarding his work with her, asked her casually if she had been to the village and informed her that now their marriage had been put in the *Haagsche Post* and *Elseviers* they might expect visitors and some invitations, and had gone on to suggest that she might like to go to Leeuwarden or Groningen and buy herself some clothes, and the following morning his secretary had given her a cheque book with a slip of paper inside it on which the Professor had scrawled: Your allowance will be paid into the bank quarterly. The sum he had written had left Caroline dumbfounded.

But it was early days yet, she reminded herself cheerfully. He would be surprised and, she hoped, delighted to discover that she could ride. The last thing she wanted to happen was for him to feel ashamed of her because of her social shortcomings, even if he didn't want her as a wife she would manage his home just as he wanted it, entertain his friends and learn to live his way of life. She owed him that, and never mind how impatient and irritable he became.

She drank her morning tea and presently went downstairs to her breakfast, to stop in the doorway of the breakfast room. Radinck was sitting at the table, a cup of coffee in one hand, a letter he was reading in the other.

He got up when he saw her, pulled out a chair and said politely: 'Do sit down; I forgot to tell you yesterday that I have given myself a day off. I thought we might go down to den Haag so that you can do some shopping. My mother always got her things from Le Bonneterie there—it's rather like a small Harrods, and you might possibly like it—if not; we can try somewhere else.'

Caroline didn't like to mention that she had never bought anything in Harrods. She agreed happily; a whole day in his company, even if he had nothing much to say to her, would be heaven, but here she was to be disappointed, for in the car, racing across the Afsluitdijk, he mentioned casually that he had a consultation at the Red Cross Hospital in den Haag and after leaving her at Le Bonneterie he would rejoin her there an hour or so later. 'I daresay it will take you that time to buy your clothes. I suggest that you get a sheepskin jacket and some boots—it can be cold once the winter comes.'

Caroline started doing sums in her head; her allowance was a generous one but she had no idea how much good clothes cost in Holland. She would need several dresses, she supposed, and more separates and some evening clothes.

'You're very silent,' remarked Radinck presently.

'Well, I was just thinking what I needed to buy. Would two evening dresses do?'

'Certainly not—there will be a hospital ball in Leeuwarden in a few weeks' time, and another one in Groningen and any number of private parties. At Christmas I invite a number of guests to the house, but before then we will have an evening reception so that you meet my friends.'

She had to get this straight. 'But you like to lead a quiet life; you told me so—you like to work and read in the evenings. You'll only be inviting them because of me.'

'That is so.' They were flying down the E 10 and there was plenty to capture her interest, only she had too much on her mind.

'Yes, but don't you see?' she persisted in her quiet voice, 'you're having to do something you don't want to do.' She went on quickly, looking straight ahead of her, 'You don't have to do it for me, you know. I'm—I'm very happy—besides, I'd feel scared at meeting so many strange people.'

'Once you have met them they won't be strange.' The calm

logic of his voice made her want to stamp her feet with temper. 'And to revert to our discussion, I suggest that you buy several dresses of a similar sort to the one you wore at our wedding.' He glanced sideways at her. 'The suit you are wearing is nice, why not get another one like it? And some casual clothes, of course.'

Caroline said tartly: 'Do you want me to change my hairstyle too? It could be tinted and cut and permed and...'

'You will leave your hair exactly as it is.' He added stiffly, 'I like it the way you wear it.'

She was so surprised that she asked quite meekly: 'How much money am I to spend? I could get a great deal with about half of my allowance.' She frowned. 'And will they take my cheque? They don't know me from Adam.'

'I shall go with you. You will have no difficulty in writing cheques for anything you want, Caroline, but this time you will leave me to pay the bill when I come to fetch you.'

'Oh—all right, and I'll pay you back afterwards.'

'I do not wish to be repaid. Caroline, did I not tell you that I was a rich man?'

'No—at least I can't remember that you did. You did say that there was plenty of money, but I don't suppose that's the same as being rich, is it?'

A muscle twitched at the corner of the Professor's firm mouth. 'No,' he agreed quietly, 'it's not quite the same.'

They were in the heavily populated area of the country now, for he had turned away from Amsterdam and was working his way round the city to pick up the motorway to den Haag on its southern side. As they took the road past Leiden which would lead them to the heart of den Haag, Caro said: 'It's very pretty here and there are some beautiful houses, only I like yours much better.'

'Ours,' Radinck reminded her.

The city was full of traffic and people and a bewildering number of narrow streets. The Professor wove his way into the heart of the shopping centre and turned away down a side street to stop after a moment or two before a large shop with elegantly dressed windows. It was quiet there, the houses all round it were old and there were few people about, and Caro took a deep breath of pure pleasure at the thought of spending the next hour or two in the dignified building, spending money without having to count every penny before she did so.

The Professor was known there. An elderly woman with a kind face listened carefully to what he had to say, smiled and nodded and without giving Caro time to do more than say, 'Goodbye,' led her away.

The next hour or so was blissful: Caro, guided discreetly by the elderly lady, became the possessor of a sheepskin jacket because Radinck had told her to buy one, a suit—dogtooth check with a short jacket and a swinging pleated skirt—three Italian print dresses and a finely pleated georgette jersey two-piece because although she didn't think she needed it she couldn't bear not to have it, a dashing bolero and skirt with a silk blouse to go with them and four evening dresses: she would probably never wear more than one of them despite what Radinck had said, but it was hard to call a halt, especially with the elderly lady egging her on in her more than adequate English. And then there was the question of suitable shoes, stockings to go with them, gloves, a little mink hat to go with her coat, and since it seemed a shame not to buy them while she had the opportunity, undies. She was wandering back from that department and had stopped to examine the baby clothes in the children's department when Radinck joined her. She flushed under his mocking eyes and said defensively: 'I was on my way back. They're adding it up—the bill, I mean—I had a few minutes...'

She put down the muslin garment she had been admiring and walked past him. 'It's a lovely shop,' she told him chattily to cover her awkwardness. 'I've bought an awful lot. Did you have a successful consultation?'

He gave some non-committal answer, made some remark to the sales lady and then studied the bill. Caro, watching his face, was unable to discover his feelings about it. His expression gave nothing away, although the total was such that if it had been handed to her she would have screamed at the amount.

But he didn't mention it. The packages and boxes loaded into the boot, Caroline was invited to get into the car, and within ten minutes she found herself in a small, very smart restaurant, drinking a sherry and eyeing a menu with an appetite sharpened by its contents. And not only did Radinck not mention it, but he talked. He told her about the hospital where he had been that morning and the patients he had seen, he even discussed the conditions he had been asked to examine. Just for a while the bland mask slipped a little and Caro, always a good listener, became a perfect one, listening intelligently, asking the right question at the right moment and never once venturing an opinion of her own, and she got her reward, for presently he observed: 'You must forgive me, I am so used to being alone—I have been uttering my thoughts and you must have been bored.'

'No, I wasn't,' said Caro forthrightly. 'I'm interested—you forget that I'm a nurse, but there are bits I don't quite understand. You were telling me about Fröhlich's syndrome—I can't quite see how hypophosphatisia can't be medically treated—if it's just a question of calcium...'

The Professor put down his coffee cup. 'Well, it's like this...'

For a bridegroom of rather more than a week, his conversation was hardly flattering: she might have been sitting there, wearing a sack and a false nose, but to Caro, it was the thin—very thin—edge of the wedge.

Back home again she went straight to her room with one of the maids bearing her various parcels. Radinck was going out again and she hoped he might tell her where, but in this she was disappointed. He was leaving the house without a word before she had reached the top of the staircase. She consoled herself by trying on every single thing she had bought, and it was only as she took off the last of the evening dresses that she remembered her daydream—playing to Radinck in a lovely pink dress, and none of the dresses were pink; she would have to go to den Haag again and buy one. Meanwhile she might do a little practising while she waited for him to come back.

He wasn't coming. Noakes met her in the hall with the news that the Professor had just telephoned to say that he wouldn't be back for dinner, and Caroline, anxious to keep her end up, said airily: 'Oh, yes, Noakes, he did say he might have to stay. I'll have mine on a tray, please, and if none of you have anything better to do, shall we get together over those carols presently?'

She was so disappointed that she could eat hardly any of the delicious food Noakes brought presently, and even though she told herself she was a fool to have expected Radinck to have changed his ways all at once, she was hard put to it to preserve a cheerful face. It helped, of course, discussing the carols with Noakes and Marta and Juffrouw Kropp and the others. She sat at the piano, trying out the various tunes to find those they knew—and when they had, she was thrilled to discover that they sang rather well. With the aid of Noakes and her dictionary, she prevailed upon some of them to sing in harmony—it was a bit ragged, but there were several weeks to go to Christmas and if Radinck was going to be away most evenings, there was ample time to rehearse.

She made herself think about her new wardrobe and the carols as she got ready for bed, banishing Radinck from her mind. Easier said than done: he kept popping up all over the place.

It was after breakfast the following morning that he telephoned her to say that he was going to Brussels and wouldn't be back until the next day, late in the evening. 'So don't wait up for me,' his voice sounded cool over the wire. 'I haven't got Rex with me, so would you mind walking him—once a day will do, he is very adaptable.'

Caroline made her voice equally cool; rather like an efficient secretary's. 'Of course.' She wanted to tell him to take care of himself, to ask what he was going to do in Brussels, but she didn't; she said goodbye in a cheerful voice and rang off.

The day went by on leaden feet. Not even her riding lesson raised her spirits, although she was doing quite well now, trotting sedately round and round the field nearest the stables, with Rex keeping pace with Jemmy. He did the same thing again on the following morning, taking upon himself the role of companion and pacemaker, and because the weather was changing with thunderous skies swallowing the chilly blue, Caroline spent the afternoon in the library, conning her Dutch and knitting away at the sweater, with Waterloo and Rex for company, and because she had to keep up appearances, she changed into one of her new dresses that evening and dined alone at the big table, feeling lost but not allowing that to show, and after an hour working away at the carols again she went up to her room, meeting Noakes' enquiry as to whether she knew at what time the Professor would be back with a serene: 'He said late, Noakes, and I wasn't to wait up. I should lock up if he's not back by eleven o'clock—ask Marta to leave a thermos jug of coffee out, would you?'

It was long after midnight when the Professor returned. Caro, lying wide awake in her bed, heard the gentle growl of the car and saw its lights flash past her windows and presently her husband's firm tread coming up the stairs and going past her door. Only then did she curl up into a ball with Waterloo as close as he could get and sleep.

It was raining when she awoke, and cold and dark as well. None of these mattered, though. Radinck was home again and she might even see him before he left the house—perhaps he would be at breakfast. She got dressed in the new suit and the wildly expensive brogue shoes she had bought to go with it, and went downstairs.

He wasn't there, and Noakes, remarking on her early appearance, observed, 'Back late, wasn't 'e, ma'am? I 'eard him come in—ever so quiet.'

'Yes, I know, though I was still awake, Noakes.'

'Pity 'e 'ad ter go again so early—no proper rest. 'E works too 'ard.'

'Yes, Noakes, I know he does.' She gave the elderly face a sweet smile. 'Noakes, it's too wet for me to go riding, I suppose?'

'Lor, yes, ma'am—best stay indoors. Juffrouw Kropp wanted to ask about some curtains that want renewing.'

'I'll see her after breakfast and then go to the kitchens.'

It was still only ten o'clock by the time she had fulfilled her household duties and the rain had lessened a little. 'I'm going for a walk,' she told Noakes. 'I won't take Rex with me and I won't go far—I just feel like some exercise.'

She put her new hooded raincoat on over the new suit, found her gloves and let herself out of a side door. The rain was falling steadily and there was a snarling wind, but they suited her mood. She walked briskly across the gardens, into the fields behind the wall, and joined the country lane, leading away to a village in the distance. She had walked barely half a mile when she saw a slow-moving group coming towards her—a cart drawn by a stout pony and surrounded by a family of tinkers. They were laughing and shouting to each other, not minding the weather, carefree and happy. Except for a small donkey tied to the back of the cart; it wasn't only wet, it was in a shocking condition, its ribs starting through its dirty matted coat, and it was heavily in foal. It was being ruthlessly beaten with a switch wielded by a shambling youth, and Caro, now abreast of the whole party, cried 'Stop!' so furiously that they did. She took the switch from the youth and flung it into the canal by the side of the lane, then she mustered her Dutch. '*Hoeveel?*' she asked imperiously, pointing at the deplorable beast, and then with a flash of inspiration, she pointed to herself and added: 'Baroness Thoe van Erckelens.'

She was pleased to see that the name meant something to
them. The leader of the party, a scruffy middle-aged man,
gave her a respectful look, even if a bit doubtful. Caroline
had to dispel the doubt; she turned and pointed again, this
time towards Huis Thoe, just visible behind its high wall.
While they were all staring at it she went over to the dejected
little beast and began to untie the rope round its neck, and
when they would have stopped her, held up a firm little hand.
'Ik koop,' she told them, and waved towards the house, the
rope in her hand, hoping that 'how much' and 'I'll buy' would
be sufficient to make them agree, for for the life of her she
couldn't think of anything else to say to the point. Yes, one
more word. She ordered briskly 'Kom' and had the satisfaction of seeing them bunch together round the cart once more,
obviously waiting for her to lead the way.

She didn't know anything about donkeys, and she prayed
that this one would answer to the gentle tug she gave its worn
bridle. It did, and she made her way to the front, not hurrying
because the donkey's hooves were in a frightful state. It took
longer to go back too, because she thought the tinkers might
be more impressed if she went in through the main gates, and
every yard of the way she was hiding panic that they might
come to their senses and make off with the donkey before she
could reach home. But the gates were reached at last and she
singled out the scruffy man, beckoning him to follow her,
leaving the rest of them grouped in the drive staring at them.
The man began to mutter to himself before they reached the
sweep before the house, but Caroline didn't listen. She was
planning what she would do; open the door and shout for
Noakes to mind the donkey and keep an eye on the man while
she fetched some money—and that was another problem; how
much did one pay for a worn out starving animal? Perhaps
Noakes would know.

The Professor, home early for his lunch and thus breaking
a rule he had adhered to for years without knowing quite why,
was standing at the drawing-room windows, staring out over

the grounds, aware of disappointment because Caro wasn't home. He frowned at the dripping landscape before him and then frowned again, staring even harder. Unless his splendid eyesight deceived him, his wife, a most disreputable man and a very battered donkey were coming up his drive, and what was more, there were people clustered round the gates, peering in. Something about the small resolute figure marching up to the front door sent him striding to open it and down the steps to meet her.

Caro, almost at the door and seeing her husband's vast form coming down the steps with deliberate speed, felt a wave of relief so strong that she could have burst into tears. She swallowed them back and cried: 'Oh, Radinck, I'm so glad you're home!' She had to raise her voice because he was barely within earshot. 'I've bought this poor little donkey, but I don't know how much to pay the man—I got him to come with me while I fetched the money. I thought Noakes would know, but now you're here you can tell me.' She looked up at him with complete confidence and added, just in case he didn't realise the urgency of the occasion: 'She's a jenny and she's going to foal soon; they were beating her, and just look at her hooves!'

The Professor looked, running a gentle hand over the bruised back, bending to examine each wretched neglected hoof, then he straightened up to tower over the tinker.

Caro couldn't understand a word he was saying. His voice was quiet and unhurried, but the tinker looked at first cowed and then downright scared. Finally, the Professor produced his notecase, selected what he wanted from its contents and handed them to the man, who grabbed them and, looking considerably shaken, made off as fast as his legs would carry him.

Caro watched him join his family at the gates and disappear. 'That was splendid of you, Radinck,' she said in deep satisfaction. 'I couldn't understand what you said, of course, but you scared him, didn't you? Oh, I'm so very glad you were here... I'll pay you back in a minute, but I ought to see to this poor thing first. What did you say to that horrid man?'

Her husband looked down at her, a half smile twitching his mouth. 'Enough to make him very careful how he treats any more animals he may own in future, and allow me to give her to you as a gift.' The half smile became a real one and she smiled back at him in delight. 'Tell me, how did you get him to come here?'

She told him and he laughed, a bellow of genuine amusement which set her hopeful heart racing, although all she said was, 'We ought to get in out of this rain. Where shall I take her?' And before he could answer: 'There's that barn next to the stables where the hay's kept...'

He gave her a questioning look. 'I didn't know you were interested in the stables—yes, the barn would do very well.'

Caroline began to lead the animal towards the back of the house. 'I'm not sure what donkeys eat. I'll ask Jan—he'll get me some carrots, though.'

Radinck gave her an amused glance. 'Jan too?' he asked, and then: 'She can go into the south field with the horses once she's rested.'

They were halfway there when Caro asked: 'What did you mean-"Jan too"?'

He answered her carelessly: 'Oh, you seem to have a way with people, don't you? The servants fall over themselves to please you and now Jan, who never does anything for anyone unless he wants to.'

'He's a dear old man,' declared Caro warmly, remembering Jan's deep elderly voice rumbling out the carols of an evening. 'He had a frightful cold, you know—I told him what to do for it.' She glanced sideways at him. 'I hope you don't mind?'

He sounded irritable. 'I don't suppose it would make any difference whether I minded or not. Give me that rope, and be good enough to go up to the house and ask Noakes to get Jan and young Willem, then telephone the vet and tell him to come out as soon as he can to examine an ill-treated donkey in foal.'

'Yes, of course.' Caroline smiled happily at his rather irritable face. 'I'll go at once. Radinck, what shall we call her?'

He was staring at her with hard eyes as though he couldn't bear the sight of her. 'What could be more appropriate than Caro?' he wanted to know mockingly.

She hadn't taken a dozen steps before he was beside her, his hands on her shoulders so that she had to stop.

'I'm sorry, that was a rotten thing to say.'

She had gone a little white and the tears were thick in her throat, but she managed a smile. 'As a matter of fact it's a very good name for her.' She added earnestly: 'It doesn't matter, really it doesn't.'

'It does—you didn't deserve it, Caroline.' His voice was gentle. 'What shall we call her? We have a Waterloo and a Rex and the kitchen cat is called Anja—how about Queenie, and if the foal is a boy we can call him Prince.'

Caro had no doubt that he was trying to placate her hurt feelings, and although it wasn't much the tiny flame of hope she kept flickering deep down inside her brightened a little; at least he had realised that he had hurt her. She smiled at him a bit crookedly. 'That's a splendid name,' she agreed. 'I'll get Noakes.'

She slipped away before he could say anything else and took care not to return until she saw Jan and Willem going towards the stables.

Radinck had fetched a bucket of water and some oats while she had been gone and now the three men stood watching the donkey making a meal. She was still happily munching when Mijnheer Stagsma arrived. Radinck explained briefly what had happened, introduced Caro and waited patiently while the vet wished her happiness in her marriage, congratulated her on her rescue of the donkey, hoped that his wife would have the pleasure of calling on her soon and enquired how she liked her new home.

He was a youngish man with a friendly face. Caro would have enjoyed talking to him, but out of the corner of her eye she saw her husband's bland face watching them. He was growing impatient, so she brought their cheerful little talk to a friendly end and indicated the patient.

Mijnheer Stagsma took a long time, muttering to himself and occasionally saying something to the Professor. At length he came upright again.

'Nothing serious, I think—starved, of course, but that can be dealt with, and I'll deal with those hooves as soon as she's stronger. I should think she'll have the foal in a week or so—it's hard to tell in her present state. I'll give her a couple of injections and some ointment for those sores on her back. Who'll be looking after her?'

Caro, striving to understand what he said, looked at Radinck. He answered the vet, spoke to Willem who grinned and nodded and then turned to Caro, telling her what the vet had said.

'Oh, good—Willem doesn't mind feeding her? I don't...'

'No, not you, Caroline. You may visit her, of course, and take her out when she is better, but Willem will tend her and clean out the barn.'

She supposed that being a baroness barred her from such chores. 'If you say so,' she said happily, 'but I simply must learn Dutch as quickly as possible.'

The glimmer of a smile touched her husband's face. 'You seem to manage very well—but I'll arrange for you to have lessons.'

They wished the vet goodbye, standing together on the sweep as he drove down the drive and out of sight.

'Oh, dear—should I have asked him in for a drink?' asked Caro.

'I already did so, but he couldn't stop—he's a very busy man.'

'And nice—so friendly.' She didn't see the look her husband shot at her. 'May I go back and look at Queenie?'

He turned away to go into the house. 'There is no need to ask my permission, Caroline. I am not your gaoler—you are free to do exactly what you like as long as you don't interfere with my work.'

'Not your work,' said Caro, suddenly passionate, 'your life—and never fear, Radinck, I'll take care never to do that.'

She marched away, her chin in the air, in one of her rare tempers.

But her tempers didn't last long. Within half an hour they were lunching together and although she didn't apologise for her outburst she tried to be friendly. She supposed that it was for Noakes' benefit that Radinck met her conversational efforts more than half way. It was a disappointment when he told her that he wouldn't be home for dinner. She spent her afternoon wrestling with an ever-lengthening list of Dutch words and the evening coaching her choir once again, and before she went to bed she went down to the stables to take a look at Queenie. The little donkey looked better already, she thought. She pulled the ragged ears gently, offered a carrot and went back to the house, where she mooned around for another hour or so before going to bed much later than usual, hoping that Radinck would come back before she did. But there was no sign of him. She fell asleep at last and didn't hear him return in the small hours of the morning.

She was up early and with Waterloo in attendance went down to see how Queenie had fared. Willem was already there, cleaning out the barn and feeding her, and Caro, trying out some of her carefully acquired Dutch, made out that the donkey had improved considerably, but Willem was busy and she didn't like to hinder him, so she wandered off again into the crisp morning—just right for a ride, she decided, and with Waterloo trotting beside her, hurried back for breakfast.

Jan was waiting for her when she got to the stables and Jemmy greeted her with a toss of the head and a playful nip. Caroline mounted his plump back and walked him out of the yard and into the field beyond. Walk round once, Jan had told her, then trot round once. She did so, watched by the old man, and then because she was feeling confident and enjoying herself she poked Jemmy's fat sides with her heels and started off again. Jemmy was enjoying himself too; his trot broke into a canter and Caro, her hair flying, let out a whoopee of delight. They were three quarters of the way round the field when she saw Radinck standing beside Jan.

CHAPTER SIX

THERE WAS ONLY one thing to do and that was to go on. Caroline finished circling the field and pulled up untidily in front of Radinck. Jan was standing beside him, but she couldn't tell from the craggy old face if anything had been said. To be on the safe side she leaned down from her saddle. 'Don't you dare be angry with Jan!' she hissed fiercely. 'I made him teach me—he thought I was doing it as a lovely surprise for you.'

'And were you?' It was impossible to tell if Radinck was angry or not.

'Well, yes—but not just for you. I thought that as you're a baron and have a lot of posh friends you might be ashamed of me if I couldn't do all the things they do...'

The gleam in Radinck's eyes became very pronounced, but he answered gravely: 'That was very thoughtful of you, Caroline. Were you going to use it as an argument in favour of inviting my—er—posh friends here?'

He was impossible! She looked away from him at the gentle countryside around them. 'No,' she said evenly, 'I promised that I wouldn't interfere with your life, didn't I? You seem to have forgotten that. It was only that I didn't want to let you down.'

'I beg your pardon, you are...' He stopped and started again. 'I should enjoy your company each morning before breakfast.'

'Would you really?' Her eyes searched his face. 'I saw you the first morning we were here, you know, that's when I made up my mind to learn to ride. But I'm not very good, it was lucky I didn't fall off just now.'

'Jan has taught you very well.' Radinck turned and spoke to the old man, who grinned at him and answered at some length, and then turned back to her. 'Jan says that all you need now is practice. It is a pity that I have an appointment this morning, otherwise I would have ridden with you.' His gaze swept over her. 'But I think you must have the right clothes. I'm free after lunch until the early evening. I'll take you into Leeuwarden and get you kitted up.'

Caro stammered a little. 'Oh, that would be s-super, but isn't it taking up your time? If you tell me where to go, I c-could go on my own.'

'We'll go together, Caroline,' and just as she was relishing this he added briskly: 'You would have no idea what to get, in the first place, and the shop is extremely hard to find.'

He was right about the shop; it was tucked away in a narrow street lined with old gabled houses, squeezed between a shirtmakers and a gentleman's hatters. Following Radinck inside, Caro wondered where on earth the customers went, and then discovered that the narrow little shop went back and back, one room opening into the next. The owner of the shop knew Radinck; he was ushered into a small room at the back, its walls lined with shelves stacked with cloth and boxes of riding boots and beautifully folded jodhpurs. Here he was given a chair while Caro was whisked into a still smaller room where, with an elderly lady to observe the conventions, she was fitted with boots, several white sweaters and shirts, a riding hat, a crop and a pair of jodhpurs, and finally the jacket. Looking at herself in the mirror she hardly recognised her image. 'Oh, very elegant,' she said out loud, and, obedient to the old tailor's beckoning finger, went rather shyly to show herself to Radinck. She stood quietly while he looked her over.

'Very nice, Caroline,' and then, to her surprise: 'What size are you?'

'In England I'm a size ten, I don't know what I am in Holland.' She was on the point of asking him why he wanted to know and then thought better of it; instead she said, 'Thank you very much, Radinck.'

He gave her a half smile. 'What else can you do, Caroline?'

She gave him a surprised look. 'Me? Well, nothing really—I can swim, but only just, if you know what I mean, and I can play the piano a bit and dance a bit...'

'You drive a car?'

She shook her head. 'No—I've never needed to, you see.'

'You shall have lessons and later on a car of your own. Tennis?'

'Well, yes.' She added waspishly: 'I hope I've passed.'

He turned away from her. 'You would have done that even if you could do none of these things. If you're quite satisfied with the things we'll get them packed up and I'll drive you back.'

She had deserved the snub, she supposed. She wondered for the hundredth time why Radinck had married her; she hadn't been a very good bargain.

Fairmindedness made her stop there; he had wanted a sheet-anchor and she had said that she would be one. She belonged in the background of his life, always there when he wanted her, and it would be a good thing if she remembered that more often.

On the way back she did her best. 'I expect,' she said carefully, 'that now you've had time to think about it, you'd rather I didn't ride with you in the mornings—it's something you hadn't reckoned on, isn't it? And that wasn't why I wanted to learn to ride,' she finished with a rush.

He had turned off the motorway and had slowed the pace a little, because the road was narrow. 'I didn't think it was; shall we try it out for a day or two and see what happens?'

Caroline agreed quietly and just as quietly wished him goodbye presently. He had already told her that he had an appointment and she forbore from asking him if he would be home for dinner. She was surprised when he told her that he would see her about seven o'clock.

She wore one of the new dresses, a silk jersey in old rose with a demure stand-up collar and long sleeves, and when he

got back she was sitting by the fire in the drawing-room en-
grossed in some tapestry work she had bought as an alternative to the sweater. She wished him a demure good evening
and set a group of stitches with care. There was a pleasantly
excited glow under the new dress, for Radinck had paused in
the doorway and was looking at her in a way he had never
looked at her before. The stitches went all wrong, but this was
no time to look anything but serene and casual. She went on
stitching, the needle going in and out, just as though she knew
what she was doing; there would be a lot of unpicking to do
later. Radinck advanced into the room, offered her a drink
and went to fetch it from the sofa table under the window.
As he handed it to her he observed, with the air of a man
trying out words he had almost forgotten: 'You look pretty,
Caroline.'

The glow rushed to her cheeks, but she answered compos-
edly: 'Thank you—this is one of my new dresses, it is charming, isn't it?'

'I was referring to you, Caroline.'

'Oh, how kind.' That sounded silly, so she added: 'The
right clothes make such a difference, you know.'

She bent to scratch Rex's woolly ear and then offered the
same service to Waterloo, sitting beside the dog. 'I went to
see Queenie this evening,' she told him. 'It's a wonder how
she's picked up, and Willem's done wonders with her coat
already.'

'I've just come from there—she's reacting very nicely to
the antibiotic.' Radinck sat down in the great winged chair
opposite her, his long legs stretched out, his glass in his hand,
and when she looked up briefly it was to find him staring at
her again, his eyes very bright. It seemed a good idea to apply
herself to her tapestry and by the time Noakes came to an-
nounce dinner was ready she had made a fine mess of it.

And to her surprised delight, after dinner, instead of going
to his study or out again, Radinck followed her into the drawing-room and sat drinking his coffee, giving no sign of want-

ing to go anywhere else. Her fingers shook as she fell upon the tapestry once again, but her face was quiet enough as she gave him a quick peep. He had stretched himself out comfortably and was reading a newspaper—perhaps he had forgotten that she was there.

But he hadn't, and presently he began to talk; observations on the news, describing an interesting case he had had at the hospital that day and going on to ask her if she would like to start Dutch lessons straight away as he had found someone suitable to teach her.

She replied suitably to everything he said and presently, loath to do so, for she could have sat there for ever with him, she declared her intention of going to bed; it would never do for him to discover that she was eager for his company. She gave him a quiet goodnight and went to the door, aware as she went through it that he was looking at her again. She was half way along the gallery above the hall when he called to her, and she stopped and leaned over the balustrade to ask 'Yes, Radinck?'

'You have forgotten that we are to ride together in the morning?'

'No, Radinck. Shall I meet you at the stables?'

'No, I shall be here at half past seven.' He said goodnight again as she turned away.

Contrary to her expectations Caroline slept dreamlessly until she was wakened by Ilke with her morning tea. She drank it while she dressed, afraid of being late. Actually she raced downstairs with a couple of minutes to spare, to find Radinck waiting for her. She thought he looked splendid in his riding kit and longed to tell him so. He wished her good morning and without wasting time they went to the stables. It was almost light with a clear sky and a cold wind and the grass was touched with frost. 'If it gets much colder you will have to stop riding—once the ground gets too hard there's more chance of a toss.'

She said, 'Yes, Radinck,' meekly. Frost or no frost, she would go on riding as long as he did.

The stables were lighted and Willem was there, busy with Jemmy and Rufus, Radinck's great bay horse. Caro, her fingers crossed, contrived to mount neatly and watched while Radinck swung himself into the saddle, whistled to Rex, and led the way out of the yard. He hadn't fussed over her at all, merely wanted to know if she were ready and carelessly told her to straighten her back. 'We'll go over the fields as far as the lane and go round the outside of the wall,' he told her. 'Don't trot Jemmy in the fields, but you may do so in the lane.'

Caro, completely overshadowed by man and horse, craned her neck to answer him. 'Yes, very well, but I expect you like a gallop, don't you?'

'Yes, I do—but not this morning. I must find a quiet little mare for you and then we can gallop together—it hardly seems fair to expect Jemmy to do more than trot.'

She patted the pony's neck. 'He's a darling—wouldn't he mind if I rode another horse?'

Radinck laughed. 'He's been here for years—he's quite elderly now, he'll be good company for Queenie and her foal.'

They reached the first field and once out of it started to trot, and presently when they reached the gate to the lane beyond Radinck said: 'Now try a canter, Caroline.'

She acquitted herself very well, although by the time they got back she was shaking with nerves, terrified that she would fall off or do something stupid, but she didn't, and had the pleasure of hearing her husband say as they went indoors: 'That went very well—do you care to ride each morning while the weather's fine?'

She tried not to sound eager. 'Oh, please, if you'd like to.'

He turned to give her a suddenly cool look. 'I should hardly have asked you if I hadn't wanted to, Caroline. Shall we have breakfast in fifteen minutes?'

'Yes, I'll tell Juffrouw Kropp.' She went along the passage

to the kitchen, gave her message and went upstairs to shower and change, her feelings mixed. Radinck had seemed so friendly, then suddenly he had drawn back and looked at her as though he didn't like her after all. She was in two minds not to go down to breakfast, but if she didn't he might think that she minded being snubbed... She changed into a tweed skirt and sweater, tied her hair back and went to join him.

He was already at the table when she got downstairs, but he got up to draw out her chair, handed her her letters, and went back to reading his own. It was to be a silent meal, she guessed; for the time being she wasn't a sheet-anchor at all, only a nuisance. She murmured a cheerful good morning to Noakes when he came with fresh coffee, and immersed herself in her post—a letter from Clare, excitedly telling her the news that she was engaged, one from her aunt, asking vaguely if she were happy and regretting that she hadn't been able to attend the wedding, and a card from Sister Pringle inviting her to her wedding in the New Year. Caroline was wondering what to do about it when Radinck leaned across and handed her a pile of opened letters. 'Invitations,' he told her. 'Will you answer them?'

She glanced through them and counted six and looked up in surprise. 'But Radinck, how strange! I mean, we've been here for almost two weeks and no one has even telephoned, and now all these on the same day.'

His smile mocked her. 'My dear girl, have you forgotten that we are supposed to be newlyweds? It would hardly have been decent to have called on us or invited us anywhere for at least a fortnight.' He tossed a letter across the table to her. 'Here's a letter from Rebecca—Tiele's wife. She wants us to go over for drinks soon—she will ring you some time today.'

'Am I to accept?'

He looked faintly surprised. 'Of course. Tiele is a close friend, and I hope you and Rebecca will be friends too. As for the others, if I tell Anna to type out the correct answer in Dutch perhaps you would copy it and get them sent off.'

Caroline glanced through them; three invitations to drinks, one to the burgermeester's reception in Leeuwarden and two for evening parties.

'But, Radinck—' she began, and stopped so he looked up rather impatiently.

'Well?'

'You don't like going out,' she observed, not mincing her words. 'You said so—you like peace and quiet and time to read and...'

'You do not need to remind me, my dear Caroline, I am aware of what I like. However, there are certain conventions which must be observed. We will accept the invitations we receive, and at Christmas I will—I beg your pardon—we will give a large party. By then you will have met everyone who is acquainted with me and we can revert to a normal life here. You will have had the opportunity of making any friends you wish and doubtless you will find life sufficiently entertaining.'

Words bubbled and boiled on Caro's tongue, and she went quite red in the face choking them back. The awful thought that she was fighting a losing battle assailed her, but not for long; she had had a glimpse just once or twice of Radinck's other self hidden away behind all that ill humour. She told herself that it needed patience and all the love she had for him, and she had plenty of both.

Rebecca telephoned later that morning and Caro liked her voice immediately. 'We're not far from you,' said Rebecca, 'and I've been dying to come and see you, but Tiele said you were entitled to a couple of weeks' peace and quiet together. Will you come over for drinks? Could Radinck manage to-morrow evening, do you think—I'm going to invite you to dinner too, but if he's got something on, ring me back, will you, and we'll be content with drinks. Have you settled down?'

'Yes, thank you, though I wish I could speak Dutch, but everyone's so kind.'

'Radinck told Tiele that you were managing very well—
have you started lessons yet?'

'No, but Radinck said he'd found someone to teach me.'

Rebecca giggled. 'Well, you've not had much time to
bother about lessons, have you?'

She rang off presently and Caro went to her room and
looked through her wardrobe, wondering what she should
wear. She came to the perfectly normal female conclusion that
she hadn't anything, and then changed her mind. The rose
pink jersey would do; it had had a good effect the other evening, and after all, it was Radinck she wanted to notice her,
not Tiele and Rebecca.

She broached the subject of going to dinner when Radinck
came home for lunch and managed not to show her disappointment when he said that it was quite impossible. He had
a hospital governors' meeting to attend at eight o'clock; he
would drive her back from the Raukema van den Ecks and
go straight on to the hospital where he would get a meal later.
He looked at her sharply as he said it, but she met the look
calmly, remarking that it would be nice to meet another English girl. 'She sounded sweet,' she declared. 'Would you like
your coffee here or in the drawing-room?'

'I'm due back in ten minutes—I won't wait. Don't wait
dinner for me either, Caroline; I'll have some sandwiches
when I get back.' He was at the door when he paused and
asked: 'Will you come riding tomorrow morning?'

'Well, yes, I should like to. The same time?'

He nodded as he went out of the room.

Caroline didn't see him for the rest of that day, but he was
waiting for her when she went downstairs the next morning.
The weather was being kind, cold and windy but dry, and the
skies were clear. She acquitted herself very well, although
Radinck had very little to say as they rode across the fields
and after a few remarks about Queenie and a request that she
should be ready that evening by half past six he fell silent. It
was when they had returned to the house and were crossing

the hall that he observed that he would be unable to get home
for lunch. He spoke in his usual austere way, but she thought
that she detected regret and her spirits rose.

They stayed that way too. The morning filled with her visit
to see Marta, a solemn consultation with Juffrouw Kropp
about the renewal of some kitchen equipment, a visit to
Queenie, now looking almost plump, and an hour at the piano.
And the afternoon went quickly too. By half past five Caroline
was upstairs in her room trying out different hair-styles and
making up her face. In the end she toned down the make-up
and decided to keep to her usual hair style, partly because she
was afraid that if she attempted anything else it would dis-
integrate half way through the evening. The pink jersey dress
was entirely satisfactory, though. She gave a final long look
in the pier glass, and went down to the sitting-room.

It wasn't quite half past six and she hadn't expected Radinck to be waiting for her, but he was, in an elegant dark
suit, looking as though he hadn't just done a day's work at
the hospital, only sat about in idleness. Caroline wondered
how he did it. He allowed himself very little recreation. One
day, she thought with real terror, he would have a coronary...

He got up as she went in, took her coat from her and held
it while she got into it and they went out together. Beyond
greeting her he had said nothing and nor had she, but once
on the sweep she was surprised into exclaiming: 'But where's
the Aston Martin?'

There was another car standing there and she went closer
to see what it was. A Panther de Ville; she had only seen one
or two before. Now she admired the elegance and choked over
its price. She hadn't quite believed Radinck when he had said
that he was rich, now she decided that she had been mistaken.
Only someone with a great deal of money could afford to
buy, let alone run such a motor car. 'What a lovely car,' she
said faintly. 'Is it yours?'

'Yes.' He opened the door and she got in, cudgelling her
brains to find some way of making him say more than yes or

no. She was still worrying about it as he drove off and since he had very little to say during the brief journey, she had time to worry some more. Perhaps it was a good thing when they arrived and she had to empty her head of worries and respond to the friendly welcome from Tiele and his wife.

Rebecca, Caro was relieved to see, wasn't pretty; beautifully made up, exquisitely dressed, but not pretty, although it was apparent at once that her husband considered her the most beautiful woman in the world.

They took to each other at once and Caro was borne away to see the new baby before they had drinks. 'A darling,' declared Caro, and meant it.

'Yes, he is,' agreed his doting mother, 'but he keeps us busy, I can tell you, although we've got a marvellous nanny.' She giggled enchantingly. 'The poor dear doesn't get a look in!' She tucked an arm into Caro's as they went down the stairs. 'Tiele's a splendid father—he's a nice husband too. Radinck's a dear, isn't he? And that's a silly question!' They had reached the drawing-room and she laughingly repeated her remark to the men. 'As though Caro's going to admit anything!' she declared. Caro was glad to see that Radinck laughed too, although he didn't look at her, which was a good thing because she had got rather pink in the face.

There seemed to be a great deal to talk about and she found herself listening to Radinck's voice, warm and friendly, teasing Becky, exchanging views with Tiele, including her punctiliously in the talk so that they gave what she hoped was a splendid impression of a happily married couple. She was sorry to leave, but since they were to see each other again at the burgermeester's reception, she was able to echo her husband's 'Tot ziens' cheerfully enough. But he showed no inclination to discuss their evening, indeed he didn't speak until they were almost half way home.

'You enjoyed your evening?' he asked her. 'You liked Becky?'

'Very much; she's sweet, and such a darling little baby.'

Her husband grunted and she wished she hadn't said that; she hurried on to cover the little silence: 'It's nice that we shall see each other at the reception.'

'Yes. You will also meet a number of my friends there. You answered the invitations?'

'Yes, and three more came with the afternoon post.'

'Will you leave them on the hall table? I'll make sure they're friends and not just acquaintances.'

'You're not coming in before you go—wherever you're going?'

'I have no time.' She couldn't help but notice how cold his voice had become. She sighed very softly and didn't speak again until they reached the house, when she said hurriedly: 'No, don't get out, Radinck, I'm sure you're pressed for time.'

She jumped out of the car and ran up the steps where the watchful Noakes was already standing by the open door. 'We'll ride in the morning?' Radinck called after her. Caroline had been afraid he wasn't going to say that, so, careful not to sound eager, she said over her shoulder: 'I'll see you then,' and ran indoors.

She saw him much sooner than that, though. Left alone, she had whipped down to the stables to see how Queenie was, gone round the outside of the house with Rex, who was feeling hurt because Radinck had gone without him, had her dinner, conducted her choir and then gone upstairs to bed. She had been there two hours or more sitting up against her pillows reviewing her evening when she heard Queenie's voice—not loud, not nearly loud enough to rouse everyone else in the house, with their rooms right on the other side. Nor would Willem hear her, living as he did in a small cottage on the estate boundary with his mother. The noise came again and Caro got out of bed, put on her quilted dressing gown, whipped a pair of boots from the closet, and crept through the house. Radinck wasn't in and she had no idea when he would return. She could take a look at Queenie and if things weren't going right, she could get a message to Willem or old Jan, who would know what to do, and if necessary she could get Mijnheer Stagsma.

She let herself out of the side door nearest the stables, into the very cold, clear night, and, glad of her boots but wishing she had put on something thicker than a dressing gown, made her way to the yard. There was a light in the barn. She switched it on and went to peer at the donkey. Queenie looked back at her with gentle eyes. She was lying down on her bed of straw and even to Caro, who didn't know much about it, it was obvious that she was about to produce her foal. But whether she was in need of help was another thing. She might have been calling for company; after all, it was a lonely business, giving birth.

Caro knelt down by Queenie's head and rubbed the long furry ears; for the moment she wasn't sure what to do. 'I'll wait just for a few minutes,' she told Queenie, 'and if something doesn't start to happen by then I'll go and get help. It's a pity that Radinck isn't here, but even if he were, I wouldn't like to bother him. You see, Queenie, he doesn't...' Her soft voice spiralled into a small shriek as her husband spoke from the dimness of the door.

'I saw the light—it's Queenie, isn't it?' He came and stood beside the pair of them, and it was difficult to see his face clearly. Caroline nodded, her heart still thumping with fright, and he took off his car coat and his jacket, rolled up his shirt sleeves and knelt down to take a closer look at the donkey. 'Any minute now,' he pronounced. 'Everything looks fine. How long have you been here?'

'Ten minutes, perhaps a little longer.'

'Did she wake you up?'

She answered without much thought. 'No—I hadn't been to sleep.'

He had his head bent. 'It's almost two o'clock.' He turned to look at her then, a slow look taking in her tousled hair and the dressing gown. 'My dear good girl, it's winter! You should have put on something warmer than that.'

'I am wearing my boots,' Caro declared as though that was a sufficient answer, and added: 'I didn't want to waste time in case Queenie was ill.'

'And what did you intend to do?' he wanted to know.

'Well, I said I'd wait just a few minutes and then if she went on groaning and looking distressed I thought I'd go and get Jan up—only he's old, I didn't want to bother him.'

He put a gentle hand on the beast's heaving flanks. 'You didn't want to bother me either, Caroline.' His voice was quiet.

'No.' For something to do she ran her fingers through her untidy hair.

'Leave your hair.' He still spoke quietly and she dropped her hands in astonishment. After a moment he said: 'Look!'

The foal was enchanting. 'We shall be able to call him Prince,' observed Radinck as they watched him get to his wobbly legs and nuzzle his mother. 'Caroline, do you think you could make some hot mash? Willem should have it ready for the morning over in the far corner. There's a Primus— just warm it up, Queenie could do with it now. I'll stay here for a minute or two just to make sure everything's as it should be.'

Caroline went obediently, found the mash and the stove and waited while it heated, and presently went back with it to find that Radinck had fetched a bucket of water which Queenie was drinking thirstily. She gobbled down the mash too, standing between the pair of them. She was still far from being in the pink of condition, but she was clean and combed and content. Caro, sitting back on her heels so that she could see more of the foal, observed: 'Oh, isn't it lovely? She's so happy.' She caught her breath. 'What would have happened to her if we hadn't taken her in?'

'Oh, she would have been left in a field to fend for herself.' Radinck didn't add to that because Caro's eyes were filled with tears.

'In a couple of days she shall go out into the fields with

the horses. She's almost strong enough—they like company, you know, and horses like them.'

Queenie finished her meal, arranged herself comfortably on the straw with the foal beside her and wagged her ears. 'She's telling us we can go,' said Radinck. 'She'll do very well until Willem comes.' He pulled Caro to her feet, draped his jacket round her and walked her back through the moonlight night to the side door. Inside she would have gone to bed, but he kept an arm round her shoulders. 'I have a fancy for a cup of tea,' he declared. 'Let's go to the kitchen and make one—it will warm you, too.'

He seemed to know where everything was. Caro, her arms in the sleeves of his jacket to make things a little easier, got mugs, sugar and milk while he fetched a tea-pot and a tea canister, found a loaf and some butter and put them on the table. 'Didn't you have any dinner?' asked Caro.

'Yes—only it was a very dainty one. I have been famished for the last hour.'

'Oh, that's a terrible feeling,' agreed Caro, 'and one always thinks of all the nicest things to eat. I've often…' She stopped herself just in time. He wouldn't want to know that she had sometimes been rather hungry; hospital meals cost money and although one could eat adequately enough if one were careful, there was never anything left over for chocolate clairs and steak and sole bonne femme.

'Well?' asked Radinck.

'Nothing.' She busied herself pouring the tea while he sliced bread and spread it lavishly with butter.

Caroline hadn't enjoyed a meal as much for a long time. It was as though Radinck was a different person. She wasn't just having a glimpse of him as he really was, he was letting her get to know him. She found herself talking to him as though she had known him all her life. She had forgotten to worry that he might, at any moment, revert to his normal severe manner. Everything was wonderful. She sat there, eating slices of bread and butter, oblivious of her tatty appearance, talking about Queenie, and her riding and how she was going to learn to speak Dutch and what fun it was to have found a friend in Becky. And Radinck did nothing to stop her—indeed, he encouraged her with cleverly put questions which she answered with all the spontaneous simplicity of a small girl. It was the old-fashioned wall clock striking a ponderous three which brought her up short. She began to collect up the mugs and plates, stammering a little. 'I'm sorry—I've kept you out of bed, I don't know what came over me.'

He took the things from her and put them back on the table. 'Leave those. Will you be too tired to ride in the morning?'

'Tired? Heavens, no, I wouldn't miss…' She stopped herself again. 'The mornings are lovely at this time of year,' she observed rather woodenly.

Radinck was staring down at her. 'I must agree with you, Caroline—the mornings are lovely.' He turned away abruptly and went over to the sink with the tea-pot and she watched him, idly sticking her hands into the pockets of his jacket which she still wore draped round her. There was something in one of them. She just had time to pull it almost out to look at it before he turned round; she only had a glimpse, but it was enough. It was a handkerchief—a woman's handkerchief, new but crumpled.

They walked out of the kitchen together and up the stairs, and all the way Caroline told herself that she had no reason to mind so much. She had taken her hands out of the pockets as though they were full of hot coals and handed him his jacket with a murmur of thanks, aware of a pain almost physical. If she was going to feel like this every time she encountered some small sign that she wasn't the only woman in his life, then she might just as well give up at once. Of course, the handkerchief could belong to an aunt or a cousin or…he had no relations living close by. It could belong, said a nasty little voice at the back of her head, to whoever it was he went to see almost every evening in the week. Then why had he married her? Couldn't the handkerchief's owner have been a sheet-anchor too? She thought of herself as a shabby, reliable coat, always at hand hanging on the back door, necessary but never worn anywhere but in the back yard in bad weather, whereas a really smart coat would be taken from the closet with care and pride and displayed to one's friends.

At the top of the stairs she wished him goodnight and was quite unprepared for his sudden swoop and his hard, quick kiss. She turned without a word and fled into her room, aware that any other girl with her wits about her would have known how to deal with the situation.

CHAPTER SEVEN

IF CARO HADN'T BEEN so sleepy she might have lain awake and pondered Radinck's behaviour, but beyond a fleeting sense of elation mixed with a good deal of puzzlement, there was no time to think at all; she was asleep as her head touched the pillow. And in the morning there was no time for anything but getting dressed by half past seven. As she went downstairs she did wonder if she would feel awkward when she saw him, but that need not have worried her. He offered her a cool good morning, led her down to the stables, watched her mount, had a word with Willem about Queenie, and led the way into the fields. They rode in almost complete silence and on their return, even the sight of Queenie and her foal called forth no more than a further businesslike discussion with Willem as to their welfare. They were back to square one, thought Caro. Last night had been an episode to be forgotten or at least ignored. She remembered the hanky with a pang of sheer envy, subdued it with difficulty and loitered to add her own remarks to Willem, who, with the rest of the staff at Huis Thoe, made a point of understanding her peculiar Dutch.

By the time she got down to breakfast, Radinck was almost ready to leave. Caroline wasn't in the least surprised when he mentioned that he wouldn't be home for lunch. She was glad that there was so much to keep her occupied. It wasn't until after lunch that the wicked little thought that she might take another look at the handkerchief in Radinck's jacket pocket entered her head. The suit was to be sent to the cleaners, along with her dressing gown; they would be in one of the small rooms leading from the passage which led to the kitchen.

They were there all right. Feeling guilty, she searched every pocket and found the handkerchief gone. It must be something very precious to Radinck and it served her right for snooping.

Feeling ashamed of herself, she put on her sheepskin jacket, pulled a woollen cap over her head and went to find Rex, prowling in discontent from room to room. He had been left behind again. They went a long way, indeed they were still only half way home in the gathering dusk when Radinck opened his house door. He had a large box under one arm and went at once to the sitting-room where Caro liked to spend her leisure.

The room was empty of course, and in answer to his summons, Noakes informed him that the Baroness had gone out with Rex. 'Been gorn a long time, too,' observed Noakes. 'Great walker, she is too.' He turned to go, adding with a trusted old friend's freedom: 'Walking away from somethin', if yer ask me.'

His employer turned cold blue eyes on him. 'And what exactly does that mean?'

Noakes threw him a quick shrewd look. 'Just me opinion, Professor, take it or leave it, as you might say.'

'She's unhappy? The Baroness is unhappy?'

'Not ter say unhappy—always busy, she is, with this and that—flowers in the rooms and ordering stores and learning Dutch all by 'erself. 'Omesick, I've no doubt, Professor.' He added defiantly: 'She's on 'er own a lot.'

The master of the house looked coldly furious. 'I have my work, Noakes.'

'And now, beggin' yer pardon, Professor, you've got 'er as well.'

The Professor looked like a thundercloud. 'It is a good thing that we are old friends, Noakes...'

His faithful butler had a prudent hand on the door. 'Yes, Professor—I'd not 'ave said any of that if we 'adn't been.'

The austere lines of the Professor's face broke into a smile. 'I know that, Noakes, and I value your friendship.'

Caro walked in half an hour later, her cheeks glowing, her hair regrettably untidy. As she came into the hall from the garden door, Rex beside her, she saw Noakes on his stately way to the kitchen.

'Noakes!' she cried. 'We've had a lovely walk, I'm as warm as toast. And don't frown at me, I've wiped Rex's feet. I went to see Queenie too and she's fine.' She had thrown off her jacket and was pulling the cap off her head when the sitting-room door opened and she saw Radinck.

Her breath left her, as it always did when she saw him. After a little silence she said: 'Hullo, Radinck, I didn't know you'd be home early. I hope you've had tea—we went further than we meant to.'

He leaned against the wall, his bland face giving nothing away. 'I waited for you, Caroline.' He nodded at Noakes who hurried kitchenwards and held the door wide for her to go in. The room looked very welcoming; the fire burned brightly in the grate and Waterloo had made himself comfortable before it, joined, after he had made much of his master, by Rex. Caro sat down on the little armchair by the work table she had made her own, smoothed her hair without bothering much about it, and picked up her tapestry work. She had painstakingly unpicked it and now had the miserable task of working it again. She smiled across at her husband. 'I hope it's scones, I've been showing Marta how to make them.'

He said gravely: 'I look forward to them. Caroline, are you lonely?'

The question was so unexpected that she pricked her finger. She said rather loudly: 'Lonely? Why, of course not—there's so much to do, and now I'm going to start Dutch lessons, tomorrow, and Juffrouw Kropp is teaching me how to be a good housekeeper, and there are the animals...' She paused, seeking something to add to her meagre list of activities. 'Oh, and now there's Becky...'

Noakes brought in the tea tray then and she busied herself pouring it from the George the Second silver bullet tea-pot into the delicate cups. It wasn't being rich that mattered, she mused, it was possessing beautiful things, lovingly made and treasured and yet used each day...

'Queenie and Prince are doing very well,' remarked Radinck.

She passed him his cup and saucer. 'Yes, aren't they? I went to see them this morning—twice, in fact... Oh, and I asked Juffrouw Kropp to see that your suit went to the cleaners.'

'I imagined you might; I emptied the pockets.' He stared at her so hard that she began to pinken, and to cover her guilty feelings about looking for that hanky, bent to lift the lid of the dish holding the scones.

'Will you have a scone?' she asked. 'Marta's such a wonderful cook...'

'And your dressing gown? That was ruined, I imagine.'

'Well, yes, but I think it'll clean—it may need several...'

'I don't think I should bother, Caroline.' He bent down and took the box from the floor beside his chair. 'I hope this will do instead.'

Caroline gave him a surprised look, undid the beribboned box slowly and gently lifted aside the layers of tissue paper, to lift out a pale pink quilted satin robe, its high neck and long sleeves edged with chiffon frills; the kind of extravagant garment she had so often stared at through shop windows and never hoped to possess.

'It's absolutely gorgeous!' she exclaimed. 'I shall love wearing it. Thank you very much, Radinck, it was most kind of you.' She smiled at him and just for once he smiled back at her.

They had a pleasant tea after that, not talking about anything much until Caro reminded him that they were to go to the burgermeester's reception the following evening.

'You have a dress?' Radinck enquired idly, 'or do you want to go to den Haag shopping—Noakes can easily drive you there.'

'Oh, I have a dress, thank you. It's—it's rather grand.'

'Too grand for my wife?' He spoke mockingly, but she didn't notice for once.

'Oh, oh, no, but it's rather—there's not a great deal of top to it.' She eyed him anxiously.

The corners of Radinck's stern mouth twitched. 'It was my impression that—er—not a great deal of top for the evening was all the fashion this season.'

'Well, it is. The sales lady said it was quite suitable, but I—I haven't been to an evening party for some time and I'm not sure...'

'The sales lady looked very knowledgeable,' said Radinck kindly, and forbore from adding that she would know better than to sell the Baroness Thoe van Erckelens anything un-suitable. 'Supposing you put it on and I'll take a look at it before we leave tomorrow—just to reassure you.'

'Oh, would you? I wouldn't like people to stare.' Caroline added reluctantly: 'I don't think I'm much good at parties.'

'Neither am I, Caroline, but you don't need to worry. Everyone is eager to meet a bride, you know.' His voice held a faint sneer and she winced and was only partly comforted by his: 'I'm sure the dress will be most suitable.'

Caro repeated this comforting observation to herself while she examined herself in the long mirror in her bedroom, dressed ready for the reception. There was no doubt about it, it was a beautiful dress; a pale smoky grey chiffon over satin with a finely pleated frill round its hem and the bodice which was causing her so much doubt, finely pleated too.

She turned away from her reflection, caught up the mink and went quickly down the staircase before she lost her nerve.

The drawing-room door was half open and Noakes, ap-pearing from nowhere opened it wide for her to go through. Radinck was standing with his back to the hearth with Rex and Waterloo sitting at his feet enjoying the warmth. Caro nipped across the stretch of carpet and came to a breathless halt. 'Well?' she asked.

Radinck studied her leisurely. 'A charming dress,' he pronounced finally, 'exactly right for the occasion.'

She waited for him to say more, even a half-hearted compliment about herself would have been better than nothing at
all, but he remained silent. And she had taken such pains with
her face and hair and hands...

She said in a quiet little voice: 'I'm ready, Radinck,' and
picked up her coat which Noakes had draped over a chair.

He didn't answer her but moved away from the fire to fetch
something lying on one of the sofa tables. She thought how
magnificent he looked in his tails and white tie, but if she told
him so, he might think that she was wishing for a compliment
in her turn.

He crossed the room to her, opened the case in his hand
and took out its contents. 'This was my mother's,' he told her.
'I think it will go very well with this dress. Turn round while
I fasten it for you.'

The touch of his fingers made her tremble although she
stood obediently still, and then went to look in the great gilded
mirror on one wall. The necklace was exquisite; sapphires
linked by an intricate chain of diamonds, a dainty, costly trifle
which went very well with her dress. She touched it lightly
with a pretty hand, acknowledging its beauty and magnificence, while at the same time aware that if it had been a bead
necklace from Woolworths given with all his love she would
have worn it for ever and loved every bead.

She turned away from the mirror and got into the coat he
was holding, picked up the grey satin purse which exactly
matched her slippers and went with him to the car. On the
way to Leeuwarden she asked: 'Is there anything special I
should know about this evening?'

'I think not. I shall remain with you and see that you meet
my friends, and once you have found your feet, I daresay you
will like to talk to as many people as possible. It will be like
any other party you have been to, Caroline.'

It was on the tip of her tongue to tell him that she had been to very few parties and certainly never to a grand reception, but pride curbed her tongue. She got out of the car presently, her determined little chin well up, and went up the steps to the burgermeester's front door, her skirts held daintily and with Radinck's hand under her elbow. She had a moment of panic in the enormous entrance hall as she was led away by a severe maid to remove her coat, and cast a longing look at the door—it was very close; she had only to turn and run...

'I shall be here waiting for you, Caroline,' said her husband quietly.

The reception rooms were on the first floor. Caroline went up the wide staircase, Radinck beside her, her heart beating fit to choke her. There were people all around them, murmuring and smiling, but Radinck didn't stop until they reached the big double doors opening on to the vast apartment where the burgermeester and his wife were receiving their guests. She had imagined that their host would be a large impressive man with a terrifying wife. He was nothing of the sort; of middle height and very stout, he had a fringe of grey hair and a round smiling face which beamed a welcome at her. She murmured politely in her carefully learned Dutch and was relieved when he addressed her in English.

'So, now I meet you, Baroness,' he chuckled, 'and how happy I am to do so. We will talk presently; I look forward to it.' He passed her on to his wife with a laughing remark to Radinck, who introduced her to a tall thin lady with a beaky nose and a sweet expression. Her English was fragmental and Caro, having repeated her few phrases, was relieved when Radinck took the conversation smoothly into his own hands before taking her arm and leading her into the room.

He seemed to know everyone there, and she shook hands and murmured, forgetting most of the names immediately until finally Radinck whisked her on to the floor to dance.

He danced well, but then so did she; not that she had had much chance to show her skill, but she had always loved dancing and it came naturally to her. She floated round in his arms, just for a little while a happy girl, although a peep at his face decided her not to talk. It was bland and faintly smiling, but the smile wasn't for her; she had the horrid feeling that he was doing his social duty without much pleasure. On the whole she was glad when the music stopped and Tiele and Becky joined them, and when the music started again it was Tiele who asked her to dance.

Unlike Radinck he chatted in an easy casual way, telling her how pretty she looked, how well she danced and wanting to know if she and Radinck would be at the hospital ball.

'Well, you know, I'm not sure about that—there were so many invitations...' And when her partner looked surprised: 'Does Radinck always go?'

Tiele studied her earnest face carefully. 'Oh, yes, though it's always been a bit of a duty for him—not much fun for a man on his own, you know. But you're sure to be there this year. We must join forces for the evening.'

He was rewarded by her smile. 'I'd like that—it's all rather strange, you know, and my Dutch isn't up to much.'

'Never mind that,' he told her kindly. 'You dance like a dream and everyone's saying that you're just right for Radinck.'

She blushed brightly. 'Oh, thank you—I hope you're right; I don't mind what people say really, only I do want Radinck to be proud of me.'

Tiele's eyes were thoughtful, but he said easily: 'He's that all right!'

And after that Caroline went from partner to partner. There seemed to be no end to them, and although she caught glimpses of Radinck from time to time he made no attempt to approach her. It wasn't until they all went down to supper that he appeared suddenly beside her, took her arm and found her a seat at a table for four, before going in search of food at the buffet. Becky and Tiele, following them in, hesitated about joining them until Becky said softly: 'Look, darling, he's only danced with her once this evening. If it had been you I'd have boxed your ears! Look at her sitting there—she's lonely.'

'I'd rather look at you, my darling, and I don't think Radinck would like his ears boxed.'

'Well, of course he wouldn't, and Caro's clever enough to know that.' Becky added darkly: 'He's been leading a bachelor life too long—she's such a dear, too.'

'Which allows us to hope that he will become a happily married man, my love.'

Caro had seen them. Becky gave her husband's arm a wifely nip and obedient to this signal, they went to join her. Tiele said easily: 'Do you mind if we join you?' He settled his wife in a chair beside Caro. 'I suppose Radinck is battling his way towards the sandwiches—I'll join him.' He touched his wife lightly on her arm. 'Anything you fancy, darling?'

Becky thought briefly. 'Well, I like vol-au-vents, but only if they've got salmon in them, and those dear little cream puffs. What are you having, Caro?'

'I don't know.' Caro smiled brightly, wishing with all her heart that Radinck would call her darling in that kind of a voice and ask her what she would like, as though he really minded. Tiele, she felt sure, would bring back salmon vol-au-vents and cream puffs even if he had to go out and bake them himself.

But it seemed that these delicacies were readily obtainable, for he was back in no time at all with a tray of food and Radinck with him. Caro accepted the chicken patties he had brought for her, had her glass filled with champagne and declared herself delighted with everything. And Radinck seemed to be enjoying himself, laughing and talking with Tiele and teasing Becky and treating herself with charming politeness. Only she wondered how much of it was social good manners, hiding his impatience of the whole evening. It wasn't until Becky remarked: 'We shall all see each other at the hospital ball, shan't we? Can't we go together?' that Caro saw the bland look on his face again and heard the sudden coolness in his voice.

'I'm not certain if we shall be going—I've that seminar in Vienna.'

'Isn't that on the following day?' asked Tiele.

'Yes, but I've one or two committees—I thought I'd go a day earlier and settle them first.' He glanced at Caro. 'I don't think Caroline will mind—we have so many parties during the next few weeks.'

Becky opened her mouth, caught her husband's quelling eye and closed it again, and Caro, anxious to do the right thing, observed with a cheerfulness she didn't feel that of course Radinck was quite right and she wouldn't mind missing the ball in the least.

'You could come with us,' suggested Becky, but was answered by Radinck's politely chilling:

'Might that not seem a little strange? We have been married for such a short time.'

'Oh, you mean that people might think you'd quarrelled or separated or something,' observed Becky forthrightly. 'Caro, let's go and tidy up for the second half,' and on their way: 'Caro, why don't you go to Vienna with Radinck?'

Caro tried to be nonchalant and failed utterly. 'Oh, he wouldn't want me around.' She went on quickly in case her companion got the wrong idea, 'He works so hard.' Which didn't quite seem adequate but was all she could think of.

Back on the dance floor, she almost gasped with relief when Radinck swept her into a waltz. She had been in a panic that he would introduce her to some dry-as-dust dignitary and leave her with him, or worse still, just leave her. They danced in silence for a few minutes before he asked her if she was enjoying herself.

'Yes, thank you,' said Caro. 'You have a great many friends, haven't you, and they are all very kind.'

'They have no reason to be otherwise.' He spoke so austerely that her champagne-induced pleasure dwindled away to nothing at all. She danced as she always did, gracefully and without fault, but her heart wasn't in it. Radinck was doing his duty again and not enjoying it, although she had to admit that nothing of his feelings showed on his face. The dance finished and he relinquished her to another partner and she didn't see him again until the last dance, when he swept her on to the floor again—but only, she thought sadly, because it was customary for the last dance to be enjoyed by married couples and sweethearts together.

They left quickly, giving Caro barely time to say goodbye to Becky. 'I'll telephone,' cried Becky, 'and anyway we'll see each other at the Hakelsmas' drinks party, won't we?'

Radinck maintained a steady flow of casual talk as they drove home. Caro listened when it seemed necessary and, once in the house, bade him a quiet goodnight and started up the staircase. She was halted half way up by his query as to whether she wouldn't like a cup of coffee with him, but she paused only long enough to shake her head, glad that he was too far away to see the tears in her eyes. The evening, despite the dress, had been a failure. He had evinced no pleasure in her company and she had no doubt at all that the moment she was out of sight he would turn away with a sigh of thankfulness and go to his study, to immerse himself in his books and papers. She undressed very quickly and took off the necklace; tomorrow she would return it to him.

Ilke, not having been told otherwise, woke her early so that she might go riding, but she drank her tea slowly and then lay, listening for the sound of Rufus's hooves on the cobblestones. Presently, after they had died away, she got up, bathed and dressed in her new suit, did her face and hair and went down to her breakfast. Radinck was back by then, already half way through his own meal, and she said at once as she went in: 'Good morning—no, don't get up, I'm sure you have no time.'

She slipped into her chair and sipped the coffee Noakes had poured for her and took a slice of toast.

'You were too tired to ride,' stated Radinck.

'Me, tired? Not in the least.' She gave him a sunny smile and buttered her toast, and after a moment or two he picked up his letters again, tossing several over to her as he did so.

'Will you answer these? Drinks mostly, I think.'

'You want me to refuse them?'

He looked impatient. 'Certainly not. Why should you think that?'

Caroline didn't answer. After all, she had told him once; she wasn't going to keep on. Instead she got on with her breakfast and when Noakes went out of the room, she got up and put the necklace carefully beside her husband's plate.

'Thank you for letting me wear it,' she said.

He put down the letter he had been reading to stare at her down his handsome nose. 'My dear Caroline, I gave it to you.'

She opened her hazel eyes wide. 'Oh, did you? I thought you'd lent it to me just for the evening. How kind—but I can't accept it, you know.'

'Why not?' Radinck's brows were drawn together in an ominous frown.

She did her best to explain. 'Well, it's not like a present, is it? I mean, one gives a present because one wants to, but you gave me the necklace to wear because your wife would be expected to have the family jewels.'

Radinck crumpled up the letter in his hand and hurled it at the wastepaper basket.

'What an abominable girl you are, Caroline! As I said some time ago, you have this gift of putting me in the wrong.'

'I'm sorry if you're annoyed, but I can't possibly accept it, though I'll wear any jewellery you like when we go out together.'

He said silkily: 'Don't count on going out too often, Caroline, I'm a busy man.'

'Well, I wasn't going to.' She gave him a thoughtful look, and added kindly: 'You're very cross—I daresay you're tired. We should have left earlier last night.'

The silkiness was still there, tinged with ice now. 'When I wish you to organise my life, Caroline, I will say so. I am not yet so elderly that I cannot decide things for myself.'

'Oh, you're not elderly at all,' said Caro soothingly. 'You're not even middle-aged. How silly of you to think that; you must know that you're...' She stopped abruptly and he urged her blandly:

'Do go on.'

'No, I won't, you'll only bite my head off if I do.' She took a roll and spread it with butter and cheese. 'What time do you want to go to Mevrouw Hakelsma's party? Only so that I'll be ready on time,' she added hastily.

'It is for half past seven, isn't it? I should be home by six o'clock. Will you see that dinner is later?'

'Would half past eight suit you? I'll tell Juffrouw Kropp.'

He nodded. 'I should like to leave the Hakelsmas' place within an hour; I've a good deal of work waiting.'

Caro kept her face cheerful. 'Of course. Just nod and wink at me when you're ready to leave.'

Radinck got up from the table. 'I shall neither nod nor wink,' he told her cuttingly. 'You are my wife, not the dog.' He stalked to the door. 'I'll see you this evening.'

She said, 'Yes, Radinck,' so meekly that he shot her a suspicious look and paused to say:

'It will be short dresses this evening.'

She said 'Yes, Radinck,' again, still so meek that he exclaimed forcefully:

'I wish you would refrain from this continuous "Yes, Radinck", as though I were a tyrant!'

'Oh, but you're not,' Caro assured him warmly. 'That's the last thing you are; it's just that you've lived so long alone that you've forgotten how to talk. Never mind, you'll soon get into the habit again now that I'm here.' She gave him a limpid smile and he said something in a subdued roar, something nasty in his own language, she judged, as she watched him go.

She finished her breakfast, inspected more cupboards under Juffrouw Kropp's guidance, discussed the evening's dinner with Marta and then arranged the flowers, a task she enjoyed even though it took a long time, and then went down to see how Queenie was getting on. Willem was there and they stood admiring the little donkey and her son, carrying on a conversation, which, while completely ungrammatical on Caro's part, Willem understood very well. She had sugar for the horses too, and Jemmy whinnied when he saw her, looking at her so reproachfully that she changed after lunch and, with Jan keeping a watchful eye on her, rode round the fields. Which didn't leave her much time for anything else. She was ready, wearing one of her new dresses, pink silk jersey with a demure neck and long sleeves, well before six o'clock, and went to sit in the smaller of the sitting-rooms, industriously knitting. It was half past six when Noakes came to tell her that Radinck was on the telephone.

He sounded austere. 'I'm sorry, Caroline, but I shall be home later than I expected. Perhaps you could ring Mevrouw Hakelsma and say all the right things. I don't expect we can get there much before eight o'clock.'

She said, 'Yes, Radinck,' before she could stop herself, but what else was there to say? 'OK, darling,' wouldn't have pleased him at all. She went along to the kitchen and prudently arranged for dinner to be delayed, then went back to her knitting.

Radinck got home at half past seven, looking tired, which somehow made him more approachable.

Caro wished him a pleasant good evening. 'Would you like a sandwich before you go upstairs?' she asked.

He had gone to the sofa table where the tray of drinks was. 'Thank you, I should—I missed lunch. What will you drink?'

'Sherry, thank you.' She pressed the old-fashioned brass bell beside the hearth and when Noakes came asked for a plate of sandwiches.

Radinck was famished. He devoured the lot with his

whisky, looking like a tired, very handsome wolf who hadn't had a square meal for days. Caro watching him, bursting with love, sighed soundlessly; he needed someone to look after him so badly.

He went away presently, to rejoin her in a little while looking immaculate in one of his beautifully cut dark suits. She got up at once, laid her knitting on the work table and went with him into the hall where Noakes was waiting with their coats. Radinck helped her into hers and shrugged on his own coat, and Caro, with a quick whisper to Noakes to be sure and have dinner ready to put on the table the moment they got back, followed Radinck out to the car.

The Hakelsmas lived on the outskirts of Leeuwarden, in a large red brick villa full of heavy, comfortable furniture. Caro had already met them at the burgermeester's reception and liked them both—in their forties, jolly, plump and kind. They had a large family, and three of them were there helping to entertain the guests, of whom there seemed to be a great many.

Caro murmured her set piece to her host and hostess, accepted a glass of sherry and something called a *bitterbal* which she didn't like at all, and was swept away to go from one group to the other, careful never to lose sight of Radinck. He seemed very popular, laughing and talking as though he liked nothing better than standing about drinking sherry and making small talk, and some of the girls there were very pretty and he appeared to be on very good terms with them. Caro, swept by a wave of jealousy, tried not to look at him too much. She had never thought of him as being likely to fall in love with anyone else, but there was no earthly reason why he shouldn't. One couldn't help these things. Of course she had every intention of trying to make him fall in love with her, but she began to wonder if the competition was too keen. Her not very pleasant thoughts were interrupted by Becky's voice.

'Hullo—you're looking wistful. Why?' She beamed at Caro. 'You're late. Did Radinck get held up?'

'Yes. There are a lot of people here, aren't there? I expect I met most of them at the burgermeester's.'

'Don't worry, it took me months to remember everyone's name, but they're all very sweet about it, and we'll all be seeing each other quite a lot during the next few weeks. Radinck gave an enormous party last year—are you having one this year too?'

'I think so.'

'Well, I expect now he's got you, he'll go out more. He's always been a bit of a recluse—well, ever since...'

'His first wife died? That's understandable, isn't it?' Caro smiled at Becky and let her see that she knew all about the first wife and it didn't matter at all.

On their way home presently, she said carefully: 'Radinck, I don't a bit mind not going to all these parties if you don't want to. After all, everyone knows you're a very busy man—mind you,' she observed thoughtfully, 'I daresay you don't need to do as much work as you do, if you see what I mean. Becky said you didn't go out much before—before we got married, and I did promise you that I'd not interfere with your life...'

She couldn't see his face, but she could tell from his voice that he was frowning. 'I thought that I had made myself clear; we will attend as many of these parties as possible, give an evening party ourselves, and then I shall be able to return to what you call my life. For most of the year there is very little social life on a big scale, only just before Christmas and at the New Year. Once that is over...' He slowed the car a little and Caro, thankful for the chance to talk to him even if only for a brief while, said unhappily: 'You hate it, don't you? I'm glad it's only for a few weeks. What a pity I can't get 'flu or something, then we couldn't go...'

'That is a singularly foolish remark, Caroline. Of course you won't get anything of the sort.'

But just for once he, who was so often right, was wrong. Caro woke up in the morning feeling faintly peculiar. She hadn't got a headache, but her head felt heavy, and moreover, when she got out of bed her feet didn't seem to touch the ground. She had no appetite for her breakfast either, but as Radinck was reading his letters and scanning the morning's papers, she didn't think that mattered. He was never chatty over the meal; she took some toast and crumbled it at intervals just in case he should look up, and drank several cups of coffee which revived her sufficiently to bid him goodbye in a perfectly normal way. They weren't going anywhere that evening and she would be able to go to bed early, as he so often went straight to his study after dinner. She went through her morning routine, visited Queenie and Prince, took Waterloo for a brief walk in the gardens and retired to the library to struggle with her Dutch. But she didn't seem able to concentrate, not even with the help of several more cups of coffee. She toyed with her lunch, which upset Noakes very much, and then went back to the sitting-room, got out her knitting and curled up in Radinck's chair with Waterloo on her lap. He was warm and comforting and after a very short time she gave up trying to knit and closed her eyes and dozed off into a troubled sleep, to be wakened by a worried Noakes with the tea tray.

'Yer not yerself, ma'am,' he declared. 'Yer ought to go ter bed.'

She eyed him hazily. 'Yes, I think I will when I've had tea, Noakes. It's just a cold.'

She drank the tea-pot dry and went off to sleep again, her cheeks flushed and her head heavy. She didn't wake when Radinck, met at the door by an anxious Noakes, came into the room.

Caro looked small and lonely and lost in his great chair and he muttered something as he bent over her, a cool hand on her hot forehead. She woke up then, staring into the blue eyes so close to hers. 'I feel very grotty,' she mumbled. 'I meant to go to bed... I'll go now.'

She began to scramble out of the chair and he picked her up with Waterloo still in her arms. 'You should have gone hours ago,' he said almost angrily. 'You weren't well at breakfast—why didn't you say so then?'

He was mounting the staircase and she muttered: 'I can walk,' and then: 'I thought I'd feel better. Besides, I didn't think you noticed.'

Noakes had gone ahead to open the door and Radinck laid her on the bed, asked Noakes to fetch Juffrouw Kropp and then pulled the coverlet over Caro, who was beginning to shiver. 'So sorry,' she told him, 'such a nuisance for you. I'll be quite all right now.'

He didn't answer but waited until Juffrouw Kropp came into the room, spoke to her quietly and went away, while that lady undressed Caro as though she had been a baby, tucked her up in her bed and went to fetch Radinck, walking up and down the gallery outside. Caro, feeling so wretched by now that she didn't care about anything at all, put out her tongue, muttered and mumbled ninety-nine and then swallowed the pills she was given. She was asleep in five minutes.

She woke a couple of hours later, feeling very peculiar in the head, and found Radinck bending over her again. He looked large and solid and very dependable, and she sighed with relief because he was there.

'Now you won't have to go to the party tomorrow,' she told him, still half asleep, 'and there's a dinner party...when? Quite soon; we needn't go to that either.' She closed her eyes and then opened them wide again. 'I'm so glad, you can have peace and quiet again.'

She dropped off again, so that she didn't hear the words wrung so reluctantly from Radinck's lips. Which was a pity.

She felt a little better in the morning, but her recollection of the night was hazy; she had wakened several times and there had been a lamp by the bed, but the rest of the room had been in shadow. And once or twice someone had given her a drink, but she had been too tired to open her eyes and see who it was. Radinck came to see her at breakfast time, pronounced himself satisfied as to her progress and went away again, leaving her with Waterloo for company. Presently Juffrouw Kropp came and washed her face and hands, brushed her hair and then brought her a tray of tea—nice strong tea with a lot of milk, and paper-thin bread and butter.

Caro dozed through the day. Lovingly tended by Juffrouw Kropp, Marta and the maids, it seemed to her that each time she opened her eyes there was someone in the room looking anxiously at her. Towards teatime Noakes came in with a vase of autumn flowers and a message from Becky and Tiele, and that was followed by a succession of notes and several more flower arrangements.

'But I've only got 'flu,' said Caro. 'I mean, there's really no need...'

'Very well liked, yer are, ma'am,' said Noakes with deep satisfaction. 'The phone's bin going on and off all afternoon with messages.'

'But how did they all know?'

'The Professor will 'ave cancelled your engagements, ma'am.'

Caro nodded. She wasn't enjoying having 'flu, but at least it was making Radinck happy. She drank her tea and after a struggle to keep awake, slept again.

She woke to find Radinck at the foot of the bed, looking at her, and she assured him before he could ask her that she was feeling a great deal better. She sat up against the pillows, happily unaware of her wan face and tousled hair. 'And look at all these flowers,' she begged him, 'and I'm not even ill. I feel a fraud!'

He said seriously: 'You have no need to—you have a quite violent virus infection of the respiratory system.'

It was silly to get upset, but somehow he had made her feel like a patient in a hospital bed; someone to be cured of an

ailment with a completely impersonal care. Her eyes filled
with tears until they dripped down her cheeks and although
she put up an impatient hand to rub them away, there seemed
no end to them. Radinck bent over her, a handkerchief in his
hand, but she pushed it away. 'I'm perfectly all right,' she
told him crossly. 'It's just that I don't feel quite the thing.'
She added peevishly: 'I think I'd like to go to sleep.'

She closed her eyes so that he would see that she really
meant that, and although the tears were still pouring from
under her lids, she kept them shut. And after a minute or so
she really did feel sleepy in a dreamy kind of way, so that
the kiss on her cheek seemed part of the dream too. She woke
much later and remembered it—it had been very pleasant;
dreams could be delightful. She dismissed the idea that Radinck had kissed her as ridiculous and wept a little before she
slept again.

CHAPTER EIGHT

Two days later Caro was on her feet again. She had been coddled and mothered by Juffrouw and Marta, ably backed by the maids and old Jan who sent in flowers each day from his cherished hothouses, the whole team master-minded by Noakes. No one could have been kinder. Even Radinck, visiting her twice a day, had been meticulous in his attentions. Although that hadn't stopped him telling her that he would be going to Vienna that evening. 'You wouldn't wish to go to the hospital ball,' he pointed out with unescapable logic, 'and much though I regret having to leave you while you are feeling under the weather, my presence is hardly necessary to your recovery. My entire—I beg your pardon—our entire staff are falling over themselves to lavish attention upon you.' He gave her a mocking little smile. 'I leave you in the best of hands.'

Caro had agreed with him in a quiet little voice. Normally she wouldn't have allowed herself to feel crushed by his high-handedness, but she wasn't quite herself. Her chances of making him fall in love with her seemed so low they hardly bore contemplation. She wished him goodbye and hoped he would have a good trip and that the seminar would be interesting, and then, unable to think of anything else to say, sat up in bed just looking at him.

'Goodbye, Caroline,' said Radinck in a quite different voice, and bent and kissed her cheek. She didn't move for quite a while after he had gone, but presently when Waterloo jumped on to the bed and gave her an enquiring butt with his head, she scratched the top of it in an absent manner. 'I didn't dream it, then,' she told him. 'He kissed me then as well. Now, I wonder...'

It was probably a false hope, but at least she could work

on it. She got bathed and dressed and went downstairs, to be fussed over by everyone in the house, and all of them remarked how much better she looked.

She felt better. Somewhere or other there was a chink in her husband's armour of cool aloofness; she would have to work on it. Much cheered by the thought, she spent her day catching up on her Dutch, knitting like a fury and entertaining Rex, who with his master gone, was feeling miserable.

'Well, I feel the same,' Caro told him, 'and at least he's glad to see you when he comes home.' She insisted on going to the servants' sitting-room to rehearse the carols after dinner too, although Noakes shook his head and said she ought to be in bed.

'Well, yes, I'm sure you're right,' Caro agreed, 'but Christmas is getting close and we do want to put on a perfect performance. I think that tomorrow evening we'd better get together in the drawing-room so that you'll all know where to stand and so on. The moment the Professor comes home on Christmas Eve, you can all file in and take up your places and the minute he comes into the room you can start. It should be a lovely surprise.'

She went to bed quite happy presently with Waterloo to keep her company and Juffrouw Kropp coming in with hot milk to sip so that she would sleep and strict instructions to ring if she wanted anything during the night.

They were all such dears, thought Caro, curled up cosily in the centre of the vast bed. Life could have been wonderful if only Radinck had loved her even a little. But that was no way to think, she scolded herself. 'Faint heart never won Radinck,' she told Waterloo, on the edge of sleep.

The weather was becoming very wintry. She woke in the morning to grey, woolly clouds, heavy with snow and the sound of the wind racing through the bare trees near the house. But the great house was warm and very comfortable and she spent her morning doing the flowers once again, with Jan bringing her armsful of them from his hothouses. There was Marta to talk to about the meals too; something special for dinner on the following day when Radinck would return. The day passed quickly. Caroline ate her dinner with appetite with Noakes brooding over her in a fatherly way, then repaired to the drawing-room.

They were all a little shy at first. The room was grand and they felt stiff and awkward and out of place until Caro said in her sparse, excruciating Dutch: 'Sing as though you were in your own sitting-room—remember it's to give the Professor pleasure and it's only because this is the best place for him to hear you.'

They loosened up after that. They were well embarked on *Silent Night* with all the harmonies just right, when the Professor unlocked his own front door. No one heard him. Even Rex, dozing by the fire, was deafened by the choir. He stood for a moment in the centre of the hall and then walked very quietly to the drawing-room door, not quite closed. The room was in shadow with only a lamp by the piano and the sconces on either side of the fireplace alight. He pushed the door cautiously a few inches so that he could look in and no one saw him. They were grouped round Caro at the piano, her mousy head lighted by the lamp beside her, one hand beating time while the other thumped out the tune. Radinck closed the door gently again and retreated to where he had cast down his coat and bag and let himself out of the house again. The car's engine made no noise above the sighing and whistling of the wind. He drove back the way he had come, all the way to the airport on the outskirts of Leeuwarden where he parked the car, telephoned his home that he had returned earlier than he had expected, then got back into the car and, for the second time, drove himself home.

Caro had received the news of Radinck's unexpected return with outward calm. 'We'll find time to rehearse again tomorrow,' she told them all. 'Now I think if Marta would warm up some of that delicious soup just in case the Professor's cold and hungry...'

She closed the piano and went to sit in the sitting-room by the fire, her tapestry in her hands. She even had time to do a row or two before she heard Radinck open the door, speak to Noakes, on the watch for him, and cross the hall to open the sitting-room door.

'What a nice surprise!' she smiled as he came into the room. 'Would you like dinner or just soup and sandwiches?'

'Coffee will do, thank you, Caroline.' He sat down opposite her. 'You are feeling better, I can see that, and being sensible, sitting quietly here.'

'Oh, I've been very sensible,' she assured him. 'Would you like coffee in your study?'

He looked annoyed. 'My dear girl, I have just this minute returned home and here you are, banishing me to my study!'

Caro went red. 'I'm sorry, I didn't mean it like that, only you so often do go there—I thought you might rather be alone.'

'Very considerate of you; I prefer to remain here. What have you been doing with yourself?'

'Oh, almost nothing—the flowers and catching up with my Dutch, and showing Marta how to make mince pies...'

'I surprised you playing the piano before we married,' he said. 'Do you remember? Don't you play any more?'

Caro's red face went pale. 'Yes—well, sometimes I do.'

He sat back in his chair, relaxed and at ease, and watched while Noakes placed the coffee tray at Caro's elbow. 'Have you any plans for Christmas?' he asked idly.

She stammered a little. 'I understand from Noakes that you don't—that is, you prefer a quiet time.'

'I am afraid that over the years I have got into the habit of doing very little about entertaining—I did mention the party which I give, did I not? Is there anything special you would enjoy? A little music perhaps?'

'Music?' Caro's needle was working overtime, regardless of wrong stitches. She took a deep breath. 'Oh, you mean going to concerts and that sort of thing; Becky was telling me…but you really don't have to bother. We did agree when we married that your life wasn't to be changed at all, but you've already had to go to these parties with me and you must have disliked them very much. I'm very happy, you know, I don't mind if I don't go out socially.'

'I thought girls liked dressing up and going out to parties.'

'Well, yes, of course, but you see I don't enjoy them if you don't.' She hadn't meant to say that. She stitched a whole row, her head bowed over her work, and wished fruitlessly that the floor would open and swallow her up.

'And what precisely do you mean by that?' asked Radinck blandly.

'Nothing, nothing at all.' And then, knowing that she wouldn't get away with that, she added: 'What I meant was that I feel guilty because you have to give up your evenings doing something you don't enjoy when you might be in your study reading…and writing.'

'Put like that I seem to be a very selfish man. I must endeavour to make amends.'

Caro gave him a surprised glance. He wasn't being sarcastic and his voice held a warm note she hadn't heard before.

'You're not selfish,' she told him in a motherly voice. 'No one would expect you to change your whole way of life, certainly I wouldn't. You've devoted yourself to your work and the staff adore you—so do the animals.'

'And what about you, Caroline?'

She took her time answering. 'You must know that I have a great regard for you, Radinck.' She looked across at him, her loving heart in her eyes and unaware of it. 'You have no need to reproach yourself; you made it very clear before we married that you didn't want to change your life, and I agreed to that. I'm very content.'

His eyes were searching. 'Are you? Perhaps I have done wrong in marrying you, Caroline—you might have found some younger man…'

'I wish you wouldn't keep harping on your great age!' declared Caro hotly. Suddenly she could stand no more of it. She threw down her embroidery carelessly, so that the wools flew in all directions, and hurried out of the room and up to her bedroom, where she burst into tears, making Waterloo's fur very damp while she hugged him. 'What am I going to do?' she asked him. 'One minute I think he likes me a little and then he says he regrets marrying me...' Which wasn't quite true, although that was how it seemed to her.

She went to bed because there was nothing else to do, but she didn't go to sleep; she lay listening to the now familiar sounds in the old house—the very faint clatter from the kitchens, Rex's occasional bark, the tread of Noakes' rather heavy feet crossing the hall, the subdued clang as he closed the gate leading to the garden from the side door, even faint horsey noises from the stables. It was a clear, cold night, and sounds carried. Presently she heard Noakes and Marta and the rest of them going up the back stairs at the end of the gallery on their way to bed, and after that the house was quiet save for the various clocks striking the hour, each in its own good time.

It was almost one o'clock and she was still awake when she heard cars travelling fast along the road at the end of the drive, and the next moment there was a kind of slow-motion crashing and banging and the sound of glass splintering and then distant faint cries. She was out of bed and pulling back the curtains within seconds and saw lights shine out as the front door was opened and Radinck went running down the drive, his bag in his hand. Caroline didn't stop to take off her nightie but pulled on a pair of slacks, bundled a sweater on top of them, and rushed downstairs in her bare feet. Her wellingtons were in one of the hall cupboards; she got into them just as Noakes came down the stairs with a dressing gown over his pyjamas.

'You'll need a coat, Noakes,' said Caro, 'and thick shoes, it's cold outside, then will you come to the gate and see if the Professor wants you to telephone.' She didn't wait for him to reply but opened the door and started down the drive.

Something was on fire now, she could smell it and see the flickering of flames somewhere on the road to the left of the gates. But there were no cries any more, although she thought she could hear voices.

There were two cars, hopelessly entangled, and one was blazing with thick black smoke pouring from it. Well away from it there were people on the grass verge of the road, some sitting and two lying, and she could see Radinck bending over them. She fetched up beside him, took the torch he was holding from him and shone it on the man lying on the ground. 'Noakes is coming as soon as he's got his coat on,' she said quietly.

'Good girl!' He was on his knees now, opening the man's jacket. 'Shine the light here, will you? There are scissors in my bag, can you reach them?'

Noakes arrived then, out of breath but calmly dignified. He listened to what Radinck had to say and with a brisk: 'OK, Professor,' turned and went back again. 'And bring some blankets and towels with you!' shouted Radinck after him.

The man was unconscious with head injuries and a fractured pelvis. They made him as comfortable as they could and moved on to the other silent figure close by. Head injuries again, and Radinck grunted as he bent to examine him, but beyond telling Caro to wrap one of the towels Noakes had brought back round the man's head and covering him with a blanket he did nothing. There were three people sitting on the frosty grass—an elderly man, a woman of the same age and a girl. Radinck looked at the older woman first, questioning her quietly as he did so. 'Shock,' he said to Caro, 'and a fractured clavicle—fix it with a towel, will you?' He moved on to the man, examined him briefly, said, 'Shock and no injuries apparent,' and then bent over the girl.

The loveliest girl Caro had ever set eyes on; small and fair with great blue eyes, and even with her hair all over the place and a dirty face she was breathtaking. 'Were you driving?' asked Radinck.

It was a pity that Caro's Dutch didn't stretch to understanding what the girl answered, nor, for that matter, what Radinck said after that. She held the torch, handed him what he wanted from his bag and wished with all her heart that she was even half as lovely as the girl sitting between them. She had looked at Radinck's face just once and although it wore the bland mask of his profession, she knew that he found the girl just as beautiful as she did; he would have been a strange man if he hadn't. The girl said something to him in a low voice and he answered her gently, putting an arm round her slim shoulders, smiling at her and then, to Caro's eyes at least, getting to his feet with reluctance.

'Stay with them, will you, Caroline?—this poor girl's had a bad shock, the others aren't too bad. I'll take a look at the other two, though there's nothing much to be done until we get them to hospital.' He stood listening for a moment. 'There are the ambulances now.'

He went away then and presently as the two ambulances slowed to a halt, Caro saw him directing the loading of the two unconscious men. The first ambulance went away and he came over to where she was waiting with the other three casualties. 'Go back to the house,' he told her. 'There's nothing more you can do. Get a warm drink and go to bed. I'll follow these people in to the hospital, there may be something I can do.' She hesitated, suddenly feeling unwanted and longing for a reassuring word. He had spoken briskly, as he might have spoken to a casual stranger who had stopped to give a hand, only she felt sure that he would have added his thanks.

'Do as I say, Caroline!' and this time he sounded urgent and coldly angry. She turned without a word and went down the drive, her feet and hands numb with cold, and climbed the steps slowly to where Juffrouw Kropp was waiting, wrapped in a dressing gown, and any neglect she had suffered at her husband's hands was instantly made up for by the care and attention she now received. Hardly knowing what was happening, she was bustled upstairs and into bed where Juffrouw Kropp tucked her in as though she had been a small girl and Marta waited with a tray of hot drinks. Both ladies stood one each side of the bed, while she sipped hot milk and brandy, reassured themselves that she had come to no harm and then told her firmly to go to sleep and not to get up in the morning until one or both of them had been to see her.

'But I'm not ill,' protested Caro weakly.

'You have had the grippe,' Juffrouw Kropp pointed out. 'The Professor will never forgive us if you are ill again.'

Caro searched her muddled head for the right words. 'He's gone to the hospital—he'll be late and cold…'

'Do not worry, Baroness, he will be cared for when he returns. Now you will sleep.'

'I ought to be there.' Caro spoke in English, not caring whether she was understood or not.

'No, no, he would not like that.'

She gave up and closed her eyes, not knowing that while Marta crept out with the tray, Juffrouw Kropp perched herself on the edge of a chair and waited until she was quite sure that Caro slept.

She wakened to find that lady standing at the foot of the bed, looking at her anxiously, but the anxious look went as Caroline sat up in bed and said good morning and then gave a small shriek when she saw the time.

'Ten o'clock?' she exclaimed, horrified. 'Why didn't someone call me? Is the Professor back?'

Juffrouw Kropp shook her head. 'He telephoned, Baroness. He will be back perhaps this afternoon, perhaps later.'

Caro plastered a cheerful smile on her face. 'Oh, yes, of course, he'll be busy. I'll get up.'

'Marta brings your breakfast at once—there is no need for you to get up, *mevrouw*, it will snow before long and it is very cold outside.'

Under Juffrouw Kropp's eagle eye Caro put her foot back in bed. 'Well, it would be nice,' she conceded. The housekeeper smiled in a satisfied way and shook up the pillows.

'There has been a telephone call for you—Baroness Rau-kema van den Eck—she heard about the accident. I asked her to telephone later, Baroness. She hopes that you are all right.'

It was nice to have a friend, reflected Caro, sitting up in bed eating a splendid breakfast, someone who wanted to know how you were and really minded. Not like Radinck. She choked on a piece of toast and pushed the tray away and got up.

It wasn't until the afternoon that Radinck telephoned, and by then any number of people had rung up. Becky, of course, wanting to know exactly what had happened, asking if Caroline were quite better, did she need anything, would she like to go over and see them soon. 'Tiele saw Radinck for a few minutes this morning,' went on Becky. 'He was getting ready to drive one of the crash people home—the girl who was driving. You'll know that, of course. I must say it's pretty good of him to go all the way to Dordrecht with her—let's hope the snow doesn't get any worse.'

Caro had made some suitable reply and put down the phone very thoughtfully. Of course, there might be some very good reason why Radinck should take the girl back home—something urgent—but there were trains, and cars to hire and buses, and most people had friends or family who rallied round at such a time. She did her best to forget about it, answered suitably when a number of other people she had met at the burgermeester's reception telephoned, took Rex for a quick walk in the garden, despite Juffrouw Kropp's protests that she would catch her death of cold, and settled down by the fire to con her Dutch lessons.

The weather worsened as the day wore on; it was snowing hard by the time Radinck telephoned. He sounded cool and rather casual and Caroline did her best to be the same. 'I'm in Dordrecht,' he told her. 'I took Juffrouw van Doorn back to her home; she had no way of reaching it otherwise and her parents must stay in hospital for a few days. I shall do my best to get back this evening, but the weather isn't too good.'

'It's snowing hard here,' said Caro, anxious not to sound anxious. 'If you'd rather not drive back—I expect you can find a hotel or something.'

'Juffrouw van Doorn has offered me a bed for the night— probably I shall accept it. You're all right?'

'Perfectly, thank you.' And even if I weren't, she added silently, I wouldn't tell you. 'Do you want me to tell anyone? Have you any appointments for the morning?'

His low laugh came very clearly over the wire. 'Realy, Caroline, you are becoming the perfect wife! No, there's no one you need telephone. I can do it all from here.'

'Very well—we'll expect you when we see you.'

'Caroline—about last night—'

She interrupted him ruthlessly. 'I'm sorry, I must go. Goodbye, Radinck.'

The rest of the day was a dead loss.

They were to go to a party the following evening. Becky had telephoned to know if they were going and Caro had improvised hurriedly and said that they expected to be there but Radinck would let her know the moment he could leave Dordrecht. 'The weather's awful there,' she invented, 'and I told him not to come home until the roads were clear.'

And Becky had said how wise she was and she hoped they'd see each other the next day.

There was no word from Radinck the next day. Caro ordered the meals as though he were expected home, took Rex for a snowy walk, rehearsed her choir and then telephoned the people whose party they were to attend and made their excuses. She was on the rug before the fire in the sitting-room when Radinck walked in, with Waterloo purring beside her and Rex leaning heavily against her. He bounded to the door as Radinck came in and Caro looked round and then got slowly to her feet. 'You didn't telephone,' she observed, quite forgetting to say hullo.

'No, I'm sorry I couldn't get back sooner—the roads are

bad.' He fended Rex off with a gentle hand and sat down. 'How quiet and peaceful you look, Caroline.'

Appearances can be deceptive, she thought. She wasn't either, inside her she boiled with rage and misery and jealousy and all the other things which were supposed to be so bad for one. 'I hope the trip wasn't too bad,' she remarked. 'Would you like some coffee?'

'Yes, thanks. Aren't we supposed to be going to the Laggemaats' this evening?'

'Yes, but I telephoned them about an hour ago and told them that as you weren't back we would probably not be able to go. I hope I did right.'

'Quite right. Did you not wonder where I was?'

She said evenly: 'When we married you particularly stressed the fact that that was something I was never to do.'

She poured the coffee Noakes had brought and handed Radinck a cup.

He said testily: 'You seem to have remembered every word I said and moreover, are determined to keep to it.'

Caroline didn't answer that but asked in her quiet little voice: 'How are the people who were hurt in the accident?'

'The first man is in intensive care, the second man died on the way to hospital—I think you may have guessed that; the two older people who were in the second car are to remain under observation for another day or so. Their daughter—Ilena—I drove home.'

Caro busied herself pouring a cup of coffee she didn't want. 'Oh, yes, Becky told me when she telephoned yesterday.' She was careful to keep all traces of reproach from her voice. 'I'm so glad she wasn't hurt; she was the loveliest girl I've ever seen.'

'Extraordinarily beautiful,' agreed Radinck blandly, 'and so young, too. She asked me to stay the night and I did.'

'Very sensible of you,' declared Caro calmly. 'Travelling back in all that snow would never have done.'

'What would you say if I told you that I've never allowed bad weather to interfere with my driving?'

She could say a great many things, thought Caro, and all of them very much to the point. She didn't utter any of them but said prudently: 'I think it was very wise of you to make an exception to your rule.'

She put down her coffee cup and picked up her work again, glad to be able to busy herself with something.

Radinck stretched out his legs and wedged his great shoulders deeply into his chair. 'Don't you want to know why I took Ilena home?'

'You must have had a good reason for doing so—I daresay she was badly shaken and not fit to travel on her own.'

'She was perfectly able to go on her own. I drove her because I wanted to prove something to myself.' He frowned. 'I seem to be in some confusion of mind—about you, Caroline.'

She looked up from her work, her eyes thoughtful as she studied his handsome and, at the moment, ill-tempered face. Her heart was thundering against her ribs. That he was about to say something important was evident, but what, exactly? She had promised herself that she would make him love her, but it seemed probable that she had failed and he was going to tell her so. She said steadily: 'If you want to talk about it I'm listening, Radinck.'

It was a pity that just at that moment the telephone on the table beside him should ring. He lifted the receiver and listened, frowning, and then embarked on what Caro took to be a list of instructions about a patient. The interruption gave her time to collect her thoughts, which were, however, instantly scattered by the entry of Noakes, announcing Tiele and Becky.

'We were on our way to the Laggemaats',' explained Becky, 'and Tiele thought it would be an idea to pop in and see how you were.'

She kissed Caro, offered a cheek to Radinck and perched

herself on a chair close to Caro, spreading the skirts of her dress as she did so.

'That's pretty,' observed Caro. 'It's new, isn't it? I love the colour. I was going to wear a rather nice green...'

Tiele had bent to kiss her cheek and said laughingly: 'Oh, lord—clothes again! Radinck, take me to your study and show me that agenda for the seminar at Brussels. Are you going? We could go together—we need only be away for a couple of days.'

The two men went away and Becky, declining coffee, remarked: 'We weren't sure if Radinck would be back. The roads are very bad further south. He telephoned Tiele about some patient or other quite late last night—said he'd gone to a hotel in Dordrecht and planned to leave early this morning, but he got held up—you know all that, of course.' She ate one of the small biscuits on the coffee tray. 'He must have been glad to have handed that girl over to her aunt—a bit of a responsibility—supposing he'd got landed in a snowdrift!' She giggled engagingly.

Caro had listened to this artless information in surprise and a mounting excitement. If what Becky had told her was true, why had Radinck let her think that he'd stayed at the girl's house? Had he wanted to make her jealous? On the other hand, did he want her to believe that he had thought better of their dry-as-dust marriage and wanted to put an end to it? More likely the latter, she considered, although that was something she would have to find out. She wasn't sure how and she had a nasty feeling that whatever it was Radinck had been going to say wouldn't be said—at least not for the moment.

In this she was perfectly right. The van den Ecks went presently and Radinck went almost at once to his study with the observation that he had a good deal of paper work to do. Which left Caro with nothing better to do than go to bed.

CHAPTER NINE

THE SNOW LAY thick on the ground when Caro looked out of her windows in the morning. It was barely light and she could see Radinck, huge in a sheepskin jacket, striding down to the stables with Rex at his heels. He would be going to see how Queenie fared before walking Rex in the fields beyond. It would have been lovely to be with him, she thought, walking in the early morning cold, talking about his work and planning a pleasant evening together. Which reminded her that there was another party that evening and presumably they would be going: a doctor from the hospital and his wife—she searched her memory and came up with their name—ter Brink, youngish if she remembered aright and rather nice. She would have to ring Becky and ask what she should wear. She bathed and dressed and went downstairs and found Radinck already at the table.

It was hardly the time or place to expect him to disclose what he had intended to say to her, but she sat down hopefully and began her breakfast. But beyond a polite good morning, the hope that she had slept well, and could he pass her the toast, he had nothing to say, but became immersed in his letters once again. Caroline was glad that she had a modest pile of post beside her plate for once. It seemed to keep her occupied and by reading each letter two or three times, she spun out her interest in them until Radinck put his own mail down and got to his feet.

'You feel well enough to go to the ter Brinks' this evening?' he asked her pleasantly.

'Oh yes, thank you. Where do they live?'

'Groningen—not far. I should be home about tea-time and we shall need to leave here about half past six.' He paused on his way to the door. 'Be careful if you go out—it's very cold and treacherous underfoot.'

'Yes, Radinck.' She smiled at him as she spoke and he came back across the room and kissed her hard and quick. Caroline sat a long while after he had gone trying to decide whether he had meant it or whether he was feeling guilty; she remembered all the books she had read where the husband had tried to make amends to his wife when he had neglected her by being kind to her, only in books they sent flowers as well.

They arrived a few hours later—a great bouquet of fragrant spring flowers; lilac, and hyacinths, tulips and daffodils, exquisitely arranged in a paper-thin porcelain bowl. The card said merely: Flowers for Caroline, and he had written it himself and scrawled Radinck at the end. Caroline eyed them at first with delight and then with suspicion. Was he, like the guilty husbands in all the best novels, feeling guilty too? She was consumed with a desire to find out more about the beautiful girl in Dordrecht. She was a satisfyingly long way away, but absence made the heart grow fonder, didn't it?

Caro spent the whole day vacillating between hope and despair, so that by the time Radinck came home she was in a thoroughly muddled state of mind—made even more muddled by his unexpected friendly attitude towards her. He had always—well, almost always—treated her with punctilious politeness, but seldom with warmth. Now he launched into an account of his day, lounging back in his great chair, looking to be the epitome of a contented man and even addressing her as Caro, which seemed to her to be a great step forward in their relationship. She went up to change her dress presently; it was to be a long dress occasion and she chose one of the dresses she had bought in den Haag. A rose pink crêpe-de-chine, patterned with deeper pink roses, it had a high neck and long tight sleeves and the bodice was finely tucked between lace insertions. She swept downstairs presently, her mink coat over her arm, and then stopped so suddenly that she very nearly tripped up. She had never thanked Radinck for his flowers.

A deep chuckle from the end of the hall made her look round. Radinck was sitting on a marble-topped side table, swinging his long legs, the picture of elegance. 'Such a magnificent entry!' he observed. 'Just like Cinderella at the ball—and then you stopped as though you'd been shot. What happened?'

'Oh, Radinck, I remembered—I'm so sorry, I never thanked you for the flowers, and they're so lovely. I hope you don't mind—I put them in my room, but I'll bring them downstairs tomorrow...'

'I'm glad they pleased you.' He swung himself off the table and came towards her. 'That is a charming dress, and you look charming in it, Caro. I have something for you; I hope you will wear it.'

He took a box from a pocket and opened it and took out a brooch, a true lovers' knot of diamonds. 'May I put it on for you?'

He held the lovely thing in the palm of his hand and she put out a finger to touch it. 'It's magnificent!' she breathed. 'Was it your mother's?'

His hand had closed gently over the brooch and her fingers. 'No—I chose it yesterday as I came through den Haag on my way home. I want to give it to you, Caro, and I want you to wear it.'

She looked up into his face; his eyes were bright and searching and his brows were raised in a questioning arc.

'Why?' asked Caro, her head full of the girl in Dordrecht. Flowers, and now this heavenly brooch—it was even worse than she had thought, although Radinck didn't look in the least like a guilty husband.

'I'm afraid to answer that,' said Radinck surprisingly, and pinned the brooch into the lace at her neck with cool steady fingers.

And when he had done it: 'It's my turn to ask a question,' he smiled down at her. 'Why did you ask why, Caroline?'

Oh dear! thought Caro, now I'm Caroline again, and said carefully: 'Well, first you sent me those heavenly flowers and now you've given me this fabulous brooch, and you see, in books the husband is always extra nice to his wife when he's been neglecting her or—or falling in love with someone else—then he buys his wife presents because he feels guilty...'

He looked utterly bewildered. 'Guilty?' he considered it for a moment. 'Well, yes, I suppose you're right.'

Caro's heart dropped like a stone into her high-heeled, very expensive satin sandals. 'So there's no need to say any more, is there?' she asked unhappily.

Strangely, Radinck was smiling. 'Not just now, perhaps— I don't really think that we have the time—we are already a little late.'

She said yes, of course, in her quiet hesitant voice and got into her coat, then sat, for the most part silent, as he drove the Panther de Ville to Groningen, almost sixty kilometres away. The roads were icy under a bright moon, but Radinck drove with relaxed ease, carrying on a desultory conversation, not seeming to notice Caroline's quiet. He certainly didn't present the appearance of a guilty husband who had just been found out by his wife. Caro stirred in her seat, frowning. She could be wrong...

There wasn't much chance to find out anything more at the party. The ter Brinks were a youngish, rather serious-minded couple living in a large modern house on the outskirts of Groningen, and Caro found herself moving round their drawing-room, getting caught up in the highbrow conversations among their guests. She had met most of them already and almost all of them spoke excellent English, but—typical of her, she thought—she got pinned into a corner by an elderly gentleman, who insisted on speaking Dutch despite her denial of all knowledge of that language, so that all she could do was to look interested, say 'neen' and 'ja' every now and then and pray for someone to rescue her.

Which Radinck did, tucking a hand under her arm and engaging the elderly man in a pleasant conversation for a few minutes before drifting her away to the other end of the room.

'My goodness,' said Caro, when they were safely out of earshot, 'I only understood one word in a hundred—thank you for rescuing me, Radinck. What was he talking about?'

Her husband's firm mouth twitched. 'Nuclear warfare and the possibility of invasion from outer space,' he told her blandly.

'Oh, my goodness—and all I said was yes and no— Oh, and once I said Niet waar in a surprised sort of way.'

Radinck's shoulders shook, but he said seriously: 'A quite suitable remark, especially if you sounded astonished. "You don't say" is an encouraging remark to make—it sounds admiring as well as astonished, which after all was what Professor Vinke expected to hear.'

'Oh, good—I'd hate to let you down.'

He had guided her to another corner, standing in front of her so that she was shut off from the room. 'I believe you, Caroline. It is a pity that you cannot return my opinion.' He took her hand briefly. 'Caro, perhaps I'm going away for a day or two. Are you going to ask me where and why?'

She stared down at his fingers clasping hers. 'No, I don't break promises.'

He sighed. 'Perhaps the incentive isn't enough for you to do that...'

And after that there was no further chance to talk. They were joined by friends, and presently Tiele and Becky came across to talk to them and although they left soon afterwards they only discussed the party on their way home. They didn't talk about anything much at dinner either, and afterwards Radinck wished her a cool goodnight and went away to his study. And yet, thought Caro, left alone to drink her coffee by the fire in the drawing-room, he had looked at her very intently once or twice during the meal, just as though he was wanting to say something and didn't know how to start.

She went to bed presently and made a point of being down in time to share breakfast with Radinck the following morning. It was hardly the best time of the day to talk to him, but she didn't feel she could bear to go on much longer without asking more questions. When he had read his post she said abruptly: 'I'm going to break my promise after all. Are you going to Dordrecht?'

Radinck put his coffee cup down very slowly. 'Why should I wish to go to Dordrecht?' His eyes narrowed. 'Ah, now I see—the flowers and brooch were to cover my neglect, were they?' His voice held a sneer. 'You really believe that I would go tearing off after a girl young enough to be my daughter, just like your precious novels?' He got to his feet, looking to her nervous gaze to be twice his normal size and in a very bad temper indeed. 'Well, Caroline, you may think what you wish.'

'When are you going?' she asked, for there seemed no point in retreating now. 'And you needn't be so very bad-tempered; you wanted to know if I was going to ask you where you were going, and now I have you're quite peevish...'

He stopped on his way to the door. 'Peevish? Peevish? I am angry, Caroline.' He came back to tower over her, still sitting at the table.

'And why do you keep on calling me Caroline?' asked Caro. She had cooked her goose and it really didn't matter what she said now. 'And sometimes you say Caro.'

He said silkily: 'Because when I call you Caroline I can try and believe that you are someone vague who has little to do with my life, only I find that I no longer can do that...'

'And what am I when I'm Caro?' she asked with interest.

'Soft and gentle and loving.' He bent and kissed her soundly. 'You have brought chaos to my life,' he told her austerely, and turned on his heel and went.

Caro sat very still after he had gone. Things, she told herself, had come to a head. It was time she did something about it. And he hadn't told her when he was going to Dordrecht, or even if he was going there. She poured herself more coffee and applied her wits to the problem.

She got up presently and went to the telephone. Radinck's secretary at his rooms was quite sure that he wasn't going anywhere, certainly not to Dordrecht, and at the hospital, in answer to her carefully worded enquiries, she was told that the Professor had a full day ahead of him. So he had been making it up...to annoy her? To get her interested in what he did? She wasn't sure, but his kiss had been, even in her inexperienced view, a very genuine one. Caroline nodded her mousy head and smiled a little, then went to the little davenport in the sitting-room and after a great deal of thought and several false starts, composed a letter. It was a nicely worded document, telling Radinck that since they didn't agree very well, perhaps it would be as well if she went away. She read it through, put it in its envelope and went in search of Willem, who, always willing, got out the Mini used by the staff for errands and rattled off to Leeuwarden, the letter in his pocket.

It was unfortunate that Radinck happened to be doing a round when Willem handed in his letter with the request that it should be delivered as soon as possible; the round took ages and it was well after lunch before a porter, tracking him down in the consultants' room, making a meal off sandwiches and beer, handed it to him. He read it quickly and then read it again, before reaching for the telephone. He had been a fool, he told himself savagely; Caro had believed that he had gone to Dordrecht because he had been attracted to that girl—and he shouldn't have let her believe that he had stayed there, either. He was too old to fall in love, he reminded himself sourly, but he had, and nothing would alter the fact that little Caro had become his world.

Noakes answered the phone and listened carefully to the Professor's instructions. The house was to be searched very thoroughly; he had reason to believe that the Baroness, who wasn't feeling quite herself, could be in one of its many rooms. Radinck himself would call at the most likely places where she might be and then come home.

He spent the rest of the afternoon going patiently from one friend's house to the next, calling at the shops he thought Caro might have visited and then finally, holding back his fear with an iron hand, going home.

Caro had been sitting working quite feverishly at her knitting for quite some time before she heard the car coming up the drive, the front door bang shut and Radinck's footsteps in the hall. It was a great pity that the speech she had prepared and rehearsed over and over again should now fly from her head, leaving it empty—not that it mattered. The door was flung open and her husband strode in, closing it quietly behind him and then leaning against it to stare across at her. Meeting his eyes, she realised that she had no need to say anything, a certainty confirmed by his: 'Caro, you baggage—how long have you been here?'

'Since—well, since Willem took my note.'

'The house was searched—where did you hide?'

'Behind the door.' She made her voice matter-of-fact, although her hands were shaking so much that stitches were being dropped right left and centre. She wished she could look away from him, but she seemed powerless to do so. Any minute now he would explode with rage, for he must be in a fine temper. His face was white and drawn and his eyes were glittering.

Caroline was completely disarmed when he said gently: 'I have been out of my mind with worry, my darling. I thought that you had left me and that I would never see you again. I wanted to kill myself for being such a fool. I had begun to think that you were beginning to love me a little and that if I had patience I could make you forget how badly I had treated you.' He smiled bleakly. 'I have just spent the worst two hours of my life...'

Caro's soft heart was wrung, but she went on ruining her knitting in what she hoped was a cool manner. 'I didn't mean you to be upset,' she explained gruffly. 'You see, I had to know...well, I thought that if you m-minded about me at all, you would look for me, but if you didn't then I'd know I had to go away.' She dropped three stitches one after the other and added mournfully: 'I haven't put it very clearly.' Not that it mattered now. He hadn't said that he loved her and everybody called everyone else darling these days.

Radinck crossed the room very fast indeed. 'Put that damned knitting down,' he commanded, 'you're hiding behind it.' She had it taken from her in a ruthless manner which completed the havoc she had already wrought, but it really didn't matter, for Radinck had wrapped her in his arms. 'To think that I had to wait half a lifetime to meet you and even then I fought against loving you, my darling Caro!' He put a finger under her chin and turned her face up to his. 'I think I fell in love with you when you told me to give you a needle and thread and you'd do it yourself...only I'd spent so many years alone and I didn't believe there was a girl like you left in the world.' He smiled a little. 'I carry one of your handkerchiefs, like a lovesick boy.'

He kissed her gently and then very hard so that she had no breath. 'My beautiful girl,' he told her, 'when I came in just now and saw you sitting there it was as though you'd been here all my life, waiting for me to come home.'

'Well, dear Radinck, that's just what I was doing.' Caroline's voice shook a little although she tried hard to sound normal. 'Only I didn't know if you would.'

He kissed her again. 'But I did, dear heart, and I shall always come home to you.'

She had a delightful picture of herself, with her delightful children, waiting in the hall for Radinck to come home...and now she would be able to wear the pink organza dress. She smiled enchantingly at the idea and Radinck smoothed the mousy hair back from her face and asked: 'Why do you smile, my love?'

She leaned up to kiss him. 'Because I'm happy and because I love you so much.'

A remark which could have only one answer.

Modern Romance™
...seduction and
passion guaranteed

Tender Romance™
...love affairs that
last a lifetime

Medical Romance™
...medical drama
on the pulse

Historical Romance™
...rich, vivid and
passionate

Sensual Romance™
...sassy, sexy and
seductive

Blaze Romance™
...the temperature's
rising

27 new titles every month.

Live the emotion

MILLS & BOON®

Betty Neels Ultimate Collection
Official Prize Draw Rules

NO PURCHASE NECESSARY

Each book in the Betty Neels Ultimate Collection will contain details for entry into the following prize draw: 4 prizes of a signed Betty Neels book and a weekend break to Amsterdam and 10 prizes of a signed Betty Neels book. No purchase necessary.

To enter the draw, hand print the words "Betty Neels Ultimate Collection Prize Draw", plus your name and address on a postcard. For UK residents please send your postcard entries to: Betty Neels Ultimate Collection Prize Draw, PO Box 236, Croydon, CR9 3RU. For ROI residents please send your postcard to Betty Neels Ultimate Collection Prize Draw, PO Box 4546, Kilcock, County Kildare.

To be eligible all entries must be received by July 31st 2003. No responsibility can be accepted for entries that are lost, delayed or damaged in the post. Proof of postage cannot be accepted as proof of delivery. No correspondence can be entered into and no entry returned. Winners will be determined in a random draw from all eligible entries received. Judges decision is final. One mailed entry per person, per household.

Amsterdam break includes return flights for two, 2 nights accommodation at a 4 star hotel, airport/hotel transfers, insurance and £150 spending money. Holiday must be taken between 1/8/03 and 1/08/04 excluding Bank holidays, Easter and Christmas periods. (Winner has the option of accepting £500 cash in lieu of holiday option.)

All travellers must sign and return a Release of Liability prior to travel and must have a valid 10 year passport. Accommodation and flights are subject to schedule and availability. The Prize Draw is open to residents of the UK and ROI, 18 years of age or older. Employees and immediate family members of Harlequin Mills & Boon Ltd., its affiliates, subsidiaries and all other agencies, entities and persons connected with the use, marketing or conduct of this Prize Draw are not eligible.

Prize winner notification will be made by letter no later than 14 days after the deadline for entry. Limit: one prize per an individual, family or organisation. All applicable laws and regulations apply. If any prize or prize notification is returned as undeliverable, an alternative winner will be drawn from eligible entries. By acceptance of a prize, winner consents to use of his/her name, photograph or other likeness for purpose of advertising, trade and promotion on behalf of Harlequin Mills & Boon Ltd., without further compensation, unless prohibited by law.

For the names of prize winners (available after 31/08/03), send a self-addressed stamped envelope to: For UK residents, Betty Neels Ultimate Collection Prize Draw Winners List, PO Box 236, Croydon, CR9 3RU. For ROI residents, Betty Neels Ultimate Collection Prize Draw Winners List, PO Box 4546, Kilcock, County Kildare.